Dream

A Novel

Jeff Trippe

Silent E Publishing Company

Cover art by: E.P. Pirt

Silent E Publishing Company
4446 Hendricks Ave, #141
Jacksonville, Florida, USA
All Rights Reserved

ISBN-13 978-1-941091-14-2

First Edition

10 9 8 7 6 5 4 3 2 1

Also by Jeff Trippe

Lawsuits of the Rich and Famous, 1994

This Brittle Existence, 2007

For Young Adult Readers

The Pride of the Panthers, 2014

Far From My Own Shore, 2015

Onward to Planet Kopius, 2015

Dream

Part One: The Shadow

One

August, 1959

A panther attack. That was what the local paper called it, even though there had been no documented sighting of a big cat on that stretch of the Little Pee Dee River since 1941. And even though life in general had not changed much for people who lived along those fourteen miles of looping blackwater and whose families had farmed and lumbered and fished there for generations, the warnings were grave: children should be kept indoors, especially after dark, and livestock and pets should be looked to.

Of course, the old swamper who found Treadwell that morning with two holes clean through his neck where the fangs had gone in would have told it differently. That it was a panther was indeed correct, but there had been no attack, really, no animal savagery in whatever had happened there under the dark webs of live oak limbs, among the drifting, humming clouds of mosquitoes, where the ground literally oozed – no vicious ripping of life from limb, and no intent to feed. The swamper, who was called Dan Byrd, had once seen a victim of such an attack, a child, and it had not been pretty, but it was what one might expect, with the lower stomach raked open, the entrails eaten, and part of the ribs exposed before the animal must have been frightened off by someone or something. This was different.

Firstly, there were just the two puncture wounds through the throat, one above the other; the blood had apparently come out in a thin stream, pooling and then coagulating in the lap of the victim, Bob Treadwell, who was seated against a tree trunk, still looking curiously out toward the river. The swamper knew him, for occasionally he had done odd jobs for him and had once sold him a stringer of catfish. He also knew of Treadwell's strange custom of tethering himself to the same broad live oak trunk whenever he had been drinking hard, using a cuff around one ankle and a heavy length of chain to restrict himself. He was not entirely certain who it was that would eventually come with the key each time, for by then Dan would almost always be headed for home, bound for the depths of the swamp with his lines and his traps, passing once again in the late afternoon to find the chain hanging limp and Treadwell gone – probably to his own home two miles or so up the highway, to supper, most likely, and the warm and merciful light of sobriety; yet he had seen the man's teenage son now and again riding his bicycle along the river road, and he suspected that he had been charged with this dire duty.

But when he had seen the fresh, deliberate prints of the big cat in the mud that morning, he had tracked it. It had moved more or less in a straight line through the cypresses and the oaks and the pines, almost as if some unerring, irresistible homing signal had called it to the place where Treadwell had chained himself. Apparently, it had killed him with a single, equally unfaltering, momentous strike to the neck with no resistance from the man, and then had sunk like a shape of night back into the dark forest whence it came, invisible but for its yellow eyes in the bandoliered shafts of moonlight.

None of it made much sense to the swamper, but he was not one to fret over such mysteries. He had hiked up to the highway, which was already shimmering with heat, and he had flagged the first car that came along – a white pickup truck driven by a shriveled little farmer – and briefly related to him what he had just seen down in the live oak grove by the river. Although Dan Byrd was not inclined to put himself in the way of the authorities on any occasion (as some of his own doings were not quite within the boundaries of the law), he and the driver agreed that the sheriff's office ought to be telephoned as soon as possible. Then the swamper had gone back to stand beside Treadwell's body until a deputy arrived.

The heat of the day was coming on, and that smell, which travels straight to the gut and which we all abhor but also recognize immediately as the dampness and darkness of our own mortality, had begun to emanate from Treadwell's corpse. Dan lit a cigarette to ward it off, and he looked into the dead man's eyes: it was as if he were still looking with disbelief at the receding form of the big cat, having arrived at the very brink of some great understanding only to be mired in confusion.

"I'd shut 'em for you," Dan said, "but I ain't supposed to touch anything."

A fat blue fly buzzed about Treadwell's head. Dan plucked the cigarette from his lips and rolled it in his fingers, holding the smoke in his throat and sinuses, savoring it.

"I reckon you musta been pretty damn surprised. I know I woulda been. Maybe she didn't tear ya' up the way she coulda, but she sure had *some*thin' against you."

As if in response, a breeze suddenly lifted the dead man's copper-colored hair and pushed it behind his ears. The swamper heard a car door slam, and gazing up to the roadway, he could just make out the top of the deputy's hat and the glint of his badge as he made his way down silently and carefully through the tall weeds.

———————

The old swamper had been wrong on both premises: There had been no malice in what had occurred, and Treadwell had not been at all surprised. In fact, he had known from his boyhood how things would turn out, though he could not have known the precise time. And although for years now he had forgotten it or else shoved it forcefully out of his memory, he had always lived with the inevitability of it, for the shadow of the big cat had haunted him for many years.

It was black, and he had seen it the first time when he was five. He and his father had been out fishing in the little outboard and were returning at dusk, with the wake running silver across the face of the inky water and rolling away to the shores in glistening crescents. Abruptly, as they were passing within twenty yards of the public pier at Sanders Landing, his father cut the engine, and they drifted, the bow dipping downward and bobbing, and his father said,

"Do you see him? On the beach?"

The cat, so black against the glowing sand that he was like a hole cut into the air in the shape of a beast, stood silently, his head following them as they drifted past, the very end of his long tail flicking ever so quickly every few seconds. His father reached under the bench, found the flashlight, and aimed its beam at the creature. Its yellow, unblinking eyes traced their slow progress; there was no wind, and the blackwater was utterly still, as if when his father had switched off the engine, the current itself had also gone dead.

"Can he swim?" he asked.

"Sure he can. But he won't."

Oddly, they said nothing more about it; when they had at last floated on around the pier and then the last bend, his father cranked the engine and took them on in among the trees where they would moor the boat. But Bobby, as he was called then, had thought about it well into the night, lying there listening to the frogs and to the insects thudding against the light over the shed door. Over and over, he saw the yellow eyes fix upon him and then draw nearer and nearer, growing ever larger, until he seemed to step abruptly into some strange, watery world which was wet and smelled of tannin, which washed over him like a wave, and afterward, looking down from above the treetops to the place where he had stood in the boat, he saw that there was no one, and he felt sure he had died.

Sometimes it would happen in his dreams, too, but it was always the same. His younger brother, Banks, was still too little to be trusted with the confession of his fears; and then by the time he was eight and Banks was six, when they might have begun having those kinds of talks that only male siblings have, about their anxieties, their fears, their intended braveries and aspirations to bright deeds, their mother left suddenly, taking the younger boy with her. This event passed without much commotion, and with little commentary from their father, but the strange, dark dreams of the panther now became a nightly torture. He thought it must all mean that he certainly would not see the age of nine, but when his birthday passed, and then Christmas, and then the school year ended, and he and his father began fishing again nearly every afternoon, he felt that perhaps his untimely death was not quite so imminent. It did not come, and it did not come, and by August he began to believe that he might survive after all. The eyes approached him less and less frequently, and finally, because he was a boy in the midst of summer, he had all but forgotten about the panther.

But the panther had not forgotten him. Bob had been drafted into the army in 1942, assigned to the Pacific, and on the night before he was to catch the bus for Fort Jackson, he walked down to the river for a smoke. He was 24 years old now, and his dad had grown old and crooked, and Mother had become a mere ghost to them, a faded memory of which neither of them ever spoke (he knew only that she had left them all those years ago for a man named Hatchet who owned a bar in Beaufort; there had been no further news of her or of Banks). He wandered out into the warm evening, the old smells of the river and the marsh coming up to him, the smell of mud, of his old life, for better or worse, seeping towards him; sleep seemed the remotest possibility, and his father kept no whiskey in the house, and the names of places such as the Coral Sea and Midway and Wake Island were only words that he could mouth but that had no grounding in his life at all. That would all change in short order, of course, but on this night there was only the river and his cigarettes and a vague sense that he would be back here again.

This time the great cat came very near to him. He did not even have to see it, at first, as he felt the shadow behind him, and he realized immediately that walking out on the dock at old man Pitts's place had been a grave error. He had also neglected to bring his old maple baseball bat, which he often carried to ward away stray dogs, though it wouldn't have helped him in this case. Then, too, he didn't want to get wet, but if the panther truly wanted him, jumping wouldn't make any difference either. He turned slowly, so as to cause as little commotion as possible, and there it was: there was only a quarter moon overhead, but the cat's eyes burned like two hot chunks of coal, and Bob stood stock still. The dock ran about a hundred feet or so into the river, and the animal had already advanced roughly half of that distance; it took a small step, and he could hear the sound of the paws' pads touch lightly against the wood, and then it took another and another, and then lay down, haunches tensed like thick coils of black rubber, ready to fling itself at him instantaneously, and he took a gulp of river air, believing it to be his last. Their eyes were locked on one another, Bob's no doubt filled with silent terror, the panther's aloof, omniscient, unbiased, gazing from a mind which was not a mind at all but rather an instrument to measure distance from its prey and the most efficient means by which to bring it down. And then, as silently and swiftly as it had appeared, the big cat rose, darted toward the woods, and vanished.

And then once again, the recollection of it, like the fog drifting above the cypresses and live oaks, had left him entirely. The army finished with him, and the boy he had been was seemingly erased, along with his memories. In their place were images of the corpses of Japanese soldiers and saltwater made cloudy with blood, and the kind of knowledge he had never wanted but now possessed, and believing he had already done the most important thing he would ever do in his life, he resolved to be married and to settle in for the long ride down. It was time to find himself a wife.

He had managed to learn a thing or two: he would not seek for her in the taverns or among the shallow, giggly girls he had known in school, some of whom were now working as waitresses at the truck stop up on Highway 57 or at the Piggly Wiggly. No. He would seek a wife in the place where, unlike many of those who lived along the river, he had spent as little time as possible, where (as he had understood later) his own mother, though she might have been grudgingly accepted, would certainly have been the object of much gossip, and where his father had never gone because he used Sundays to pursue the simpler pleasures of fishing, drinking coffee, and trading manly stories.

He would find her in the church.

––––––––––

Many years later, in those very moments that Dan Byrd, a self-appointed watcher of the dead, stood waiting by the lifeless shell that had been Bob Treadwell, the dead man's only son, Frank – all of 15 and with barely ten dollars in his pocket but with three meatloaf sandwiches and a thermos of coffee tucked into his canvas backpack – was acting upon momentous decisions of his own. Now he stood contemplating first the dark stretch of the Little Pee Dee, which was behind him, and then the path that led up the hill and away from it, blurring ultimately into cloud-wrapped sunlight and the shadows above him.

He knew already that he would always remember this, the river, most clearly out of everything. When he had crossed it that morning in the wooden johnboat, the bumping of the oars floating back to him from the far trees, all had been quite still. But in the hour or so that he had stood looking back, the wind had picked up and the water had begun to shift in what seemed to be large metallic sheets, and he began to feel anxious. A hawk, a dark gash against the veiled sky, struggled around the looping bend, hung over him on the wind for a few moments, gave a single cry, and then flew on.

He had not even brought a change of clothes, but for some reason, that didn't worry him. When he had made himself the three sandwiches and the coffee this morning, and then had gone back to his room to inspect the pile of dirty clothes in the corner, he could imagine his mother's voice: "The Lord will provide." Fine, and if He didn't, no doubt some fastidious country lady with a backyard clothesline would. No, he was much more concerned about the objects he had deliberately left behind, for he was a superstitious boy and believed in the luck of objects. First, there had been her Bible to consider. It was worn and frayed along its spine, but it was leather-bound and very much intact and filled with her neat handwriting – not just with family history, birth and death dates and such, but also with her marginal notes throughout. She was an expert on all those stories, all right, and a bit of a critic, and she'd had some thought or other to offer on nearly every verse. But it was heavy, and not good for the sort of traveling he intended to do; perhaps he could come back and fetch it someday, in a few years. Then there was the key on the kitchen counter, next to the three empty liquor bottles. It was old and rusted, but it still turned in his father's special cuff as smoothly as if it had been minted and oiled yesterday. He would have liked to take it, to remind himself of why he had left (or of one of the reasons, anyway), to take it out and handle it if he were ever to doubt himself. However, he knew that the old man was still on the drink and had no doubt chained himself up again, and that he would need to direct someone to the key's location on the kitchen counter, whenever he might finally realize that Frank wasn't coming this time. Then he had thought how it might have made a pretty good joke to take it with him, but in the end he could not bring himself to do it.

Lastly, there was his glove. It was an excellent piece of craftsmanship, especially made for outfielders, and it had cost him an entire summer of yard work and trash-hauling to get it. Mr. McGuire at the sporting goods shop in Dillon had had to order it for him, and he had stopped in at the shop day after day for six weeks to see if it had come (not that he minded that, for it was cool in the shop and it smelled of polished wood and fine leather and horsehide), and when it finally did come, he had raced home, oiled it, nestled a baseball in it with twine around it and put it under his pillow. Of course, his mother had chided him later about the oil stain on the pillowcase, but when he had at last put the glove on his right hand, understanding for the first time the true meaning of a tool, of a thing well crafted for a particular use, then nothing she could say would ever bother him again. There had been that moment, too, when she had turned with a huff and marched out of his room, and his father was standing there in the hallway, grinning at him. That was almost two years ago now.

Nevertheless, he had left that behind, too, thinking, "Well, if I am meant to do anything…that is, if I ever do play ball again, I can come fetch that, too. I'll take that and her Bible in one swoop."

In truth, it seemed to him the purest and best way to go was with as little as possible. There were lots of things he could have fit into the pack, such as his trading card collection, two or three 45-rpm records he was fond of, and especially the picture of his friend Liza…but he had realized with startling, grownup clarity that these things had no utility, and anyway, if he was really to do this the right way, he must strip himself of that old life. To take things with him would be to tie himself to this place – chain himself, really – and he wanted only to break free. His life would be his own, even if it came to nothing at all in the end.

He did not know how long he had stood there on the grassy bank, thinking, but the light had changed again. Along his arm now he felt the stiffness of the tree upon which he had been leaning – it was a black tupelo – and he looked up into the veiny, purplish leaves above him. Out there, above the river, the hawk had returned to hover on the warm, damp, rising air, and was looking down at him expectantly, anxiously, as if to remind him that up there was the road, Route 9, and beyond that the state line. Time to go.

He picked up the backpack, tossed it easily in one smooth half-circle across one shoulder, and moved along up the little path.

––––––––

Oh, that glove, though. Not only had it been the sweetest, best thing he'd ever owned, it was the first thing of any value he'd ever purchased for himself. It was caramel-colored, soft and pliant, and it fit him like…well, like a glove. So, when he was thirteen, with the old maple bat that Dad had given him and a good pair of spikes, and little suspecting all that the next two years would hold for him, he felt that he at last had everything he needed. It was not just that he knew his life was simple and therefore good – he deliberately sought to make it so.

It was early on that he had realized he had the ability to play ball, and after that, everything made much more sense to him: here was a round object in flight, but it was not aimless flight, for once set in motion, it had purpose. If it had been struck by the round stick, it must be caught and thrown someplace else, or if he had the round stick in his hands, he must be the one to strike it, as fiercely as he could. The ball came in, and the ball went out again, on and on, for such is the nature of all round things, including, as he would see later, the earth itself and the moon and sun and all other things in the sky. The other motions involved, the running and the knowing where to throw and the watching of the ball all merely served the idea of sending the ball where it ought to go or stopping it where it ought to be stopped. That's how it was when he was small.

He could not recall how or why he had started to play. He knew that it had been his father who had first noticed that he could do those kinds of things, but he did not know the circumstances. Early in life, every child is involved with a ball at some point, in some way, and luckily enough for him, Frankie's father had been able to see that he was good.

When he was seven years old, he took him to a youth baseball tryout (it wasn't Little League, yet; it was called Dad's Club baseball, and they had to drive all the way to Florence for it). It was a chilly, bright morning in late March, and there were traces of frost in the grass, and he had to wear his corduroy coat and his boots because he had nothing else warm, but something in his boy's heart had responded to the smell of the damp clay, the praiseful, happy shouts of the men who were to be their coaches, to the sun slanting over the outfield, which he had thought at first was somebody's barnyard, to the sounds (the plock! of bat on ball, the thudding of the ball in the pocket of someone's glove), but most of all to the magnificent feeling in his own hands every time he swung and hit the ball solidly, sending the first one zipping over the head of the dad who had tossed it to him, and then the second, third, and fourth ones into the green meadows well beyond the scraggly edge of the clay infield.

After twelve swings, the dad on the mound said, "Okay. That's a good deal. Just take a seat in the dugout."

He wasn't sure what the dugout was, until he heard his own father's voice: "Frankie. Over there with them other fellas."

All the rest came to him with the same easiness, the catching, the throwing, and the running, and anyway it wouldn't have mattered that much because there was so much fun in it and it meant that every Saturday morning, after bacon and eggs, he got to climb into the Chevy with his father and make the drive to Florence, where he would hit the ball and run in the meadows and where afterward everyone seemed to like him a great deal, though all he really cared about besides the running and the ball were the free soda and hot dog he always got when it was over. His dad would stand there by the fence smiling and winking as the other men swatted him on the back and said merry things, and his dad would say, "I'm not sure where he got it from. I always had that bat, all right, long as I can remember, but I never did get to play any ball. Fact is, I climbed out the schoolhouse window in the eighth grade and never went back. I swear, I don't know where he got the talent from."

After the third game, when Frankie had hit it over the centerfield fence for the second game in a row, his father drove all the way home in utter silence, shaking his head and barely able to speak, not grinning at him this time but looking over at him every few minutes as if he did not know him, as if he were some odd little animal he had found by the roadside and was bringing home for the curiosity of it. Frankie was holding the ball he had hit, which someone had retrieved and given to him.

"What's wrong?" he finally asked.

His father looked over. "How'd you hit that one so far?"

"I thought I was s'posed to," he said.

At supper that evening, as usual, his mother said the blessing and then began by passing the biscuits and butter to him. Father took a sip of his iced tea, still regarding him with that same bewildered expression. Mother put a scoop of mashed potatoes on his plate.

"How was the game?" she asked.

"Good," he said.

"That's it?"

"It was fun. I had Coke."

His father propped his elbows on the table and placed his chin on his folded hands, chewing slowly. "Frank hit another home run," he said.

She smiled and touched the boy's arm. "Very nice, Frankie."

His father went on: "It's startin' to get a little scary, to tell the truth. I never did play no sports. Don't know where he's getting it from."

Later that evening, when they were sitting in the living room under soft lamplight, as they often did back then, he with his Tom Swift and his father with his newspaper and mother with her tatting, every so often, the man would peak at him over the corner of the paper, until finally she put down her needle and thread and said, "Oh, all right, then. Just a minute."

She came back with a small photo, no longer black and white but in antique shades of sienna, and she placed it on the sofa cushion where they could both see it. It showed a stunningly handsome, rawboned young man in a cap and white cotton uniform with the number 10 stitched on the chest. He had white teeth, a thin mustache, and soft but intelligent dark eyes. The picture was dated in the lower right-hand corner, 1924.

"Who's that?" he asked.

"That's your great uncle on my side of the family."

"Oh."

His father studied the photo skeptically for a half-minute or so, and then with a great rattling of paper, he buried himself in the week's news once again.

————

When he was fifteen, his mother got sick. When they had brought in the hospital bed and put it in the den for her, on another of those frosty spring days in the Pee Dee region, when Bob had gone off reluctantly and halfheartedly to his work at the hardware store, and Frank was at school, Della lay thinking, trying to remember what she had thought about when she first saw her future husband's face. There was confusion in her: she saw him looking around the paper, the way he would always do, but then she saw him looking up from the hymnal, too, and she could not remember which had been first.

Most likely it was the hymnal. Yes, certainly it was. He had come into the United Methodist Church that Sunday with his friend, that big boy with the blond hair who drowned during the summer of '47, and Bob had looked measly and uneasy standing next to him, in a shirt that was way too big for him and a tie which had obviously come out of his daddy's closet. He wasn't even singing, he was just looking at the page, and glancing up occasionally at Penny Hardaker, whom she knew he had spotted in his first five minutes inside the door. She had not thought he was particularly good-looking, but she liked the way his reddish-brown hair fell stubbornly over his eyebrows no matter how many times he brushed it back with his hand. Penny was down at the end of the choir box, and Della was more or less in the middle, but his eyes never drifted her way even once, that first Sunday.

That's just fine, she had thought at the time. I certainly do not need to be looking at him, and Lord knows I don't want him looking at me. Of the four high-school girls in the choir back then, it had always been Penny they wanted to meet, Penny with her platinum hair and her face shiny with makeup. Bob Treadwell was not the first boy in these parts to take a sudden interest in the Gospel when he came to marriageable age and realized that the girls at the truck stop and in the taverns were not the sort they wanted raising their children. Clearly, there would be someone for her, in God's own time, and she was in no hurry, as she had just been accepted to Converse College with a full scholarship, and she had a lot to do before she was to pack and be delivered there by her parents in August. It was already April.

Looking back, as if through a long, twisting and dented tunnel, Della could not even begin to imagine how life might have happened had she gone away after all. If he had not stayed for the coffee and doughnuts on his fourth Sunday in attendance, and if she had not been helping her mother serve, and if Preacher Laite had not walked him over personally and introduced him...if she had gone on to Converse and then become a teacher or a paralegal and had gone away to Raleigh or Charleston or Atlanta... Well, what did it matter? You put your best years into whatever life you get, and you still end up in your own downstairs in a bed that plugs in and holding onto a button you push in order to sit up.

During those lonely hours, when the bitterness started to work on her this way, she would pick up the Bible from the table, not to read but to have its weight on her chest or lap. That helped. It would have been hard to describe how she felt about all of this, and she was glad that neither Bob nor Frankie asked too many questions or talked too much. But if she had to say, she would say it was just all very odd to sense herself shrinking, withering, sinking back into the earth, bodily. There wasn't much pain now, now that they had given her these latest pills, but there was this strange sensation of slowly disappearing, and the weight of the book on top of her showed her she was still here. She did not need to read the words inside it again, for they had been her companions all of her life, the language of her heart, but now the only question was the way in which she would actually go. Would it be like a door opening on a light-filled room? Would the Savior appear to her in robes, or would He simply be some sort of presence, a sort of mist? And most importantly, would she be able to let go and proceed with dignity?

For, if she had done nothing else, she had loved them, Bob and Frankie, however imperfectly. In truth, they had been her life, even in the unhappy days and in those times (which were many) when it seemed Bob barely knew she existed. And Frank, he had been her great love, and her great mystery; he was quiet like his father, but he had always seemed older, in some way, and sometimes he seemed very sad. What things did he know deep down that he could not express? She had known, from the instant he came squalling and sprawling out of her own body, grasping at the air with tiny hands, that there must have been reasons for the life she had agreed to.

Still, she did not really know what they were. As she had grown into this life, this long aching curve, she found she had many more questions than answers: why does the body fail, for instance? Why give something to the object of your love, as He had given the body, and then have it simply wear out this way? Oh, she knew the easy answers, all right – that sin had brought decay and despair, that our bodies are made of the earth while our souls are meant for something else – but she wanted to know what it was all for. It was like this, she thought: I get hungry, and behold, a pot of stew appears on the stove, with corn fritters to boot; I get thirsty, and I get myself some sweet tea or lemonade or plain old water; I am filled up with love to give, so brutal that it hurts me in this big gaping place inside me, and I am given a child. So, it would be reasonable, eventually, to deserve to know why she had reeled out her own life in laundry loads and scrambled eggs and PTA meetings and Wednesday choir practices and the endless Sundays at church. What had it been for?

The fog came upon her, but when she opened her eyes again, there was Frankie's face, so grownup-looking even though he was only 15, and with the old expression of curious concern, the same as his father's, floating above her with the darkening afternoon shadows all around.

"Hey, Momma. Do you want the TV on?"

Her mouth was so dry. "No, hon', just reach me my water, please."

He took the glass over to the sink, poured it out, put in fresh water, and brought it to her.

"You're home late," she said.

"We started baseball practice this week."

She nodded. "Your Dad home yet?"

"No, ma'am. I'll start dinner. I think there's some fish left over in there."

Men in the kitchen – that's what it all came to. She turned her face toward the window and traced the final decline of the sun through the black tree trunks, as she listened to the pots and plates clunking and clanging just like broken bells.

———

The preacher himself, Luther Laite, had not given them a chance in hell when he married them, but driving out to the Treadwell house in his rumbling old Ford wagon, he had to admit it, now that her time was almost up: they had surprised him, especially Bob. Sometimes Luther thought that the greater part of being a pastor (as he preferred to think of himself, unlike some of the boys at seminary who had wanted to be called ministers or reverends) was just getting people to see things through to the end. There was great value in finishing any job, and the rituals as he saw them were all about closing the deal, crass as that seemed. But human beings were inclined to be lazy and to leave things hanging, especially some of these folks around here who often could not even clean up their own yards or show up on time for anything.

He had always liked Bob and Della. It was a clear-cut case of a very fortunate man stumbling into a chance at his own salvation because he had somehow connected himself to a woman who knew what to do. There was a time when Treadwell would wander off and do his drinking (oh, yes – Luther knew about that, though he was not typically the sort of shepherd to take his staff and beat a dumb animal) and make light of her devotion and try to ruin things sometimes for everybody else, but by God, she would be in that choir box come Sunday whether he actually chose to come through the door or to stand outside under that crepe myrtle smoking his cigarettes, the way he liked to do. And that boy, Frank, seemed to have more of her in him than of his old man, and that was reason enough for jubilation right there.

Still, he liked Bob. He had known Treadwells, it seemed, from the beginning of time. Bob was a good deal like his father, but a little more easygoing and with a better sense of humor. The real irony, however, was that Bob's daddy, even in the face of his wife leaving him for that rogue from Beaufort and taking the younger boy, and everything going to hell that way, had never touched liquor, probably knew he'd like it too much; yet here was Bob, with one of the best women in all of Marion County for a wife, one of the best human beings Luther had known, and he had at least once gone and climbed completely inside a bottle when things didn't go just so. Still, there was no great riddle in human fallibility; in fact, it was the most predictable thing in life, as far as he knew, and this was true for himself as well. Oh, Luther disdained drink and he only swore when he was by himself and if he had ever looked at the girls in the choir box it was only for a moment and only because he was human and had the same plumbing as the worst kind of wretch. That was what people couldn't seem to comprehend about Christ's remark about the sins of the heart: He wasn't trying to make us feel even worse about ourselves but was merely telling us that we ought not to feel so righteous when we don't give in to temptation, because believe you me, we are all of us only a short step away from a royal screw-up.

Now, he did worry some for the boy, for Frankie. There were some who said he was a little slow in the head, but Luther knew this was far from true. Every time he went out to the house, as he was doing now, the kid seemed to have a schoolbook in his hands. And when Bob was late coming in, he took care of his mother with so much tenderness and meticulousness that it made the preacher want to weep. And of course, everybody in the entire state who paid any attention at all to such things knew about Frankie's prospects as an athlete. Downright freakish, it was said, but Luther knew a thing or two about that as well: he knew that the boy had it in his head that playing ball was what he was supposed to do, that he was meant for it, and when coupled with a healthy intelligence that wasn't overly critical or analytical – why, that was the sort of kid who really could go a long way, barring corrupting influences.

He turned down the river road and pulled up in front of the Treadwell place just as twilight was turning to darkness and one long shadow lay across the land, spreading itself toward the water. The lights were on, but he noticed that Bob's pickup was not in the carport. He swung his door open to the cool spring night and the hiccupping of frogs and the softer song of crickets, and he went up to the house.

The boy answered the door. "Hey, Pastor Laite," he said. "Come on in. She's dozing right now. She just ate."

"Thank ye. Is your daddy home?"

"No, sir, not yet."

Luther looked around the room. A familiar smell came to him, and he knew it as the smell of a house in which someone was going to die soon – a kind of muskiness, almost stale but not quite. Nevertheless, he thought it was heroic, the way the boy and his father (he assumed) kept the place up. There was dust, to be sure, along the baseboards, and old newspapers strewn here and there, but the place was neat and there were no dirty dishes on the stove or counter. A better job than he himself could have done.

He looked in on Della, who appeared small and withered but seemed to be sleeping quite serenely, and he let her be. He sat down on the sofa out front; Frankie had gone back to his mathematics book at the table.

"I'd offer my assistance," Luther said, "but I'm sure I'd cause more harm than good. I nearly flunked algebra in high school."

Frankie smiled but said nothing.

"So, I hear you boys started baseball today."

"Yes, sir, pitchers and catchers."

"Seems like y'all start earlier every season."

Frank nodded. "It does seem that way. Care for anything to eat or drink, Pastor?"

"No, thanks, son. You go on and do your work now. I'll be quiet. I just wanted to wait here a while and get in a word with your father when he gets home."

"Okay, sir. Whatever you'd like."

Yep, that's a good fella right there, Luther thought. Turning out all right, he is. I just wish he had some clue as to what's about to happen to him. He put his head back on the sofa, listening to the crickets and to Frankie's pencil scratching its way across the page, and just underneath those sounds, the woman's steady, soft breathing coming from the next room.

————

When Frank had gotten home that afternoon around five, he was not much concerned to see the empty space in the carport where his father's truck should have been. Sometimes he worked late at the store, stocking shelves, unpacking boxes of nails, hanging the gleaming new tools up on hooks, taking inventory... If he had known, in fact, Frank would have stopped in there himself, detouring from the bike path to the main street in Dillon, as he sometimes did, because he loved the hardware store. He knew nothing about tools or machinery or fertilizer, but he loved the cool concrete floors, the smells of iron and oil, and the easy conversation between the men who worked there.

On those occasions, his father would hoist Frank's bicycle into the bed of his truck and they would ride home together.

At least he would be able to get some work done. Even so, he was glad when the pastor arrived, for to have sat there by himself, with her in there in a dead sleep, and with that feeling of just waiting for something, anything, to happen, was all just too tedious for him; he found he could actually concentrate better on schoolwork these days with someone else around, especially when it came to math. Reading had always come quite naturally to him, and so English and History weren't so bad, but numbers on paper didn't mean much to him. Now, comprehending the angle between his position in center field or on the mound and the arc of a fly ball or the streaking line of a grounder, understanding the mechanics and the applied physics of baseball – that was another matter. He was Albert Einstein when it came to that.

Of course, he knew that Pastor Laite would ask him about the team. Everyone did. Frank certainly enjoyed playing for the high school, but there was a lot more baseball around than people seemed to realize: there was the Dixie Youth League and the American Legion team in Marion, and this past winter he had gotten a letter from a man with the Greenville Spinners, who were in the Tri-State League, "expressing interest" in him. When he showed the letter to his mother, she pressed the little button to sit herself up so she could hold it under the light, and she had said, "Isn't this for grown-ups? You're only fifteen." Frank had merely shrugged his shoulders and then put the letter away in a desk drawer.

It had always been like that, with people wanting him to "play up" with the older fellows. Last year, as a ninth grader, still in junior high school, he had crossed the street every afternoon to practice with the varsity team, and after a while they started putting him in the games. His aloof teammates had seldom spoken to him, and he had no place in their conversations anyway, with their mysterious references to this or that girl and their swear words and their talk of the cars they wanted to buy. When eventually he was given the starting position of one of the seniors, a tall, skinny boy named Ricky, he felt awful about it, because that boy then spent the rest of the season down at the end of the dugout, sulking, expressing his annoyance in quiet, sinister tones to anyone who walked past, and glaring at Frank. Still, most everyone had told him it wasn't his fault that he was good, and his father had said, "Just go out and have a little fun, Frankie, like you usually do." Indeed, it was fun, though he always imagined that baseball would still be fun even if he weren't very good. On the other hand, if being good meant he got to play more, then he supposed he was glad.

But there was more than just the playing. Playing was the best thing, of course, but he also relished the calm moments right before something would happen, right before everyone would spring into motion and there would be shouting and he would have to think and act very quickly and yet not think; and when the inning was over, he liked sprinting to the dugout and throwing himself down on the bench, chest heaving, trying to calm himself for the moment when he would have to take up a bat and get ready to hit, telling his still-racing heart to slow down. He liked the warm smells from the concession stand and the moist odors that arose from the infield dirt on particularly hot days, of the sour sulfur water that shot from the chugging sprinklers in long arcs that flashed in rainbows out across the green expanse. He liked coming out to the on-deck circle, sliding the heavy lead donut over the bat's handle, and then as he swung it whiplash-fashion, he liked looking up into the stands and finding the people he knew. Of course, his father was nearly always there, and his mother, too, if there were no church activities, and sometimes they brought along the neighbor girl, Liza, whom he had regarded at the time as his best friend; for a while everyone laughed and talked and seemed able to forget all the things that might have bothered them, just as he did.

None of this was to say that he did not understand the objective of winning the game. Often Frank was as mystified as anyone as to why opposing hitters struggled to hit his pitching, for he did not feel that he threw all that well. Coach Bass, the high school coach, had shown him how to break his curve off a bit more and how to throw from different angles, but otherwise, he just "rared back and threw," as the old-timers would say. The truth was he preferred playing center field, where he could roam and sprint after tall fly balls or scoop up a base hit and fire the ball off of a crow-hop to second or third, or in the most exhilarating instances, to home plate to try and catch a runner. And now, with his beloved glove and his well-scuffed, well-broken spikes, he believed he could make a play on just about any ball from the edge of the infield to the deepest section of outfield fence.

Still, he found himself trading off starts on the mound with only one other pitcher, Hal Yates, who had much better control than he had but did not throw with the same power. Consequently, Coach Bass was always worrying after his arm, always having him wear his jacket in the dugout and ice down his elbow afterwards, but Frank hardly ever even felt any soreness. He did not exactly like Coach Bass, but he respected him, and that was as it should be. He knew that his inquiries and doting reflected only his wish to win the state championship but did not stem from any sincere caring for his well-being, and that was perfectly fine with Frank. He preferred that to a false show of concern and affection, and he had seen plenty of that. That was one thing that had been worth learning – that being especially good at doing a thing sometimes brought out the worst in those who came out to watch you do it.

That accounted in part for his fondness for the preacher, he supposed, for he was a man who seemed completely uncorrupted by hidden motives.

Now, as Frank finished up his last math problem and closed the book, he looked over to where Pastor Laite had fallen asleep with his head leaned back on the couch, his bald pate glowing in the soft lamplight. It was late – 9:00, and his father had not come home yet. He stood up and went over and touched the man on the sleeve of his rumpled white dress shirt, and the pastor stirred and sputtered, then gazed at him uncomprehendingly for a few seconds.

"He ain't come home yet," Frank said. "I guess he worked real late or stopped off at the diner for a bite or something."

Pastor Laite gazed around the room and then rubbed his eyes. "Well, that's odd," he said. "I reckon you're right, though." He looked toward the den. "And how 'bout your momma?"

"Still sleeping. She'll probably sleep straight through till morning, now."

"So much the better. I should be getting on home myself." He stood up, steadying himself against the back of the couch, still trying to rouse himself. He was tall for a preacher, Frank thought.

"You best get some rest, too, Frankie. It's gonna be a busy spring for you. Tell your daddy I'll try and catch him tomorrow."

"Yes, sir, I will."

When Pastor Laite was gone, he wrapped up the catfish he had been saving for his father and then washed, dried, and put away the pan. He looked in one last time on his mother, whose breathing was not strong but was at least still steady. Then he went down the short, paneled hallway which his mother had adorned with family portraits, to seek the small citadel of his own room.

———

Della had been dreaming, but this one was not like so many of the dreams she'd been having lately, the ones she could not distinguish from her own true memories of the past. The doctors said it was because of the tumor pushing on her brain, but sometimes she woke up and did not know she was at home, sick; she would believe she was in the outboard with Bob, floating over dark water, or sitting on a quilt at a church picnic. This time, however, she knew it was a dream, in part because she was frustrated that it had not been real after all and because she wanted to see how it ended.

She was looking through the little window in the United Methodist Church's big oak door, watching someone praying at the altar. Then she realized it was herself who was praying there, and suddenly her awareness had shifted to that spot: she felt the cushion under her knees and her elbows on the polished wood. Ahead of her, someone was moving behind the lectern, where Pastor Laite usually sat when someone else was reading aloud or speaking, but it was not Pastor Laite. She couldn't see who it was.

But she knew. It was the Savior. He was there, but she could not see His face or His eyes or His gleaming smile, as she had expected. There was only an aura, growing brighter by the moment, and a movement back behind the lectern, beneath the tall cross mounted there. As the light began to fall across her own hands, arms, and face, she began to be lost in joy, and to lose all sense of herself. But then it was as if someone else, who must have been behind her, dropped a dark veil over her face, and she could not see anything at all. Then she was awake, her dry throat aching and her forehead burning. She heard Frank's voice:

"Momma? I got some water here for you. And I made some eggs, if you want any." He pushed the little button, and her upper half rose slowly, painfully, as she opened her eyes. She took the glass of water from him and drank, and after a minute or so, she could speak.

"No eggs, please," she said.

"I gotta go to school, Momma. Your pills are right there. Do you want the TV on?"

She shook her head, but he put it on anyway, telling her it would keep her company. The weatherman was waving his arms in front of a big map, but the volume was way down.

"Where's your father?" she asked.

Frankie looked at the floor. "He didn't come home last night." Before he could move away from the bed, Della put her hand on his forearm.

"Wait. There's somethin' you gotta do for me.

"Yes, ma'am."

She sat up and fixed his eyes to make sure he would understand her clearly. "Over there in the kitchen, in the drawer with the tools in it, there's a key at the bottom. I think it's black. Take that key with you and go look for him by the river. Do it this morning. He might be there."

Frank looked away. "By the river?"

"Yes. Down by Sanders Landing in that little grove of trees. You know the place?"

He nodded. "They'll count me tardy, though."

"It's all right," she said. "I'll send a note along with you tomorrow. Go on now, son."

He gathered up his book satchel and his baseball gear and left the house, taking care not to let the screen door slam.

———

It was the first of many mornings that Frank would carry the key to his father, so that very soon Della would not even need to ask him. There had been no frost that first time, and even at such an early hour, Frank could feel the promised warmth of spring. He pedaled his bike up Sanders Road, and though his tires did not like the shells and gravel and the hard, muddy clumps, he pointed it into the stand of live oaks. It was cooler in here, but not unpleasantly so, and he made a little game of veering in and out amongst the shadows.

He found his father seated on the ground against a good-sized tree trunk, staring philosophically out toward the Little Pee Dee. There were two empty bottles beside him, glistening like gigantic jewels in a shard of sunlight, and Frank wheeled his bike over to him straightaway.

"Hey," he said.

"Hello," his father replied.

"What are you doing there?"

"Who, me?" His father looked up at him now, and Frank noticed the thick iron cuff around his ankle and the length of chain, which was in turn coiled twice about the bottom of the tree. His hair was all mussed, and his eyes had an odd look, as if he had been deep in thought.

"Yeah, you."

"I'm not doin' nothin'. I came out here for a walk."

"All night?"

"I guess I fell asleep," his father said.

"Guess so."

The two bottles, which were dark green, were obviously quite empty, but Frank could smell the whiskey. He knew the smell – he smelled it once in a while on Coach Bass's breath on Monday mornings. It was not altogether bad – a little sweet, but sharp, and a little rancid, like rotten apples or peaches.

"Momma sent me to give you this," he said, and held out the black key.

His father gazed up at him, and then with a motion that was at once both an admonition and an apology, he reached up and took it. Frank sat there on his bicycle waiting, but then the man said gruffly, "I'll take it from here."

Frank nodded. Then he wheeled back out through the same little ruts he had made in the mud coming in, pedaling faster and faster once he made the road again, for fear of missing too much of his first class of the day.

———

Maxwell Bass sat back in his squeaky office chair, his feet up on the desk, as he gazed out at the students arriving for school. The bus wheezed up to the curb, and a dozen or so kids got off, among them...one...two...three of the girls in his afternoon gym class. They were dolled up in their green and pink and yellow dresses and sweaters, flipping their freshly washed hair to and fro as they chatted excitedly about some nonsense, boys, sex...who knew what?

Who was dumber? he wondered to himself. That Jeanine, from out on Zion Road, or her cousin, Estelle, who lived across the river? What he really wanted to say to both of them was that if their brains were even half the size and quality of their titties, they'd be a couple of damn geniuses, but of course, he couldn't say that. Well, he probably could say it, and they would just laugh it off, and the boys in the class would guffaw and smack each other on their backs, but then it might get back to somebody's parents. The school principal was a coward, but Bass did not want to get into it with any of these country bumpkins around here. If you said the wrong thing to somebody's daughter, you could get shot. No, there was only one girl he trusted at the present time, and that was the Billings girl, who was in the first-period group; granted, she was not very curvy – she was skinny, to tell the truth – but her daddy was in jail and her momma worked afternoons and evenings, and so he felt safe meeting her out by the field house in the twilight, after everyone else was gone. He ought to have felt worse about it, he guessed, but hell, for all he knew he might have been in love with Sarah Billings, who was a senior, after all, and nearly eighteen. He was not too old for that; thirty was by no means too old. There was a time when such a thing would have been completely acceptable. In a year, he might marry her, and then some of these church people would have to keep their mouths shut. That could all happen; he could see it.

Still, on those evenings, when he would walk back from the field house with the scent of Sarah Billings on him, which had intoxicated him only an hour or so ago, he felt like the lowest sort of skunk. It felt like the walk of a condemned man – no, not a man at all – a dirty, lowdown son of a bitch. He would slide into his car, put his head down on the steering wheel, and wonder what was wrong with him. And yet, there she would be again the next morning, sitting on the gymnasium floor among the other students, on her smooth, young haunches, smiling up at him, her eyes glistening and her blonde hair tumbling down her back in a stream, and he would think: Maybe you *are* in love, Max, you old dog. Maybe she is the one. And then, without thinking, later, as the light grew dim, and without allowing himself to think about it, he would lock up the gym and his office, having put away the kick balls and the badminton net and the basketballs, and he would take the walk out to the field house.

It was a little trickier now, though, now that baseball tryouts had begun. Some of the boys liked to stay as late as possible, and he had to pitch batting practice, going through bucket after bucket of balls, whipping them up to these idiots who had no hope of playing ball beyond high school anyway. They had won some games last year, and were in the running to win a state title this season, but Max knew that meant little in the big picture. None of his boys had the tools to make it as professionals, except maybe for one, the Treadwell kid, who had some natural talent, but Bass thought him none too bright. No, even the Treadwell kid…who did have good instincts and some athletic ability and who was still growing…even he would come up against the inevitable wall, and on the other side of that wall would be some bastard pulling the strings to make sure you never got your shot. He could speak from experience on that one.

The Braves organization was the one that had screwed him over worst. All right, he had hurt his back that spring in Florida, and it was true he had not done all that the trainer had instructed him to do (nor had he refrained from doing things he was *not* supposed to do) in order for it to heal properly; but he had only been twenty-three then himself, and he was just figuring out how much certain women enjoy hanging around pro baseball players; there had been plenty of liquor, too, and it had turned out to be a short road for him from the Charlotte Knights triple-A team to Dillon High School. Ironically enough, his back had healed up fine and he felt stronger now than he ever had in his life, but now he couldn't get so much as a cup of coffee with any team.

The homeroom period passed, and the bell for first period rang. "Time to go mold some young minds," Max said aloud, as he snapped the chair upright, stood, and scooped his clipboard and whistle up off the desk all in one coordinated motion. Then he stepped out into the hallway.

He always tried not to let his glance fall on her first, just in case there was any trace of suspicion among any of the other girls, but her hair was so bright in its golden allure, her eyes so fawning, her skin so fine, it was difficult. He had noticed her on the first day of school, way back in September, and even though her body was not as fully developed as those of some of the others, she carried herself with a certain maturity that had appealed to him. She had terrific posture, and she just seemed to know more than most girls her age, and as he would eventually find out, she certainly did know a few things, all right. He tried to appreciate the knowing without wondering about where she had acquired such knowledge, and so far, he had not made the mistake of raising that question. All you need to know, Max, he said to himself, is that you are a lucky bastard. Think how many men would like to be in your circumstances. Screw the Milwaukee Braves.

"All right," he said, "please respond appropriately as I call your name." He didn't need to call the names, as he knew all the kids, but it helped to kill off five minutes or so of class time.

"Aikens."

"Here."

"Applewhite."

"Here."

"Atkins."

"Here."

"Bassett."

"Here."

"Billings."

"Here." Good – that's it, chime right in with no hesitation, he thought; yet in her tone, he heard something else, something liquid, some kind of sonic spark that bespoke the glory, the passion, the intensity of a young heart in love for the first time with a real man. All of that weight was hung upon a single word uttered by her lips.

Mercifully, the class went by quickly, and she was the last one through the gym door as he held it open. She lingered there for just a moment, not long enough to arouse any notice, but just hesitating and tossing her head ever so slightly, so that her hair brushed his arm and her pretty scent came up to him softly, and she whispered, "What time?"

For an instant, he saw that this was the moment for strength, to displace his desire with patience, and if they were really meant to be together, to think not of the thrilling anticipation and the walk out to the field house but of the self-loathing which would follow, the mortifying guilt of the walk back. But he found on his tongue only a single syllable:

"Six."

———

My wife is dying.

Now that Bob Treadwell had finally admitted it to himself, he abruptly realized that those same words would now be tumbling around in his head like this for weeks, maybe months, like a jagged rock in one of those motorized tumblers, but this rock never would turn into a smooth stone. That made him think of the tumor in Della's head, growing bigger and bigger until at last it would simply squeeze her brain hard enough to kill it. In this day and age, he thought – how is it the rock still wins?

He had not wanted to go back on the bottle, but when he had driven by the liquor store in Marion yesterday, those lovely green bottles in the window seemed to speak to him, and he remembered the way good whiskey (or for that matter, no-so-good whiskey) could soften up the world for you, smooth out the stones. But he had forgotten the rest, that the softening would continue for a little while, but then something else would happen; it would be like stepping through a door and suddenly seeing with painful clarity the harshest truths he knew. In this case, his wife was dying. So then you had to get another bottle and start all over again.

He could say with pride, however, that it had been a long time that he had refrained, had been virtually a teetotaler, had worked as hard as any man and had been a good husband and a good father, and if he fell down now, well, at least he had gotten somewhere. He had no delusions about his condition; he was not inclined to lie to folks and say he had just lapsed a bit and everybody makes mistakes and he would be fine today. That was not how it took him.

There had been that two-month binge fifteen years ago, when Frankie was newborn, when he had felt overwhelmed and had seriously doubted whether he had the stamina for all this…this domestication, and he had deliberately tried to sabotage himself and his marriage. Lucky for him, Howard, his boss down at the hardware, was an understanding man.

That time, in '44, he didn't see at first what his time in the Pacific had had to do with it. Even when Della, who had been watching with silent horror as he unraveled and trying to care for an infant at the same time, even when she told him he had been murmuring about strange things and strange places she had never heard of, he thought they were just bad dreams. But then one night he woke up and he was kneeling in the kitchen with the big carving knife in his hand, but he was sure that he was on the beach at the island of Rabaul, with his unfixed bayonet. He had been ordered to crawl down to the shoreline and exterminate any surviving Japanese soldiers he could find. It was a clear morning with a warm ocean breeze, and it turned out that there were lots of survivors bleeding in the sand, and he had stopped counting after a while as he slithered among them, but somehow he had completely forgotten about the entire episode until he woke up in his kitchen in Dillon, South Carolina. That was the day he had gone down to the hardware and fetched a length of chain and a locking iron cuff, and he had shown Della the key and then put it away in the drawer. As foolish as it might have seemed to chain himself up down there in the live oak grove, from his whiskey-clouded point of view, it was a sensible precautionary measure: he desperately wanted not to hurt anyone.

Then one morning, it had not been Della who came down through the trees with the key; though he could not see who it was at first, he knew it was not her light footfall he heard approaching, but a much heavier, more deliberate one. And then suddenly, Luther Laite, the pastor from the Methodist church, was standing before him in his light blue suit, black shirt and collar, towering over him, really. He dropped the key onto Bob's lap and said,

"If you ever do this again – if you put her through this again, you won't need to chain yourself to a tree, because I will personally drown your sorry ass in that river right over there."

So it was that he had gone home, gone back to work, put away the chain in the shed, collected the empty bottles and hauled them to the dump, and returned to the life he and Della had made for themselves, humble though it was. He had to like that preacher, and that was twice now he had brought Bob to her, in a way, and maybe this second time was even more binding. He went back to church for a time, too, which he had not done with any regularity since their wedding – for five years he attended, to be exact, although he was never one to get overly involved, never was inclined to be in the men's club or prayer group or to help with the fundraisers or any of that kind of thing, but at least he went, and Frankie went to the nursery and then to Sunday School when he was old enough. And even when he did start to drift away, to find other pressing duties on Sunday mornings, Pastor Laite did not pester him. Sometimes, Bob would go and stand outside the church, in summer when the windows were open, and he would stand beside a huge, flaming crepe myrtle tree and smoke a couple of cigarettes. He knew that the preacher probably thought he was making some sort of statement of rebellion when he did that, but it was only because he still liked to hear the music; he could even single out his wife's voice as the choir swelled over the old familiar lines.

Now as he sauntered up Main Street, past the Methodist and Baptist churches, past the town offices, past the general store, past the hardware where his pickup was still parked out front (quickening his pace in case Howard happened to glance out the window and see him), he was a free man, a rounder, a born loser and happy to be such. Maybe he would just walk up and down this street all day till he got thirsty again, or maybe he would go get his truck and pay another visit to the liquor store in Marion, or else head up to Silky's Bar on the state highway and spend the day in that cool, windowless room and have as many beers as he wanted. In any case, he would have to make sure he'd be able to get back to the tree, where he'd left the chain wrapped around it. It had been the boy who had come with the key this morning, and although that didn't surprise him any, he half-heartedly wished it had been the pastor, as that might have brought some excitement to the mix.

But it was Frank who had come, and after he had gone on to school, Bob had unlocked himself and walked up to the house. Della had been asleep in the den, of course, with the television flickering noiselessly, but he purposely did not look directly in but slipped past the doorway and into the kitchen where he carefully and quietly put the black key back in the drawer. As he had turned to go out again, he was seized by an impulse to go in and look at her as she slept, look down into that face which would now be ever more gaunt but still as sweet as it had been on the day of their wedding. He had not been able to bring himself to do it, and as the coward he now knew himself to be, he went out again into the bright light of day.

———

Della awakened once again from the dream in which she knelt at the altar, and once again, before she could fully realize the presence moving toward her from under the large mounted cross behind the oaken lectern, the veil had descended over her eyes. That euphoric sense of becoming one with the purest sort of light imaginable had touched her once more, and she lay there feeling that she floated on an incoming tide, which now set her down once again in the living world. She struggled to bring air into her lungs and moisture to her throat, and it was with sadness that she realized she was still in the big bed with the white metal header and footer and the little button on the end of a cord that was practically her only means of movement now.

She looked at the bedpan on the table, and reached for it, though she had hardly eaten or drunk anything today, but she hesitated. With Bob being gone or coming in very late now – as she suspected would be the case – it meant that her fifteen-year old son would have to attend to these personal matters for her, and she couldn't have that. Perhaps the pastor would come by today, and he could ask one of the church ladies to drop in a couple of times a day for a few weeks. Of course, he would, and she had lots of friends there, some of whom had already come by with hot meals and to help with odd chores, and she had no doubt that one of them would agree to help, unpleasant as the job might be. She had done the same for some of them herself, when Penny's husband was ill, for instance, and Jackie's, and besides, it wouldn't be for long, she thought.

It was unfortunate about Bob. She didn't want to leave things this way with him, but the truth was she wasn't all that surprised by his behavior. He had never been very good at dealing with these kinds of things. It came from his own upbringing, she knew; his own mother had left them when Bob was young, claiming the younger brother for herself, and his father, of course, had had no idea how to make his son feel loved. It was more difficult with men, as she had seen; silly things got in the way, and it was all about pride and not ever appearing weak. There was the finest irony of all: he thought the drinking and the carousing at a time like this made it seem as if it didn't matter that much to him, that he would go on strutting through the world like a peacock even after she was gone, but she knew that wasn't so. And in her way, that was something she had tried to impress upon Frankie – that it is all right sometimes, anytime, for a male to let his feelings show a little bit. Maybe he'd gotten it, or maybe he was too wrapped up in his sports and in being fifteen or in whatever else he was into, and so maybe he hated having to do a few things for her now. It was hard to tell with him, he said so little.

But what fun they'd had once, the three of them. On Saturdays when Frank was small, they would take the boat upriver to Lake Norton and picnic and fish, and watch the boy waddle around and splash in the water. You couldn't have knocked that smile off of Bob's face with a hammer, and then in the late afternoon they would make a fire and cook up some beans and weenies. The breeze would come up, then, to keep away the mosquitoes, and the moon would rise over the lake and the tall pines and cast a long white reflection like a flaming arrow. Somehow, with one running light, Bob found his way with ease back home again, drifting over the glossy blackwater and cutting the engine every so often so that they could just drift and enjoy the quiet. She remembered how, when they got home, Frank would be too tired for a bath, and she would put him in bed and the smell of the river and the wood smoke was on him, and she sat on the edge of the bed stroking his hair and thinking how cruel it was that he would get bigger, much bigger. And then Bob would come in and put his hand on her shoulder, and there they were, looking like a *Saturday Evening Post* cover, she knew, but so what? Some things were true and of value even if they were corny.

Bob had sold that boat when he got the new truck, and that was a sad day. They still had the jonboat, and he always said he'd get another outboard one day, but then the whole sports thing started and weekends were taken up forever after. She had no real objection: she was glad that Frank had found something he really loved and was good at, something Bob could take part in, too, though it still struck her as amusing that whatever talent the boy had came through her side and was the same gift which had been given to her Uncle Wayne, specifically, whom family lore recalled as a successful professional ballplayer. She couldn't have said with what team or for how long or any of that because she had never cared for ballgames, really, and she knew nothing except what little she learned going to Frankie's games. But she had sorely missed that boat.

Who was that little girl from up the road that they used to take with them, the pretty little one with the curly brown hair? The one who'd had such awful family trouble later on. Oh, of course – Liza Applewhite. She was two years older than Frankie, but even at five she was very protective of him; she always kept a close eye on him and made sure he didn't get too close to the fire, and she always helped him find a good stick for roasting marshmallows. Her family had moved into town a few years ago, and after that she didn't come around.

Anyway, the past was one more thing you couldn't change. Because she knew that, she had thought that it would be easy to let it all go. She had watched her own parents (Bob's dad had passed away not long before they got married) just fade, fade, one piece of them after another sliding away: no more Friday night dinners with all of them together, and then no more of the big, happy Thanksgivings, all just dwindling and dwindling with no renewal or replenishment, and she wondered at how quietly and with such dignity her mother, the last to go, had lain down and accepted her own mortality. The old people understood some things that we cannot, Della thought. Maybe they had ridden in wagons, many of them, and used funny sayings, but by and large they did not fear what they couldn't control. It was like living with the weather, on the old tobacco and cotton farms: you did your best but there was only so much you could do, and if the drought came, or the flood, you didn't curse your fate. You accepted the mystery of it. And oh, how poor they had been sometimes. She recalled one Christmas when all she had gotten was a single pencil – a pencil! – and the look on her father's face when she opened it was worse than it would have been had she gotten nothing at all. So maybe she and Bob had never had very much, but at least there had always been more between them and utter despair than a little sliver of wood with lead in it, and she was thankful for that. Still, she wished she had her mother's strength now, as she waited through these shadowy hours.

That afternoon, when baseball practice was over and the twilight was thickening, Frank trotted over to the bicycle rack and was startled and disturbed at what he found there: someone had slashed his bike's tires. He stood with his book satchel over one shoulder and his baseball bag slung across his back, staring at the two jagged breaches in the rubber, and he wondered who might have done such a thing. It was true that he didn't have many friends outside of the team (if any), but he was not aware of any enemies either. Had it happened last year, Ricky Simpson, the senior whose position he had taken in the outfield, would have been the immediate suspect, but when Ricky's family had lost their house to the bank last summer, they had moved away to Raleigh. He couldn't think of anyone else who might have a grudge against him, and since he had no choice, he shrugged his shoulders, yanked the bike out of the rack, and began pushing it up the school's driveway.

When he made it to the dirt path alongside the main road, it was very dark. There would be no moon tonight, and all seemed oddly silent. He had gone perhaps half a mile when a set of headlights approached him from behind, causing the shadow of himself and his bike to veer and distort itself into maniacal shapes as the lights rounded the big curve. A dark pickup pulled up beside him and slowed. The passenger side window went down, and from behind the wheel, a face leaned over and hung there, staring at him.

"Hey," said a girl's voice.

He glanced over. "Hey yourself," he said.

"What's wrong with your bike?"

He shook his head. "Tires are flat."

"Well, that ain't no good, is it." She pulled the truck closer to the road's bank. "Hey, boy. Do you know who I am?"

He looked over again. "Can't say I do," he said.

"Well, if you'd stop for just a minute, you might could see."

He halted and gazed intently at the pale oval eerily lit by green dashboard light. Then he shook his head.

"Come closer," she said. He took a step; she was pretty, with short-cropped, wavy hair, and white teeth, but he still felt no spark of recognition. She smiled. "It's me. It's Liza. Liza Applewhite. We used to be friends a long time ago."

Of course. He did know her. As young children, they had once been neighbors, but her family had moved away years ago, to Greenville, if he recalled correctly. Anyway, now she would be a senior, two years ahead of him, and even if she had lately moved back to Dillon, the likelihood that they would share any classes or the same circles of friends would be remote. Their lives had taken such divergent paths, and he found he could barely even conjure up the past that they had once shared. And she was an older woman now, and the gulf between 15 and 17 – no, in fact, she would be 18 already – was, naturally, impassable.

"So, do you need a ride, or what?" she asked.

He looked away and started trudging up the path again. "No, thanks. It ain't that far."

She edged the truck along. "Frankie," she said, and hearing his own name on her lips, something came suddenly rushing back to him, and the sound of it nosed at his heart. "Just get in."

He hoisted his bike into the truck's bed and did as she told him, climbing in beside her and muttering a thanks, but keeping his eyes fixed on the road.

"You still living at the same place?"

He nodded. He was trying to figure out how long it had been since he had seen her. Her family had moved when she was eleven and he was nine, and after that they had lost touch with one another. But before that, they had been together nearly every day, as there were only a few houses scattered along the dirt road that ran beside the Little Pee Dee, and playmates were rare. Together they had explored the piney woods, the rivulets, the hidden glades, and he had been only vaguely aware that she was a girl then, with her short brown hair and her toughness and the way she ran and shouted and played – she had been his best and only friend in those days. And well, despite the promises they had made to stay in touch with one another, when she had moved, it was like closing a book, or walking into a different room.

As if she read his thoughts, she said, "You do remember me, right?"

"'Course I do."

"Then why ain't you looked at me yet?"

He looked. She sure had turned out pretty, he thought. She wore jeans and a light windbreaker, and she was still on the small side, but she had grown into a distinct poise. Her hands were slender and quite long for her size, and they lightly goaded the steering wheel with genuine competence. Her hair looked much the same as it always had – she had always preferred it short – and her eyes shone, even though there was no light in the cab other than that of the dashboard; they gave off their own light.

"Is this your truck?" he asked.

"Belongs to my momma's new boyfriend. He says I can use it pretty much any time I want."

"Oh."

She peered at him. "So how come you never speak to me at school?"

"I...I guess I didn't know you'd moved back to Dillon. When did you, anyway?"

"Just after Christmas."

"Well, I don't think I even woulda' recognized you anyway."

"Or it might be you've got too famous to be seen talking to the likes of me. My momma and I read about you in the paper."

It was true – the local weekly had done a write-up about him in advance of the baseball season, though mostly it was Coach Bass who did the talking in the story, and that was fine, for when the reporter had come to the school and Frank had been called down to the athletic office, he found he was no good at answering questions about himself. He knew that his clipped and sometimes even one-syllable replies had made him sound stupid, so he was relieved a few days later, when the paper came out, to see that he had not been quoted directly.

"Oh, I hated that article," he said. "Besides, the *Dillon Register* is a long way from being famous."

"Still," she said, slowing as she came to the turnoff for the river, "you've got to admit, around these parts, you've made a splash. I mean, it seems around here everyone knows who you are."

"Do they really?"

She studied him a moment. "Frank Treadwell, do you honestly mean to say that you are not aware of the fact that you're the most famous boy at school?"

"That's..." He groped for a word... "that's ridiculous. It's only baseball. I mean, I been playing it my whole life."

"Well, now, that's not entirely true. You and I used to do a lot of stuff before you got so carried away with sports. Do you remember those times, Frankie?" She was looking over at him again, her eyes shiny, and even though he couldn't see their color in the dim light, he remembered that they'd be brown.

"I remember Momma and Daddy used to bring you to my games."

"Oh, your family and me goes back further than that. Do you remember our picnics?"

He tried, but his earliest recollection of Liza was of her sitting beside his mother in the stands, with her hair up in a ponytail. "I don't. I'm sorry."

She eased into the Treadwells' driveway. His father's pickup was once again missing from its spot.

"That's all right," she said. "You were pretty little then. Say, I heard your momma was sick."

He nodded. "She's doing a bit better here lately, I think. We got her a bed downstairs now."

"Do you think she'd mind if I came in to say hello? It's been so long since I seen her, and it ain't that late."

"I don't know," Frank said. "She sleeps a lot. And my dad's not home yet, so I guess I'll have to fix supper, plus I got a science test to study for."

She cut the engine and opened her door. "In that case, I won't stay too long."

He was surprised to find his mother wide awake, with the bed in the upright position. She was staring at the muted television, and her closed Bible was upon her lap, with her hands folded across it. She turned and smiled at them.

"Hey there, Mrs. Treadwell. It's me, Liza Applewhite."

Frank watched as true delight filled his mother's face; she literally beamed and stretched out her hand toward the girl. "Well, of course I do. How are you, Liza? And how's your momma?"

So just like that, he realized, a spark was rekindled. Here was a bond which had not been defeated by time and circumstance. And now that he had a good look at Liza with her strong limbs and her sturdy woman's figure – for she was no girl anymore, despite the vestiges of her tomboyishness – he saw that this had been a stroke of good fortune all around, and thought that if he could find out who had ruined his bike's tires, he might end up owing him a debt of gratitude. He would mind even less now the walk up to the main road to catch the bus for a couple of days until he could patch them up or else buy some new tubes.

The catching-up went on for a while between the two of them, and then Liza turned to him: "Tell you what, Frank, why don't you go ahead and get started on that homework you were talking about earlier. You're probably bored with all this girl-talk."

He muttered in agreement and went out to the dining room table. He took out the fat science book and opened it to the chapter on the respiratory system, and after a few minutes, she came out of the den with the bedpan and the top sheet and shut the door behind her. "Frank," she said, "where's the clean linens?" He pointed to the closet in the hall, and then for several minutes Liza bustled back and forth from den to closet to den to bathroom in a flurry of towels and sheets and pillowcases, and then she disappeared into the den again and shut the door.

A half-hour or so later, when she came out and said softly, "She's sleeping now, but she might be a little bit hungry when she wakes up," he did not really know what to say. He knew he ought to thank her, admit that there were plenty of things he hadn't thought of and probably couldn't have done for her anyway, but he found he could not; then he wished he might be able to tell her how she had brought with her a... a flame, or something like it, that he hadn't seen his mother so alert and happy in weeks, that just having her in the house for a short while had made a tremendous difference, but again, those words got stuck somewhere back in his throat. She had tossed her keys on the dining room table, and when she walked over to retrieve them, he stood up awkwardly.

He managed to say, "I'm glad I ran into you. I mean, I'm glad you stopped and picked me up and all."

"It was no trouble. Your mom was always nice to me."

He walked with her to the door, where she turned to him. Her face was quite close to his, and he carefully watched her lips moving, her fine white teeth. "Oh, listen, Frank. If you don't mind, I thought I'd maybe drop by again tomorrow evening. Just do a bit of laundry for her, see how she's feeling. In fact, I can pick you up on your way home again, if you want."

"Sure," he said. "Great."

"Okay. See you tomorrow. Maybe I'll even run into you at school." She smiled, a little pink half-smile, and went out, and he stood there dumbly, his hand on the doorknob, his head like a big, empty jar, or a blank screen with no edges, and he whispered to himself, "Well, now, then, there." Then he went back to the kitchen, opened the pantry, and began fumbling through layers of cans and boxes, immersing himself once more in the nightly hunt for something to make for dinner.

———

Della had been sleeping off and on. It was not a fitful sleep, but rather as if she were floating in a pleasant stream from one island of consciousness to another, and upon one of those landings, she had actually eaten some of the tomato soup and crackers that Frank must have brought in around eight. When she woke again at the sound of voices, around ten, she wasn't sure whether it was the same night, for the girl's voice was definitely not among them now.

One of the voices was quite loud, in fact, and at first she thought that Bob had come home finally, but then she realized its timbre was a good deal deeper than his. And then, of course, she realized that it was Pastor Luther Laite, and that he seemed quite agitated. The other voice was Frankie's – not the voice of the boy she had raised, but instead the husky tone of a young man.

"Where is he?" the pastor said.

Frank: "He ain't home yet."

Luther: "Home yet? He ain't? No, I reckon he ain't home yet. Don't think for a minute that I don't know what's been going on, Frankie. I didn't drive all the way out here at this time of night to hear you pretend to be dumb."

"I really don't know, Pastor. I mean, I don't know where he went to today. I don't think he went to work. Have you heard anything?"

"Work? Work? No, when I get a call from Howard Beamon at the hardware store asking *me* for his whereabouts, and then three more calls throughout the day and evening from various members of my own congregation saying they saw him stumbling – *stumbling* – around town and also in the parking lot at Silky's Bar, well, I'd say it's a safe bet he didn't show up to work. Wouldn't you?"

A few seconds ticked off, and then she heard Frank say, "I guess not."

"No, I guess not, too. Now, Frank, I think you might actually know something about this after all. Are you familiar with that little stand of live oak trees down near Sanders Landing?"

Pause. "Yes, sir," Frank said softly.

"And what about a certain length of chain your daddy keeps around here for the odd occasion...oh, say about four foot in length. And an iron shackle, like the kind prisoners wear? Are you familiar with those, too?"

"Yes. Sir."

"All right, then. Now we're getting somewhere, aren't we? Now, I want that key. I want the key to that cuff. Where is it, Frankie?"

Again, pause. "No disrespect, Pastor, but what do you want that for?"

"What do I want that for? I'll tell you why. Because I am personally going to go down there, unlock the son of a bitch, and personally – *in person* – knock the shit out of your daddy, pardon my language. And I would not strike a man at a disadvantage, so I need that key. And believe me, he won't be too quick getting up again, when I'm done with him."

She could picture Frank taking that one in, and she smiled when he said, "Well, I'm sorry, Pastor Laite. In that case, I can't give it to you."

"Can't give it to me? Can't give it to me? That's just fine. Don't think I won't go down there anyway, and if it means beating a man who has locked himself to a tree, dumb ass that he is, then my conscience will be clear. Now, I'll bid you good evening, Frank."

She heard his angry steps moving toward the door, and then Frankie said, "Wait, Pastor. I'd ask you not to do that. Don't go down there. Please, sir."

"Please, sir? *Please, sir?* Hell, son, you'll thank me for it after it's done. He'll either straighten up, or he won't come back around here no more, and that'll be good for all of you."

"Wait, Pastor Laite. I'm just askin' you to give me a chance to deal with it. It's a family matter."

"Oh, hell, Frank, I know that. I been knowing Bob Treadwell a whole lot longer than you have. I know your family, all right, and believe me, I'm saving you's all some trouble here. Now, do you want to give me that key or shall I just go on down there?"

The moments dribbled away. Della thought about how still the night was outside her window. Then Frank said, "It's family. No disrespect intended, sir, but I'm askin' you to let me handle him. I'll go down there in the morning, and I'll take care of it. I'll get him straightened out. Just give me a chance. I know what to do."

She could feel the pastor's will begin to give now, if only slightly. "You know what to do, do you?"

"Yes, sir."

Silence. Then: "You know what to do. You. Well, then do it, then. I swear, I don't know why I waste my time with you people. But I'll tell you this: if I come around here tomorrow night and he's not sitting in there by her bedside looking like the model spouse, there will be hell to pay. I hope you understand that, Frank."

"I do."

"I hope you do."

The front door opened, slammed, and he was gone.

A few more minutes had passed before Frank opened the door to the den, just a hair, and the kitchen light seeped across the ceiling, and he said, "Momma? You awake?"

I am awake, she thought. I am here. I am still with all of you. But she said nothing, and only a few moments later (or perhaps it was much longer – she couldn't tell), she found herself drifting in that warm current once again, hardly knowing how many more islands lay between her and the open sea.

Two

April/May, 1959

As he swung open the door to Silky's Bar and then covered himself in the shroud of that dim interior, Bob Treadwell had never been gladder to escape the glare of midday. It wasn't merely because of the stickiness of a spring that had turned from crisp to dank in a matter of days (they would be steaming by June); he was also relieved to get out from under all those eyes: he could feel them on him now, everywhere he went, and even though he knew that there were some in town who did not know him and would not have cared, there were also plenty who did, who watched him with the sourest, most righteous disdain and shook their heads as he passed by. If nothing else, the sight of an able-bodied man strolling at his leisure through a town where everybody worked except for the sick, lame and lazy would have registered general disapproval.

They could all go jump. He had done nothing wrong. Even when the sheriff's deputy's cruiser had pulled alongside him yesterday, and he was greeted and then questioned by a chunky fellow with whom he had gone to high school, who looked at him as if he were a piece of trash blowing along the road, he knew that the only code he had violated was the unwritten one of his own small, pitiable society: he was drunk during the day, with a sick wife at home and a boy still in school. No, he did not need nor want a ride home, and he was not creating a nuisance. He could always walk as straight as anybody, and he had bathed in the river for three mornings in a row now, so no one could say that he stank or was vagrant. As long as the boy came with the key each morning, good boy that he was, this life was not so bad, and by God, why couldn't they just let him alone?

He was regretful, a little, about the story he had told Frank, who had come – on foot this time – with the black key early this morning. He had come to with a start, not realizing at first where he was, and the ground was damp, and his pants' cuffs were dirty, and there was Frank, standing over him.

"You gotta come home today," he said.

He looked up but the glowing morning mist behind the boy and around his head made him squint. Thank God, he thought to himself: I can't remember a goddamn thing. How lucky can a man be?

Frank held the key in front of his face, and when Treadwell reached for it, he drew it away. "You gotta come home today," he said again. "The preacher is layin' for you."

"Course I will," he said.

"You're promising?"

He nodded; Frank dropped the key onto his lap and then turned and walked away.

Bob hoisted himself onto the tall stool and prepared to ride out the afternoon. He signaled Old Jack for a beer, and the old man looked up from his auto magazine and nodded. He came down along the bar, his wiry arms swaying, the heavy green navy tattoos undulating like snakeskin, and he popped open a beer bottle and set it in front of him.

"Hey, Bobby, how they treatin' you?"

"Been worse."

"Tell you what, it's goddamn hot out there already, ain't it?

Ah, Bob thought. Now he could open his mouth, sip on the beer, enjoy the cool, let the words and the beer swirl around, and talk about anything in the world besides the trouble – cars, the fishing, the weather, it didn't matter. And later, when Old Jack went back down the bar to restock the register or wash the glasses, he could stare at the labels again on the shelf behind the bar, shut his eyes, test himself (let's see, Johnny Walker Red, Johnny Walker Black, Cutty Sark, Wild Turkey...), until some of the boys came in and maybe a couple of girls and somebody fed the jukebox and maybe somebody would start to dance and he'd get into the whiskey then, and he'd be home free for another night, or so he hoped. There was always that dangerous time – the very dark hour or so between the bar and the place by the river, when all the windows along the streets would be dark, when he would try and let the hypnotic buzzing of the crickets and the frogs in the marsh fill up his brain.

He lit a cigarette. "Aw, hell, yeah," he said. "Hot. Gonna be a hot one."

Liza Applewhite slipped into her seat in the third row of Mr. Dillingham's biology class. He glanced over at her with those distant, colorless eyes, and it was clear that he saw she was tardy, but he turned wordlessly back to the lectern and looked down. She carefully took her notebook out of her satchel and opened it on the desktop.

This was the one class she was always sure to attend. She made her first-period gym class as often as she could because she liked exercising, even though she did not care much for Coach Bass – she had seen the way he leered at the girls, and of course, most everyone knew what was going on between him and Sarah Billings, or at least suspected it. But she would never miss Mr. Dillingham's Biology class.

The teacher peered up at them, his eyebrows forming a sharp V over thick, professorial glasses, his eyes rolling like small blue globes as he surveyed the thirty or so bodies ranged around the room. To his left, the lab table and sink stood like a great black monolith, or a tomb, and the flame of a Bunsen burner gave off a soft hiss.

"There is something you should all know," Mr. Dillingham said suddenly, his voice low but very clear. "This…" he said, raising his right hand, "and this…" Now he pointed at his own head with his left index finger. "These are your undoing." He let the words hang there for a few moments, the way he often began, and immediately, the class was entirely drawn in.

"I know I could stop there, as that is really all you need to know. We could roll up our sleeves, pick our lab partners, and go about performing all of the little experiments to show you how a tornado happens or what's on the inside of a toad or how to burn magnesium… That's what your counterparts around the nation are doing right now, these heady spring days, in *their* science classes: little Johnny and Janie are cutting open toads and lighting little fires. But I intend to actually do my job as the state asks me to: I intend to teach you something today. I'm going to tell you how to cut open *people* and how to start *big* fires – because that's what you're going to need to know."

A ripple of murmuring traveled around the room. He had been talking this way for weeks now, but since Liza had arrived at school in January, he had gotten progressively worse – or better, depending on how you looked at it. But there was definitely something wrong with Mr. Dillingham; no one ever knew what he was going to say anymore, but the principal and the school board hadn't yet figured out what to do with him. She had overheard a girl at lunch the other day say: "Oh, I think it's just sad. What we're seeing is a man unraveling right before our eyes. My momma said it's a matter of time before they take him away to the booby hatch."

Nonetheless, in the meantime, it was damn good entertainment. The teacher stared at them again, and a smile crept slowly onto his face. "What do I mean? This, the human hand, and this, the human brain. Think of it: all the might of the universe, the cosmic explosions, the terrible struggles of slimy half-fish to drag themselves onto the muddy shores, the swarming of cells to organize themselves over the eons, all of it conspiring to give you these two incomparable mechanisms. And for what?

"Now, you may argue that a man of science cannot be a man of faith and religion. But I beg to differ. I am indeed a religious man and my religion gives me the faith, the faith that these things have a purpose. Who can tell me what is distinctive about this tool?" He raised his hand again and fluttered it in the air.

A boy in the front row muttered halfheartedly: "Opposable thumb?"

Mr. Dillingham looked pityingly down upon him. "Little Johnny has come up with an answer… and he is wrong once again. Monkeys have thumbs, do they not? In fact, a gorilla can crush your skull like an acorn, and he might enjoy that very much, as would I. And then even a dog knows how to use his paws to hold his bone in place while he gnaws on it. And think of the ingenuity and relevant might in the tiny legs of a tiny ant. No. NO. The distinctive quality in this hand, these two hands, is their obedience to this…" He raised his finger to his own head again, and his thumb snapped downward like the hammer of a pistol. "The connection between my mind and these hands is the most powerful conspiracy of forces in the known universe, my friends. These hands do not act and react out of instinct alone, they are not mere flexors. As the tragic history of mankind has shown us with chilling clarity, every thought which occurs here, in the brain, however godlike or diabolical, eventually manifests itself in the actions of these two devices, these ingeniously sculpted machines, these makers of violins, these conductors of tactile compassion – these slitters of throats. Picasso used his to create some of the most important paintings of the twentieth century; Hermann Goering…on the other hand…chose to pop a cyanide tablet into his mouth on the night before he was to be hanged for crimes against humanity. Think of it, ladies and gentlemen."

Liza studied the teacher's face. He was around fifty, she thought, with pleasant smile creases around his mouth and a gallant swoop of graying hair thrown back behind his ears; he was handsome, actually, or at least he must have been, not so long ago. His light-blue tie was neatly knotted, and his crisp white shirt was freshly ironed: he certainly did not appear to be insane.

"Now," he continued, "allow me to impart to you where all this checkered history is taking us." He lowered his voice to a whisper: "The bus is careening out of control, little ones. The driver has passed out. We are about to go over the side of the mountain. And there is nothing we can do about it." Now loudly: "NOTHING. It was all set in motion long ago… The philosophers call it Determinism. It means that these clumps of atoms that make up our reality have been on a collision course since they first appeared, and nothing can keep them from crashing into each other. From the instant that one of our primal ancestors used this magnificent mechanism – which your very insightful school chum recently identified as a thumb moving in opposition to the hand's other digits – to pick up a rock and deliver a splintering, shattering blow to the skull of his fellow cave dweller, from that instant we started down the long, painful road to self-destruction. And now, at last, the best modern scientific minds, at the behest of and with the full approval of our own leaders, have given us the capability to wipe ourselves off the face of the earth forever. And make no mistake, boys and girls: we will do it, and although it may not occur in my lifetime, it will most certainly occur in yours.

"To what do I refer, exactly? Our leaders say that we are in the midst of a Cold War, a war without actual fighting or bloodshed, a war of willpower and intimidation. But please believe me when I say that when the moment of truth arrives, it will be anything but cold. A nuclear explosion produces temperatures near one thousand degrees at the point of impact. Even if you are two miles away when the bomb strikes, your clothes will ignite spontaneously.

And even if you at first survive such an attack, you will not escape the resulting toxins in the water, the air we breathe, in the food we raise; they will seep down into your bones, and within six years, you, too, will join in the ongoing carnival of death. Our precious Little Pee Dee River will become a bubbling stream of poison, as multitudes of fish turn their rotting bellies to its surface, and our lovely blue sky will turn to perpetual twilight – a darkness visible, as Milton described his notion of hell, a shadowland.

"Or perhaps the enemy will choose instead to invade us – a thing we have never known in this society, and the terror of which we have never had to endure. If those great countries far to our east, with their determination, their resources, their diligence, their party members who care only for the party, who spawn and nurture and sustain and grow its bacterial ideology until it cannot be contained – if they should decide to build up their army once again, it shall be the cruelest military machine the world has known, and they will come to our shores. And then the blade of execution and the lead pipe of tyranny shall fall upon us, children. Perhaps one day you will be in your father's fishing boat, laughing and lolling in the sunlight, or at the fruits of your mothers' tables, and then the next, you will find yourself in chains. Most assuredly, you will find yourself wishing you had met with swift and blinding annihilation instead."

He eyed them over the thick black frames. "I do not offer these scenarios merely to frighten you, children. These are not campfire ghost stories or sensationalist tales. I have myself witnessed the swirling effects of these inevitabilities, in places whose names you do not know. We speak of two world wars as if these were somehow fundamental conflicts, clashes of great ideologies, and finally the resolutions of conflicts, but I tell you, it isn't so. They are merely further evidence of the long, sad, drawn-out self-induced demise. But the next battle, friends, the *next* one will be unlike any recorded in the history books thus far, and there is a third possible landscape which I hesitate to paint for you, for it is the most terrible of all. But I have come this far, haven't I? Suppose that you were to lose all sense of yourself, and I do not mean it in the sense of becoming selfless. I mean it in the sense of a kind of sleeping condition: a numb sleep, the sleep of oblivion, wherein you will be unable to dream (and even your dog dreams), a sleep in which you are vaguely aware that there is life and color around you, but you are separated from it as if by a veil. Right now you cannot imagine the world without yourself in it. But in the world I speak of there will be no you, and no self. You will become the small parts of a big machine, or perhaps little flashes along a great electronic circuitry. I do not pretend to know how you will be suspended in this walking sleep, but I know that you will. And the authorities – or shall we say the forces, for they will be equally mindless – that will put you to sleep will do it so subtly, so quietly, that the battle will never truly be fought. You will have no will to resist, because they will use things which delight you in order to deaden you. You will be brainwashed, with your own identity scrubbed away like so much mold."

Liza looked about the room. A girl in the back was yawning. Two fellows in white t-shirts next to her were whispering and grinning at each other. This was how it usually happened: when he would begin, he had them, but after a while their attention would falter, although she still hung on every word; it was as if the rest of them had become desensitized to his ravings. Nevertheless, because of what happened next, this time would be different – this time, he would enter into the school's history, and they would remember it as vividly as anything that had happened thus far in their young lives. Some would say it was a trick, that Mr. Dillingham could not possibly have done what he seemed to do, and others would say he had only been able to do it because he really was insane. In any event, as things turned out, today would be his last day at Dillon High School. No one ever learned where he went, exactly.

It was nearly time for the bell, and the school's principal, Mr. Horace Babcock, suddenly slipped in through the door at the back of the lecture hall, his black blazer blending with the heavy shadows along the wall. He stood there with his arms folded, watching. After a few moments, Mr. Dillingham looked up at him, smiled, and kept right on speaking:

"Now, I don't know about you boys and girls, but I know Death when I see him. And of his many forms, the one that frightens me most is the one who seeks to numb your mind, to take away your identity, and to steal your soul. Personally, I prefer the fire." And with that, quite abruptly, as if he suddenly knew exactly what he wanted, the teacher strode briskly over to the black lab table with the lit Bunsen burner atop it, and held his palm over the hissing blue flame. He looked around at them, still smiling, his blue eyes flashing merrily behind the thick frames. When the students realized what he was up to, there was a collective gasp.

"My God!" someone shouted.

At that instant, the sleeve of Mr. Dillingham's clean white shirt burst into flame. He made no move, and his face was very calm.

Then someone else yelled, "FIRE!" Spontaneous turmoil ensued. Desks were overturned and books tumbled into the aisles as students scrambled for the doors. Over the din of chaos, as Liza squeezed through the exit between two flailing cheerleader types, she thought she heard the sound of Mr. Dillingham's laughter.

————

As he crossed the parking lot adjacent to the baseball field, Frank listened to the clattering of his spikes on the blacktop, and he thought to himself: "Everything is all crooked right now."

Beforehand, it seemed that there had never been any gaps or deviances in the way his time went. There was never any need to stop and linger in the noisy locker bays, to talk to the girls or joke with the boys, no need to waste time at all. You went from the school building to the field house, where you changed into your practice clothes, which had that sour smell of stale sweat in them, but which you didn't mind because it reminded you that this was work, this was your job, and by the time you had gotten loose and had broken a sweat, you decided you liked that smell anyway. And it all began with simple arcs – the swift, sharp throwing motion and the quick loop of the bat, for instance, and the never-ending flight of the ball – but it led to lots of details. You could see the curveball, for instance, if you sat back and deliberately slowed everything down until the instant you slashed at it with a kind of controlled savagery; and in the outfield, if you timed it so that you were in a dead sprint as you came to gather in the fly ball, and then if you executed the crow-hop perfectly, so that your shoulders rolled right into the throw, the ball really did explode away from you as if it had been shot from a rocket, and it would go hissing past the shortstop's head and bury itself with a pop in the catcher's glove just to the catcher's left of home plate. And if you got the runner, the cheer would go up, and Josh, the catcher, would hold up the ball and grin at you. Because it was beautiful and simple and yet it was difficult. It was not just a sport.

And afterward, the going home had always been good, too. He did like to stay late sometimes with a couple of other guys for extra hitting and shagging and throwing, but that was only if he had a fairly light load of homework. But he did not feel bereft when he left the practice field, for home had always been good, too, and when she was able to, his mother made the best food he had ever eaten, would ever eat, all from a little blue notebook of recipes that *her* mother had kept. To come home tired, have a cool bath, eat a supper consisting, for example, of snap beans cooked with pork, fresh bread and butter (or else corn fritters), and fried chicken, with sweet tea to drink, finished off with big, fluffy teacakes or chess pie, then to put on his pajamas and do his schoolwork at the table, and lastly to brush his teeth and with the sharp minty taste in his mouth and to burrow into the covers and go to sleep thinking about the superb details – the fact that if you were on second base and someone hit a ground ball and you took one step back toward the bag, showing your back to the third baseman, he considered you checked and made his long throw and then you could take off for third anyway – to have all of that affirmed that it was after all a very good life.

But things had changed. He had never regarded playing ball as a sort of escape from anything, for his life had been all one piece up till now. His boy's heart had always been wild, but that had not meant it was in chaos or was unfocused; it was wild in the way that an animal's heart is wild, with mysterious yearnings and things he could never talk about because they would sound foolish, with a brilliant intensity which had always pushed him outside of himself and into someplace where he was unaware of his own being and yet at once entirely himself, and with an acumen that only animals possess and that singleness of mind that will drive an animal to fight to its death or to run until it drops in its tracks. Nonetheless, and especially once he had become aware that he had such gifts, all the rest of the day and the night he had thought of as the hours that buffered and propped up that brief, wild time when he could do the thing he loved most. Now he could sense a change; something fell away from him as he approached the field, and something heavy had been brushed away from his shoulders as he had put on his practice tee shirt; and then, this sensation turned to exhilaration when he stepped onto the bright green grass, slipped the glove onto his right hand, and pounded it with his fist.

He was not the first one there today. Randy Wilson, the tall first baseman, was in the dugout, arranging several bats against the chain-link fence.

"Hey, Stretch," he called.

"Oh, hey there, Frankie."

Frank had known this boy for a long time. They had played on teams together since Dad's Club baseball, and sometimes during summer they would ride their bikes down to the ice cream stand in town or to Beamon's Hardware, where they would sit on the cool, smooth cement floor beside the big metal trays of nails and screws and listen to his father and the other men talk. Randy was an easy friend to be around: their conversations were without depth or nuance, and they both appreciated that. Oh, Frank had never regarded himself as a scholar, and he certainly was not quick-witted like Josh and some of the other comedians on the team, but he had always known that Randy really was "slow." He recalled vividly the day in fourth grade when the assistant principal had come into their classroom and called out Randy and two others (another boy and a girl), told them to get their books, and spirited them away to a separate classroom behind the library.

"Where they goin'?" Frank had asked.

"Retard class," someone said.

"Oh."

It had made little difference. Everything was the same at practice, and in fact, Randy even seemed to get better as a player. Granted, at first base, his duties were not as cerebral as some, although he did have to remind himself to get lined up for the cutoff throw from right and to listen for the catcher's instructions, but he was very good at making the stretch on a long throw for the out and at scooping up the short hopper, and he was a good power hitter.

Once, during the summer after seventh grade, they had been riding their bikes along a narrow brick lane that ran up between two old brick apartment buildings on their way to the hardware. They had been seeking to avoid the main road, which in the broad, tar-melting sunlight was sending up heat in shimmering waves. Abruptly they rode up on three boys who were lolling on a wooden step beside a warped screen door; Frank knew them, though not by name – they were in the grade above them, and the biggest of them, who had hit his growth, was already burly with a thin shadow of a beard around the edge of his face. And as they rode past, it was this boy who, with a quick, stabbing motion, shoved a broomstick into the spokes of Randy's front wheel, so that as Frank watched what seemed like a slow motion film, his friend left the bike's seat, made one clean somersault over the handlebars, and landed sitting upright on the brick surface. He looked around in bewilderment, as if he had just been shaken awake from a dream, and then slowly he rolled over onto his side and moaned.

Frank jerked his bike to a stop, laid it down, and walked up to the step where the three boys were gripping their bellies in maniacal gales of laughter. The other two, he saw, were rather thin and certainly were no taller or stronger than he was, but it was the big boy that hopped to his feet and met him in the road, still holding the broom handle.

"Whatta you want, queer bait?" he snarled. His big, drooping face was only a few inches away.

"Why'd you do that?" Frank demanded.

"Seen you jerk-offs comin' from clear up at the corner. We don't allow no retards on our street."

"Yeah? Who's a retard?"

The boy jerked this thumb over his left shoulder and was forming his mouth in order to say the words "He is," when there was a sudden thudding noise and the boy's lips seemed to freeze in mid-air and his eyes instantaneously turned into small, glassy beads. He uttered no sound, and then Frank looked down just in time to see the worn sole of Randy's sneaker just before it was withdrawn from the boy's crotch; a moment later there was another thud, and the sneaker was there again as Randy kicked him once more from behind, and this time the boy let go of the broomstick and Frank reached out and grabbed it as it fell. Frank turned his body, drew the stick back with both hands like a baseball bat, and then uncoiled. It was a good, thick handle, probably oak or some other kind of hardwood, but he was still surprised when it did not break across the boy's kneecap; still, it was enough to send him crumpling down like a paper lantern. Frank turned and looked over to the wooden step; one of the other two had already gotten up and slipped into the shadows beyond the screen door, but the remaining one scowled at him and started to rise; he flipped the stick over, and with the same sort of stabbing motion the big fellow had used to jam the spokes of Randy's bike, he used the blunt end to strike the boy briskly on the breastbone. The color drained from his face in one alarming, downward swoop, and he sat back down again.

When they were on their bikes again and had come out at the other end of the alley into the brilliant but smothering light, Frank said,

"Man, son. You must have kicked his nuts up into his throat."

"Me? Hell, you probably crippled him for life with that stick."

"Yeah, well. How 'bout we not say anything to my dad about this?"

"Say anything about what?'

Frank grinned. "You're smarter than you look, you know that?"

Could that truly have been almost three years ago now? He trotted over to the dugout, where Randy had gotten the bats in an order that suited him and had picked up his big mitt.

"Wanna throw?" he asked.

Luther Laite pulled hard at the wheel of the old white Ford station wagon, ultimately wrestling it into submission as he ascended the short incline and wagged out onto Highway 9. It was too hot for mid-April, and his white shirt was sticking to him, but putting the windows down served only to suck a warm, damp breeze through the car and across his face and neck and on out the other side. At this rate, he thought, they would all suffocate by June.

He had a number of errands before him, including a trip to the bank to deposit money for the Sunday school field trip to Lumber River State Park in May, as well as junket to the food pantry in Dillon, but he had put those things off. He had acknowledged the selfishness in such neglect, but he would indulge himself for now. He was on a different sort of mission today.

He could also acknowledge the weakness in himself that compelled him to feed his own anger, for it was the old one with which he had lived and battled for a long time now: it was the sin of wrath. The color and the seam of it in him went deep, and it dated back for as long as he could remember, even to the tantrums he threw as a child. He believed he had put away all other childish things, as Paul instructed, except for that one. Instead, his youthful volatility had grown into a man's anger, and he knew it could be a dangerous thing. It had almost gotten the better of him many times, and since he had gotten involved in this mess with the Treadwells, he felt he was quite literally clinging to his last limb of self-control.

So, he was not at all sure what he would do if he saw Bob's beat-up blue pickup in the parking lot of Silky's Bar. He would find out, though, in about five minutes, and he shuddered at the possibilities. He feared the violence of which he knew he was capable, and he knew himself to be quite formidable, physically, when set off, but that was not the worst of it. The worst, of course, was the sinfulness; he had prayed over it, on his knees and in the car and in the night and while walking with God in the garden behind his house – he had taken up gardening in the hope that a hobby that required nurturing might defray his anger, but it just seemed that when the foam and the brilliant, blinding rage began to take him, he became someone else. Why? He could not say, for there was nothing in his past, as far as he could recall, which might have twisted him in such a way. He figured he had been born with it, as some men are born with a proclivity to drink or to sleep with lots of women or to over-eat, and he saw how so much of his long journey through the ministry had really been a struggle to defeat his wrath. Even as a youth, he had been much more absorbed by the Old Testament stories, the crashing of temples and the dispensing of vengeance, the crumbling of entire cites and the decimation of armies. With a certain sick savoring, he looked at artistic renderings of Samson toppling the columns after having been mocked by the Philistines, a prone Goliath with blood seeping from his cracked skull, an angry God like a muscular wrestler casting a writhing Satan from the heavens, and his heart raced. He admired Michael, the warrior angel, and sometimes his vision was filled with images of a blood-red sun.

He sometimes wished he had gotten married, for that would have softened him some, no doubt. And what if he had had a daughter? How can a man fail to learn to turn away his anger with a sweet baby girl in the house? But no, the time for such things had passed him (though there might have been a woman or two in these parts, once, who would have had him), and in the gap where the blessings of a wife and children would have grown he had stoked a tireless devotion to his work, and the meetings, the sermons, the charity work, the food pantry, the counseling, and most shamefully for him, the pandering when special church projects needed funding, all of it soaked up every minute of his waking life. So, he asked himself, what was he doing now, riding up to a roadhouse with darkness and ill will in his heart?

He knew: much as he had tried to convince himself that he was doing it for the well-being of a local family, that it was an effort to fix something that had somehow gotten broken, he knew the truth: he was awaiting his opportunity to hurt Treadwell, for Treadwell represented all those who throw away their gifts, who waste the good things God gives them merely because they are weak or lazy or dumb (or all three), and only a stiff backhand or a kick in the gut will get their attention. And so, in his moment of darkness, the preacher turned in at Silky's Bar, threw the wagon into neutral, cut the engine, and coasted into the parking lot. Then around the corner of the building, and there it was – Bob Treadwell's beat-up pickup, once perhaps a shiny blue but now turned a flat gray with an over-abundance of South Carolina sun and a distinct lack of wax.

He sat and stared at it for a few moments, and then he stared at the windowless building before him; he could hear the jukebox inside, the roil of drums and the sweep of a pedal steel guitar, and he thought, "Well, now you're here. You got to go in." Still, he sat absolutely still, feeling in his writhing soul the strange yawning blankness of a hot spring afternoon: it seemed a dull and harmless time and place, but the preacher was aware of the mortal danger that lay just below him.

———

She was slowly growing to hate the unnatural flicker of that TV screen, but Della always forgot to ask Frank to turn it off in the morning before he left for school. She considered getting up and traversing the six or seven feet in order to get her own hand on the knob, but she worried about falling. This darned bed was so high, she felt as if she were atop some sort of cushiony sepulcher.

Now, this was not to say she didn't have a couple of shows: she enjoyed *The Adventures of Rin Tin Tin* and *My Friend Flicka* because she had always liked animals, though the family had never owned any; and she also looked forward to the languid summer Saturdays ahead when Frank would be able to come in and sit on the bed and watch the *Game of the Week*. He would be happy to explain everything that happened on the field, and she would feign a keen interest in baseball, as she had always done.

That boy. She tried to look into her son's future sometimes, but she couldn't bring things into focus. She was aware that all he had ever really cared about, outside of his family, was only a game meant for children, and the few silly objects that went along with it, but because she could see the joy in him, she had never objected to his involvement. And like everybody else, she had heard how so many folks cheered for him when he walked up to the plate or out to the pitcher's mound (it wasn't a swagger so much as the rolling gait of a boy who thinks he is already a man), the way they nodded and smiled and spoke quietly and confidently to one another, even when he was still little, as if they saw in him something... something they recognized immediately but could never name; it wasn't just that he was good at it – it had to do with the pure joy, too. Of course, she also read the things they wrote about him every so often in the local papers, and she wondered how that could do anyone any good: it might make him prideful. Besides, couldn't grown men find something better to write and talk about than the doings of a fifteen-year old? Now it struck her that they had all gradually come under the presumption that Frankie would become a professional ballplayer, but she had no earthly idea how things like that actually happened. True, her own father's brother, her Uncle Wayne, had done it, but life must have been so much simpler back then. How does anybody these days go from Dillon, South Carolina, to the *Game of the Week*?

Still, it was her motherly duty to support him, and she always had. Still, Bob was the one who had gotten up early all those weekends, who had done the driving, who had stood there at the fence at every game, and it was Bob who would continue to be there for him after she was...after all this was done. Oh, she knew Bob was having a rough time of it right now, but he would be back. Bob'll come back, she thought. He always does. Her husband's weaknesses were as well known to her as her own, and she never hesitated to forgive them, for she knew he had been through far worse things than she had. For one, his own mother (who had been given by certain women in the church that most dismissive moniker, "white trash") had just up and left him and his daddy for a known rake and a drunkard, and that's all he would ever have to say on that subject. And nobody had ever given Bob anything, as far as she knew – he never got so much as a birthday card from anybody else in his own family, but he never talked about that either. But the most awful thing he never talked about, no doubt, was whatever it was he had been through in the war, on that island in the Pacific. Whatever he had seen or had done to him or was made to do himself was so terrible it had been shoved very far down inside him, and the only time it ever floated again to the surface of his memory was in his nightmares. It had taken a few years for her to know how to wake him up properly, for he did not scream the way some men were said to do: the sounds he sometimes made in the night were unearthly, like those of an animal suffering horribly, and if she shook him, his eyelids would fly open and his heart would be thudding so wildly she could feel their mattress shaking, and he choked for breath, and she was afraid he was going to die of a heart attack right there in the bed beside her. Gradually she had learned to rouse him slowly, stroking his arm gently, touching his fingertips, bringing him up gently from the shadows as she might lift a troubled child.

"Where am I?" he would say then.

"In bed with me," she would answer.

"Thank God."

Just at that instant, the front door opened, and her heart gave a little leap. "Bob?" she called.

But it was Frank's voice: "It's just me, Mama." His face appeared in the doorway. "I've got Liza with me."

Then Liza's voice: "Hey, Mrs. Treadwell."

"Hello, Miss."

She did like that girl. It appeared she had turned out to be sweet, despite her family's troubles. Della recalled very well how things had been when she was small – or at least how they had seemed, and in her view, things like that were usually worse than they seemed. Even though Liza's family's house had been nearly a mile upriver from theirs, sometimes, with the window open at night, you could hear yelling coming from up there, mostly a man's voice, full of the awfulness of vitriol, bitter as heat lightning across a dark summer sky, and she had worried about the little girl. No wonder Liza had spent so many afternoons and evenings with them in those days: she probably would have done about anything to get away from such a hell. The mother in her reached out, an invisible pair of arms, but whenever she tried a subtle question, the girl's face went blank and she would gaze out towards the woods.

"So, Miss, how's things at your house these days?" she would ask.

"Fine."

"How's your mama and daddy?"

"They're fine."

But then they had moved away. The last she had heard, Liza's father had taken a job down in Florida, and the girl and her mother had gone to stay with relatives in Greenville, and Della had thought at the time: Well, whatever the snares and dangers may be, there's nothing more I can do for her now.

But now here she was again, and it was as if a dusty cloak of dark feelings was removed, because she seemed to be happy and grown-up, and it could be nothing but good for Frankie to be around her again.

"You hungry yet, Mama?"

"Not yet, thanks. I'll eat a little something later on."

"Okay. If you don't mind, then, Liza and I have got to go out for a bit. Got some errands to run."

"Oh, sure. I'll be fine. Go on and do what you need to."

Errands to run – she wasn't sure she had ever heard Frank use that expression before. What errands might he have? None of my business, I suppose. Let the young folks do as they please, it's their time now. I've had mine. I must admit, though, I miss it when they were small and we could put them in the boat and go on those picnics and Bob would make the fire and the tall trees would become like great, silent guardians of the glowing group within. She was as close to a big sister as Frank ever had, and I often wished that she had been my own daughter. But every child must leave sometime or other; I don't begin to know why the world has to be that way. You love them that way, in ways you can't even talk about, and they only get bigger and smarter and stronger and then they go away. At least... (and now here came the hard part again) at least this way I won't have the heartache of seeing him go off on his own. There's selfishness in that, but I can't help it.

She heard the front door close, and suddenly she felt a great desperation. More than anything, she wanted to stay on here with all the familiar things and with her little one and with Bob, to get up in the morning and see the sunlight gleaming on the river and on their bright faces. Something in her was being made dull by a terrible impending loneliness, and her mind and heart attempted with all their might to rebel against it. It was a sorrow too deep to grant her any tears, and she could only lie there as the twilight crowded in at her window.

She remembered something Luther Laite had said to her. She could hear him: "We are all just pilgrims here. We think we are permanent, but we can only stay for a while and then we travel on." The hardness of it tore at her, but at the same time, the veracity of it was an odd comfort. To travel. To move on. How things are.

Still, she thought, I've had my time. Yes, indeed, I have.

She was calm. She drifted off, wondering if this time the veil in her dream would be lifted and she would see the Savior.

The truck's engine grumbled to life, and Frankie climbed up on the seat beside her, but he said nothing.

Liza had expected, of course, that getting to know the Treadwells once more after seven years or so would take some time, but she certainly had not prepared herself for these kinds of complications. All the same, she knew what she was about; from January until April she had waited for her chance to approach Frank, but their paths and schedules at school never seemed to cross, and so she had come up with the idea of cutting the tires on his bicycle and then offering him a ride, and she smiled again, thinking how well it had worked. It was a little strange, she realized, and she had not yet fully come to understand her sense of purpose, of deliberateness, in re-injecting herself, as it were, into the lives of these people. The fact that Frank had apparently become even more painfully shy than ever didn't help matters.

For one thing, she had heard that his mother was ill, but she had not known that she was on her deathbed. That was plain to see the instant she entered the house; there was the smell of sickness, and at first Liza had not known if she had the stomach to enter the room where someone who had been so alive in her mind was literally dwindling away from one moment to the next. But she also knew immediately that she had to go in, that she had been brought here for a reason, and besides, it was her deeply rooted belief that she owed something to this woman. Remnants of memory and experience drifted through her conscience, a sense of unspoken trust and safety left over from her childhood and connected to this person who had somehow conveyed to her the only shreds of dignity she had known back then. Back then, Liza had been very small in every way, and when her own mother and father had gotten into it, and the yelling had become unbearable, and then the real fighting had started, she had tried to make herself even smaller, so that if they looked at her at all they might see only a small harmless creature hiding in the shadows. But whenever she had gone over to her friend Frankie's house, her heart was calmed, and she turned into a girl again; she always had the vague sense that she had just barely escaped the teeth of some imminent disaster.

Frank rolled down the window and hung his arm out. The warmth of the night washed over them. He said, "Do you know where this place is at?"

She nodded.

When she and her mother had moved to Greenville and her father (whom she would not see again for nearly three years) had gone to Florida to work, things had been a whole lot better at first. They had lived with her Aunt Beth for a few weeks, and that had been a little cramped, but there were no loud voices and nothing got broken, and the dark bruises on her mother's arms had healed. But then, everything changed once again, as easily as you might flip the dial on a radio: her mother met a man, a Mr. Melvin, at the diner where she had found work, and within another month, they had moved into his house. That in itself was not so bad – he was a well-groomed man with a friendly smile, and although he didn't have much to say to Liza, he wasn't ever mean to her: a pat on the head, a stick of gum offered, sometimes a ride to her new school in the morning. But Mr. Melvin had a boy who had come to live with them the following summer – Mickey, who was fifteen at that time (Frank's age now, she thought) and who arrived with his clothes in a grocery sack and a scowl on his face. His arrival had marked the start of the darkest part of her journey so far.

"There. There's his truck," Frank said. She eased up behind it and shut off the engine. They could hear the clinking of bottles and the swooping sounds of the jukebox coming from inside Silky's Bar. The door swung open, the noise swelled, and a couple staggered out into the night, laughing. They wandered off down the highway.

"You want me to go in with you?"

"Nah," he said. "It'll be all right. He'll either come or he won't."

He got out, slammed the door, and went up the steps. She thought he might take a quick look back at her before he put his hand on the door's handle and went in, but he didn't.

As she waited, she could not fend off the memories that clutched at her. Mickey had just gotten out of a center for juvenile offenders, but when she was only ten, she barely had any idea what that meant. "Oh," her mother had said, "he made a couple of rotten decisions and got into some trouble. It's very important we all give him a chance to make a fresh start." Apparently, Mickey's own mother would not accept him at her home across town, so Mr. Melvin put down a mattress in the den at the back of the house, and that became Mickey's room. He was a skinny, sullen boy; he said little at the dinner table – just a mumbled request for seconds here and there, and in those first few weeks, he barely even looked at her, not because he was shy like Frank, but because as always, she assumed she was insignificant, an appendage, barely visible. She didn't care; she had learned to be wary of those she lived with.

It was August before he had actually spoken to her. Almost every night that summer, a black convertible pulled up in front of the house with two boys in it, and Mickey would get in the back and they would go roaring off. Then, typically around one in the morning or so, the convertible would pull up again; she would peek out through the blinds in her room, and Mickey would come back in. If she had to use the one bathroom in the house, she made sure to go before midnight, because it was down the hallway and across from the entryway and she was afraid of running into him. But one night, she had just been coming out of the bathroom, closing the door softly, and she had turned around, and there he was. She wasn't startled, and later she had understood that she had somehow known that this would happen.

"You're up kinda late, ain't ya?" he had said.

"Reckon so."

He folded his arms, halfway blocking the hallway. "You don't talk much, do ya?"

"Speak for your own self," she said.

"Well, I was just thinking that since we're stepbrother and sister now, we ought to try to communicate a little bit."

"They ain't married."

"Near enough. You oughta try and be nice to me, anyway. An older brother can be a worthwhile thing to have around here. Believe you me, there's some mean kids at that school, and you're gonna need somebody to take care of you, little miss."

"I can take care of me just fine. Now I'm going back to bed." She brushed past him and went quickly down the hallway. The smell of sweat and cigarettes was stuck to him. Just before she shut her bedroom door and locked it, she heard his raspy whisper:

"Okay, you get your beauty rest then. This conversation ain't over."

Nighttime, darkened hallways, doors closing, doors being locked, sounds in the shadows, and the secrets and silence of a darkened house. It was as if a labyrinthine, visible darkness had appeared before her, and for a brief moment, lying there at age ten in a strange bed, her body had shuddered once.

Now the door to the saloon swung open again, and Frankie came out. His face was utterly blank, and at first she thought he had failed to do what he had come here to do, but then she saw the small man walking behind him and looking sheepishly down at his shoes. The two of them did not converse until Frank put down the tailgate, and his father mumbled, "I don't need any help," and he hoisted himself into the truck's bed.

When Frank was beside her again on the seat, she sat looking at him, studying him, but he had his face turned toward the window. Finally he said, "Well, what are you waiting for?"

"What about your dad's truck?"

"We'll get it tomorrow." He put his head out the window and spat onto the pavement, and then he looked at her; his eyes were dull, black stones. "Let's get the hell out of here," he said.

Morning, and the boy tossed his satchel of books over his right shoulder, swung the dark-green metal locker door to, and turned to face the noise of the hallway. As always, he had two distinct and sharply conflicting sensations: he felt, foremost, that he did not belong to this place, that he was displaced, alien to this commotion, and yet he also felt a great longing to be a part of it, to know the things they knew, to be privy to the gossip and the news of the day and all of the angst-ridden give and take, and to ride the same tense wave which seemed to buoy them all through the routine of the day. But he knew as well that he had made his choice and his compromises long ago in order to be the one thing he wanted to be above all else, and this had necessitated his acceptance of their regard for him as an oddity.

Yet he knew that some of them admired him, too. And he knew some of them believed him to be dumb. This he did not care about. Ironically, it freed him from the fear of failure, and he found that with each marking period, he did better and better in his classes. He was getting to be much better in science, a subject that made a great deal of sense to him lately if he came at it in the same way he thought about baseball: if you understood the littlest things, all the big things ultimately added up correctly. There were hard facts, reliable percentages, probabilities in an uncertain universe, and one had only to put one's faith in these. Do your homework, repeat, practice, swing the bat, train your hands and arms and legs and brain to do the same things time and again, and you'll come out all right.

Today, however, he was troubled. Even now, as his sneakers moaned softly on the freshly polished floor, his science teacher, Mr. Spagnola, was laying upon their desks a test for which Frank was unprepared. The previous night, he had been up late, he and Liza, going first to fetch his father, getting him home, getting him inside the house and settled, then making supper, then waiting while she went in and tended to his mother for a while, so that by the time Liza had left and his father had flopped into a heavy sleep, he was too exhausted to study; he had managed to get his book out and open it to the right chapter, but the next thing he knew, he lifted his head from the table to see that the clock said midnight. At that point, all he could do was stumble into his room and fall down on the bed.

There had also been that stuff with the preacher. When he had remembered it this morning, he thought at first that it had been a dream, but finally he had decided that part had actually happened, too. The knock at the door must have come some time after he had opened the science text, when blurry, black words were floating across his eyes like leaves on water, and he got up to answer it, and there was Pastor Laite, looking like a big, mad bear in the doorway.

"Give me that key, boy," the bear had growled.

Frankie could not recall whether he had actually said anything in reply. All he remembered was Pastor Laite coming on inside, and then himself walking over to the room where she was and opening the door just far enough so that the preacher could see his father asleep in the recliner, and then shutting it. The bear had blinked, grunted, mumbled something that sounded like "Well...hallelujah," and left.

Trepidation welled in him now as he approached the science room, where Mr. Spagnola was standing in front of the chalkboard underneath the command: "Wait for my instructions to begin." Each desk bore a test with a light-blue cover, and Frank nervously found his seat among the other kids; he set out two pencils and then looked out the window to where the sun was slanting across the cars in the faculty parking lot, and just beyond that he could make out the silvery arc of the sprinkler loping out over the outfield at the baseball grounds, though he could not hear its chugging. The other students shuffled their feet on the floor, murmured amongst themselves – little whisperings of lament and fear – and then Mr. Spagnola's sharp voice brought their eyes forward:

"All right, you may open your booklets and begin. I will keep you apprised as to the time."

The deadly sound of pages being turned ensued, and the first feeble scratchings of pencils on paper.

Frank could not keep his focus on the task at hand. He did his best guessing on the multiple choice section, but he began to lose hope utterly on the short answers. He would read the problem, realize he did not know the answer, and then his gaze would wander to the window again and the shimmering car hoods and the staccato jetting of the sprinkler's water. When once he looked back to the front of the room, he was met by Mr. Spagnola's steely gaze, and he looked back down quickly. He had been carrying a B average in the class, and his heart sank as he realized the results of this particular disaster would pull him into the C range: Average.

Strange word, now that he considered it. It meant you were somewhere in the mid-range, of course, but in reality it meant that you became faceless and without distinction; you passed on in the midst of the herd, one more domestic beast. So, how was it one could hit for a "good average" in baseball? It was an amusing contradiction, but it was consistent, too, when you thought further about it, for if you could hit safely only three times in ten, you were said to have a good average, whereas if you could hit five times in ten, as Frank had done last year as a ninth-grader, even though five is smack in the middle of ten, you were perceived as a very good hitter indeed. He had been hitting well again this year in batting practice and in pre-season scrimmages, and he found now that he could hit the ball from anyplace in the strike zone, be it curve, fastball, slider, or change-up, and that much of the time he could place his hits where he chose, more or less – drill the liner through the spot vacated by the second baseman on a hit-and-run, or launch a towering fly ball deep into the outfield with a runner at third. It was fun, but Coach Bass was still always on him nevertheless: "Treadwell, if you don't learn to get the bunt down better than that, we won't win a single game... Treadwell, wipe that shit-eating grin off your face and start making a bigger turn at first base like I told you to..." But all of that only made Frank smile more, for he had never minded being pushed.

"Damn," Randy Wilson said, as he had placed his foot along the base and made ready to try and hold Frankie close. "What does he want you to do, for Christ sake?"

"He's just trying to help."

"Well, if that's what he calls helping, let's hope you don't really mess things up one of these days."

He had heard it said many times that this was a game based upon failure, or at least on attempting not to fail most of the time, but he had never quite understood that, The law of averages proved that if you found the right way to do a thing, the proper motion to make a curveball tail away from the hitter, say, and you did it that way each time, then ultimately everything would turn out fine.

Mr. Spagnola's voice cracked across the silence: "There are now fifteen minutes remaining before the bell."

Frank stared pitifully at the last three questions, but they were riddles to him. He had read the chapter when it was assigned, but he had not had time to review it. He put down his pencil, closed the booklet, stood up and carried his test up to the teacher's desk; he was the first to do so, and as he passed, a few of the other kids glanced up at him, mournful and empathetic looks on their faces. Mr. Spagnola nodded toward the metal tray but said nothing; Frankie liked him well enough, liked the way he stuck to the book without too much digression, and the way his lessons were entirely void of theatrics (unlike the instructor for senior science courses, the crazy Mr. Dillingham – Frank had heard the story of his abrupt departure). He felt an affinity for Spagnola's attachment to rote and repetition.

Well…English was next, and fortunately Mrs. Becker was out sick this week, and the sub would probably give them "silent reading time" again. Then lunch, then math, then history, and then practice. He had no doubt that routine would restore and cleanse him.

———

It was around ten that morning when Bob awakened from a dreamless sleep and realized he was at home. He was only slightly stiff from the recliner, and for the first time in three days, he did not have a headache. Rather, he felt he had been in some faraway place, away from everyone and everything he knew; looking down at his hands, he saw that they were cut and badly bruised, and a sickening wave of dread emanated from deep within him, for he did not know how it had happened.

Then he heard his wife's voice: "Morning, Bobby." He looked up at her, and to his relief, her eyes did not seem to loathe him or even to search him, but of course, it had been so every time this had ever happened. It was the same familiar, everyday look, with the spark of youth in it and that will to comfort which seemed to come right out of the blue irises.

"Morning," he said. "How are you feeling?"

"Not too bad today," she said. "I think that new medication is having an effect."

He nodded. He attempted to recall something of the previous night, and images of Frankie's face emerging out of the moiling and noise of the barroom came to him, and then a strong hand on his shoulder, and then a thick wind rushing over him as he rode in the back of somebody's pickup truck, and then after that there was nothing else – only blackness. He lowered his head again and spoke almost in a whisper:

"Did I… did I hurt anybody?"

"Of course not, Bob. You were fine."

Then the thing he had been hoping would leave him be, would perhaps somehow flow around him and away like running water – the sudden stream of shame – overcame him. He put his face in his hands and suppressed a terrible sob.

"It's all right," she said. "You were fine."

He swallowed a choking lump. "No, it's just – I just wish sometimes you'd get mad at me. Give me hell. Just give me what I deserve. Tell me how no-good I am."

"Because it's not true."

"I've ruined things around here," he said. He could not keep the water from filling his eyes.

"Everything is fine here."

"My own son... had to come and fetch me. Bring home his broken-down drunkard of a father..."

Her eyes were softened now with pity and pathos. "But think of this: would he have been brave enough to do that, to go in there, if you hadn't raised him right? Let it go. You're back now. That's all that matters."

He shook his head. He wanted to tell her that he had only done it because he was afraid for them, and because he cared so much for her, and because he did not know how he would ever get along without her, but he knew that none of that made any real sense; he was really just a coward.

The coward stood, shuffled over to her, and instinctively and automatically and with some effort, she sidled over so that he could get in the bed beside her. He placed his head along the fragile curve of her shoulder, ran his fingers across her ribs, and realized with the most ancient kind of sorrow just how thin she had gotten.

———

"Time to go home, Treadwell. You're overdoing everything. A player gets too tired, and that's when he's liable to get hurt."

"I ain't tired, Coach."

"I ain't asking you. I'm telling you. Besides, it's dark out here."

"Yes, sir."

Damn bumpkins around here, Max Bass thought. Don't even have enough sense to know when practice is over. There was one more ball in the wooden bucket, and so he plucked it out, reached back, and threw it up towards the plate with some bite on it. It rode up inside on Frank and he took a quick step, turned his swing inside out, and swatted it over the left field fence. They watched the ball plummet and disappear into the twilight like a rock falling through dark water. "All right," Bass said. "There's a good one to quit on."

He'd be the first to admit he had been much the same way, but he had always thought of his own doggedness as being deliberate and full of purpose, whereas this kid seemed to do it only because he liked it; that was it exactly – it wasn't work to him. Or maybe he just couldn't think of anything else to do with himself. In any event, he expected that Treadwell was good enough to carry them to the state title this year or the next, but he still did not believe he had a future in the professional ranks. That took being somewhat of a sonofabitch, or at least having a sonofabitch in your corner, and he hadn't seen any of that sort of savvy around these parts.

Bass knew that he did not have a natural coach's affinity for his players, but hell, he had not been meant for this; he had been born to be a big leaguer. Only he had not known that the road to one's own destiny is fraught with potholes, and those bastards in Milwaukee had put him in the ditch. But all right, he hadn't taken very good care of himself in those days either: he would admit to some of the responsibility. The point was, he knew what it took to really make it – the luck combined with the skills and the mindset and the... hell, just the opportunity was hard enough to come by.

At last the kid had gathered up his gear and was heading toward the gate in the outfield fence.

"All right, Treadwell. Pop quiz. What is happening this Friday?"

The boy turned around and grinned. "First game of the season. See ya, Coach."

"Yep. Now go home."

He watched the boy's white tee shirt turn to gray and then at last disappear among the pine trunks, and he thought, Well, I suppose it's a shame he's such a nice, simple kid; he don't know the dark road that awaits him if he expects to keep playing ball. He certainly does have a rifle for an arm, I'll admit, and I've never seen a kid his age who could track down a fly ball that way. Now, as far as his pitching, he's pretty raw, but he throws hard enough to where these kids can't hit it. Natural hitter, too. Damn shame he ain't got a mean bone in him.

That was one component of his own makeup that Bass knew had been adequate to his aspirations: he could be mean as hell. In his first game in spring training with the Braves back in 1950, he had been brushed back at the plate by the Cardinals pitcher and had charged the mound. Something about the sound of that fastball hissing by right under his jaw had set him off. No one could quite believe it at the time – both benches sat there for half a minute or so watching them roll around in the dirt on the mound before the other players came sprinting out. God damn if he hadn't shaken their world up a little bit.

He carried the two duffel bags full of gear out to the field house and unlocked the door, and he knew in his gut that when he came out again she would be waiting at the edge of the woods once again. There was a little clearing and a slab of cool, smooth stone there, as if it had been placed there for the purpose. She would have a blanket with her. His heart lurched at the thought of what was about to occur; he was frightened and thrilled at once, and he struggled to gain control of himself, for he mustn't let her see that he had any doubts about this, for if *she* got scared, then everything would surely go to hell, and by everything he did not mean just his job, most likely, and his reputation, but also any chance of rationalizing – no, of legitimizing – his relationship with the Billings girl. He still believed he might truly be in love with her.

How had it started? She had come out to the field one evening a couple of months ago, when he was seeding the grass and watering it down in anticipation of the spring, and she had inquired about serving as equipment manager for the team to earn another P.E. credit. She was in his class this semester, she reminded him, but she had discovered she was an hour short and didn't want to have to make it up, she said. He was sorry, but Andy Buckley ("You know Buckley? Dorky-looking kid?") had already applied for the job, but if she wanted she could help with the scorebook once things got underway; he couldn't give her the credit, though. He remembered that she had stood very close to him, so that when she had said, "Oh, that's all right, Coach Bass. Maybe the dean of girls can find some work for me after school," and when she turned to go with a little toss of her head, her long blond hair had brushed across his forearm.

"Hey, wait a sec." She had stopped and turned back towards him. "I'll see what I can do for you. Check with me again tomorrow."

But the next evening, there had been no talk of school credits. First there had been a small, almost avuncular kiss, and then lots of other things after that. And then, even as he trudged from the field house to his car, the disgust for himself and the sense of mortification and dread had come upon him like a suffocating fog, and he had sat there gripping the steering wheel like a man desperate for...for redemption. The next day, on her way out of the gym after class, she had tried to slip him a little note, which he refused, and when they had met again, he had told her in no uncertain terms that there could be no notes or letters. "There'll be a time for all that stuff," he'd said. "But not right now."

Now he deliberately put those thoughts away from himself, as he turned off the lights and shut and locked the door. He went around the corner of the building, and there she was, waiting by the path, the shadows receding behind her in the pine forest. Her hair appeared to be of soft gold in the elfin light, and her skin gave off its own moist sheen. She was barefoot, and she wore a thin, short lavender dress. She raised her hand and waved at him girlishly, as she might have done had they encountered one another by chance on a crowded street someplace, as if all of this were happening by the wildest of chances and she had never intended to come here in the first place and he had never intended to find her. Oh, love, desire, failure, fear... this was the twisted existence that awaits a man once his true destiny has failed him, once the dream of the big cities and the crowds and the adulation has perished. He had never expected to be a man like any other, subjected to the tortures within his own soul.

Nevertheless, he thought to himself, She is beautiful. She might be exactly what you need after all. Come along now, Max. Get aholt of yourself, boy.

By the time he had covered the final few yards and was reaching for her, he felt once again the old confidence, the old glow.

––––––––

As in countless other towns across the Carolinas, but especially in the Piedmont region, the lowlands, along the coast, and in the ramshackle communities scattered like broken teeth along the Great Pee Dee River and the Little Pee Dee, the opening of the high-school baseball season marked a new beginning in various ways. For the boys, of course, it was the fresh pursuit of one brand of the so-called American Dream unique to the 20th century – sports stardom – so that even those who knew they would not see much playing time beyond warm-ups and perhaps in the late innings of a lopsided victory, even they clung grimly to the thought that fate might suddenly turn for them. For their relatives and friends, it marked the opening of an odd (and again, uniquely American) social season; they loved to come and sit out in the wooden bleachers or on blankets along the fence with their picnics, deftly employing their ability to talk about many things at once – family doings, town gossip, potato salad, as well as the temporal but dramatic events of the game itself. And as did their male offspring, most of them exhibited that determinedly optimistic attitude whenever someone failed, offering consolation and support rather than giving voice to the truth of the dark and hopeless feelings within them, and in general holding their tongues whenever the umpire made a poor call, if only because these men were also likely to be people they knew well:

"Ah, c'mon now, Blue. That pitch looked pretty good to me."

And maybe at worst: "Say, Blue, you're missing a good game here."

Now, for some of the girls, the new season marked the beginning of a strange courtship ritual which they would follow over the course of the spring and on into the first languid days of summer. It was not that they did not understand or enjoy the game, for most of them did; yet they also understood innately that at some point during the steady and pleasant pace of the game, some young man would be granted a chance to perform a heroic deed, someone would burst upward on firm thighs and calves, dart sideways, dive through the air, or with one quick and mighty blow of a weapon bend the course of destiny to his own will. Inevitably, it would happen, and there were some of these girls who wished to be here when it did, so that they might stand up with the crowd and become a part of the glory of a moment, and for several of them with boyfriends on the team, why, the boy of the moment might be her own, and she could stand like Athena, magical guide to Telemachus on his journey around the bases and back home again.

Liza Applewhite, on the other hand, was here for one reason alone (all right, two, then, for it was also her intent to return to the Treadwells' home afterward with a detailed report for Frankie's mother, since her son was so reluctant to speak): she was attempting to back her life up, in a sense, to a point in her own past, and start it again from there. She was well aware of this, and she believed it was possible. As a young girl, she had attended many of his games, and as she took her place in the stands, she luxuriated in the smells of roasting frankfurters and cheeseburgers and in the pleasant laughter of this place where old and young came together and time did not seem to matter much for anything. Excitement stirred in her, yet she also had to push away from her a sense of sorrow, for something very wrong had happened: the brilliant days of green, green grass and red dirt and cheerful talk had somehow turned into the long and dreadful night of her adolescence, and she was deliberately seeking to capture the remnants of it before it was gone entirely.

She had been harmed. She knew this now, and her anger over it was blunted by a sense of shame and a sense of foolishness that she had allowed it to happen to her. Only a year ago, self-loathing had brought her to the brink of self-destruction. What had begun with Mickey's ominous words – "Okay, you get your beauty rest then. But this conversation ain't over" – in the darkened hallway of the little house in Greenville had turned into a black vortex through which she had fallen slowly and from which she had ultimately emerged on the other side, she believed. But at the true bottom of it, she had not wanted to live.

As she sat now in the sun, her sneakers crossed on the next bench down, she tried, as ever, to push the old memories away. Still, they were always there, and often they swarmed at her like wild shadows on a wall, and she could only sit still and wait for them to abate. It was always very odd but familiar to her: even now it seemed that the cheerful sounds and images of the ballpark – the parents and students waving and greeting one another, the players jogging in pairs across the outfield, the popping of their mitts as they played catch – all seemed merely to drift about her like errant scraps, or clips from a disjointed newsreel, and she existed only in the twilight of her recollections once more. She had been eleven and he had been fifteen, but it took him a year to get around to touching her, not because he was afraid of any consequence or of hurting her, but because (as she realized later) he found some kind of pleasure in the waiting and in the anxiety it caused her. She had known someplace inside her that it would happen ultimately, that he would try something, and she had imagined many scenarios, many ways in which she would be brave and fend him off; but when it had happened, not too long after her twelfth birthday, she had been frozen. That was the first time she had known of her ability to be suspended outside of herself, to cast her mind into some realm where there were no thoughts or feelings: his hands were on her, but she thought and felt nothing – only that she could not move. And afterward, because she had not resisted him, she had felt guilt, and a terrible shame had come over her that rendered her unable to say anything to anyone – certainly not to her mother. And the next time… well, when Mickey saw the blood on the sheet over the couch cushions where he slept, he had told her gruffly to get the shovel out of the shed and to take the sheet to the woods behind the house and bury it, and she had done so. And as she had begun to dig, the pain shot up into her stomach and she felt faint, but she had not cried, being frozen.

A voice broke through to her now, and sunlight, wonderful sunlight, tumbled across her: "Hey, kid." It was Frankie's father. He sat beside her.

"Oh, hi, Mr. Treadwell."

"How are they looking?"

"Real good. I don't think he's pitching today, though."

"Naw, they'll save him for a couple of games. That one there is interested in hitters anyway. Chatted with him at the end of last season. Scout for the Orioles organization." She looked in the direction in which he had nodded, and down there by the fence at field level was a man in a brown suit and a white hat with a black band. He stood utterly still as he watched the outfielders, who were now shagging fly balls in the deepest part of the yawning green.

"He ain't from around here, that's for sure," Liza said.

"Nope. There'll be others, too."

"But Frank's just a kid."

"He acts like a kid. But he don't hit like one."

"I s'pose I haven't seen him play in a while."

Treadwell smiled at her. She had been very pleased, of course, when they had gotten him home earlier that week, and even more so to see that he had still been there the next day, and the next. He was back to work as well, Frank had said, and his mama had looked better than she had in months – more color to her, and she had an appetite.

The Dillon Tigers pitcher struck out the first opposing batter, and the second, and then the number three hitter raked a skittering ground ball to the second baseman, who threw to first with one quick, snakelike motion that was little more than a gesture, and the crowd clapped and whistled pleasantly as the players charged toward the dugout. My God, Liza thought, how could I have forgotten about all of this? It's so simple, really: you come out on a warm afternoon and watch some boys toss a ball around and suddenly your life is put back in order again; you don't even have to understand what you're seeing (and even though she comprehended the game very well, the grace, the immediacy of it, the sudden tensions bursting across the long expanses of dreamlike ease, always astonished her), but you are a part of it all simply because you're here. It was too good, and a kind of gratitude she could not identify filled her and seemed to spill out and dissolve into the golden light.

When Frank's first turn to hit came around, anticipation seemed to tauten like a straight line across the cloudless blue sky, but then it disappeared in the lulls between pitches to the batter ahead of him. Most everyone glanced over at him in the on-deck circle, where he smudged the darkened tar rag across the handle of the old maple bat and then slid the lead donut down the barrel and tamped it on the ground, just as all the other players did. There was nothing at all especially distinct about his movements, except that maybe when he swung the weighted bat, his shoulders seemed to hump up a bit, as if his muscles actually expanded a little before their eyes; otherwise, he was quite ordinary as he watched and waited and fidgeted. The Bluffton pitcher coiled and uncoiled, and a fastball flashed up to the plate and veered out of control, and the Dillon hitter, Hal Yates, had just time to turn and take the ball on the right side of his back, so that he was unharmed; without hesitation he tossed his bat toward the dugout and trotted up the foul line to first base.

Frank approached the plate, and all the little rituals of stepping into the batter's box were set into motion: the tapping of sticky clay from the shoes with the end of the bat, the circular, birdlike stretching of the head and neck, the waving of the thick stick of hardwood behind his shoulders and back like a flag caught in a violent wind, the scraping of two small troughs for both the front and back foot, and then the raising of his left hand to tell the umpire he was not yet ready, and then at last, after what seemed like half a minute but which was actually only three seconds, the dropping of the hand, the cocking of the bat, and the rock-still posture with only a barely perceptible twitching, like a cat's tail, to indicate alertness, all of which seemed trivial and random but which, like asteroids drifting in an abyss, led onward to some as yet unknown destiny which would involve either near misses or fantastic collisions. Liza watched the Bluffton pitcher's face, which was stony but which below its surface gave away the anxiousness of a child, and she thought, They're all so young, aren't they? So young to have to act so tough. There'll be plenty of use for the tough later on. For now they ought to still be allowed to have a bit of fun. But as the pitcher threw from the stretch, lifting his big bony knee to his chest, pushing off the rubber and driving toward the plate, his arm unfurling, and as Frank in turn raised his right foot a few inches off the ground and then set it down again like a man taking great care to step on a bug, she suddenly felt she understood something: this was indeed fun, but it was a fun that belonged neither to the child's world nor the adult's; it was unto itself. It was the joy, in fact, that comes with doing difficult things correctly.

And all of them, Liza and Frankie's father and Max and the scout for the Orioles and all of the other students and the other parents and the players on both teams had a brief, sharp taste of that same joy in those milliseconds when the ball zoomed up toward the plate and the polished barrel of the bat sparked in the sun, in that increment of time so small as to be immeasurable, when they were able to forget themselves utterly and see into the only thing that mattered: the assertion of a human will.

————

For the first time in quite a long while, Luther Laite felt very good about things. He sat at his desk in the church office, where he was supposed to be working on his sermon for this Sunday. Instead he was ruminating on the ways in which his long career as pastor for the United Methodist Church had often seemed only a great struggle. Leading a spiritual community was one thing, but for many years he had dealt with people who presented problems of two essential varieties: there were those who were simply recalcitrant and who resented him because they believed he wished to force them to come to services, like some kind of truant officer, but who were then even more resentful when he did not do so (they were usually the husbands of the most devout ladies); and then there were those people who wanted the church and were even aware that they *needed* the church, but who because of their own inclinations to debauchery and laziness and the weight of generations of debauched and lazy people, somehow managed to screw things up for themselves and for those around them.

By "church," he did not mean the building or the congregation or even the Methodist way of doing things; he meant some sort of structured communion with God. Luther knew lots of Christians who claimed to have "personal" relationships with Christ, and that was well and good, but he had never been able to think of Him as someone akin to a fishing buddy. He thought of it in this way: if you were a student and you wanted to learn something from a great teacher, you'd attend the class and do the work and learn the method and take the tests, and when you failed, you'd take them again until you passed, and then you'd move on to the next set of harder questions; but you'd have to do all this knowing the grade would never matter too much and the class would never really be over during your lifetime. The church presented the same idea, he thought, except that after a while, something happened between you and the teacher that can only be called love, although it is not a love born of mutual attraction or filial ties but of an ultimate belief in the subject itself. Then, when you were ready, that love became something more, and you stepped through another door, and it became all one – teacher and student and subject – like bathing in pure light. Probably that was what the Buddhists meant by enlightenment.

Luther had wanted to be the great teacher, and he had failed, but he still believed in the method. He had started out with lofty ambitions, but the complaints and foibles and weaknesses in human beings had pulled him down, and to be sure, he counted himself among the weak and depraved. Frequently these days his most salient thought was: *I am just another sinner. Always was, always will be.* It was true, for his thoughts and lusts and compulsions and especially his anger were no different from those of any man, but he thanked God that he had been able to control his actions, for the most part, and had never gotten himself into real trouble. For instance, he was glad he had not gone into that saloon after Bob Treadwell the other night, for things would have gotten ugly.

Treadwell. He fell into the second category of problems, for he knew he needed the church, the structure of communion, but his past, and all the misery that he had inherited, prevented him from seeing clearly. However, the idea that he could straighten up now, when circumstances demanded it, was encouraging; that time fifteen years or so ago, he had allowed the bottle to have its way with him, to wring him out and leave him utterly useless for a time before he would at last pick himself up again, but this time was different. With a little help from the boy, he'd had a cold bucketful of Grace dumped on his head, and he had awakened and come on home where he was needed.

The boy. That could go either way. It was hard to know what was going on inside his head, whether he really understood what was happening or not, whether he would fall apart when his mother's time came or lean on the simple things he had in his life – school, playing ball, and such things as are given to young people to keep them out of trouble. Maybe he would even finally discover girls; there was the Applewhite girl, who had been around their house quite a bit lately, and that was very good. He sensed that she had been through a few things in her life already, even though he had not had much opportunity yet to speak with her. It was curious: when she looked at him, he could see something in her eyes – there was sorrow there, but also a need to comfort, and he believed that whatever she had been through had taught her something worth knowing.

Well, praise God then. He had set the table, and all was in place for the events yet to come. Della certainly deserved to have it that way, and it was clear that she intended to go out with her dignity intact, and that was the most that any of us could ask for. And he felt that he would be ready, too, whenever it should come to pass.

His glance fell upon the pad of paper and the fountain pen on the desk before him, and he said aloud, "Oh, all right, then." He found the making of a sermon laborious, and as he had so often over the years, he thought: I missed my calling. I really ought to have turned Catholic, or at the very least Episcopalian. They got a book and a set of rules for everything, and there's never any gray area.

The gray area. That was what took it out of him. He picked up the pen and made a single black mark on the unscathed, white sheet of notebook paper.

———

Bob was assembling wheelbarrows when he got the message. Since he had gotten back to work, he had thrown himself into every meticulous task he could find, especially anything that involved small screws, bolts, nuts, slots, clips, and the like. He also felt less inclined to shoot the bull with the other men who worked at the hardware store, some of whom were inclined to take long lunches laced with whiskey and beer in the back room.

Howard, his portly, red-faced boss, came out to the parking lot and said, "Bob. Some boy just brought a note for you."

It was from the high school coach, Max Bass, asking him to come down to the field. Apparently, the scout from Baltimore had stuck around and wanted to speak to the both of them about Frankie. "Well," he mumbled to himself as he washed his hands at the big iron sink, "why the hell not?"

But when he arrived at the field, Frank was there, too, seated in the dugout. "What are you doing here?" Bob asked "Thought this was a grownups' meeting."

"Coach fetched me."

Bob walked on over to where the scout and Bass were standing opposite one another with the chain-link fence between them; the scout's arms were folded along the top of the fence, and Max was looking down at the ground, nodding his head and waving a narrow fungo bat across the top of the grass. It was around 11 a.m., and he could almost see the steam beginning to emanate from the hot clay. The base paths, infield and mound had been neatly raked and watered down.

"Mornin', Bob. This here is Mr. Eddie Robinson from the Baltimore Orioles organization. He's taken an interest in your boy's ball playing abilities." The tall man in the baggy chocolate-colored suit grinned at him and shook his hand.

"He's kinda young, ain't he?" Bob said. "Only in the tenth grade."

Now the scout paused, leaned back very slightly from the waist, and took in Treadwell's small, taut figure. "Well, yessir, he is, but that's exactly why I asked that you come down here today. I don't want to do or say anything that might make you folks uncomfortable, so the first thing I said to Coach Bass this morning was that we have to get Frank's father down here and get his permission on this."

Bob's mouth felt dry. Of course, he had known this sort of thing would occur, but he hadn't really thought about what his reaction might be when it did. He didn't know whether to be excited and affable or to play the protective and reluctant father. Instead he said, "What is it I'm giving my permission to do? We don't have to sign anything, do we?"

The scout smiled. "Positively not. Nothing of the kind. I'm only here to watch him a little more."

Bob shrugged. "I guess it's all right by me. What do you want to watch him do?"

"Well, first I'd like to see him run a bit, if you don't mind."

Bob looked at Max Bass, who had said so little and in fact now seemed somewhat disinterested in the whole matter, but he gave him a quick nod anyway, and then Max turned and called down to the dugout:

"Treadwell! Hustle up, now!"

Frankie came trotting over, and Bass said, "Stand right here on the this line and sprint over to the right field fence. Then count to ten and sprint back."

Like a man trying to read a distant billboard, the scout watched Frank run. Bob watched the scout, and Max Bass looked down at his shoes and spit into the grass. The boy returned, barely winded, and put his hands on his hips.

"Can we see him catch and throw a little? From his position, if you don't object."

Bass turned to Frank. "Trot on out to your position, kid." Then turning to Bob: "Catch me up, Mr. Treadwell? There's a catcher's mitt on the bench over there."

As the scout watched with the same sort of detached study, Max stroked several one hoppers on a line into center field, and just as he had always done (or so it seemed to Bob), Frankie scooped each one on the run, took one long but quick hop and rolled his shoulders over behind his throw, so that on his follow-through his right-hand fingers brushed the outfield grass each time. Each time, with only a very slight arc, the ball rocketed towards the plate and smacked into the mitt where his father held it just a couple of feet above the plate. Then the coach whacked two tall drives into the deep pasture, the first one well to Frank's left and then the second to his right. The boy made a long sprint for the first one but arrived in time to gain a little extra ground so that he could come back in, make the catch on the run, and then execute the crow hop once again; the second one was well-drilled and Frankie turned his back and started on a dead run at an angle away from home.

"That one's gone," Bob said. "He'll never reach it." Yet, in his heart, he knew he was wrong.

He watched his son cover the last few yards of available outfield, peel off, and run at full speed parallel to the curve of the fence. And just as the ball was fading, clearly falling too far, seeming to rush wildly to the free and boundless space beyond the park, the boy leapt perhaps three feet and plucked it cleanly out of the air, never touching the metal fence. This time, without breaking stride at all, he lobbed the ball in one quick darting motion, and it rose up again against the sky and then plopped into the mitt with surprising velocity.

"Okay," the scout called out. "That's enough. I appreciate it, gentlemen."

With the fungo bat on his shoulder, Max Bass turned to him. "Do you want to see him hit?"

"No, thanks," Eddie Robinson said. "Saw all I needed of that yesterday. Four for four with two home runs is not too shabby."

Bass turned back and spit into the clay. "Nah, I guess it ain't," he said.

Frank came trotting up, his cheeks vaguely flushed, his eyes clear and sharp, finally breathing hard from his effort.

————

"I don't want Frank moving to Baltimore," Della said. "He's got to finish school."

Bob leaned in the doorway with his hands in his pockets. "I told you already, that ain't the way it works. We make an agreement, and then after he's done with high school, he goes."

Now Frank's voice echoed from the other room: "I like the Cubs."

Bob turned and spoke over his right shoulder: "You just hush and do your math. What makes you think the Cubs will want anything to do with you?"

"I don't know. I just always liked the Cubs. I like Ernie Banks."

"Well, Ernie Banks don't care nothing about you. Do your math."

"That's still two years away," Della said. "S'pose he decides to do something else with himself? He could go play baseball for the state college. Or s'pose he decides he wants to be a doctor or a…a lawyer? I mean to say, I don't want to be sitting there on his graduation day wondering if he's about to make a big mistake."

"Well, then, I guess we'll just jump off that bridge when we get to it. He's got two years."

"Cubs could win it all this year," Frank called.

"Sure they could," said Bob. "And I might run for governor. Get back to work."

He walked over and placed his hand on Della's forehead. "You're a little warm. How you feeling?"

"I feel fine," she said. "I'm about to get up from here and get back in that kitchen. The Lord knows what it looks like by now."

"Now, let's not overdo it, Della. I gotta get back to the hardware. You wait for me, and if you want to get up again for a while this afternoon, I'll help you."

"Frankie's here."

Louder, so that the boy could hear him: "Frank's busy right now. I'll see y'all later."

When he had left, Della thought about swinging her legs over the side of the bed, standing up, and walking straight out to the kitchen. She could just imagine the look on Frankie's face as she walked past him just as smart as you please. Still, Bob was right. She had made some progress these last couple of weeks, had actually gotten up and around, with his help; she'd even sat out back yesterday and had looked down to the river – now there was a sight she'd thought she'd never see again. It was lovely, more blue than brown or black this time of the year, what with the spring rains washing down from upcountry, and farther up, way up there to the west in those tall old mountains, the ice was still thawing. Of course, she couldn't see it, but she knew that it was so.

In any event, it had given her something. Hope was the only word for it. Or maybe relief. She had things yet to do, and she would not yet have to learn how her dream ended, the dream which seemed so real, down to the feel of the polished altar against her elbows; she would not yet know what happened once the dark veil was lifted from her face, though she believed she knew how it would turn out. Still, it was not the time for that.

Now Frankie appeared in the doorway. "Mama?"

Her big boy. He really had begun to look all grown up and handsome, and that curious mixture of pride and regret filled her throat. "Yes, son?"

"I was just wondering. You know, what you were saying about graduation and all…" He looked down at the floor, embarrassed.

"I know what you want to ask me," she said, "and the answer is yes."

He grinned, and like that, he was her child again. "All right, then," he said, and he went back out.

A few minutes later, Della slid slowly into sleep, the occasional shuffling of pages from the other room like the small waves upon which she rode.

———

Liza had begun spending more of her time at the Treadwells' home than at the small apartment her mother had rented for them in town. That was fine with all concerned: she knew that Della liked her a great deal and that Bob needed her help; Frankie seemed a little uncertain about it all yet, but he had always been ginger about such things – he'd come around. As for her own mother, she and Liza knew each other so well now that they didn't even have to talk much, and these days they felt more like roommates with different lives, different obligations, and besides, her mom was putting in so many hours waiting tables at the truck stop up on Route 9 and then out dancing with her new boyfriend, Roger, that they hardly saw one another. And especially since Roger had handed her the keys to his old truck, she now had greater independence and sovereignty over her own time than she had ever known. For reasons she was not even sure of herself, she chose to spend much of that time down by the river, with the Treadwells.

She knew it didn't take a psychiatrist to figure out that part of it was her need to backtrack, to come to know once again the person she had been before, the girl in her that had been lost. Every time she came down here, she drove past her old house, and she felt nothing, no regret, no longing, no sense of tragic loss, so tonight, as she started home, she actually pulled into the overgrown yard of the old place, which was still vacant. She shone the truck's headlights into the window of the room that had been hers, and still she felt only numbness. One might have said that was advantageous, but she knew it only meant that she had buried something that would ultimately have to be dug up and reckoned with. Her childhood, the girl she had been – that was the good ghost who would chase away the specter of the past six years, the all-too-vivid recollections of her life in Greenville and of Mickey and then of everything else that had happened. She had tried many times to hate him, that leering boy who had demolished her innocence, and she had even thought of ways in which she might have killed him: she could have plunged the big carving knife right through his ribs and heart, for instance, as he lay in his drunken, stinking sleep on his stinking mattress, and the blade was so long and sharp it would have gone straight through and into the floor below, impaling him. But she knew that she could never have done so, for she thought that she was also at fault, in that she had not fought him, never fought him whenever it happened, and it had happened over and over as time went on, and at times she wondered whether she had not somehow willed it all upon herself.

And what about everything that came later? The things she had done? Mickey had gone away again when he was seventeen and she was thirteen, because he had gotten into an altercation with another boy and had hurt him very badly (she never knew the details), and he had been sent away again. She had thought at the time, *This is it – I have escaped at last.* But when she got to Greenville High School the following year, at first to her shock and then to her terror, she found that a kind of reputation had preceded her, for he had told everyone there what they had done, had boasted and gloated, apparently. And the deadness came over her again, and she could say nothing, could do nothing except grip her books to her chest and scurry from one class to the next while the clusters of boys or girls stood in the shadows of the lockers and hallways, smiling, staring at her as she passed. *Slut, whore, dirty bitch…* these were the words that hung in the air about her as she moved through this alien world. And for reasons she could not articulate, finally, she had accepted this as her lot in life, and finally, driven by loneliness and despair, she had become that which they said she was. She had used to watch with loathing in her soul as Mickey would leave the house and get into the black car each night to carouse with his friends, and now she had become the prodigal child, the one who sought the darkness, who rode with the boys deep into the night to places she ought not to have gone, giving whatever was asked of her in the thick shadows by the lake and in dimly lit vacant lots, fouling herself but feeling nothing except the surface bubbling of the self-hatred that simmered within her. For two years, this had been her pitiable existence.

Eventually, in December of her senior year, when she was inevitably trapped by the hideous lies she had told, when she had been almost entirely crushed by the weight of her guilt, the school's principal asked her mother to come in and meet with him. Liza was not allowed to be present, but she knew from the expression on her mother's face when she came home that afternoon that all had been revealed.

Her mother's voice came out muffled and throaty, but she somehow managed to push her emotions back: "I knew something bad was gonna happen," she said. "But I didn't know it would be this."

Liza had said nothing, but had only thought, *Thank God. Thank God it's out. Now it will end.*

Then her mother took her roughly by the shoulders, and Liza had thought she was going to shake her, but instead she stared into her face and said, "He touched you, didn't he? What did he do to you?"

Her heart spun and the breath went out of her. "Who?" she gasped.

"Mr. Melvin. Mickey's daddy. He did, didn't he? What did he do to you?"

Mickey's filmy, crooked grin flashed though her mind. What if he came back? *This conversation ain't over...* She couldn't face him. She had to get away. "Yes," she said. "He touched me."

Her mother's eyes flinched, and she dug her fingernails into her daughter's shoulders. "What did he do?"

Hot tears seemed to leap from Liza's eyes. "I told you," she said. "He touched me."

Now her mother did shake her, vigorously, and she forced her words through tightly clenched teeth. "You'd better tell me. I want to know. You'd better say, right now."

"All right. He stuck it in me. He fucked me. Lots of times."

Now her mother let go, and it was as if Liza felt herself falling, not drifting or floating but shooting feet-first straight down into a long black tunnel with no bottom. The woman before her suddenly shrank from her view, crumpled to the kitchen floor like a bag of empty clothes, and a wailing sound that seemed to come from above them reached out like a very long hand, and as she fell, Liza grabbed at it, clung to it. She looked down at her mother, who seemed very far away. As the wailing became louder, the long fingers flexed, slipped, and again she felt herself plunging ever downward.

That night, she had locked her door and placed the long, gleaming carving knife on the little table by her bed. She lay there for two hours with her thumb upon the pumping vein in her neck, and then she fell asleep.

The next morning, her mother had put all of their possessions into two extra-large garbage bags, and they left Greenville on the 6:45 bus.

———

It was a Saturday afternoon, and for the first time in many months, Frankie had the house to himself. He and his father had helped his mother into the pickup, and he had watched them drive away, waving at them from the front step. It seemed she was now well enough to go in to the county hospital for various tests.

They had watched her clearly getting better, but as yet no one had really said as much except for Della herself, as if to talk about it might somehow curse them and break the spell of the gradual improvements they saw in her condition from day to day. Only a few days ago her physician, at the behest of Frank's dad, had come to the house to see about her. When he arrived, his demeanor was that of a man accustomed to delivering bad news – his eyes tried to be sorrowful but only looked tired, and he was abrupt, almost impatient with them. But when he had examined her, he came out of the room and stood for a few moments with his hands on his hips, before gazing up at them and saying,

"I don't think I can explain this right off. I certainly don't want to jump the gun, but there does seem to be some change for the better."

Frankie's father hooted and then slammed his fist on the dining room table. "I *told* you!" he said. "Didn't I say it, Frank?"

Frank was smiling. "*She* said it. I didn't hear you say anything."

"Aw, c'mon now, I… So Doc, how long you think it'll be before she's back to her old self again?"

The doctor waved his hand. "Hold on there, now, Bob. I merely said there has been some sort of a change. Let's not overreact. I have to say, there's such a thing as misdiagnosis. She could have the chronic form of the disease rather than the acute. I just wouldn't speculate at this point."

"And sometimes a person just gets better," Frank's father chirped. "Ain't that right?"

"It happens on the rare occasion. The *very* rare occasion."

"This is one of them occasions, I reckon."

The doctor shook his head. "Again, we can't know just yet. If she continues to feel better, see if you can get her into the car and over to the county hospital on Saturday for a more thorough exam. Give my office a call and we'll set it up."

"Yes, sir. Yes indeed we will."

And this morning, his dad had gotten her into her navy blue church dress, and they had each taken an arm, even though he could have lifted her up and put her in, really, for she was still as light as a milkweed; they had guided her out to the truck and into the front seat, and she had looked up at Frank and winked. "Hold the fort," she had said.

So, he had been alone for most of the day. He was supposed to be icing down his elbow, as he had pitched in a game the previous day, but he didn't feel at all sore. Instead, he sat on his bed, where he had spread out some trading cards featuring a few of his favorite baseball players. Almost every time he rode his bike down to the hardware store to see his father, he would stop in at the market three shops down and spend a few cents on a wax pack, tearing them open as soon as he got outside, shoving the pink stick of gum into his mouth and then leaning against the brick wall to peruse the enclosed cards. Today he had taken out Ernie Banks, Harmon Killebrew, Mickey Mantle, Henry Aaron, Bobby Friend, and Rocky Colavito, all from the previous season, 1958. The sweet smell of gum still clung to them, and he picked up each one in turn and studied the information on the back for perhaps the thousandth time.

He heard a vehicle outside, but it was a little early for them to be back, he thought; the front door opened, and he heard Liza's voice: "Yoohoo! Anyone home?" It had become her custom of late to let herself in this way, and nobody minded, of course, for she had become practically a part of the household again.

"Hey," he called. "In here."

She appeared in his bedroom doorway. She was wearing a tan skirt and a light blue tee shirt. "Where *is* everybody?"

"She went to the hospital. Don't you remember? I told you yesterday she was going."

"Oh, that's right. I guess I forgot. Oh, hey, stay right there. I got a surprise for you."

"What is it?"

"It's in the truck. Wait here."

He sat on the bed and looked around at his room: it was a boy's room, with several model airplanes suspended from the ceiling over his bed, an autographed football on top of his chest of drawers, a couple of posters of sports cars on the wall, and a cowboy motif on his bedspread. He started to reach for the baseball cards to put them away when she reappeared carrying a grey and white box.

"What's that thing?"

"Duh. It's a record player. Haven't you ever seen one?"

"Oh. Course I have."

She dragged the straight-backed chair over from the corner and set the box down on it, carefully opening the hasps and flipping the top over to reveal the turntable, and she plugged it into the room's lone electrical outlet.

"And..." She reached in and pulled out two 45-rpm records. "I brought these. I got the Everly Brothers. Do you like them?"

"I think so," he said. "I'm not sure I've heard it."

"This one has 'Claudette' on it, and this other one is 'Wake Up Little Susie' and 'Maybe Tomorrow.'" She held them out for him to see.

"Looks pretty good," he said.

"I like 'All I Have to do Is Dream,'" Liza said. "I'll put that one on."

She turned on the player and fitted a record over the center-hole adaptor and set the needle down on it. There was a quick spurt of sound, like a faucet being turned on, and then a chord from an electric guitar went spidering out upon the air. Then two male voices came wavering across the room, and Frankie had never heard such a thing before: with aching sweetness, they sang about holding a girl in their arms, tasting her lips... It was like a dream itself - dark, dangerous, a forbidden room in a grown-up's world.

She closed her eyes and let her head sway in a little half circle, her short brown hair playing across her forehead, her shoulders making a little rolling motion.

"Just like honey, ain't it?" She sang along with Don and Phil Everly for a few lines, then said, "Kinda just drips right off your tongue."

"Sure does."

She perched on the foot of his bed and examined the trading cards laid out there. "Whatcha doing with these?" she asked.

"I was just looking at some of my baseball cards."

"Oh." She pointed at one of them. "Who's that colored man?"

"That's Hank Aaron. He plays for the Milwaukee Braves."

She nodded. "I've heard of him. Is that where you want to go? Milwaukee? It gets cold up there, you know."

"I'm gonna play for the Chicago Cubs," he said.

"Cold in Chicago, too."

"Well, you only have to live there during the baseball season. I'd come back to Dillon in the wintertime. Besides, during the season, you get to go all over – New York, St. Louis, and now even to Los Angeles, since the Dodgers moved out there."

She leaned over and picked up the Aaron card, and as she did so, Frankie caught a scent – it was lily-flavored, definitely. But there was something else mixed in with it; was it vanilla? Maybe it was the sweet smell of gum on the cards. He thought of putting his nose down closer to her long, tanned arm for a better whiff, but thought better of it. "Is he your favorite?" she asked.

She looked up at him over the edge of the card, brown eyes behind a red screen. "Um, no. Ernie Banks is my favorite."

"Oh, right. Chicago Cubs."

Had he been thinking clearly, he might have been surprised by her interest in professional baseball, but he was not thinking clearly. He was thinking about the way she had one leg folded under the other as she sat there on his bed, with the calf muscle flexing under her taffy-colored skin as she leaned over to hand back the Henry Aaron card, and about the way the tips of her fingers touched his as he took it from her, and about the way her brown eyes came up again and the way she always seemed just about to smile, though he could not tell what kind of smile it would be. Maybe she just thought him stupid; or maybe she only cared about the Everly Brothers.

Now she leaned over again, farther this time, to reach Rocky Colavito, and this time her arm brushed his and her face and neck were quite close to him. "Hmm," she said. "It says he plays for Cleveland. Batting average was .303 last year."

He could feel her breath on his cheek. "With 41 homers," he said.

"That's pretty good, huh?"

"Second in the league behind Mantle."

The Everly Brothers wound around and down through their last chorus, and in the sudden silence that followed he wondered what he ought to do. Did she want him to kiss her? He'd never sat this close to a girl except for his science lab partner at school. He was certain she was too old for him – she seemed so grown-up, in fact, and he was afraid she would laugh at him if he tried anything.

So it was with something like relief that he heard his father's truck outside. Like a man rising through warm water, palliating though unknown, back to the reality of air, as if even his breathing had been suspended, Frank stood up beside the bed.

"I gotta go help get her in," he said.

"I'll come, too," she said. "Maybe I can help carry something. Then I better get going."

"Don't forget your record player."

"How about if I leave it here for a while? Maybe we'll listen to some more. I got some Ray Charles I'll bring over."

"Sure."

Together they went out and down the front step into the bright light of Saturday afternoon.

———

Luther Laite was as anxious as anyone about Della's trip to the Marion County Hospital, but as was always the case on Saturdays, he had other obligations. He would carry groceries to a few homes in the outlying areas, to those who couldn't get to town on their own for one reason or another, the helpless and handicapped. He would drive down rutted, muddy roads, his car grinding and thrashing through potholes, the early-May heat beating in on him through the scrubby pines, to visit the ramshackle homes in which the forgotten had been entombed by circumstance. As he delivered eggs, milk, toilet paper, and other staples, some of them expressed profuse gratitude from their back bedrooms or the old torn and battered easy chairs on their porches, but many were too proud to do much but cough and say, "Thank ye, Preacher."

Today, as he often did, he had arranged to pick up the minister of Mount Olive Baptist Church of Mullins at his neat little house just inside the town line, and together they would drive out to the homes of colored folks around Marion County as well. He felt that he had a great deal in common with the Reverend James Jenkins: he wasn't married either, and as did Luther, he sometimes had trouble suppressing his frustration with certain of his parishioners, namely those who could do for themselves but who allowed others to carry them along. "Those people" especially galled him on these days, when the two of them saw up close the sharp contrast, the real measure of real misery, the real poverty of those who had been rendered twisted and in pain, physically, by the storms of their lives.

"Morning, Luther," he said, slamming the station wagon's door. "How goes it this morning?"

"It goes, James. It goes. How about for yourself?"

"Oh, just fine." He nodded and straightened up his narrow black tie; he was a serious fellow, with silver-rimmed glasses and a disinclination to smiling too much, but Luther could certainly appreciate that, for given the problems he himself faced in the white Christian community, he could only imagine the complexities Jenkins encountered amongst his poorer negro congregation. As far as his actual parishioners, Luther's most common annoyances were busybodies and scoundrels, but he knew that James dealt daily with people who sometimes lacked proper food, parents who had no access to medical care when their children got sick, elderly folks whose only social connection was the church itself but who were too broken down to get there very often.

"If you don't object," Reverend Jenkins said, "I'd like to drive on out to Nettie Russell's house first. She didn't look too well last Saturday."

"You got it."

If they had been surveyors making maps to illustrate economic demographics, they would not have needed any fancy equipment. They knew that as one drove outward from either town center in Mullins or Dillon, the rings of poverty became thicker and thornier. Over the years, James had taken them down red dirt roads whose existence Luther would never have known otherwise. Nettie Russell's shack was the last vestige of humanity on the last ring to which clung the lame and the sick, and beyond it was only wilderness.

"And how is your special project goin'?" James asked. "Your Mrs. Treadwell?"

Luther shook his head. "I'm somewhat in awe at the moment. Her condition actually seems to be improving."

"Well, God is good. I've certainly held her up in my own prayers."

"And for that I thank you, and she would, too, if she knew anything about it. You and yours do some of the best praying I've heard around these parts, that's for sure."

Jenkins allowed himself a slight smile, and Luther thought to himself: I could use some of those praying skills myself. The bare truth was that sometimes prayer, for him, merely meant going through the motions, and the spark, that sense of kinetic energy and connection that he felt when he was younger, was often absent in these days. He certainly had never considered himself a crusader for the rights of colored people, and he was acutely aware that his friendship with James and these Saturday visits would likely alienate many of his own members at United Methodist, were they to learn of it, and so he kept quiet about it (ironically, he believed that James probably did the same for much the same reason). He believed in a universal, apostolic and evangelical church, but he also knew that a man could hope to accomplish only so much in his lifetime; if he wished to continue to lead or at least to contribute anything, there were certain attitudes and conventions he must not address or resist. Status quo, it was called... but if Christ had worried about status quo, we'd be in a far worse fix. Why couldn't something get easier once in a while?

They turned down the narrow dirt drive that led to Nettie's dwelling. It was tucked in an ancient stand of tall pines on a lot that had once been part of a turpentine farm, where the great, thick trunks had been tapped seasonally and the runoff transported to giant kettles for cooking at the center of what had been a thriving camp. When the turpentine business had shut down, naturally the camp closed, but the negroes who had been hired to do the tapping and hauling had been allowed to remain in the flimsy camp homes, if they chose, and given a small pension. A few of the old folks had remained, and Nettie had outlived them all; as for her pension, it had run out years ago.

She was sitting on her porch, and as usual, when they had parked and gotten out, she seemed to be gazing far beyond them into an invisible horizon, for she was blind. Still she called to them:

"Good mornin', Reverend Jenkins, Pastor Laite."

"Now, how'd you know it'd be us?" Jenkins asked, glancing at Luther and winking.

"You tryin' to be funny, but you know, y'alls ain't the only callers I ever get. My nephew was here just last week. Laid up in bed all week wid' a bad head, he did. Done gone back to Charleston, now."

"That so? Good thing, then, 'cause we only brought enough for one today."

Every Saturday she spoke of this disappearing nephew. Luther had finally understood that her memory had betrayed her, had gotten scratched up like some old record and could no longer put events in their proper sequence; James had confirmed that none of her family – if indeed there were any left – had come to see her in many years.

She stood up on thin legs which looked like they might splinter any moment, her frayed housecoat hanging loosely about her like a tattered pink flag. A number of the old clay turpentine pots with artificial flowers in them adorned the edge of the porch. "Just put the groceries on the step there, Preacher. Ah can get 'em inside."

"Now, Nettie, don't be stubborn. You know I'm gonna bring 'em in and put 'em on the table for you."

"I ain't had a chance to clean in there."

"Never you mind. And set back down before you fall down."

She did so, muttering, and Luther said, "Here, I'm going to take and fill your bucket here for you, Nettie. 'Spect you need some fresh water."

"Thank you, Pastor. They's another empty one out by the pump, if you please."

When he had filled the buckets and brought them inside, he looked around: there was not much she might have cleaned anyway – a small kitchen table, a narrow counter, one straight-backed chair, and a single bed shoved over against the opposite wall, which was neatly made; there was a small carpet remnant in the middle of the unfinished wooden floor. In one corner sat a small, badly corroded wood-burning stove, and wraithlike burlap sacks blew loose in the window frames.

The two men stood on the porch and chatted with her for a while, about goings-on in Mullins, about what additional supplies she might need next week, about the elders in the congregation that she still remembered ("And how is Lena Evans doin' these days? And her boy, what he been up to?"), about precautions she might take when the *real* hot weather should arrive, until at last James said,

"Well, we gotta get on back now. But don't forget what I said, Nettie – anytime you feel like coming in town for services, just let me know. I'll come fetch you tomorrow morning if you like."

"Oh, tha's all right, Preacher. Seem like the longer I stay out here, the better I feel. I got a understanding wid' these woods around here. Don't need no church prayin' these days. Been doin' me some tree prayin'."

Tree prayin', Luther thought on the drive back. Now that might just work... whatever it is. Nonetheless, he didn't dare complain. As soon as he had dropped off Reverend Jenkins, he drove back through Dillon, and with the old station wagon rumbling under the strain, he barreled straight down to the Little Pee Dee River to the Treadwell house for news about Della. Bob opened the door and met his eyes with an utterly benign expression, a sheepish tilt to his eyes that might have meant anything, and so Luther blurted out:

"Okay, so what are they saying at the hospital?"

Treadwell shrugged (Luther hated it when he put on this hang-dog demeanor) and said, "Nothing definite, of course. As usual, it's hurry up and wait. Blood work and x-ray results'll be in next week, though they did say the signs look good. She's way underweight, but the good news is she's hungry. Frankie and I are just about to make up some ham sandwiches. Come on inside, Pastor Laite."

As father and son rummaged about in the kitchen, banging plates about, Luther headed for the little room at the side of the house. He found Della with the automatic bed in the fully upright position. Her color was good, and she looked up at him and smiled around the rim of the tumbler of water she was sipping from. She swallowed and said,

"Well, look who the cat dragged in."

"You're looking well today," he said.

"I'm feeling well. Better than I deserve to."

"Let's not get in too much of a hurry, Della. You've been laid up here for quite a while, and it's gonna take some time to get your legs under you again."

"Really? I was hoping to go for a swim today. Honestly, the only reason I'm a bit tired right now is from the mill they ran me through down at the county. Never been scraped and prodded so much in my life."

"Guess we need to have a little faith that they know what they're about, these doctors."

She did still seem quite frail, but the air in the room had changed since he had been in here last. That murky oppressiveness had lifted, and even the window seemed clearer, as if someone had just wiped the glass; outside, the sunlight came off the grass in bright speckles. He sat down in the armchair, and cool air from the fan in the next room flowed in and over them, and he wondered: Is this the wind of healing? He thought of John's metaphor in Chapter 3: *The wind bloweth where it listeth, and thou hearest the sound thereof, but canst not tell whence it cometh, and whither it goeth: so is every one that is born of the Spirit.*

I'm with John on this, he thought. The wind will blow, and where it's going, I have no idea. But at least it's blowing.

———

Della believed that if she could do two things – eat and listen to Liza's voice – then she would continue to get better. She was not nearly as groggy as she had been these past few weeks, though she knew that much of that had been due to the stronger pain medication, which she had cut back on substantially. As a matter of fact, today she felt no pain at all.

It was Wednesday, and since her visit to Marion County Hospital on Saturday, she had felt herself gaining strength by the day. Food actually had some taste to her now, and she had gotten up and about numerous times, had gone out on the porch, and even all the way down to their little dock. She had done this with Bob and Frank's assistance, but she had not told them that she had also gotten out of bed when they were away at work and school or at Frank's ballgames, though everyone had warned her against this: "What if you fell?" Bob had asked. "Just what if you fell?" But she had never had it in her to lie in bed if she could help it.

The second and more recent form of sustenance, Liza's increasingly busy chattering and especially her vivid narratives rendering the Dillon team's performances on the ball field seemed to reconnect her to the world, to infuse her once again with an awareness that she was a part of a town, a community, loose-knit and hapless though it might be in spots. She believed she could see the other parents, the kids, smell the roasting frankfurters, hear the happy clapping and shouted praise when a boy did something well, and could especially sense the pride she would certainly have felt in her own child had she been sitting in those bleachers next to Bob and this delightful girl who had come suddenly back into their lives.

There was a third source for her improving strength – her regular Bible reading, though she felt that should go without saying. It was something she had always done, but it had taken a long time for her to figure out that it's like anything else you do to feed certain parts of yourself – it's not because you've forgotten anything that's in there or because you're just passing the time or even despite the fact that you know it all by heart: it's because it is nourishment.

One evening, after Liza had left, she lay thinking: mostly she looked forward to the time (and it now seemed that it wouldn't be too long) when she could cease to be at the center of all this, when she could return to being a mother and a wife and no longer the patient, the one they spoke about in the other room, in those quiet, deadly voices, when getting to the bathroom would no longer be an ordeal, and when her dignity would be restored to her. And she thought about Frankie and relished the idea that he could go back to being a boy again and not have to concern himself any longer with things that were so hard and so unfair for him.

At that moment Bob came into the room, and anxiousness filled his face. "What's wrong?" he asked. "You hurting?"

"What? Why?"

He reached down and blotted at her cheek with his finger. Water was flowing from her eyes.

She wiped her sleeve across her face, looked at the moisture there, and nearly broke into laughter. "No, it's silliness," she said. "I can't really explain. I guess I'm just happy for a change."

Now he covered her hand with his and said, "You ain't got to explain nothin'."

He stood looking down at her. That was all he had to say, but for her, it was enough.

———

Liza was excited. She had just watched Frank pitch in another home game, this time against Conway, and he had only allowed one hit and struck out thirteen batters; plus, he had hit a triple. She had begun to think that she enjoyed telling the story of the game to Mrs. Treadwell more than the actual watching of it. She was only a decent spectator, but she was an excellent narrator, and she was just now climbing into the red truck in order that she might go to the place where she could be just that.

She knew that Della was warming up to her, and the better she felt, the warmer things got. She had not intended to become a surrogate daughter or confidante, but rather just to try and help out the family a little bit while there was illness in the house. She knew something about illness, though that which had afflicted her family had been of a different sort. Her own mother, she had finally realized, would never recover from the colossal failures of her marriage and then her lengthy cohabitation with Mr. Melvin, and whatever else she had been through in her past. Now she was with Roger, and although Liza got along fine with Roger, experience had taught her to doubt and distrust the people who came into their lives. With the Treadwells, though, she felt that she had some control – first off, she could come and go, and when she was there she could choose to do kind things, and she believed that helped to make up for some of the things she herself had done in Greenville.

She liked Frankie but had little idea what he thought of her. She certainly did not think him thickheaded, but it was as if no one had ever taught him how to talk to people. Or maybe it was because when someone was so good at one thing, better than anybody else around, people treated you as somewhat of a freak of nature. Of course, in turn, that only made him shyer, and likely more confused, since he thought baseball was easy and couldn't understand why other boys believed it difficult. It would certainly help matters if everyone could remember that he was still only in tenth grade, including those scouts who were now coming out in groups, little hungry packs, with their little notepads, standing at the fence and watching him like foxes eyeing a chicken.

Nevertheless, this all felt right to her, this life she was creating for herself, and that was something she had never known before. She had realized one thing, and that was that her own mother's life was not likely to change in any significant way: she would still be waiting on tables ten years from now, and still involving herself with men who were essentially no good for her, and if Liza weren't careful, she'd still be the daughter who always got dragged along. But at the Treadwells', things seemed to be moving in a different way, there was recovery and redemption, and an air of destiny; it wasn't just Frank's very specific gifts and all the places they might eventually take him, it was the idea that if folks worked hard and there was unity and hopefulness, you could get somewhere. And within her, she knew that in order to be part of that, to feel that way, too, she would have to dismiss the demons inside of her; someday, she would have to tell someone her story and be forgiven in order to move on. Della was the only one who could possibly listen and understand.

It was late afternoon as she pulled out of the school parking lot. Frank had stayed to help rake the infield, and then he would have to shower and change, so she would go ahead to report the news of the game. Mr. Treadwell had been unable to leave work, so she would have two avid listeners today. The sun was just above the trees off over her left shoulder, painting the underside of the clouds in gold, and as she took the road down to the river, the light played in shifting, golden bars through the trunks of the tall pines. It was the best time of day, when things began to cool off and the wind came off of the dark water, and all the promise of a weekend in late May filled the blue and green spaces. The truck threw up a cloud of brown dust as it rattled along.

There were three vehicles in front of the Treadwell home: she recognized Bob's pickup and Pastor Laite's station wagon, but there was another car, a big black Chevy, that she didn't know. Had they invited guests for dinner? Some of the church people maybe? She pulled up onto the edge of the yard and then went on inside without knocking, as she had gotten used to doing.

The house was silent. One light was burning, the lamp on the dining room table by which Frankie did his studying, but otherwise, all was eerily dark. Abruptly, the door to the room where Della slept was opened, and Pastor Laite stepped out. He looked very tall, in his seersucker suit with the black cloth and white collar, and he seemed not even to see her. Behind him, the door swung inward a bit, and she could see Bob in there, sitting in the chair with his head down, staring at his own knees. She could see the two little hills of Della's feet under the bed sheet, and above that, a bald man with a stethoscope around his neck stood utterly motionless. It struck her that with the muted colors, the surreal lighting, and the stillness of the scene, she might well be looking at a photograph.

Luther walked very slowly and carefully over to the kitchen sink, teetering slightly as if treading along a narrow beam, and he took down a glass and filled it with water.

"Pastor Laite." He turned slowly and saw her now for the first time. "What is it?" she asked. "What's the matter with everybody?"

Looking down at her, with the lamplight shining up and across his chin and cheekbones, he looked quite old and tired. He took a swallow of water and then said, "It's Mrs. Treadwell. I'm afraid she has passed away."

She heard the word "Oh," come out of her own mouth. She looked out the window; the last smudges of the sun were just fading across the little slope of grass leading down to the river, and the crickets had taken their cue in the deepening shadows along the bank.

Three

July, 1959

Deputy Reuben Sasser of the Dillon County Sheriff's Office edged his car through the alley that ran past Beamon's Hardware and spilled out onto Main, squeezing to a stop as Howard Beamon approached him across the back lot. He lowered his window as Howard, his face already sheened in sweat at 10 a.m., put his hands on the cruiser's roof and leaned over.

"He's already been by here," he said. "Picked up his check and then disappeared out the front door."

"Say what his plans were?"

"Didn't say hardly anything."

"Okay," Reuben said. "Thanks."

Reuben figured he would find Bob Treadwell somewhere between here and Silky's Bar, but he wondered whether he ought to go back to the office, get another thermos of coffee, and chip away at some paperwork for an hour or so. Silky wouldn't open till eleven, anyway, and then he could go in under some pretense ("Heard tell of some bad bills bein' passed around town lately..."). He did not want to accost Treadwell along the highway or sidewalk again, as he had done twice in the last two weeks – not because he feared any violent reaction from the man at all but because he hadn't really broken any laws, as Bob had clearly pointed out to him the last time. Sasser knew that in the public's view it was a narrow line he walked between public servant and professional agitator, but in fifteen years on patrol he had learned that things like this were best nipped at the earliest possible time; for instance, whenever he saw a couple of kids heading for the path that led from the back of the school building down through those woods, he wouldn't hesitate to swoop down on them and ask them how their day was going. This was different, though: he couldn't say he had ever really been friends with Bob Treadwell, but he had known him for a long time to be a decent sort, and that counted for a lot around these parts.

He put the car window down again and kept it down this time. It was that hour when it no longer mattered, for any remaining coolness from the previous night had been blasted by the midmorning sun. Reuben felt a sudden trickle of perspiration slide down the inside of his left arm. He decided to take one more tour around the town.

Small-town cop. People thought it was easy, but all things being relative, it had its complexities. Most of these had to do with alcohol and the occasional domestic dispute (usually also involving alcohol), and if it wasn't Silky's or one of the colored taverns over in Mullins, it was moonshine. The trick was knowing when to laugh with somebody, slap him on the shoulder, tell him to mind his p's and q's, and then get back in the car and drive on, and when to put on the strong arm, because when you got the cuffs out, you had to go all the way. But when a man's wife died... how should he handle that one?

He pulled over to the curb, picked up the newspaper from the seat beside him, and killed off another twenty minutes or so. Then he put the car into gear and followed the treeless, sweltering road that led up to Highway 9, and sure enough, there he was, walking along almost in the ditch, his white tee shirt sticking to his narrow shoulders in wet patches of sweat. *Damned, insufferable heat*, Reuben thought; he had lived here his whole life but felt that he never got used to it.

He eased up alongside Treadwell, who did not look over at him, of course. "Morning, Bob," he said. Treadwell, his short legs covering oddly long stretches of ground, did glance over now, but did not speak. Inconspicuously,

Reuben sniffed the air, but from here he could not scent any liquor smells emanating from him.

Sasser took off his sunglasses. *Try and look sensitive, dumbass,* he told himself. "Where we headed this morning, Bob?"

Treadwell looked at the horizon. "*We* ain't headed nowhere. *I* am out for a walk in the country. But I don't see where that's any of your business."

"I'd be happy to give you a lift."

"Well, now, then I wouldn't really be out for a walk, would I?"

All right, then. "I guess you got me there. Get plenty of water in you, Bob, and stay to the shade when you can. It's gonna be a scorcher."

He would go back to town and get some lunch, and then maybe take a drive out past Silky's this afternoon. He accelerated past him, and at the very next place where the road's shoulder flattened out into baking gravel, he turned around. He waved as he passed Treadwell, but the determined walker did not look at him.

Stubborn fella, he thought.

———

"Order up."

Liza rang the little bell on the counter, stuck the check on the side of the plate, turned back to the sizzling griddle, and with the spatula shoveled waves of dark grease over to the edges of the metal sheet. That was the last breakfast order of the day – a western omelet, and it was time to switch over to lunch. The weekday clientele at Trudy's Diner, mostly broad, bearded men in overalls, tended to come steadily in clusters throughout the day, and she seldom got a break until well into the afternoon, when her mother would arrive and put on one of the stained pink aprons, and then the two of them would be on shift together until Liza left at five, provided the prep work for dinner was all finished.

So far things had worked out better than she had imagined they would. She and her mother seldom conversed, since Liza was in the kitchen and her mother was out front, but that was all in keeping with the strange dynamics they had adopted at home as well; the idea of merely greeting one another in passing had become so habitual that even when they were sitting in the same room together, it always seemed that one of them was on the verge of departure. She had never cooked very much before, but she now found that what she lacked in culinary creativity she made up for with finesse, for she was quick with the spatula and the chopping knife, and she kept things running efficiently when she was at the griddle. The one thing she truly despised was the grease: every evening she arrived home with a coating of grease on her – even on her hair, though she wore a hairnet, and grease clogged her skin's pores so insidiously that it seemed no amount of scrubbing could cleanse them. Otherwise, it gave her something to do through the languid Carolina summer, as well as a small stream of income; and it gave her a whole block of hours in the day when she would not have to think at all.

Unless, of course, she allowed herself to think. Then the chopping of potatoes and onions and the flipping of hamburgers made for a perfunctory activity that gave her mind the freedom to wander as it might. Nonetheless, her thoughts always took the same path back to the events of the spring, when things had gone so badly, beginning with the death of Mrs. Treadwell. To start with, she had not seen Frank since mid-June, and that had left her with a jagged hole in the life she had managed to rebuild for herself since she and her mother had returned to Dillon, but that had all been his decision, really, and so she had had no control over that. At least she could honestly say that she had learned this one thing: that her own choices were the only ones over which she could hope to gain any mastery. It stung, though; there was no questioning that, and nearly every time she replayed those days and nights of only a few weeks ago, she wondered whether she ought to have done something differently.

As for Frankie's father, she had seen him many times as he walked the streets of the town, seemingly aimlessly, though he always moved with a sense of purpose, as if he saw a destination to which others were blind. Even when she drove right past him and honked the truck's horn, he would not meet her eyes, and finally she had given up, watching him in the rear view mirror as he faded and then vanished in the steam and the shimmering waves of heat. She had been giving up, she knew, for some time now; at first, she had tried to help the two of them, just as the preacher had, she thought, for they had floundered like drowning men, but she had come to realize that the Treadwell males were difficult – far more so than she had imagined. And when things had become too grim, when the shadows had grown too thick and the cabinets were bare and there was no more light in that house, her instinct for self-preservation had been triggered, and she had stopped going. She had held herself together and graduated from high school, and now she knew, to her great relief, that everything could always be temporary – this job, her living arrangements, all of it; she could leave whenever she chose. She felt sorry for those who could not understand this as she did. The ability to leave would finally be her redemption.

Now Robley, the elderly colored man who washed the dishes, stuck his tufted gray head around the kitchen doorway and called out: "All right, now, Queen Bee. You gon' give the worker bees a chance to catch up or not?" He was smiling, the flesh of his bottom gum shining pinkly under the bright utility light.

"Sorry, Robley, but no rest for the weary. I got a business to run here."

His grin widened: "Wouldn't surprise me no-ways if you really *wuz* to take over. I mean this *whole* place. You the Queen Bee." Then he disappeared.

He had taken a liking to her, she knew, and she liked him. She felt that his kindness and good humor toward her were genuine, though of course, she had known plenty of colored people (and especially older ones) who simply "put on" in this way but who, deep down, didn't trust or like whites, and with good reason. Anyway, it didn't really matter; she could only believe in what she had experienced herself, only trust what she saw for herself, and she had seen a lot, from the bottom up. The bottom had been Greenville, that night with the gleaming blade that Mr. Melvin had honed so sharp, she could drop one of her hairs on it and it would float away in two pieces. It was on the nightstand, and she had easily found the big vein in her neck with the pad of her thumb, but when she thought about that now, it seemed as if someone else had done those things, some very sad, very sick young girl.

Sometimes she thought about Mr. Melvin, and then a terrible guilt would overtake her because of the lie she had told her mother about him. Nonetheless, she had known at the time that it was her only chance to get out of Greenville. She was sorry, and she regretted that she had perhaps ruined Mr. Melvin's life, but in essence, her survival instinct had kicked in.

In any case, since the beginning of the summer, her greatest dread had been that Della Treadwell's death would cast her backward into that abyss again, but such had not been the case. Certainly it was hard: she had even gone to Pastor Laite, but even the bitter truth – the fact that he had been unable to give her anything, to impart any strength to her at all – had not distressed her beyond hope, and then she knew, she *knew* that she was moving ahead. She had the strength to leave this place, too, to start fresh again, and to leave them all behind, including Frank. Still, she had not wanted to be the sort of person who would abandon others, as in the stories of would-be rescuers of drowning victims, who ultimately have to kick themselves away from those they would save simply to preserve their own lives. A voice in her spoke: *Don't worry, it's not too late*, it said. *He might still come around.*

"Maybe so," she said aloud. "But I could be long gone by then."

———

Saturday. Luther Laite sat at his desk in the pastor's office at the United Methodist Church of Dillon, the tyranny of sermonizing upon him once again. The blank sheet of paper stared back at him like a cold devil. He had picked up his pencil and set it down again several times already, and the heavy dread filled him as he realized that these past six weeks (which he had called a sabbatical but which had really turned into the longest spate of slothfulness he had ever undertaken) had not renewed and recharged him; it had had the opposite effect, and continually, like a distressed man who checks his hairbrush every day to see how quickly he is balding, Luther saw his own willpower thinning before his eyes.

Dear God, he murmured, *help me with this. If I can just get a few words down on paper, maybe it'll make sense.* He picked up the pencil again, which was freshly sharpened to a crisp point, but the circuitry from his brain to his hand had gone dead, and the hollow place in him had grown even more empty than the page in front of him. He set the pencil back down.

He still could not believe that the death of one congregation member had so decimated his spirit, for he had been through it many times; there were some that he had baptized when they were infants and for whom he had later performed funeral services. Strange as that might have seemed sometimes, it also had brought him a curious kind of comfort, and for a while he had believed he understood, had seen some meaning in the arc of any life, small and insignificant as it might appear. *We are all like babies*, he had thought back then, *all the way through. We can't do diddley on our own.* Back then, at least, he knew he could do and say a few things that could help; now, he was the helpless one.

That first week away from the church, following Della's death, he had sat at home, slumped on the back porch in his tattered green and white lawn chair, looking out at the azalea bushes, where it seemed the blooms had already come and gone and he had never known about it. Then on Sunday morning, an idea had come to him, and he had put on his blue seersucker (but with a dress shirt and tie this time) and he had cranked up the old wagon and driven across the county line to James Jenkins's Mt. Olive Baptist Church, arriving just in time for the opening hymn. He had slipped into a pew near the back, but it was impossible, of course, for him to be anonymous here – not merely because his skin was a different color but because this was another indigenous congregation, like his own. The people sang in what seemed to be ancient voices, full of the wavering of time and pain, but there was something soothing in it, too, and Luther felt desperate to become part of that. Some of those in attendance knew him already, and they would turn and smile at him, while the others simply glanced over at him curiously or bemusedly, but not suspiciously. He wondered – doubtfully – whether his own congregation might be as tolerant, should the shoe ever be wrangled onto the other foot.

The hymn ended in a long, reverberating gathering of rich tones, and then all sat down, as Reverend Jenkins approached the old, battered lectern, adjusted his sliver-rimmed glasses, and opened the book before him.

His voice rolled out in those familiar inflections, the rising and falling and the distinct rhythms which were the stock in trade of the country preacher; Luther had heard it in colored churches and white ones, and even though he had never been able to achieve the same sort of dramatic tension with his own voice, it took him back to his boyhood immediately, to his father's little clapboard church in the South Carolina woods. But it was Jenkins he heard:

"The first reading today is from the Gospel according to John: 'Let not your heart be troubled; you believe in God, believe also in me. In my Father's house are many mansions; if *it were* not *so,* I would have told you. I go to prepare a place for you. And if I go and prepare a place for you, I will come again and receive you to myself; that where I am, *there* you may be also. And where I go you know, and the way you know.' Thomas said to Him, 'Lord, we do not know where you are going, and how can we know the way?' Jesus said to him, 'I am the way, the truth, and the life. No one comes to the Father except through me.' That's the Gospel according to John."

Jenkins stepped back and bowed his head. He had not yet looked at him directly, but Luther knew he had marked that passage for him – or maybe it only seemed so, for it was in the nature of things uttered in a church that they almost always appeared to be relevant to the individual in some way. His own heart was certainly troubled, and he knew that when Christ had spoken to the grieving disciples, He had understood the essence of comfort: I have not abandoned you, you are not alone, I go ahead to prepare your place, too. Luther had often quoted those same remarks to sobbing widows and bereft children, but this time the loss had been his own, and apparently James had known that instinctively. Still, that wasn't all there was to it: he had not been able to explain, even to himself, what had happened in that room with Della on the day she died.

He had wanted to stay for Jenkins's homily, to sing, to pray, to sweat with all of them and find refuge, but he had found that he could not. At that moment, as his friend James stood there looking down at the pine-plank floor and the believers waited, he was seized again by the same mortifying, paralyzing dread he had felt at Della's bedside that day, and he set the hymnal on the pew behind him and quickly made his way back to the big doors and out into the blazing sunlight which seemed to strike him over the head like a burning fist, and sweating and breathing hard, he climbed behind the wheel of the station wagon.

At that moment, he had not realized what was wrong, had not begun to realize what it meant. But now, seated at his desk, with only the useless paper in front of him and the unused pencil mocking him, waiting, and the air hanging silent and shroud-like about him, he had to confess to himself at last, after six weeks of wallowing in the sludge of self-pity, that he had lost his faith.

———

Frank sat on his bike at the corner of Dillon's Main Street. The town yawned out empty and sleepy before him, and metal-colored clouds sat well behind the brick facades and tar roofs; by afternoon, those clouds would bulk and darken up nearly to black, as they were in that part of the summer now when daily thunderstorms would lash the countryside and then give way once again to a murky steam bath. A slight, warm wind touched his face as he glanced down toward the front of Beamon's Hardware; although he had no thought of going down there today (or any other day, for that matter), he couldn't help looking.

It wasn't that he expected to see his father's small, wiry figure hauling boxes or assembling machinery in the lot; he knew quite well, in fact, that he would miss work today. But something from that place harkened to him, even haunted him – the cool, polished cement floor, the smell of the bags of fertilizer leaned against the wall, the metal shelves filled with metal bins, the racks of saw blades, drill bits, mallets and hammers, and the deep, drawling voices of the salesmen…the sense of safety it had once given him. He had used to stop in at least once a week, and his father would always get a Coke for him out of the big, bright-red cooler and sit on a crate as the on-going conversation among the men went on well into the afternoon, broken only by the occasional customer who would come in, locate what he wanted, and then inevitably become part of the measured banter. It seemed that no women ever intruded there.

That all seemed a lifetime ago to Frank. Since the Fourth of July, the town had seemed especially quiet and empty. There seemed to be fewer cars and trucks in the angled spaces along the storefronts, fewer farmers in their overalls and shirt sleeves ambling about, fewer mothers marching determinedly toward the Piggly Wiggly to buy their groceries for the week. It wasn't just the heat, he figured – people must be moving away. Even though he had dreamt many times of playing big-league ball in the great, golden cities, of trotting out across those fabled green meadows beneath tens of thousands of gazes and the electric hum of crowd noise broken now and again by an ecstatic roar, even though he had seen himself time and again in those dugouts and clubhouses and in the magnificent hotels and on the trains streaking over the countryside, now he saw that here was his life. He could never escape, and this would never be the town to which he would return from some grand adventure, his haven for the off-season.

For there could be no off-season if there were no more seasons, and he felt about as certain about that as he possibly could, in the midst of all the other uncertainties that now characterized his existence. It had not so much been because of his mother's death at the time of their keenest hopes; rather, it was what had come after – his father's unraveling, Pastor Laite's conspicuous and abrupt absence from their affairs, and a general lack of any order, any method by which to cope and to put all troubling things into one place in his mind where he could begin to comprehend them; he knew all of this, and for a while he had wished to say as much to somebody at first, but now he no longer cared. The thing he *had* cared most about, and which might have saved him, had gotten dirtied (or more correctly, it had been dirtied by his own actions), and now he felt as empty and purposeless as the vacant streets now set before him.

Granted, her death had been unfair. But of course, he could see that death was always unfair, except maybe for someone who had done terrible things. And in the thudding of his methodical brain, he had then understood that this could only mean one thing, if it were to make any sense at all: that we had all done something wrong. And then: if we were all already guilty enough that we must die, then what does it matter what else you do? Through this reasoning, which was as sound as any he knew, he had sabotaged his baseball season, and then some. He realized that there were those who pitied him and who said it was simply a boy's natural reaction to the loss of his mother, but he knew that in truth it was reasonable that if the end to everything came inevitably, it could hardly matter when it came. And realizing this, he had found he did not need to cry; thus, his newborn indifference was mistaken by many for manly courage.

He looked at the town and saw it for the vacuous, timeless limbo it truly was, but he let his memory carry him back to another time – seven years ago, when he had been only eight. Ordinarily he found that he could not recall very much before the age of twelve or so, when the only waking meaning for him concerned whatever would happen on a given day on the baseball field, but now he clearly saw himself on that Fourth of July; in fact, he had been on his bicycle then, too, at this very corner, and the sidewalks had been filled with spectators waiting for the parade put on by the Lions Club. Red, white and blue streamers swirled about every lamppost, American flags were draped on every storefront, and he was waiting for his mother and father to meet him with the picnic basket and the big quilt, and he could hear the high school's marching band toodling and honking and booming down the street and around the corner from which they would momentarily emerge. The glory of it all had come tumbling down over him, the firemen in their shiny red hats smiling down from their tall, glistening trucks, the flower-laden floats, the pretty high-school girls, and then afterwards they had gone to the park to spread out the quilt and eat the chicken sandwiches and listen to the brass band in the pleasant wane of the afternoon, until he had fallen asleep with his head on his mother's thigh while his father, propped comfortably on his elbow and smoking cigarettes, looked approvingly out over the scene.

He truly could not say how things had gotten so twisted around.

For a few moments he wished that he could go back, even if only to last May, and if he couldn't have prevented everything that had happened, then at least he could have helped. If he had known that his mother's apparent recovery had been just another trick, another example of the unfairness, he could have prepared himself. They said it had been a heart attack, that her tumor had indeed ceased growing and that the disease was even in remission, but her body and heart had gotten too weak, that lying in that bed – that damned bed (and the first thing his father had done afterward had been to put that damned bed in the back of his pickup and haul it to the dump) – had essentially ruined her. And if he had known how things would go at the funeral with Pastor Laite, he could have been ready for that, too. If he had known, if he had only known, he would not have made a fool of himself with the girl, Liza, either. And then there was that game with Greenville.

But none of it mattered, finally. It had taken the game with Greenville to show him that. What he had thought was the purposeful and predictable flight of a ball had turned out to be another deception. He could no longer waste his time – his *life!* – with it. The only trouble was, as Mr. Spagnola had often told his tenth-grade students, nature abhors a vacuum. Something will always rush in to fill up a void, he had said. Frank wondered, in his particular case, what that something would be.

———

This old boy wasn't having any of it.

Coach Max Bass was seated on a stiff leather-covered bench aboard the Charleston and Western Carolina Railway train, watching the scrub oaks, pines, the corn and bean fields, and the oily backwaters rush past him in runny gray, brown, and jade swirls. He held a glass of bourbon suspended just beneath his lips, as if some hypnotist or conjuror had touched him on the shoulder some time ago, but in fact he was deep in thought.

By late afternoon – maybe at Beaufort, if he recalled correctly, he would switch to the Atlantic Coast Line and then ride northward all the way to Richmond, where he would meet with representatives of the Washington Senators about a position as a scout with that club, and then the entire population of Dillon could kiss his white ass.

Still, there were only a handful of them against whom he bore a grudge, but it satisfied him to lump them together as a bunch of ignorant river rats. Mainly it was that little sonofabitch, the Treadwell kid, who had tried to ruin him; he had no proof of it, but he believed it. When things had gotten out, the Billings girl's parents had actually had very little to say about it (though he had never been able to determine how much they really knew, and the principal had essentially given him a mere rap on the knuckles; and the county school board – they had offered him a raise, for Christ's sake! But that Treadwell kid, little shit that he was, had not only tried to ruin him by running his mouth – this kid who had hardly ever said *anything to anybody*, he was so dull – but he had also undertaken to smash Bass's season (and what would have been his state championship) to bits in the game against Greenville High School. He had picked a fine damn time to show that he had a temper after all.

Yet he believed he had already put all that behind him, and if he could secure this scouting position (and he was sure he was qualified), he'd never have to see any of them again. Baseball might be a very young man's game, but it could also be an older man's game, and it was his time, he felt. He had even halfway expected Sarah Billings to come up to his rented house in town over the summer, given her appetite and the things she had said to him, but she had not; he supposed that she had suffered some embarrassment, but hell, so had he, for that matter. At least it had all hit the fan only a couple of days before graduation, so that classes had been pretty much all done with, and he hadn't had to walk down the halls with all of their eyes burning into his back. By fall, it would probably all be forgotten, but he hoped to be far away by then, regardless.

So he had been right about one thing, but wrong about the other. Not a bad average. He had known that Frank Treadwell did not have the mental toughness, the savvy, to last for very long in baseball, and when the crack-up had begun, he had known it immediately and had watched it…not with pleasure, really, but with a sense of vindication and the contentment that comes with knowing such things and seeing them affirmed. True, the boy's mother had died and his father had turned out to be worthless, but Max could have told them stories that would have broken their hearts: players who had been abandoned in the streets as kids, some who had lost *both* parents, and one or two who had been raised in orphanages and had never known their families at all. Just look at the Babe, for instance – there was a case in point. And those who stuck it out and didn't let it get to them, those who learned to take it out on that white ball with the red stitches, they became men, they were ballplayers.

Not so much, the Treadwell kid. All the talent in the world couldn't have helped him.

The silent triumph of having been dead on the mark about that one was somewhat tainted by his having been mistaken about the other thing, which was the girl. He could not now believe that he had thought he might be in love with her. He saw clearly that those distorted feelings had been motivated by guilt, but slowly, as he had gotten things into perspective over the past few weeks, he had been able to shed that guilt as one might dust off his hat or shoes, comprehending that these things were never the fault of one person alone. She had come to him first, hadn't she, with her woman's body and her girl's brain, and Max was a man like any other. Yes, he had made a mistake, but it was understandable.

As the train sagged back and rolled with a high-pitched lament into another small town, he snapped back into the moment and took a sip of the bourbon. For the first time in several years, he felt he was getting someplace.

———

Robley withdrew a cigarette from the crinkly pack, and holding it delicately between his chunky, dark-brown thumb and forefinger, he extended it towards Liza. With equal care, she accepted it, put it between her lips, and leaned over to the match he had struck along the seam of his pants. She wasn't much of a smoker, but it had become part of the ritual of their mid-afternoon breaks out behind the diner: they would sit on two wooden crates beside the brick wall and smoke two cigarettes apiece, talk if one or both of them felt like it (or otherwise sit in comfortable silence), and then they would go back inside to finish up the late-lunch shift.

Today she was chatty. "I don't know nothin' about your family, Robley," she said. "Or where y'all live."

"Down to the river," he said. "Got two grown-up sons, but they livin' up in Raleigh, so it's just me and my wife."

"Whereabouts on the river?"

"Moccasin Bluff."

She nodded. "I know where it is. Not too far from where my mom and I used to stay. It's nice there."

He took in a chestful of blue smoke. "Nobody bothers us at least," he said. "Now what about you, Queen Bee? I know somethin' like you got to have a little boyfriend."

She laughed with a smoky hiccup. "Me? I *been* done with boys for a while now."

"Well, that I cannot comprehend. Fact, I seen you maybe a month or so ago with somebody. He come up here on a bicycle and then got in your truck with you when you took outa here that day."

"Oh...that. He's just a friend of mine. He ain't my boyfriend."

"Mm-hmm." Robley lifted one eyebrow and glanced upward at her.

"I don't know," she said, "He mighta been my boyfriend, kinda. I'm still not sure what happened between us."

"Some a' these boys 'round here ain't too smart."

"It wasn't like that," Liza said. "See, his – his mama died this past spring, and that really messed everything up, bad."

"Sho' will. *Sho'* will."

"But things were okay, I mean, I thought they were gonna be all right. But then he just sorta snapped."

"Snapped?"

"Lost his mind." The cigarette had burned to the filter, and she dropped it on the pavement and crushed it with her shoe. Robley handed her another one. "He plays for the school baseball team, or he did. He went nuts in the game against Greenville High. Hit a boy in the head with a pitch and cracked his skull open."

"What he done that for?"

"This boy said somethin' mean about me. Somethin' pretty bad."

"Oh, okay. Now I start to understand. He was defendin' your honor. That ought to made you like him all the more."

She paused, looking down at the grey pavement, which was wet with runoff from the gutter above them. "Yeah, but…it's embarrassing to admit, but the things the other boy said were true. He was just saying what was true. I used to go to Greenville, before my mother and I moved back here."

Robley shook his head. "Don't matter. A gentleman don't say stuff like that about a lady."

"Well, he ain't saying nothing now. Still in the county hospital."

"Dang, Queen Bee. Your boy throw *hard*. Must be a good ballplayer."

"'Except that he almost caused a riot and then got kicked off the team."

Robley shook his furry head, snuffed out cigarette number two, and leaned back against the wall. "Sometimes that happens when somebody dies. Still, I will say this: we all got to live with whatever it is we decide to do." After another moment, he smiled up at her. "That ain't very good wisdom, but I guess it's all I got for you today, baby girl."

She smiled back, but she thought, *He's righter than he knows. I didn't have to go to that game. I knew they were playing Greenville, and it was my choice to go, even though I knew how it might turn out. I was just being pigheaded, trying to prove something to myself – that they couldn't hurt me anymore.* She had not been able to forget the sound of that boy's head splitting open; it was like a melon being dropped on the sidewalk. And then there was the blood, all over his shirt and pants, and then the big fight that came right after. Some of it had been her fault, she believed. It had to be.

Robley stood up. "Time to go to work, Queen Bee," he said. He opened the door for her, and they traipsed back up the tiled corridor to the kitchen and the smell of grease smoking on the big steel griddle.

————

As for Frank himself, whenever he thought about the incident, he felt not even a twinge of regret. When he had decided to throw at the Greenville third baseman's head, he knew he would hit him and hurt him, and so to a great degree he had been prepared for the aftermath. It was the ensuing brawl he had not anticipated, for he had never seen that happen in a high school game. Neither had anyone else in attendance that afternoon.

It had begun forebodingly enough, when he had singled in the bottom of the first inning, stolen second, and then advanced to third on a fielder's choice. One out. Randy Wilson, who had only gotten taller and lankier as the season had worn on, ambled slowly up to the plate, somehow making his knees, hips and elbows all move in the same direction, and Frank clapped his hands and called out, "Here we go, Randy. Little base hit."

He said that because Max Bass, who was coaching third base, had given Wilson the sign for the squeeze play. As he took his walking lead off of third, Frank envisioned himself charging toward home in ten or twelve driving strides and diving in under the catcher's tag.

Instead, something else was happening. The Greenville third baseman grinned at him, then glanced past him to where Liza was sitting in the bleachers next to his father. He gestured towards her with his glove. "So, I hear you been gettin' you some, Treadwell."

"How's that?" Frank wasn't sure he had heard correctly.

The pitcher put his back foot on the rubber, brought his ball and glove to his belt, and stared at Frank. "The Applewhite girl," the third baseman said. "I hear you're gettin' a *lot* of it."

"It?"

The Greenville player grinned at him again. "Now, you ain't gonna try and tell me you ain't knockin' the bottom outa that little slut."

Frank said nothing, but tried to focus on the pitcher's feet. He heard Coach Bass's voice: "Get a couple more feet, Treadwell. Get out there."

He took two steps in foul territory, and the third baseman stood over the bag, though he was not in the ready position, but had his hands on his hips, and he said in a louder voice, "Well, I hope you are gettin' it, Treadwell. Lord knows we all had plenty of it when she was at our school. Best pussy in both Carolinas." Frank looked back to the pitcher, who had not moved or blinked. Now the voice was lower, more lurid: "She must have sucked you off, at least, hasn't she?"

He turned to say something, but when he did, there was a sudden "whop!" and the ball shown white in the third baseman's glove, and Frank did not even have time to duck and grab for the bag with his hand before the tag hit him in the chest. He had been picked off.

Bass, trotting to the dugout after Wilson popped out, was grim-faced, his lips in a tight, thin line across his jaw – always a bad sign. Frank looked up to the stands, and Liza was still there: he was hoping for a wave or a smile or something, anything, to indicate that she had not heard any of it, but she was gazing toward the outfield, her face an utter blank.

He ran out to the mound as always, picked up the rosin bag, jostled it in his palm, and dropped it with a soft thud in the dirt. He took his warm-up pitches, and then squatted down as the catcher made the throw down to second.

He stood up and scanned the green and brown palette around him, taking note, in particular, of the outfielders' positioning. A lively chatter kicked up:

"Go after 'em, Frank…"

"One-two-three, here we go…"

When he faced the plate, he saw that the third baseman, Greenville's number four hitter, was stepping into the batter's box - a stroke of truly ill fortune for him, as it would turn out. A righty, he scuffed at the dirt with his cleats, dug in, set his bat on his shoulder, and then stood up straight again, hand raised to the umpire for time; then he took two steps backward and looked back over his right shoulder to where Liza sat. He removed the bat from under his arm, put it between his legs with the barrel jutting into the air, and ran both hands up and down the length of it, smiling at Frank as he did so. Several players on the Greenville bench laughed.

"Play ball," the umpire said.

Frankie went into his windup. When the ball left his hand, he believed it to be the hardest fastball he had ever thrown. It tailed upward like a bottle rocket and caught the hitter on the left side of his face, right along the eye socket. He'd had no chance even to see the ball, much less to get out of the way, and he dropped as if he had been shot. Later, some people would say it was the most vicious thing they had ever seen, but Frank could only think how glad he was that no one had been dumb enough to say something about his mother, too; he'd have killed someone over that.

As it was, several seconds elapsed before anyone grasped what had just occurred. The umpire was the first to react, removing his mask and kneeling over the injured boy, and then, as though on cue, all players on both benches seemed to explode from their respective dugouts like shrapnel, or thick foam rushing from two upended soda bottles, and charged the mound in one convulsive retching, writhing, wrapping in snakes of white and cream-colored uniforms about one another, clawing, flinging fists, and snarling. Frank found himself underneath three or four twisting bodies, and he could hear Coach Bass's voice above the melee:

"GET BACK TO YOUR POSITIONS! YOU, TREADWELL, GET OUT FROM UNDER THERE! EVERYBODY BACK IN THE DUGOUT, GODDAM IT!"

But it was too late. The dam had broken, and Frank fell into the grip of his anger and began striking out blindly with his fists at every movement, friendly or not, until at last a few parents – some of the bigger men – entered the fray and began pulling players apart, and between them and the coaches on either side, they at last managed to separate the two teams, with two of them pinning Franks arms to his sides. As they stood restlessly in the dugouts, scuffing about and panting, hearts still racing, an ambulance came wailing down along the third-base fence-line. The Greenville third baseman, whose copiously bleeding head had been wrapped in a towel, was lifted onto a stretcher and slid into the back. Once it was gone, its siren trailing off in the distance like a sound in a dream, a deadly silence fell over the field and stands.

Frank had been ejected from the game, of course, and he was only slightly surprised to find out two days later that the school's principal had also suspended him for the season, along with Randy Wilson, who had carried a bat out to the mound with him, though he had not hit anyone with it.

During his slow, meandering ride through town and then out to the river road and home, without caring to, he had gone over it in his head again. There was little doubt that he had ruined the season; that in itself was sorry enough, but now he could think of nothing to do with himself. He knew his body was too big now to be on this stupid bicycle, and that he must have looked idiotic, but aside from walking, he had no other choice, for he had royally, irreparably wrecked everything with Liza as well. To hell with the riddle of girls in general – he couldn't even solve this *one*. But he was coming up to the house now, and through force of will, he was able to tuck her away in his brain for the time being, before the shame (which was far greater than anything he had felt about the Greenville game) could begin soaking through him once more.

The house would be stiflingly hot, with dirty dishes stacked in the kitchen and dirty clothes strewn over the floors, but at least he could retreat to his own room, where he might perform some small, meaningless task to keep from thinking about the bad things again. Anyway, it was certain he would have the place to himself.

———

Such was not the case for Liza when she got off of work at five that afternoon. The apartment building where she and her mother lived was noisy, an abode for the dispossessed, the disenfranchised mothers and their fatherless children, and Roger often worked a night shift, and so he would likely just be getting up when she got there. She had been thinking about Frank off and on all day as she labored over the grill, and now she relished a few more minutes on the front seat of her truck (or rather, Roger's truck) outside the diner to turn things over in her head.

Had she overreacted? Had she been unsympathetic? Probably, but in another sense, she was proud of herself. She had withstood an essential test, she had been able to put things in perspective when it mattered, and she had known at last that the old Liza was truly dead and gone and no words or actions of that sort would ever again sting her so badly. Still, there were one or two other things that bothered her: supposing she really did care for him? Then nothing that had happened would matter, ultimately. He was young, he was immature, he knew nothing, but whatever there was on the inside of him would win out if it were meant to. She believed that. If he found that she really mattered to him – and it might take him years – he would move heaven and earth to get to her. She believed that, too.

She had longed to do something more for him after Mrs. Treadwell had died, but the risks to herself and her sanity were great. She knew that he was suffering, that he was reeling, plummeting, impaled upon the point of his grief without knowing what any of it was about, but she also had known that she could not be the one to help him. Nonetheless, she watched the unraveling with dread, and it certainly had not started with the game against Greenville. She had deliberately gone to that game as a prideful act, to show them all something, so she had to accept some of the blame, but she had not anticipated that this would be the moment when it would all become too much for him. It was not as if he hadn't shown signs of the impending explosion, for there had been a series of things prior to the real disaster: he had gotten up and walked out of a math test and had walked all the way home; he would no longer answer the front door when Pastor Laite came by; and when someone had asked about his father's well-being, Frank had replied, "I don't care if he runs off now. I hope he does." As far as baseball, for a while he had looked like the old Frank, and she had thought, *This is just what he needs, this will help him, the consistency of it;* but then he had started saying and doing things that were uncharacteristic of his behavior on the field. In one game, after he had struck out, he had smashed the old maple bat (which had snapped cleanly and shown its white splinters like a crisply broken bone) across the side of the dugout. He had taken to sitting by himself on the bus and on the end of the bench when Dillon was up to bat, peering out suspiciously from under the bill of his cap. It was a doomed season.

Once it was all said and done, he had come looking for her. It was three days after graduation, and she had just started working at the diner. It had been raining all day, and when she saw him looking in the big window, there was mud on his bike and on his clothes and even a few spatters on his face. She waved at him and indicated that he should wait for her, and ten minutes later, she came out. Steam was rising from the sidewalk.

"You done?" he asked.

"Yep."

"How was it?"

"Good. How's things with you?"

"Good. You wanna go somewhere?"

"Sure. Where do you wanna go?"

"You remember that little beach up to Lake Norton where we used to go when we were little?'

"'Course I do," she said. "I would never have thought you'd remember that, though."

"Things just come back on you sometimes," he said.

They took her truck along the river road and up to the lake, and there they spread the tarp from the truck bed on the wet sand. Frank gathered a bit of wood and attempted to build a fire, but things were still too damp. So, they sat on the tarp, and the mist collected on their faces and bare arms. She could hear the tree limbs ticking with moisture, and a gray fog hung over the middle of the lake.

"Your folks used to bring us out here," she said. "We'd come up in the boat and stay till after dark, roasting weenies and marshmallows."

Frankie nodded. He had barely spoken during the ride, and not at all since they had arrived here. He had his legs folded under him and was twirling a stick on his palm.

"Do you wanna talk about her?" Liza asked.

He shook his head.

"It might help."

"I'm okay with all that," he said. "It doesn't matter. I'm over it."

"Over it? That's a good one. Yeah, you're over it, just like I am and just like your daddy is."

"I don't wanna talk about him either. And it ain't for you to worry about. You're not even in our family." She saw by his face that he was immediately sorry he had said it; she made no reply but looked up over his head at the dark, wet leaves and pine needles. "I have decided on one thing, though," he said.

"And what might that be?"

"I decided it's time for you and me to try something different."

"Oh?"

He was looking at her now with an odd expression, as if he had been about to say something else but had changed his mind. He leaned toward her and put his hand on her knee. "It's time for us to do what everybody else does."

"And what does everybody do?" He brought his face close to hers, his lips slightly parted. "What's the matter with you, Frankie?" she asked.

"I mean I want what everybody else has already gotten." He moved closer, and she put her hand on his chest and pushed at him away.

"Nothing like that is going to happen, Frank, Especially not right here. I can see where you might have gotten the idea that it could, given how people talk, but I'm different now. I'm not the same as I was, and you should be glad about that."

"How many of those fellas on the Greenville baseball team did you actually...date?"

"I don't recall. A few of them, I guess, but I told you, I'm not that person anymore. Why can't you understand that?"

"What about that time in my room, then? When you brought your records over and sat on my bed?"

"What? I don't know what you thought, but I was trying to have a little fun. I was trying to get you to have a little fun. Things were so depressing."

"That's what I'm talking about," he said. "Having fun. Now, I want you to just sit there and be still." Clumsily, he groped at her, and his hand seemed like a dead thing fumbling blindly at her in a dream. She stood up quickly.

"I'm warning you, Frankie. Don't touch me again. I have to get back to town now."

He shook his head slowly and ran his fingers roughly through his hair and said, "It's just my damn luck. I wish't I had known you before, instead of right now."

"You did," she said. "You knew me when I was seven."

"Oh, hell," he said, standing up, too. "Let's just go."

There had been no further conversation. The cab of the truck was stuffy and warm, but when she put down the window the dampness flailed in at her, and so they traveled in a sticky silence all the way back to Dillon so Frank could get his bicycle. She had not seen him since.

She put the key in the ignition and realized that time, the patient yet oblivious physician, had begun to bind up the small cuts from that day. Maybe she would go out to the Treadwell house later. For the immediate future, a warm shower and a magazine on the sofa seemed the best the world could offer her.

———

Luther Laite sat on his porch with his iced tea, looking at his back garden, which was now choked with thick, blue-gray weeds. It was Sunday morning, and he still had not returned to his congregation. Naturally, he knew that he couldn't go on this way; the United Brethren would be inquiring with him soon, he believed, and then things would really get gruesome very quickly. He had seen it before.

He had been giving serious thought to stepping down from his appointment in Dillon. He had long been under the impression that he had friends here, that he was needed, but strangely, no one had come out to see him during his absence except for Liza Applewhite. He knew that the district superintendent had sent an interim minister, but Luther had not had contact with him either. It seemed he had rapidly become invisible in town; he was clearly not much missed, if at all, and thus he might as well leave. But where would he go?

He had christened them, married them, buried them, prayed for them and with them, suffered with them, tried to lead them…and now he sat here in his open-collared shirt and wondered what it had all been for, all these years. He wished he could feel angry about it, but that impulse had left him, too. He had come to recognize that what he had thought was the sin of anger had actually been an underlying and important part of his passion for the faith. Anger had moved him many times to action, which had in turn changed a few people for the better. But that was gone now, and in its place, complacency and passivity had collected in a slow pool, sinking him more and more heavily into this sagging lawn chair on a weathered porch. If nothing else, he ought to have been disgusted with Bob Treadwell's complete collapse in the aftermath of Della's death, and in the way he had allowed the boy to founder, but instead he could not muster anything other than complete indifference. It was as if someone had taken a hose and blasted away everything in him that had been of any substance. All that was left was an empty receptacle.

He thought it was very telling that only a young girl, a high-school senior, one who had never struck him as particularly "Christian," had even bothered to seek him out. Liza had come to his house, and he had made her a glass of sweet tea with lemon, and then they had sat in silence, mostly, out on his back porch. Oh, he had known what she wanted to talk about all right, but when the moment had come, he found he had nothing more to say about Mrs. Treadwell. An opening inside him that had always been a fountain for words had run dry, and although he wanted to offer her something besides iced tea, he had no heart for it; he knew he would not be able to live with the hollowness of his own voice. At last, after a half hour or so of uncomfortable silence, she had thanked him for the drink and left.

It was not quite as bad as it had been at the funeral: when he had stood up and walked up to the lectern, he could feel the blood draining from his head and face. He gripped the wooden edges and tried to focus on the open book in front of him, but suddenly the pages went blank. He knew the service by heart anyway, and sought to call upon his memory, but when he attempted to speak, he could only mutter a couple verses before his mouth was entirely dry. He turned his back to the congregation, and struggling not to pass out, fumbled his way back to his chair. Several of those in attendance glanced up at one another in confusion. Fortunately, one of the deacons, old Fred Strother, rose from his chair at the left of the altar, read the appropriate passages, and then concluded the service.

He did not know what had brought on such paralysis, but looking back, those few minutes in the downstairs room at the Treadwell house, on the afternoon of her death, had certainly been a turning point in his life and career. However, he saw that it had all really begun long before that. He had been slowly slipping away from the faith for quite some time, as the things of the world had gradually worn him down and eroded his belief. The awareness that death was all-powerful had walked with him for many years, was connected and extended from him but had grown steadily closer to the rest of him until it had swallowed him. Death had shown itself to him in that room on that day, but he had known all along that it was there, all-consuming, devouring, laying low all that had once been bright and quick and returning it to the inert pile of carbon from which it had pathetically, briefly arisen. He found little proof that his life had carried any meaning thus far, but oblivion, silence, nothingness – he now saw ample evidence that these are the conditions which await us all.

He had seen it that day most clearly. He had come immediately when Bob had telephoned him, practically bolting from the church office to the station wagon and then barreling through town and out to the Treadwell place on the Little Pee Dee. He had entered the house without knocking, finding Bob on his knees beside the bed, his face buried in the quilt, looking for all the world like a frightened child. Della herself lay absolutely still on her back, legs stretched out straight as two thin columns of stone; she was gulping air, trying to get her breath, her neck straining each time and her chin thrusting out alarmingly, grotesquely, quite pale around her lips. One hand clutched her right breast, and the other arm was close against her side, the old, torn Bible underneath the palm. Her eyes were shut tight.

"Have you called her doctor?" he asked.

Bob nodded into the quilt, and a sob leapt from him so that he suddenly gripped his own throat in an effort to cut off any further sound. Luther leaned over Della.

"Can you hear me?" he whispered.

Her lips moved fractionally, and he leaned even closer. Her wrinkled, dry tongue daubed at her upper lip, and in a low rasp, she said, "It hurts."

"Just hold on for a few minutes. Doc is on his way."

She did not say a word or even nod. Her chin pressed outward once again, and a long, grotesque rattle, a sound which did not seem to come from her small body at all but from some dark space below the bed, issued from her mouth. Her eyes snapped open: they were already void of light, covered in a milky reptilian film. Her legs bowed out oddly and then settled back into rigid lines again, her feet arching distinctly under the covers.

Luther began the recitation, the old words that were so deeply etched in his mind: "The Lord is my shepherd; I shall not want. He maketh me to lay down in green pastures. He leadeth me beside the still waters. He restoreth my soul. He leadeth me in the paths of righteousness for His name' sake. Yea, though I walk through the valley of the shadow of death, I will fear no evil; for Thou art with me..."

He waited for some movement, some subtle shift in the room. He had felt it before at such times: a feeling that, at one time in his own life, he might have called the transit of a soul, a moment in ephemera, when body and spirit diverge. Long ago, after the night in the Upper Room, the Cenacle at Jerusalem, and the following day of derision and the worst of all pain, it had occurred on Golgotha, the triumph of faith in the place of the skull. And then the greatest mystery of all occurred behind the round stone, of course, in the tomb where His body was lain, to which only the angels were privy. But Luther believed he had had a fleeting comprehension of that mystery when he attended to the dying, a sense that the end of the body, the strange stillness that entered the room when the believer's heart and breath had ceased, was actually the beginning of something radically different from what the body knows. Otherwise, what was any of this about? The faith had given him the only answers that had ever made sense to him and offered clarity, for it affirmed the identity and the worth of the human being and the greater worth of the mind and the soul, and without it, he knew, he himself would shrivel and die. This time, however, on the occasion of Della Treadwell's death, none of it had happened. The stillness arrived, yes, but it was an utter, smothering silence. He looked down at her and saw with terror that her lips were dry and stretched thin and her eyes were no longer eyes but mere blank orbs turned upward to the ceiling. He felt an overwhelming oblivion settling over him like an impervious veil, and a new voice in his head said to him: "You see? This is all there is – a collection of cells all come to nothing, a pitiful stringing together of bones, muscle, skin, and nerves, all of which had been animated a short time ago and which had been driven by its lone adaptation to a hard world, a brain; the brain had housed that set of experiences and memory that we had called Della, but now that the brain was dead, 'Della' has become merely a piece of your own experience and memory. There is nothing beyond this." A powerful sense of dread and near-panic set upon him, but to his relief, he felt someone in the room moving. Bob had risen to a half-crouch and was groping for the chair against the wall. He sat down in it and pressed his hands to his face.

A few moments later, the doctor came in, closing the door behind him. He looked down at Della, then at Luther, and shook his head. He moved over to the bed and lifted her arm at the wrist. Luther could see the blue shadow along its underside, where the blood had begun to collect.

Luther's throat was scorchingly dry, his collar choking him; he had to have some water, and he went out to the kitchen. He had not seen the girl, Liza, until she spoke to him, and even then he did not really recognize her. He was blinded, besotted. "Pastor Laite," she said, "what is it? What's the matter with everybody?"

The words struggled out of his craw like pieces of ash: "It's Mrs. Treadwell. I'm afraid she has passed away."

"Oh."

By the time the boy arrived home, Luther had pulled himself together enough to speak coherently and was prepared to inform him of his mother's passing, but it was Liza who acted first. She went to him; he was smiling, and his face was flushed, his hair damp. They were so still, their embrace so beautiful they reminded him of paintings of saints by Titian; their only movement for several moments was the slow dissipation of Frank's smile, as she whispered in his ear, until he looked up and spied Luther. *He has no idea what has happened here*, Luther thought. *And no idea what sorts of things are going to happen.*

"Hello, sir," the boy said. "Can you pray with us?"

"Certainly," he said. "Of course, I will. I mean...I can. Yes, I certainly will."

Now she turned, too, and they both gazed at him expectantly, as the awful silence between and around them threatened to sweep them all away in its dark current, or else crush them where they stood in this house over which death now had complete dominion.

———

In the days that had followed his wife's passing, Bob Treadwell fell back gratefully upon the routine of the hardware store as well as all the loose ends around the house that needed tying. Some of the church members had helped him with the funeral arrangements, and somehow, though to him it was merely a blur of black suits and dresses and bibles and red eyes and swollen cheeks and a lot of words he didn't remember and somber music and people shaking his hand or putting their arms about his small, taut shoulders, he had gotten through it all. But on the third day, when she was in the ground and the plates of food had been thrown away and all the furniture put back where it belonged and he had hauled that damned mechanical bed down to the town dump – that was when things had taken a turn.

It wasn't just that those green bottles with all their little refracted shapes of light like windows into various dimensions of both memory and forgetfulness; the truth of the matter was that he knew it gave his cowardliness a kind of near-legitimacy, pathetic as it was. It was as if he himself were sick and could lie abed without any real guilt or consequence, or as if his house had been destroyed by fire and he could now simply throw himself upon the mercies of the world. There was danger in it, of course, and on the morning of the fourth day, when he had driven on past Beamon's Hardware and had lit out on the highway for the liquor store in Marion, he felt a bit like a man preparing for a fight, perhaps, or for a perilous journey, for he never knew when one of those little green windows might, in his dreaming or waking hours, open upon some terror in his past. Nevertheless, his only other choice was to face the crushing hours, the rote tasks, the silences, the minutes when the absence of love crowded in on him like empty coat hangers in a closet, and that was far worse.

It only saddened him even more to recall how empathetic they all had been for those three days. He kept seeing Howard's face as it had looked when he said, "Bob, you'll be fine. Don't forget you've still got that boy to raise. He's gonna need you." But people turn back to their lives anyway, don't they, because they have their own worries. As for Frankie, he had proven that he could do all right by himself, and besides, every time Bob asked if he needed anything, he just looked out the window and shook his head. He hadn't even cried, that Bob had seen; maybe he had gotten used to the idea long ago when she first got sick, maybe he was strong enough underneath that naivety, or maybe he had buried it all up so deeply it would take years for anything to come back out; but whatever the case might be, it was clear he didn't need or want his father now. Somehow, the boy managed to get himself up and fed and off to school, and on the nights that Bob spent chained in the live oak grove by the river, Frank still never failed to arrive the next morning with the key. Most often Bob would still be asleep there on the damp ground, and he would awaken to find the cuff he had clamped on his own leg unlocked, hanging there loose; but if not, he would pretend, so as not to have to open his eyes and meet his son's gaze.

Sitting at the bar in Silky's, Bob thought: Maybe someday I'll be able to tell him about it, tell him why it all had to be this way. Even then, though, he won't know what it was like. He'll never have to do what I done, and I thank God for that. To crawl down there on that beach and to do to them what I done. He'll never know the feeling of the knife going in. It don't matter that they were just Japs. Their blood was as red on the sand as mine was. How will I tell him about that?

It wasn't always the bad places that the little green reflected windows led him to. Even just sitting here early in the day, at this bar, with only Old Jack perched over there by the register with his magazine and happy to leave him be, his thoughts sometimes took him back to better times: those days out on the water in the little outboard, those warm evenings on the beach at Lake Norton; and the baseball, which hadn't been just about the going and the watching and the pride he had felt in his boy but had also been about the coming home again and having supper and talking it all over. He had been to only one of the high school games since the funeral but had not stayed long, as he could not abide the way people stared at him; it made him want to stand up and shout, "All right, it's true! She's dead, so now look at me and get it all out of your systems." Or sometimes his mind would cast way back to the old church and the early days when he had just met her and everyone did what they were supposed to do, including himself – the preacher preached, the people sang, and Della stood with her elbow against his, and she laughed quietly at the silly jokes he whispered in her ear, and that was how love had happened to him, because whenever you thought about what you were doing or actually tried to do it a certain way, it never seemed to work out right. Whatever control he had once held had simply slipped away.

Already his fellow townsmen had begun to see him as a man in decline. He, who had grown up in Dillon and had spent nearly his entire life here as a working man and a husband, father, friend, part-time churchgoer, and now a widower, found himself an outcast. It was only by virtue of this that he now saw how tenuous his own existence had been, how peripheral, how much her strength had been his, too; the man is supposed to be the one with roots plunged deep into the earth, unshakeable as an oak, but now Bob saw himself as feeble and trembling, and Della as the foundation to which he and the boy had clung all these years. So, now he was a strange man, a curiosity, the odd little fellow who would either drive his beaten old pickup over to Marion and then who, when he could no longer see over the wheel into the sharp glare of the sun, would walk in the roasting midday up to Silky's and then back again. He hardly cared.

Old Jack peered up over his racing magazine. "Need another down there, Bobby?"

"Always," he said.

———

It had taken a few days of debating with herself, but Liza had finally decided to go and see Frank again.

She found that she couldn't stop thinking of him – not because her feelings about him had grown any stronger but because she was connected to him by the threads of her own past, and she believed that in some way their lives would always be bound up together. She did not doubt that they had a good deal of unfinished business, and this was both troubling and reassuring to her at once. Earlier in the week, she had stopped in for the second time at the preacher's house to sit with him on his back porch, and although he still hadn't had much to say (in fact, he had just stared at her, mostly), seeing Luther Laite again had brought back the turmoil and unrealized joy of those recent days.

Now it was Monday morning, and she tapped on the door of the Treadwell home, knowing he would be there. His father's truck was gone, as usual, but Frank's bike was leaned up against the front steps. The grass and weeds had grown tall around the house, and the paint on the door was flaking – it truly did not appear to be the same home she had come to know all over again this past spring. It was shocking how quickly a place could become dilapidated.

When he answered, she could not tell whether the look he wore was one of scorn, condescension, amusement, or confusion. He stared at her for a few moments, and then at last she said, "Gonna ask me in?"

"Nope," he said. "That wouldn't be a good idea. The place is kind of a mess."

She looked down at her sneakers, her pigeon-toed feet there on the cracked cement step. "All right then," she said softly, and turned to go.

"But what can I do for you?" he asked.

"I can see you're still mad at me. I just wanted to say hello and to give you something."

"I don't need anything."

"Look, Frank," she said. "We have to still be friends before we can be anything else. That's all I know."

Ever so slightly, he opened the door a little more, and she could feel him softening. "Let me get my shoes," he said. "We can go for a walk if you want."

They took the old road, the one she knew so well, and when they reached the house where her family had lived when she was very young, when her father was still around, they stopped. It stood as forlorn and yawning as it had been on the day she and her mother had left for Greenville.

"Surprised this old place hasn't caved in yet," Frank said.

"Give it a couple more days. Or maybe my mom'll buy it back someday, you never know."

"How is your mama?"

"She told me last week that she and Roger are moving to Myrtle Beach, but you can't tell with her. She says a lot of stuff."

"What about yourself? Still hoping to get out of Dillon again?"

"I decided I'll probably stay for a while. I been thinking it over. I like it here."

"Well, that's funny," he said. "I hate it here, and I've decided to leave." He picked up a pebble and tossed it at the mailbox in front of the house, where it ricocheted with a sharp ping back into the road.

"You? Now, where on earth do *you* plan to go to?"

"I got places."

"What about your dad?"

"I don't know. What about him? I ain't seen him for a while, thought maybe you had."

She glanced away, embarrassed for him. "I see him once in a while. Around town… just walking around town."

"Just walking," Frank echoed. "All around town. He's a walker, all right." He tossed another rock, heavier this time, and it struck with a heavy clank, denting the side of the decrepit box.

"When you planning to go, then?"

"I don't know. Pretty soon."

"Well, then I reckon I should give you this now." She reached into the front pocket of her shirt and handed him the picture. It was a wallet-sized photo, her senior portrait. "I signed the back of it," she said.

As he looked down at it, the edges of his mouth inched toward a smile. "Thanks," he said. "I saw this in the yearbook. I like this picture." He turned it over. "That's nice," he said.

"In case you forget what I look like when you're on your great journey," she said.

Later, as she drove home, she would wonder whether she ought to have kissed him at that moment. He was still looking down at the photo, so he wouldn't have been ready for that, but his reaction might have told her a great deal. Undoubtedly it would have been his first kiss. Maybe it would have fixed something, maybe it would have been a small break in the cloud that seemed to be smothering him now. If he imagined that he had to leave because he had done something wrong, then kissing him might have shown him it was all okay. *People always think they've done something wrong*, she thought, *and that's their ruination.* Certainly he should not have hurt that boy in the baseball game that way, but she understood why he had done it. As for Mrs. Treadwell dying, maybe in his young boy's brain he had somehow got the idea that he was to blame. Or maybe he thought he ought to have gone out and forced the old man to come home again, as they had done that time back in the spring. *It is human nature to regret, but you can only regret so much and for so long before it starts to kill you. Maybe it would be good for him to get away for a while after all. But to where? He's only fifteen.*

And then it struck her that he would never leave. And so there would be time. He would still be here, and she would, too. Anything – quite literally *anything* – might happen.

———

"Done let your garden go to weed, I see."

Ordinarily, Luther would have been delighted that his old friend James Jenkins had come to call; as things were, he had at least managed a smile and invited the man in and made a pitcher of sweet tea. Then they had adjourned to the back porch.

"Got no time for that," he said, glancing absently down at the unkempt yard.

"Mm-hmm. And how is your sabbatical getting along, Luther?"

"It's not bad. Trying to do some writing."

"I see." Jenkins took a long sip of tea, sucked a piece of ice into his mouth, and leaned forward. "If I may..." he said, "I'd be neglectful if I came here today and didn't address my concerns."

"Concerns?"

"Word travels, even between our communities, Luther. Some of my congregation's members have told me that you've been having some troubles."

"Troubles."

"They say that since Mrs. Treadwell passed, you haven't been able to attend to your duties here. That you haven't been back to the pulpit at all."

Luther set his glass down and leaned forward also, elbows to knees. "To tell you the truth, James, I was experiencing some...thoughts and feelings I'd never had before. I can't quite explain it."

"I think we all go through it at some time or another. You'll be all right with some time and a lot of prayer."

He shook his head. "That's a problem, as it turns out. The time – I've had plenty. The prayer – well, let's just say that lately it hasn't been as easy as it used to be."

"I will say that I could see something was wrong when you came out to Mt. Olive that last time. I haven't seen a man leave a church in such a hurry in many years. I thought you'd seen a ghost, or else you'd suddenly decided you didn't care for colored people after all." James smiled.

"Ha! Well, I think you know where I stand on that – colored people, I mean. In any case, you're right – I was having a tough time."

"Was?"

Luther leaned toward Jenkins, as if he feared that someone might overhear what he was about to say. "Something rather strange happened to me the other day. Now, James, I think you know me pretty well. My approach to all of this has always been somewhat orderly and even practical. I think that what we do serves many other purposes besides just whipping up a little excitement on a Sunday morning. Whenever I've had a congregation member pass on, it has always been just that: a passing, and I've found the quicker we get back to the work at hand, the better things go. But I'll tell you…this thing that happened to me…"

"I'm listening."

"All right. What you've heard is true. The loss of Della Treadwell threw me for quite a loop, for reasons I won't go into at the moment. But twice now this girl, Liza, has come here. I'm in no way bitter, mind you, but the fact remains that she is the only one besides you who has bothered to come here. But she's not even a regular at church."

"Does that matter to you?"

"I suppose not. She does seem to have some history with the family, and I know she helped them quite a lot in those last few weeks. But she came here, afterward, you see, and the second time, when I opened the door and saw her there on the steps, I… I'm not sure how to put this. I believed it was Della.

As a young person, you know, when I first met her. I mean, I honestly nearly fell over. I would have sworn to it."

"Are they similar in appearance?"

"That's just it. They don't look at all alike. Anyway, I'm not even sure it was her appearance so much as…so much as a sense of reality I had, in that moment, if that makes any sense. It was very clear in my mind that this was the young Della Treadwell."

Jenkins sat back and considered. "Our minds can play tricks on us sometimes. Especially when we're under stress."

"Maybe. I'm sure she thought I'd lost my mind altogether. I couldn't stop staring at her there on the front step. Finally she said, 'Mornin', Pastor Laite. It's me, Liza.' I tell you, it was eerie."

"What did you do then?"

"Invited her in. Gave her some tea. My usual inept social ritual. But in the entire time we sat right here, and she kept trying to make small talk, I was absolutely convinced that I was face to face with Della."

"I don't doubt it. 'There are more things in heaven and earth.'"

"Oh, but that's just it. When Hamlet says that, he's just seen his father's ghost. This was nothing like that. I had absolute clarity of mind."

Jenkins cleared his throat, sifted another piece of ice off the top of his glass, and replied, "Luther, I've always thought that you and I have a great deal in common. Like you, I am not one to profess a belief in haints, or even to shake the burning bush too often, for that matter. However, I do believe in messages and messengers. That's integral to our faith. Maybe this was somebody's way of letting you know that everything is all right."

"Or maybe I really am just losing my mind. In any event, it brought me some peace, I must say. In general, I'm feeling better. My hope is to return to my office this weekend."

"And to your congregation on Sunday?"

"We shall see. I hope so. It's not as if they seem to have missed me."

Jenkins smiled. "They may not know it, but they have. You and I must never be the ones to express a need, you know that. Are we weak? Certainly. Do we question our own abilities? Often. Do we become tired, like anyone else? Of course. But we go on and do our work. It's what we chose, Luther."

He nodded.

"And what about the boy, Della's son? How's he coping with things? And the husband?"

"Last I knew, not very well. Frankie just has no idea how to deal with it. He's in free fall, near as I can tell. And his daddy has gone back on the bottle."

"Well, then I guess you know where to start, once you get back. I heard the boy was a good ballplayer. Honestly, I don't know much about athletics, but that might prove to be some respite to him."

Luther frowned and gazed off toward the yellowing lawn. "I'm afraid he's all done with that now. There was an incident at one of the high school games. Seems he hurt another boy pretty badly."

"Hmm. It's a rough age anyhow, but with a situation like that... Now, we have this kid who comes out to Mount Olive Baptist – name of Sampson. You haven't heard of him, I'm sure, but he plays for the Marion team, and they say he's the next Willie Mays. Boy's had all kinds of problems, his daddy's in jail, momma took off with some sort of card player, on and on like that. Yet somehow he continues to play and to play well."

"I guess some are stronger than others," Luther said. "Or maybe they're just more mature."

Jenkins smiled again, that boyish crook of his mouth below the gray mustache, and his brown face seemed visibly to soak in the warm sunlight that slanted across the porch. "And some never grow up at all," he said, setting his empty glass on the unpolished floorboards and rising from his chair.

———

Bob carefully climbed back up on the barstool, which somehow had grown ever taller since he had walked over and slipped another dime into the jukebox.

Hank Williams' voice filled the tavern, warm and yet disappearing somehow, like fog on the river. Bob had heard the song before: it was about a bird who was so lonely he couldn't even fly.

Damned if that wasn't so. Bob had heard whippoorwills aplenty down by the Little Pee Dee, and he always envisioned them hunkered down under one of the low-hanging live oaks, all wrapped up in and blinded by some nameless sorrow. He'd forgotten how much he liked that song, until in the tedium of early afternoon, he had ambled over to the jukebox to have a look-see, and had lit upon it. Silkey might have slapped this place together with cinder block and the cheapest lumber he could find, but he had not scrimped on that box: it was big and shiny with great bright loops of blue and yellow neon running through it, a brilliant piece of sonic machinery. A few other folks, all regulars, had trickled in over the past hour or so, and no one had complained so far that he had played the same song six times already.

The truth was it put him in mind of a morning long ago, when he had gone grocery shopping with his mother. It was one of a very few clear memories he had of her, though he could not remember where the little store was or whether it had been bought out or gone broke of even been torn down; still, he could recall the light shimmering off of the glass entrance and the soft tar of the parking lot, and the feel of his mother's hand around his own; in the crook of her other arm, clutched against her breast and shoulder, was Banks, in a furious sleep. And then the sound had come to him: there was an elderly blind fellow, a white man, sitting on a bench by the door, playing a guitar and singing. The guitar was worn and scuffed and even had a wide crack in the top, but it was loud, and his singing was loud, too, and mournful, and it seemed to fill the air like a...like a broken church organ. Bob, who had been around five at the time, had stood riveted by the sound and the sight of the old man, who did not wear sunglasses but let his eyes roll helplessly about in their sockets like warped marbles, whose skin was not pale and loose but was ruddy and taut and criss-crossed by tiny, bright-red veins, and who was both terrifying and alluring at once. He had not been singing the whippoorwill song that Hank Williams sang, but it was something like that; there was a bird in it, and the same low, crying sound, and he had been so entranced by it that finally his mother had pulled him by his arm into the store.

It was so strange about these memories. Lately they came at him out of nowhere, it seemed, out of the sky, dropping into his brain in all their nakedness and disregard. It was like stepping right into a Polaroid and walking around, except he had to walk the way the memory went, as there was no changing it. His recollections of Della and the days when they were young together were quite vivid, though they did not distress him at all, since those times seemed to belong now to someone else's life. He could barely believe that such a life had been his: it seemed that some other man had done those things, had gotten married and worked so hard and had raised a boy and taken him places and given him things; when he thought of their long-ago Saturday evenings on the lakeshore with the fire flickering orange against the pine trunks and of all the ballgames he and Della had watched, it was inconceivable that he had done any of it. He could not shake the feeling that all of that had been the dream, and that coming back to this stool was his inevitable reality. The man with the bayonet down on the beach at Rabaul, with the blood of the dying Japs soaking into his shirt as he crawled from one to the next, turning it from fatigue green to black – that was the realest man of all, and everything that had come after that had been some sort of elaborate trick designed not by God but by certain forces which, as he was just now coming to understand, had been set in motion against him long ago. Conspirators, too self-absorbed even to know his name or acknowledge his individuality, had made it impossible for him to succeed at anything finally. He had tried at times to be a good man, and it had gotten him nowhere, with nothing except loss.

Some noise broke upon his sad reverie. He looked over to a booth where three people were seated, a large woman with stiff, dark-brown hair, and two men in straw hats. One of the men was leaning across the table and talking very loudly to the woman, who was flinching pitifully at every word; he had a broad, wet patch of sweat on the back of his shirt. He was practically shouting: "I don't give a good goddam about that! You tell that bitch that if she wants to, she can go back!"

Bob slid down from the stool slowly – he seemed to be up several feet in the air – and when his feet finally touched the floor, he gathered himself, tucked in his shirt, and made his way over to the booth. As he stood there, the fellow who had been yelling looked up at him.

"What do you want?"

"I'm awful sorry to interrupt," Bob said. He gestured with clumsy fingers toward the jukebox. "It's just I'm trying to listen to that there song."

"So?"

"So I was wondering if you might shut the hell up for five minutes."

The man, a regular customer whom Bob had seen here many times, slowly got up. He was quite tall, with ropy arms and blue, popping veins; he looked down at him narrowly from under the shadow of the straw hat, and his chest bumped Bob's chin.

"You wanna say that to me one more time?"

He was about to reply when Old Jack, the bartender, approached him quickly and silently from behind and put his hand on Bob's shoulder. "It's time for you to go on home now, Bob," he said. "I cain't serve you no more."

He turned around; Old Jack's eyes were apologetic, but his hand gripped his shoulder even more firmly. "Please, Bob. Go home and get some rest."

He looked back up at the straw-hatted man, whose eyes were now minute pins of light, and then at Jack again, and he shrugged. "Okay," he said.

Thank God the truck had learned the way. He'd made this drive many times in the last few weeks, and had had a few near misses, sideswiping a speed limit sign once and almost rolling off into a ditch on another occasion. He certainly would not count on Frank and that girl to come and fetch him anymore: Frankie's got his own life to live now, he mumbled to himself. He ain't got no need for the likes of me. Gonna be a ballplayer. Big-time. He'll be all right – he knows how to take care of himself. Hell, they ought to a' give him a trophy for knocking that kid down. Still, it's mighty tender of him to remember to bring that key every morning the way he does. Bob teared up for just a moment, thinking of his son. What would I do without that boy?

He turned down the old river road and followed it into the deepest shadows of the night, where only the crickets and the bullfrogs and nightjars and whippoorwills and the other creatures of the dark dwelt, until he came to the old stand of trees. They were like sentries, set there to guard him alone, as he came among them with his secret store of pain like white-hot gold, which had been dull and unseen all day but which now seemed to begin to burn so brightly in him that he felt it glowing amidst the dark trunks. He took the chain from the bed of the truck and dragged it behind him down to the biggest tree; it scraped in the reeds like a wounded animal pulling itself along desperately in search of safety. He sat on the damp ground, wound the chain around his chest once, and then clamped the heavy cuff on his ankle and snapped it closed, and all the worry ran away from him in a little stream. He did not know whether he had again had the nightmare lately about the beach at Rabaul, but that was just it – he couldn't be sure, and he'd be damned if he would take another chance of waking up on the kitchen floor with the butcher knife. It was sheer terror to lose one's self that way.

He had no way to tell how long he had slept, but he awoke to silence and near-total darkness. He felt himself to be an empty shell, and he thought of Della. For weeks she had seemed so far from him in every way, so that sometimes he even struggled to bring her face to mind, much less recollect the specifics of their life together; yet it had all happened, and it had absorbed so much of his being, and everything he'd had and everything he'd been, as he knew now, had been because of her. But it seemed now that she was close by, a scent hung in the air that was like hers. Must only be just after midnight, he guessed, since there was no trace of dawn breaking downriver to his right, and no vestige of the evening before still fading off in the other direction. Yet it was the utter silence that was so strange, for ordinarily, the insects and frogs and such should be reaching the first crescendo of their nightly ruckus right about now, but instead he could only hear the little gurgling of the slow tide; even the marsh beyond the far bank had gone dead. And he felt her fading, as the scent moved over and beyond him and drifted away through the pines and the oaks.

"Don't go," he said. "I'm sorry. I'm sorry for what I never was. I'm sorry I never done right by you or the boy. I tried, I really did."

Damn, he wished he had a drink, but all the green bottles had gone dry. The first small ache or the lack thereof skirted his brain, and his throat throbbed, and he had a moment of dread. A hangover: that was something he absolutely wanted to avoid if at all possible. After the month he'd had, it might kill him.

He had heard no noise, but something drew his gaze down toward the river. Two bright yellow eyes appeared there, about fifty yards away, unblinking and utterly still and locked upon his own. His first response, before the abrupt, bitterly cold awareness of his own helplessness, was to smile, as if an old acquaintance of whom he had not thought for many years had suddenly appeared to him. Not piece by piece, but rather in a miraculous totality, the memory of it came to him: it had been 1942, out on the Pitts' dock near the old man's house, both of which had finally fallen in on themselves years ago, the night before he left for Fort Jackson and then the Pacific. That was the last time it had happened, but now that he was fully conscious that it really was the big cat again, the panther, that sinister shadow of his youth, the icy dread of those times rushed back upon him. Then the mortal fear he had known as a child, when he had lain awake at night expecting that at any moment this wild thing, this thick, black killing machine with its black heart, would burst through his bedroom window and bury its claws and teeth in him, came over him, and for a few moments he was that cowering child once again; he jerked at the chain, but it only tightened and pinned him more closely against the tree. He kicked his leg out straight, but the iron cuff seemed immensely heavy. And then...then...something else happened: all in one instant, he accepted that the end.

He said aloud: "I just hope you'll make it quick."

The eyes, now burning coal-like and orange, suddenly moved toward him, growing bigger in what must have been only a couple of seconds, until they were a few yards away. He raised his head and looked out toward the Little Pee Dee River, even though, in this darkness, he could not have hoped to see it, and he lifted his chin slightly to expose the flesh of his throat.

––––––––

Once Frank had made up his mind to leave, he didn't think there would be any changing it. However, when he remembered that he had never traveled any farther than Greenville and Columbia, and had never even crossed the border to North Carolina – part of which was formed by the Little Pee Dee – he paused. He would not merely be leaving the house by the river, and not merely the town of Dillon; he must also leave behind all remembrance and the very essence of the only life he had known, for good or bad, and make of himself an orphan. He must be willing to toss away his identity, but exactly who had he been up till now anyway? An unformed boy, a child beloved by his mother, and in truth abandoned by his father, whom he could only regard with pity for his broken heart, but frankly unknown to himself. He wavered; yet when he looked around at the dirty dishes and the gray sheets and the grime on the floors, he felt resolutely that there was nothing more for him here. The only way was to leave; once he got up to the highway, one of the drivers in the big trucks might pick him up, and in just a few hours he would be far away from all of this. With sudden exhilaration, he saw himself sitting up in the tall cab, his knapsack on the floorboards.

There was still Liza, though. If she were to come by here, he thought, just seeing her again might be enough for him to decide to stay. She wouldn't come, though. There was a pride in her that demanded from him some response he could not give. Instead, he went to his desk drawer and took out the picture she had given him; he considered putting it in his pocket, but then he placed it back in the drawer. Better not start handling things, he thought, or looking at them, for that matter. He would try and do this the same way he had played ball: with a kind of blind faith and a boy's willingness to trust his instincts. Neither must there be any looking at or handling of his baseball glove, nor her 45-rpm records, nor his mother's Bible, nor any of those few objects which had marked the lives of Treadwells in this place. He must let those things go.

He went into the kitchen and sliced the rest of the meatloaf he had made the previous week for sandwiches, and after putting some coffee on to brew, he rummaged through the cabinet until he found the thermos his father had used to carry to work. That would all fit nicely in his pack. Once again, in a flashing vision like a photo, he saw himself as a passenger in one of the great shiny trucks that he had seen booming along Highway 9, the pack at his feet, the silent driver glancing over and wondering about this young kid, this runaway. What was his story? Where was he headed? How old was he anyway?

Yet they would ride on for many miles, hardly ever even speaking, out under the swaddling sky and then over the great rivers, bursting at long last, hours and hours hence, onto the dark plains of night.

―――――

Reuben Sasser had been on his way to the sheriff's office around nine that morning when the call came over the two-way: a body had been found down by the river.

Of course, he had thought at the time that it could only be Bob Treadwell. He had seen enough to know that the man was marked for death, walking down busy truck routes by dark, drinking himself comatose, and ending up in places he really ought not to have been. He had considered arresting him on any one of a variety of charges: loitering, public drunkenness, disturbing the peace (though that one would have been a stretch) – but he had not done so. Now he wished he had.

What he had not been ready for was the manner of death. He had pulled onto the embankment, hauled his big body out of the car, and then descended through the tall weeds until he came to the grove of pines and scrub oaks, and there, right where the dispatcher had said he would be, was old Dan Byrd, a swamp denizen, and behind him was visible a pair of sprawled legs on the other side of a fairly thick tree trunk.

Byrd had waved, and Reuben nodded back. "What have we got here?" he asked.

"Got us a Bob Treadwell," Byrd said. His tone was a bit too sardonic, Reuben thought, for one who was supposed to be a social dunce.

He came around to the other side of the tree and looked at the dead man, as the odor that suddenly reached upward at him caused him to pinch his nose shut. There was a line of hardened blood leading from two puncture wounds in his throat down to his lap, where a significant amount of blood had also begun to congeal and become dark. Treadwell's gaze was fixed on the river, though the eyes had filmed over and were now surrounded by gnats.

"What the hell happened to him?"

"Panther," Byrd said.

"How do you know?"

"Tracked it." The swamper pointed with a crooked finger at several over-sized paw prints in the wet ground.

"I'll be damned. Somebody chained him up here."

"Chained his self," Byrd remarked.

"And how do you know *that*?"

"He done it lots of times. Gets to drinkin' and don't wanna hurt nobody, I reckon. Or fall in the river."

Sasser shook his head. "I never knew about the chain. I'll be damned. Still, I'll have to investigate for foul play, just in case."

"Ask the boy," Byrd said. "He's the one always brung the key."

Reuben nodded, and after he had taken Byrd's statement, and after he had radioed the office and told them to send the coroner out here, and after the coroner had arrived with his assistant and they had begun to clean things up, he had driven up to the Treadwell place. It was not a thing he wanted to do, to tell a boy who had recently lost his mother that his father had been killed in such a peculiar way; there was no fair way to do it except just to tell exactly what had happened. And now the pong of the corpse, which seemed to have settled in his own lungs, turned his attitude of reluctance into a distinct, grim dread.

So it was that like a man approaching the gallows, he had parked in the drive and then walked slowly across the lawn and up to the Treadwells' front door. He had raised his knuckles, hesitated for just a moment, and then rapped sharply. No answer. He knocked again, louder. Still no answer. He tried the knob, found it unlocked, and pondered going on in, but then decided against that, for now.

Reuben got back in his car, removed his hat, the band of which was already dark with sweat despite the overcast sky and the wind, and thought it over. There was no other family around, that he knew of. I could wait a bit, he thought. Or drive up town and see if he's up there – ice cream shop maybe? He is a boy, and it is summertime. Or maybe he would go up to Howard Beamon's hardware, see if they knew anything about it. Somewhere he had heard talk of a brother of Bob's, too, but he had no idea how to try and reach him, at the moment. Then it came to him: he would need to get their pastor, Luther Laite, in on things sooner or later anyway. And he might know where to find the kid or the brother or both.

Hell of a situation, he thought. Who'd have thought that things could go to hell in such a hurry for a decent family like that?

As he arrived at the Methodist church, by chance he saw that Luther Laite was striding up the front walkway with his briefcase: he was really quite an elegant man, in his light blue seersucker suit with the jet-black vest and white collar, tall and straight as a book's spine. Though Reuben and his wife were Baptists, the sense of authority suggested by the man's appearance was almost enough to make him want to switch horses, as it were. You couldn't do that, though, around these parts. Once you were in with one congregation, you were in for the duration.

Again he swung open the door of the cruiser, grabbed the window frame, and pulled himself upright.

"Pastor Laite," he called. "Could I get a word with you, sir?"

———

Frank followed the trail up the bank. With the low, gray clouds overhead, humidity hung in patches among the trees as he moved along steadily; the pack was light, though, and he felt that he could run if he chose to, but there was no need for hurry. It was now difficult for him to believe that although life along this river had been his only existence, he had never ventured even this far above its northern bank. The trunks thickened for a time – bald cypresses and pines, the ubiquitous scrub oaks, and the occasional tupelo – but then they thinned out again, straggling over the ever-rising terrain like old, stranded skeletons. At last the ground suddenly became level, and he emerged from the woods; the highway was there, yawning out into the never-ending, flat country that faded, faded, faded into muted colorings. He put the pack at his feet and looked up and down the long blue-gray strip.

It had rained up here recently, and silvery puddles randomly marked up the roadside as far as he could see. This seemed odd, since he had only been walking for a half-hour or so, but it contributed to the feeling that had been growing in him that he was already far away from his home.

"Home?" Once he had known that word, and it had held meaning. Yet when he had it, he had never had to think about it. It was only when you didn't have something any longer that you had to begin to think it out. He saw sadly that this was true for most everything: people you knew, things you loved to touch and use, the food you liked, and even for something as simple as running across a field of green grass.

Abruptly he understood that he must not come back here again, that the only thing was to keep on going for a long while. Because who would notice or care? Even Liza would forget him ultimately, and he did not want to have to come back someday and find her married to some shop clerk or salesman, another whole, sad cycle of misery beginning again. Now he regretted leaving those things at the house behind; he wished he had burned them, even his mother's Bible, for he knew that they were pieces of his old life which would harken to him, point towards him like compass needles, when in truth he wanted all of it to slide into the jumbled images of a forgotten life, houses and stick figures in some child's crude drawing. And what if his father tried to find him? No, he must keep on going no matter what, and he now felt desperate to get away, though he did not feel at all worried over having so little money or food or even the vaguest sense of where he was heading. It's no good planning for anything anyway, he thought.

A distant winding noise came to him, and he thought at first that it was an airplane flying far overhead, and he squinted up into the opaque sky; but then he realized that a truck was coming from the east, headlights ablaze in the gray morning like the eyes of some wild animal. It appeared as a dark speck at first, but it rapidly grew larger, and he saw that it was booming along, a happy machine with no care at all except for going, for making an incomprehensible streak out of all that surrounded it but could not stop it.

He lifted the pack, slung it back over his shoulder once more, and turned expectantly toward the ever-loudening roar.

Part Two: Animus and Anima

One

October/November, 1959

The South Carolina State Penitentiary, a gigantic tombstone-gray structure that seemed, despite the tidy lawns that bordered it, to rise out of a barren earth from which all else of any weight had been worn away by time, cast a dense black shadow across its own gates. Anyone who approached, rather than feeling relief from the sharp glare of the October sun, gained the distinct impression of sinking, of stepping downward into shadow, even though the brick steps rose up to the entrance, where employees as well as visitors were each one made to stand within a cage-like rotunda where he was scrutinized like a specimen under glass, and then having submitted papers or an ID card or otherwise stating his business, each would hear the unmistakable dull clanking of iron tumblers and would then be admitted.

On this particular morning, Jacquin Anders, or Jack as he was called, looked down from the narrow window (it was a slit, in truth) at the back of his cell and watched them come and go: the familiar guards, the prisoners' wives with boxes of food or new socks and underwear, mothers, fathers, one official-looking group of men in coats and ties... And though he had stared down this way for hours at a time on many mornings – two years and three days worth of mornings, to be precise – today a new thought crossed his mind. It happened when he watched a newly-released inmate, dressed in a bright blue blazer, black pants and startlingly brilliant white shoes, descend the steps with a paper sack in hand, walk out of the prison's shadow, and embrace an elderly woman beside a gleaming station wagon. This was a white man, but nonetheless, Jack said to himself:

"That's me right there, in three more weeks."

It was true. His own freedom was at hand. But oddly, he had not actually envisioned himself departing, walking out into the light of day, striding across the green grass, and putting the great gray bone of this place at his back. It was almost too much to imagine, too luxurious, like stretching his body out in a cool stream on a hot day, and he suddenly realized that it must be terribly bad luck to think too much about it. He must try and put it away from his mind.

And yet, a minute or so later, he found himself wondering who would be there to meet him when he passed through those gates. His family did not own a car, and anyway, he was uncertain whether they even knew of the day of his release. He knew of other men, also mostly negroes, who had mis-stepped somehow in their final days and ended up with extra time tacked on. There was one guard in particular, Markel, who was known to take eager delight in tripping up certain inmates, in tricking them, somehow, as their sentences waned. Sometimes he accomplished this with liquor, smuggling it in to them and then turning evidence on them, and sometimes there was a woman involved. Or so Jack had heard.

Often he had wished that he had been assigned to one of the work farms, where he could have been out in the sun all day, as his cousin Tol had once done. True, he had seen the smooth, dark-pink scars on Tol's ankles where the shackles had cut them, and on Tol's back the straight, slashing scars of whip strokes where the walkin' boss had left his exclamations of anger, but he believed he still would have preferred the out-of-doors to the dull, impenetrable walls of the state pen. He hated it here. All of his life, he had been taught to walk quietly among white people, to keep his head down and hope to remain unnoticed, an invisibility he had been able to sustain for many years. But here, that was nearly impossible, for the evils, serpentine and aqueous, sought you here, found you out in the dimly lit corridors, or the catwalks, in the corners of your cell:

Did you wanna buy some smokes?

Got no money.

Well, you could make up my bunk ever' day for a month or so, nigger, and earn a few smokes that-a-way.

Don't smoke no ways.

Hey, Leonard, this nigger says he don't smoke.

And so it would go until they would lose interest in him and move along.

Generally, because he was a big man, he did not run into physical confrontations; but there were other big men here, and of course, there were small ones, too, who wished to prove their toughness by fighting a big man. Inevitably, then, it had been one of these who had challenged him, a stringy, rat-like, vicious fellow called Buck, very dark-skinned with dark-green, indecipherable tattoos streaming down his wiry arms. Every day, in Jack's first three weeks inside the wire, Buck had glared at him – from across the yard, across the chow hall, and through the bars of his cell, and when it was about to happen, in that unspoken ritual, the other inmates, both white and black, turned their backs, cleared the space between them, and ceased talking. Buck strode quickly up to him, a man with a dark purpose.

He said, "Got that money you owes me, boy?"

"I don't even know you," Jack said.

Buck moved his hand to the back of his pants' waist. "Don't you know you just renting that bed you sleeping on? I'm the landlord. Pay up or get cut up."

"I don't – "

As the blade came around, arcing like a swift, bright bird, Jack instinctively lurched backward; it passed an inch or so from his eyes, and then, instinctively again, he lurched forward, head-butting his attacker along the edge of his skull, just above the right temple. Buck crumpled, bent at the hips, then tottered over, sliding on his face across the smooth cement floor. Someone's loud, barking laughter broke the dead quiet, and then the guards rushed in.

They each had gotten two months in the hole – isolated confinement – tacked onto their sentences. It had been his only conflict; still, he kept to himself, mostly, doing the jobs they gave him: raking the yard, moving building materials, laundry duty, polishing the floors. Sometimes he looked at the pictures in the magazines in the prison library. In essence, he did what men in his circumstance have always learned to do – he passed the time.

Aside from this, the only time he actually suffered was when he watched the prison baseball team practicing. The colored inmates were not allowed to play, and so he watched from the yard as these fortunate men played like schoolboys in the emerald, well-watered field beyond the fence. The players whistled, shouted, laughed, jogged, took fungos, took hitting, and tossed the gleaming ball about until it was stained. He saw absolutely no difference between the game they practiced and the one he had known in the traveling colored leagues he had played in since he was fifteen, save for the complexions of the men who played. And now Saturdays, a dark-blue bus would take them away for games against teams at others of South Carolina's many regional lockups. And worst of all, on some Saturdays, another team would come here. The inmates would line up along the fence, and all – even the guards in their towers, and often the warden himself on the grandiose observation deck adjacent to his office – would be treated to the spectacle of baseball. Only Jack, in the sharpness of his pain and envy, would sit by himself at a picnic table in the yard, hearing the old sounds: the popping of leather, the click of hardwood on stiff horsehide, and the bursts of excited chatter.

Now it was October, however; the baseball gear had been put away, and this eased him somewhat. Now there was only the waiting. Three more weeks.

Jack watched from his cell window as an open-bed truck pulled up and five new prisoners got off, staggering in an uneven line, shackles clanking, as the guard strode along behind them, seemingly indifferent, his rifle's long barrel across his shoulder.

––––––––––

Luther Laite's old station wagon rattled along the unnamed road – or rather, it seemed to be sucked further and further into the remote, sparsely populated areas beyond Dillon and Marion, the unnamed backwater and backwoods communities, and further yet, the feeble shacks floating like debris in a tidal pool and washing up against the edges of civilization. Dust blasted from the rear end of the car, a plume that, from a distance, rose briefly above the thick green foliage and then quickly settled again.

It was October, but except for an occasional dry breeze, the long summer still held all in its clutches. Luther looked over at his passenger, the Reverend James Jackson, who was sweating profusely, and he remarked,

"Maybe we should stop and get us a Co-Cola."

"I would not object to it," James said, glancing at him over befogged spectacles.

"I'll pull in at the next gas station."

They had one more load of groceries to deliver, for Nettie Russell, as always, whose tiny cabin tottered at the ragged fringe of the county.

"Anyway," James said, recovering the thread of the conversation, "How come they're so sure it was a panther killed Treadwell? Could've been lots of things – wild dog…wild pig maybe."

"Shape of the teeth marks and the tracks," Luther said. "But you're right. In essence, nobody really knows for sure. It had nothing at all in common with other documented panther attacks. None of the gore. No evidence of feeding. It was all just very strange."

That was about the best he had been able to do, even in his own mind. Still, it hadn't been merely strange. "Mysterious" might have been a better word, and mystery was something he was interested in. He found it mysterious that his own faith, which had been for so long at the core of his existence, had been nearly decimated by the death of Della Treadwell, only to be fully restored thereafter in the curious demise of her husband. His loss had not been a blow, in comparison, for he had not expected Bob to last long, given his condition in the aftermath of Della's long, exhausting trial; he'd have drunk himself to death within a year anyhow. But for it to happen in such a stunning and swift way... Was it providential? Ominous? Demonic? Symbolic? Merely a quirk of nature? We will never have the answer in this life, he thought.

He had also come to realize that in truth he had been in rebellion against death, that the loss of Della, who had meant more to him than just about anyone else he had known in his life, to whom he had been minister, father, brother, was the sort of event that could have destroyed him, and in turn he saw with keen lucidity that indeed that was the purpose in that grand ploy – the introduction of death into the Garden, the ripping of the body, the fragility of our flesh, so traumatic that only ultimate faith, faith that ultimately sustains us despite terrible pain and loss, can carry us through. And Christ had done all of that for us already. He had already shown the way.

Luther felt that in some way, through her death, he had crossed over into oblivion and darkness and had come back again. Oftentimes, he had an undeniable sense that she was nearby, as when the girl, Liza Applewhite, had come to his house and he had believed it *was* Della, that somehow time had hiccupped and she had returned, young and healthy once again; it was far short, of course, of the joy the disciples must have felt when they saw Christ's smiling face among them once again after the crucifixion, but it must have been akin to that. Then, Bob's death had affirmed that the mystery was alive and well. Some part of him wanted to use the word "mystical," but he was not quite prepared to forge into that sort of terrain.

"Well," James said, "strange or not, the Lord works away in us. Great tinker that he is, he's got the tools needed."

A faded sign and then two old, flat-pink gas pumps appeared around the road's next bend. "Here we are, Luther. Just on the left here. I believe I might know these here folks."

The little country store was almost cool inside: a small electric fan hummed in a window, and the big red Coke box at the front glistened with condensation. The interior was immaculate, with its smooth, swept floor, its neat shelves with local goods, boiled peanuts, late-season vegetables, and broad coolers with fresh meats – sausages, chicken, and bacon, and fresh-caught catfish.

"My treat," James said, drawing two bottles from the shiny box and placing them on the counter. Now an elderly colored man, so small that Luther had not seen him before, rose from his chair.

His light-brown face was creased by time, but he smiled at them. "Reverend," he said, nodding.

"Sir. Ring us up, please. Cash on the barrel head."

Back in the station wagon again, Luther said, "So I reckon you must know just about everybody around these parts."

"There may be a few young'uns I don't know," James said. "Lots of these colored folk look alike to me."

Luther guffawed into his Coke bottle. "Damn racists everywhere these days," he said.

"So, tell me about the boy. That ballplayer. Any news on him?"

Luther shook his head. "Clean gone. That girl said he swore he would run away, but apparently she didn't believe him. Carl Sasser found the boat on the other side of the river and tracked him up to the highway, but there the trail was lost. Obviously got picked up by some driver."

"He'll be truant from school, I reckon."

"That won't be the worst of it, if he gets very far. He's not but fifteen."

James gazed philosophically out toward the trees. "Still, you know," he said, "I recall I left my own home when I was about fourteen. My mama died, just like Frankie's, and we had no idea where Daddy was. I guess I could have stayed with my Aunt Bev, but... I don't know, I just had this yearning. I wanted to get off by myself for awhile."

"I understand that."

"Ended up putting myself through seminary, folding newspapers, sweeping floors. Things worked out all right."

"Sure enough. Likely the boy will find his way."

"Likely will, praise God."

The battered wagon labored on, rumbling deep into the ancient wilderness, the red dust billowing and sinking, disappearing again below the tree line.

The young man – or so he appeared from where McDougal sat – stood uncertainly in the doorway. It was a figure of hesitancy, the shape of a face peering into unknown quarters, the angles of elbows and arms signaling reluctance against the brilliant background of sunlight.

"Come in, then, if you're coming," McDougal shouted, "and the shut the damn door."

Wordlessly, the figure came forward, and a boy's sunburnt face emerged, lean-jawed, smooth. He wore a khaki hat with a shank of sandy hair over his forehead.

"Well?" McDougal said.

"I seen the sign," he said. "Help wanted."

He scrutinized the kid: he was thin but solidly built, raw-boned, as were many of the country boys who came through.

"How old are you?" McDougal asked.

"Seventeen, sir."

"Hm." It was hard to tell these days; they all looked young to him, and they all acted like boys. McDougal himself had gone to work full-time at the age of thirteen, and at seventeen he had been on active duty in the military. He could not remember ever having looked in the mirror and not seen the shadow of a beard and a man's hard gaze. These kids today took their sweet time growing up.

"Can you lift up a hundred pounds without spraining something or herniating yourself?"

"Yes, sir."

"Can you read and write? Do math?"

"Yes, sir."

Now he took off his glasses and looked the boy up and down: he wasn't exactly skinny, but his pants were baggy and frayed around the bottoms and he looked hungry.

"We sell everything from pickles to hardware in here. Ain't no five and dime, either. No junk. Quality stock. There's some heavy lifting involved."

"I like heavy lifting," the boy said.

"And taking inventory."

"I like taking inventory."

"M-hm. How old did you say you are?"

"Seventeen."

Suddenly a little wave of pity ran through him. He'd seen kids like this before. Probably a stray. "Where's your parents at?" he asked.

The boy looked at his feet. "My mama got sick this past summer. Daddy's out of work right now. Said I have to earn some money to help with the family's bills and all."

"And you said they live where?"

"They live down in...in Horry County."

"Horry County, is it?"

"Yes, sir. On the Wacamaw River."

"I see. And what's your name son?"

"Frank Johnson."

MacDougal jotted it down at the bottom of his ledger and then leaned back in his chair with a long creaking of the springs. "All right, Mr. Johnson. I can give you a job. But if I find out you've told me any untruths here, I'm going to have to bring in the law on this. I can't have a runaway on the place."

"I understand, sir."

"You'll start this afternoon. Where you staying, anyway?"

"Been staying down to the bus station these three nights now. It ain't half-bad. They been letting me sleep on the bench."

"Well," McDougal sighed, rubbing his face. "If it'd suit you any better, I got a little room back there in the warehouse. Got a cot, a sink, and a toilet."

"Yes, sir, that'd be fine."

"Well?"

"Sir?"

"Go on down to the bus station and fetch your stuff."

"All right. Thanks."

He was much like the other boys who'd wandered in over the years, McDougal judged. It always happened in the fall, after the harvest had passed. But most every one he'd ever hired had been gone before Christmas. It was nothing new – it had always been a hardscrabble life around these parts, and people just perpetually drifted through; it had always been so, as far as he recalled.

McDougal's was not the only long-standing store in Columbia that was more than your typical farm and tractor supply, of course, but the Depression had nearly done them all in, way back when. Something had changed, however, in the past ten to fifteen years. Somehow people had more money, and he was able to stock items he never had before: the nice felt Stetsons, the thick, engraved belts, even chocolates from San Francisco. It was sheer pleasure opening those particular boxes, and he liked to save that task for himself. They smelt of faraway manufacturers' shops, and of...profit. The black phone on his desk issued a long, dull rattle, and he swatted at it and thrust it towards his ear.

"McDougal's."

It was his wife. Could he remember to bring home some squash for her casserole? Yes, he could.

He was short with her for no reason, and as always, he regretted it right away. He simply found it impossible to talk sweetly. Ever. To anybody. He was not a mean man, but anytime he made a deliberate effort to speak sweetly, he found himself appalling. In his own head, it sounded grotesquely artificial, like the voice that came out of a doll when you pulled the string.

But he would bring her squash and maybe something extra. Maybe some chocolates. Though she was a good churchgoing woman, she was quite a bit younger than he was, and little presents still made her happy; and as long as he could do that, there was a reason behind all this.

He rose and walked to the back to make sure that the little cot had fresh sheets and that the toilet worked. The kid could use the hose out back to bathe, or hell, if McDougal really felt soft, he might bring him up to the house sometime for a hot shower. He looked like he could use it.

When Frankie had retrieved his knapsack from the bus station and was headed back up the main street, he felt light, for a change. He could sense a slight change in the air, which was still heavy with the vestiges of summer but which seemed dryer and perhaps a tick or two cooler. In more than two months of traveling on his own, his own sweat had become a second, slimy skin, and his principle objective, in all places and situations, had been to escape the sun's ubiquitous tyranny. Even in more northerly climates – Maryland, Virginia, and Pennsylvania – the heat had smothered him, cooking his bare shoulders on the highways, and forcing him like an animal to go slithering and groveling to the nearest shade, to soak his head in foul ditches, to drink from hoses and spickets wherever he found them. He had grown accustomed to the smell of his own body; he saw now the fortuitousness of his having been allowed to sleep for three nights on one of the benches at the Columbia bus station, for he had been able to use the drivers' shower, and to rinse out one of his two shirts and a set of underwear. Simply placing his hand on a rectangular block of new white soap, with its wonderful beveled edges and its sweet smell, brought back to him a sense of domestic comfort he had all but forgotten.

So, at least he had been clean when he appeared before McDougal this morning. Even the death of his mother back in the spring had not prepared him for the horrors of a feral existence; for all the physical discomforts of his self-prescribed exile, the truest terror was in loss of identity: could it be himself – Frank Treadwell, Frankie, high-school sophomore, a well-loved son, a teammate, the boy who lived by the river, who had barely been out of the town of Dillon – who was now the aimless vagabond, invisible to most, object of scorn to others, chased by dogs, sleeping behind billboards, friendless and furtive against a backdrop of scrubby towns and scorching heat? For a while, he had wondered why he had done this to himself, when he had at least had a home and a bed, and a father who had at least had a job sometimes, and who might have, by now, shaken himself out of his funk. He would wonder, in the nights, by the roadside, if he went back, whether his father would be there waiting, clean and sober again, with that little half-smile which had been unseen for so long.

He was not a bad man. Frank knew that now. But he was a weak man, and his regard for his father had shifted irrevocably on the night he had gone in to retrieve him from that saloon up on Route 9. Nothing would ever be the same after that. In any event, it could only be a good thing now for them to be away from each other for a while.

Today, for the first time since he had left home, perhaps for the first time in roughly five months, he felt almost happy. He was a working man, and he would even have a little space of his own, with running water. When he reached the door to McDougal's again, he paused for a moment and quickly examined his reflection in the window, adjusting his rumpled shirt. Once inside, his eyes struggled again with the dark, after the brilliant street; after a moment, he realized that there was no one here. Mr. McDougal must have stepped out, or gone someplace for lunch. He approached McDougal's desk and saw the sports section of *The State* spread over the dark, polished wood. The thick headline proclaimed that the Dodgers had taken game three of the World Series, 4-3, over the Chicago White Sox. Then he saw the date along the top edge of the paper, and a sudden realization nearly made him laugh out loud.

Today was his sixteenth birthday, by God.

———————

"My Uncle Banks is a very rich man."

Banks Berenger stretched out on the chaise lounge and rolled over on one shoulder to gaze at the green and red running lights of a passing sailboat. It was a sleek white sliver in the vast shadow of the ocean, and its inboard motor hummed softly beneath the soft purple-grey dome of the sky.

"Uncle Banks is a very rich man," he mumbled, "and he is very happy. He has never been sad, once he had all the money he would ever need."

He felt contentedly drunk, drunkenly content – not thoroughly tanked but with a pleasant buzzing in his head and the fumes of good whiskey in his chest. He looked over at the girl in the hammock slung between two posts and saw that she was already sound asleep. She had covered herself with his bathrobe, but the soft moonlight ran over her bare shoulder and down her arm, and even that was enough to move something, slightly, down in his groin. He could hear her steady, even breathing, the respirations of a strong, young girl.

He enjoyed this one very much, but he would acknowledge that his approach to women was somewhat crass and simple-minded, rather like his enjoyment of automobiles. He thought that he might try and hang on to this one, for even her name – Karen – put him in mind of elegant restaurants and limousines, but he knew that complacency and ultimately non-commitment were more in his nature. He would have to move on soon.

One of the many secrets he had discovered through the acquisition of wealth was just this: that women of this caliber, so fine, as fine as exquisite sculpture, understood that they were the moving pieces in the temporary collections of powerful men. She might not go willingly, when the time came, but the dignity of her beauty and style would give her the strength to leave with her head up.

Oh, there were many secrets. In addition to the years of grueling labor, the scraping, the clearing by hand of the small parcels of land he'd bought in the beginning, there was also the work it took, early on, for him to reconcile himself to the money once it had begun to flow in. He had dreamed of it for so long, but when it had actually happened, the old ideas, the mores buried deep in his conscience that said not only was money the root of evil, but that he and his kind do not deserve monetary success anyway. He had had to eradicate from his mind his notion of himself as a social victim, a backwater rat whose only means of subsistence were government charity and outright thievery. He had come to see himself as a new man, for whom the only alternative to forging a living and accruing money was death. Once he had been able to do that, the rest was a matter of effort on his part – along with a measure of ruthlessness. But he could still make up for the ruthlessness, he believed.

He had started with small slashes of coastal land that he bought cheap, cleared, groomed, and then sold off to members of a new breed of folks who were trickling into the state: tourists, rusticators from up north, who were seeking nothing more than waterfront property on which to build vacation homes. And then when he could afford it, he bought machinery, chainsaws, backhoes, bulldozers, stump removers, and so on, to cut his time and labor in half. And then, with the return on that, he had started a construction company and begun building the houses himself, on the cheap because he now knew where to go to find all the surplus materials he needed, roofing, tiles, and sometimes he bought broken-down cabins out in the sticks, tore them down and used those materials to make "quaint" bungalows along the seashore. The rules were simple: a). you never spent money unless you knew you'd get more back on your investment, b). you learned every aspect of the business, every skill involved, even when you could afford to hire a crew, and c). you tried to be nice to everybody, but when somebody purposely got in your way, you took him down right away, no hesitating.

He realized that on occasion, he had overdone that last part. It struck him that this proclivity had perhaps been his sole inheritance, besides a surname, from his real father, Bill 'Hatchet' Berenger, whom his mother had finally married when Banks had been almost grown. That was a long time ago, and they were all dead now – his mother, her first husband, and now his older half-brother, Bob, all cast back again into the thick, mosquito-clouded fens and woods from which they had emerged.

He had thought many times over the years of going back to see Bob, perhaps just to re-establish kinship, or perhaps to inform him at last of the circumstances of his lengthy absence; for he was certain that he was unaware that Banks was only his half-blood brother, born out of wedlock, the son of his mother's lover. That in itself would not have been earth-shattering news among these people, but in large part he wanted to see for himself the life from which he had been extricated at the age of five. Had it been a merciful gesture on the old woman's part? Was there only squalor and hopelessness there, a legacy of worthless scrub trees, mud, and toothless proletariat? Once he had made his fortune, the fantasy had appeared in his brain, a tale of pathos: he would return to the place where he had been born, find his brother at the brink of starvation, and with a sum of money which to Banks would have been approximately the same as his account balance at his favorite restaurant, become the benevolent and unexpected savior, a Dickensian hero. Nevertheless, as so often occurs in such cases of family estrangement, it turned out that the only ensuing contact he would have with that forgotten part of his life had come this past August, arriving in the form of a letter from the Dillon Sheriff's Office, informing him of his brother's death.

At the funeral, it was some relief that no one seemed to remember him or recall his connection to the Treadwell family, except for Pastor Laite. It was not a well attended event, in any case: present were the minister, a couple of elderly churchgoers, Howard Beamon from the hardware store, a uniformed sheriff's deputy, and a young girl of about eighteen. After this mercifully brief graveside service, Luther Laite had approached him and invited him back to his home for a glass of iced tea.

Banks looked up and down the smooth, well-swept porch and then out at the trim garden, still colorful with autumn flowers. Modest but tidy: he liked that. Everything about the man bespoke order and calm.

"So," Luther had said, "It's been a while since I've had the pleasure. You were about seven, I believe. I'm sorry our reunion had to occur on such a somber occasion."

"Well, now, let's not sugar-coat it." Banks smiled. "I should have been back long ago. After all, a man's brother... I ought to have been here."

"Not much any of us could have done. The circumstances of his death were so strange."

"I don't mean just for that. I should have been in touch a long time ago. Twenty-nine years is a long time."

"As I recall, you didn't have much choice in that."

"I grew up to be a man with my own choices."

"Mm-hmm. That is true, I guess." Luther nodded towards him, a gesture taking in not merely Banks's tailored suit and freshly shined shoes, but his entire identity, his very essence, the measure of a man who had made something of his life. "I'd say you've done pretty well for yourself."

"Thank you, Pastor. Is it that obvious? I've never been one to flaunt it. I find having money prejudices some people against you. But believe me, I earned every dollar."

"No doubt."

"I wish I could've done something for Bob. From what I hear, he was in pretty bad shape around the time it happened."

"That big cat didn't care much about that, I guess," Luther said. "Besides, when a man's wife dies, he becomes unreasonable. It's the boy that worries me."

Banks had been watching a pileated woodpecker swoop from trunk to trunk at the back of the property, in search of an appropriate wood for hammering; it took a few seconds for Luther's last remark to sink in.

"Boy?"

Luther gazed back at him. "You didn't know? Bob had a son. He'd be sixteen now. Name of Frank."

"I- I didn't. I'll be damned – excuse my language, Pastor. What I mean to say is, where is this boy now?"

Luther shook his head. "I wish I knew. Nobody knows. The kid just disappeared, about the same day they found Bob. Sheriff organized a search party, APB went out, posters, everything. Apparently he's a runaway. The girl you saw at the burial, Liza Applewhite, she says he'd been talking about just taking off. Seems he meant it."

"I'll be." Banks whistled softly. "So I have a nephew. What's the kid like?"

"Very nice boy. Loved his mama and daddy. Did pretty well in school, I believe. Absolutely lived for baseball."

"I'm sorry I never met him. Did he know about what happened to his father?"

"We're not sure. Not sure exactly when he high-tailed it."

"Well, maybe he'll turn out smarter than I was and come on back before too long."

"We're hoping and praying. It's a big world out there – not all of it kind."

On the drive back (he had brought the Plymouth and left the flashy red Cadillac in the garage), the old feelings of regret and accountability, singed slightly by bitterness, began to bubble in him. He had never imagined having any children of his own, but a nephew was something different. You could take him fishing, to a ballgame, take him to dinner, give him pocketknives at Christmas. Thanks, Uncle Banks. Then when you were done with him, you could drop him off again at home... that is, you could have done those things if you hadn't been a selfish bastard.

An idea began to take shape in him: he had influence; he knew civil court judges in every county in the state, and in turn they knew sheriffs and police chiefs and marine patrol and others in authority. Maybe he could help locate the boy. Maybe he could do some good in this case after all.

He shifted back on the chaise lounge and looked over again at Karen. She was so comely, even in sleep, that for a moment he considered reaching over to touch her bare shoulder; then he changed his mind.

He mouthed the words again: "My Uncle Banks is a very rich man."

Uncle Banks. It did have a nice ring to it.

———

Liza Applewhite sat on the sofa in the apartment she shared with her mother and Roger, thumbing through the thick *Good Housekeeping* magazine for the month of October. The irony in this did not escape her. The crowded little room in which she found herself was neat and clean, but it bore little resemblance to the pictures before her of the two-story suburban homes with broad, sloping lawns and boxy cars in front; and their kitchen was a simple galley with only a toaster and a hot plate, whereas the elegantly attired mothers in the ads leaned towards cavernous ovens built into brick walls. She had never known her own mother to wear anything other than her old blue bathrobe at mealtimes, usually while Roger, large and awkward, flopped about behind her, battering his knuckles against the drawers and cabinets and swearing as he searched for the bottle opener.

Tonight, though, she was the only one in. They had gone over to Marion, to the drive-in movie. That in itself was not unusual, but tonight she found herself in an anxious state of mind. Three weeks ago, she had met a boy, Carl. He worked construction out of Marion and had been passing through town on his way to the job site when he had come into the diner early on a Wednesday morning. She had been moved from kitchen duty to waitressing, so certainly he had caught her eye, swaggering across the terrazzo floor like the chief male in a band of apes, in his sleeveless undershirt, but such was the exact demeanor of the boys she had learned to despise the most. She had waited on him quite deliberately and brusquely, not allowing any pauses for casual conversation. But by the end of his omelet, he had made no attempt whatsoever to talk with her, even when she lingered for a moment to total up his check. And suddenly it struck her: why, he was just shy.

So she said, "Ain't seen you in here before."

He was looking down at his empty plate. "No'm. Never been in. Heard y'all serve good food."

"By the looks of your plate, I'd say you heard right."

"Yes'm."

And that was that. He had come back again for lunch, and the same thing again on Thursday. On Friday he asked if he might come into town on

Saturday, his day off, and pick her up when her shift was over. They might ride out to the lake together. She said that sounded fine, but she wanted to go home first and shower; she had returned and met him out front.

Now, for two weeks, they had done nothing more than talk and hold hands. His hand was dry and warm, if somewhat calloused from his work, and she could feel the strength of his whole arm in its easy touch. But tonight they had planned for him to come to the apartment to watch television with her, and she knew in her heart that something different could very well happen.

She had told her mother that he was coming. She no longer hesitated to speak frankly to her mother in all situations, for they had been through too much together. This was not to say that she regarded her mother as a confidant or even a sympathetic companion – it was merely more expedient to be upfront. She had hovered over Liza for a moment, a confused angel, and then she had turned away, saying, "Well, I reckon you know what you're doing. Just don't get   into any trouble."

"Carl's a very nice boy."

"I'm sure he is, hon'. But you can get in trouble with a nice boy, too."

Liza could not recollect whether she had ever been on a real date before Carl. She had never considered her excursions with the Greenville High boys "dates," and the hours she had spent with Frankie had never seemed like any sort of courtship – not even his absurd fumblings at the lake that time. She felt no sense of obligation or loyalty to him. But Carl had treated her to dinner, and quiet as he was, he had a nice, easygoing way about him; she found him extremely attractive, in fact: his dark eyes seemed to say a lot to her, and his skin, despite his rugged occupation and exposure to the daily elements, was wrought of smooth bronze. The more she looked at him, the more she thought he must have Latin or Italian blood in him somewhere.

Perhaps it was time for her to have a little real fun in her life, she thought. Could anyone begrudge her that? After all, she had been through the mill, she had been walked over, and she had taken that like some little dog out in the rain, and then she had come back here and tried to do some good for people, for Della and for those incorrigible Treadwell men. She certainly was not thinking of anything terribly long-term, and she had no aspirations to the kind of life proffered by *Good Housekeeping*, but she felt she did deserve for something good to happen to her for a change.

And just then, there was a knocking at the front door, and she jumped and caught her breath. She stood up, smoothed her dress, and ran a finger through her bangs, and with a last look around the neat little room, she went to let him in.

———

Jacquin Anders had only three days to wait before his release from the state pen. Three days, and the sun would go up, down, the switch would be thrown twice more, and then the last hours, minutes, and seconds would trickle away, scattering over the dry yard like the leaves, and his time would be all served. He would be unleashed upon the world again. He had heard plenty about those men who, once they had been in prison, were inclined to come back again; they got used to it, even welcomed it – it was regular food and a bed, and the truth was that for some it was safer in here than on the outside. They came from the bleakest, most destitute sides of the poorest towns, "nigger-towns," as even the colored folk called them, where casual drinking on a given afternoon usually led to a card game in the evening, which in turn usually led to drawn razors by midnight.

Not Jack. His mama had taught him how to do. Once he left this place, he said to himself, he would make sure never to come back.

In fact, it had taken him many months of puzzling to understand how he had really gotten here to begin with. The charge against him had been theft, but he had finally come to understand that his real crime had been of an entirely different sort. It had happened during a Columbia Reds minor-league game, in the shambling old Capital City ballpark; Jack had always loved it there, the open vistas, great swaths of green and brown, the men in straw hats with their cigars and beer, the cool cement floors beneath the overhangs down below, littered with blowing hot dog wrappers. As was the case with everyplace else in town, seating was segregated, so that the colored folks had their gate and their own bleachers in the outfield; however, on this day, he had lit on a bit of luck when his cousin Eugene had asked him to sell bags of peanuts in his stead. He had asked his mother:

"Can I? Eugene say it's easy. You just wear this box around your neck and give out the bags, and they give you the money."

She had smiled. "Well, I reckon it's better than picking cotton."

And so, quite proudly, he had retrieved the big wooden box from his cousin and put the strap over his shoulders, and then tied the change sack around his waist, below that. He looked at himself in the little mirror that hung by the front door. He called out to himself: "Peanuts here!"

He had done well that day, working the colored section and then venturing into the general admission seats behind first base, where the white people sat. Gradually, magically, the sack grew heavy with quarters, most of which would go back to the peanut company, of course, but he would still make a pretty good haul for himself, even with Eugene getting a cut. He sold his last bag during the top of the eighth inning, with the Reds leading by three runs, and he went downstairs to find relief from the heat in the cool shadows below the grandstand. He leaned back against the cool tiles, the chilly sweat on the back of his shirt easing his tired shoulders as he removed the box and set it at his feet. On top of that, he placed the bulging black money belt.

A boy came down the steps – a white boy about his own age – with a box just like his own strapped across him, and a black waistband for the money, just like his own. He glanced over at Jack, nodded, and then headed in his direction, taking off his burden as well and setting it on the floor. He leaned back against the wall, groaned, and wiped at his forehead with his bare forearm. "Damn hot one, ain't it?" he said.

Jack nodded and smiled. He was trying to determine whether he knew this boy or not. He didn't look familiar.

"How'd you do today?" the kid asked. "Sell much?"

"Sold all," he said.

"Yeah, me, too. Hey, buy us a Coke over there?" He gestured toward the concession stand. "I'll mind your stuff."

What to do? He couldn't leave the box and the money belt, that was clear. On the other hand, a cold Coca-Cola would certainly suit him right now. But after a moment or two, he said, "I can't. Got to split everything with my cousin, Eugene."

"Aw, now, Eugene ain't gonna begrudge you a cold Coke."

Jack looked down at his shoes and swallowed. "Sorry," he said.

"Hm."

There was a sudden commotion in the game: the sharp sound of wood against ball snapped across the air above them, and a mad roar went up. Instantly excited, Jack leaned forward, stood on his tiptoes, and tried to see beyond the top of the short flight of steps; he thought maybe he could just catch a glimpse of the scoreboard, but instead all he could see were hats and arms waving wildly. "Somebody done something," he said. When he looked down again, he saw that the other boy was crouched over the two money belts, his hand stuck deep into the pocket of one of them; it took him a few seconds to realize that it was *his* belt, and not the kid's own.

"Hey!" Instinctively, he reached down and grabbed the boy's wrist, not gruffly, but certainly firmly enough, and had he known that this would be the moment of his undoing, he might have left it all alone, might have let him rummage to his satisfaction and take what he wished. As it was, the kid froze, then pulled his arm away as if it had been touched by a soldering iron, or punctured by the fangs of a snake. Then he stood up straight and drew back, and Jack thought for a moment that he was winding up to punch him, and he flinched.

The kid tried to speak but was so flustered that only indecipherable pieces of words burst from between his clenched teeth. Finally he managed to say, "Oh...you...you just wait right there! Don't you go nowhere!"

Everything happened fairly quickly after that. The boy returned a few minutes later with two men, one of whom turned out to be his father, who was also so angry he was literally spitting, and a frowning policeman, who seemed to be as big and wide as the other three of them combined.

"This is the nigger right here," the boy said. "Caught him red-handed going into my money belt. Getting so's you can't even go to a ballgame no more without some nigger trying to steal your last dime."

And that was that. Within the month, despite his mother's protests over his age (he had just turned eighteen), he found himself here, doing his time, a ward of the state. Still, it was almost finished now, and as he sat down to dinner in the mess hall, he imagined the meal he would have when he got home: his mother's chicken, of course, would come first, and around the side of the plate would be fresh fried tomatoes, some macaroni and cheese, two biscuits overflowing with butter, cole slaw, and in a separate bowl would be the mashed potatoes and gravy. Then he picked up his fork and prepared to force-feed himself, savoring the loathsomeness of the congealing prison food before him.

––––––––––

Frank had been an employee of McDougal's shop for exactly ten days, but in that odd warping of time that comes at the beginning of any new experience, he felt like an old hand around the place. He already knew the stock inside out, every fountain pen, every smoked ham on the shelves, and now McDougal was training him to use the cash register and keep the books.

He liked the work, and he liked McDougal. He liked his little room in the back with the sink (hot water, too), toilet, and cot; or course, it wasn't as big or as comfortable as his old room at home, but it was his own space, and once he was finished in the shop, he could come and go as he pleased. Often, in the evenings, he would walk the streets of Columbia, sometimes going in the brightly decorated candy store across the way, or perhaps buying a hamburger at the little stand down on the corner, peaking into the dark saloons as he passed them and hearing the low voices of the men inside. It was a much bigger and more lively town than Dillon, though not as big as some of those he had traveled through in the weeks after he had rowed the johnboat across the Little PeeDee River and caught a long ride with a trucker heading north. Still, he had only seen those places as a perpetual outsider who was merely trying to get by, with no sense whatsoever of attachment and no purpose. But here he was beginning to experience a feeling of belonging.

McDougal was a big part of that; he seemed to have a natural paternal streak in him, and he often took Frank out for lunch or sat and talked with him in the afternoons when things got slow. Their conversations where somewhat trivial, as they spoke of little more than the weather and the front page of the local paper, and that suited Frank just fine, for he certainly was in no position to divulge personal details concerning himself. And today was special: as promised, McDougal had planned to take Frank home with him and treat him to a hot bath and a home-cooked meal.

"I ain't saying the wife is a gourmet chef, but she does all right considering her youth," he'd said. "She'll get better as time goes on."

"I'm sure it'll be good, whatever she makes," Frank said.

The McDougal home, settled back from an otherwise empty stretch of road roughly three miles from town, was sizable, but not as plush as he had thought it might be. It reminded Frank of the western ranches he had seen on television and in magazines; it was somewhat sprawling, with big, open rooms and a fireplace surround made of great blue and brown stones, lovely to look at. A fire hissed and popped dryly on the grating.

Mrs. McDougal, by contrast, was a small, compact woman, about twenty-five, with that sort of attractiveness that often eluded certain men, at first, who met her. Frank, however, was stunned, besotted to silence, when she extended her hand to him and said, "Please call me Allison." The more he studied her face, the prettier she became; it had a peculiar angularity to it, and her long, dark-brown hair hung down her back in a rich mane. There was something exotic in her looks: her skin was of a slightly darker tone, and her dark eyes were quite large. Her hand was small and strong.

"I'm Frank."

"Yes, I know," she said. "Would you care for a glass of wine?"

"Hold on now," McDougal broke in. "He ain't but seventeen, honey."

"I was drinking wine from the time I was six," she said. "It's done me no harm that I know of."

"Well, I suppose it's up to him." They both looked at Frank.

"Geez," he said. "I never had any, but I guess I'll try it."

It was a strong red, very dark in the glass. In that moment, at that first taste of alcohol, he could not help but think of his father and all of the green bottles. It somehow seemed a faraway thought, the naïve reflections of a child. Or perhaps his father had been the childish one, for he had merely indulged a pathetic weakness; but in this wine there was a strength he had never expected. It fortified, it nurtured.

"This stuff is not bad," he said.

"Mac gets it for me through the shop," she said. "It's Spanish."

"Oh."

"It's called La Donna Rosa. The Red Woman."

"Oh."

"But you're only getting one," McDougal said, "so make it last."

"Yes, sir."

They sat down at the big oak dining table to a dinner of Mediterranean chicken and steamed broccoli. Allison McDougal made the bulk of the conversation, with occasional grunts of agreement or disapproval from her husband. Frank could tell that she was hungry to talk, that she probably didn't get much opportunity for that ordinarily, he imagined. Her white teeth flashed merrily as she ate and talked, and her eyes were as dark as the olives on her plate.

"So, what sorts of things do you like to do, Frank?" she asked.

"Let's see. Well... I've done a lot of traveling since I... since I got out of high school."

"Wonderful. What places have you been to?"

"Maryland, Virginia, West Virginia, Pennsylvania. Also Washington D.C."

"Fascinating. And what kinds of things did you like to do when you were in school?"

"I played baseball." It felt strange on his lips; it was the first time he had even uttered the word in months.

She clapped her hands. "I love baseball," she effused. "So does Mac. It's our favorite. Columbia has a team, you know. Minor league, but they're good. We'll all have to go to a game together in the spring. Do you still play?"

He shook his head. "Haven't touched ball nor bat in a really long time." Or glove. Instantly he thought of his old glove, forlorn on the dresser where he had left it at home.

"What position?"

"Center field. Pitched, too."

"I'll bet you were good."

"I reckon I did all right."

It seemed a lifetime ago, though it had only been about five months. Even as he sat at the big table, with Allison McDougal chattering away, he felt the old rush of freedom as he saw himself sprinting across the verdant field, gazing up at the ball in flight, thoughtlessly calibrating the spot where he and it would converge. For an instant he smelt the old smells, felt the surging blood in his thighs... Then he saw the Greenville third baseman rolling in the dusty, blood-spattered clay, holding his head.

"Frankie? Are you all right?" Mrs. McDougal was stretching her hand towards him across the table.

"I'm fine," he said. "Just tired."

McDougal cleared his throat. "I'd say it's bedtime," he declared.

They gave him the downstairs guest room. It was the finest bedroom he had ever seen: walls with royal blue wallpaper, paintings – watercolors of arches and canals, a thick rug, a great, soft bed with iron posts, into which he sank like a sack of heavy bones, and even a private bathroom with silver fixtures. He could learn to like this, for the king and queen lay just above him, and he was their adopted prince.

He drifted in the first shallow tide of sleep, and what happened in that little bubble of time, what he believed he saw and heard, would seem to him an impossibility in the clear light of the morning that followed. Was he dreaming? He wasn't sure. He stirred, opened his eyes, and there she was, at the foot of the bed, looking back at him.

"Mrs. McDougal?"

"Shh." She put a slender finger to her lips, and as she did so, the loose nightgown fell off of one shoulder, and he realized that the gown was unbuttoned, and she was bare-breasted. A thin light from somewhere fell across her hair. "I just wanted to say how glad I am that you're here." Her whisper was so soft, so fragile, it was barely audible, but his ears took in every syllable.

"Yes, ma'am," he said.

"And I want you to come back very soon."

"Yes, ma'am. I'll do that."

"Sleep well, Frank."

Still uncertain whether he was fully awake, he closed his eyes. When he opened them once again, she was gone.

The old labors of his calling, for Luther, were not as torturous anymore. He sat back at his desk in the church office, arms lifted above his head in an attempt to dry out the soaked underarms of his shirt. He was exhausted, having just finished writing his sermon for tomorrow, but it was a good feeling. Before him were the last stumps of two pencils and his writing tablet, smeared by his toil.

It had all come back to him again in recent weeks, his passion for his work, but especially since Bob Treadwell's death. He knew not the reason for this. Perhaps it had all been so strange that it simply defied any sense of reason, and for a man interested in the spirit, reason could cut two ways. It had cut him badly when Della died, because what his reason had told him then – that living cells, life itself, is feeble and always in inevitable decay, and that people talk of a soul which the eyes cannot perceive – had demolished his belief. But only temporarily; without his asking for it or praying over it, his faith had been restored to him. It had returned in a slow trickle at first, like a thin course of rain in a dry riverbed, then mounting to a steady surge. It was something different, something more, actually, than a love of his work, this feeling; it harkened back to the days of his youth when he had first begun to perceive the complexities of the Faith, to understand that it was about more than a child's belief in Heaven as a place where one goes as a reward for good behavior. It took a certain intellectual capacity to grasp the concept of a miracle as a suspension of physical laws, for example, but a child's vision in order allow for one actually occurring. Whether the restoration of his belief had been miraculous, he could not now say, but he felt deeply that the child in him, somewhere, had not gone completely blind. Or here was another way to think of it: for every need we have in our lives, we have also a means by which to fulfill it. A thirsty man needs water, for instance, and if he doesn't have it, then eventually his body will dry out, shrivel up, and so we are driven towards water. The same was true for love: when someone is in need of love, he finds it in the generosity of others, and we flourish, but if we find it not, we die. Every person needs God, and therefore, our basic humanity being a state of helplessness, we are inevitably driven towards Him. Either way, Luther could feel the fullness of his faith in ways he never had before.

Somehow it was all connected to Bob's death. The incident itself had already passed into legend. Even old Nettie Russell had heard of it, and on Luther's most recent visit to her place with James Jenkins, she had told them that the panther that had killed Treadwell was an evil spirit:

"It's a demon," she'd said, her nearly sightless eyes lolling backwards like eggs in a jar. "I seen it around here many times, too. Heard it. Black as the devil hisself."

Part of Luther, perhaps the child again, wanted to believe her and to know the thrill of fear, but the reason upon which his faith was based resisted.

"Now, Nettie," he had replied, "everybody around here knows there might still be big cats in these woods, despite what the experts say. But they're way too scared of you to be a bother. And as far as the color, nobody knows for sure if it was black or brown... or purple, for that matter."

She had tapped her porch with her chipped cane. "It's a thing made out of the night and the shadow. Dark thing made for a dark deed. Don't you doubt it, Preacher. Fact, if you wants to see for yourself, you come on back out here one a these nights. You'll see."

It was an alluring notion, and again the boy in him egged him on, but he knew that Christ had dispensed with such things long ago. Luther thought that demons were real, certainly – he was not yet that progressive. But it had only taken one or two illustrations to show the indomitable power of truth and light; before God, all such perversions, including death itself, float away like so much ash.

He raised his head, glanced out the window, and observed a figure out on the sidewalk. It was Liza Applewhite; the weather had cooled down, and she was attired in jeans and a dark-green and white flannel shirt, but something in her demeanor, perhaps the tilt of her head, still put him in mind of Della each time he saw her, though not with the same raw force as when she had first come to his house last May.

She looked awkward and uncertain, even a little disoriented, standing there staring blankly at the church building. That was unusual: he had last seen her in August at Bob's funeral service, and at that time, despite the sobriety of the occasion, she had looked quite well. She was at that age when her body had ceased developing, but her appearance was still evolving; her face was more womanly, less babyish, her eyes deeper and more self-aware. On that day, her physical ease had still implied the tomboy she had once been, but she also seemed quite comfortable in heels and a dress. And she'd had something else about her – a sense of ambition, perhaps, an energy that needed only a hint of purpose to begin its unfolding.

He could not imagine what had brought her here, though, in such a state of distraction, seemingly. Now she placed her hands on her hips and paced about twenty feet up the sidewalk, scrutinizing the cement as if she had dropped something there. Then she paused, turned around, and paced in the other direction, looking up at the sky.

"All right," he said, "that's enough of that." He rose, closing the notebook. On his way out, in the outer office, the church secretary, Myra Biggs, stopped him.

"You had a phone call," she said, her tall beehive hairdo tottering unsteadily. "Banks Berenger. Of Hilton Head, to be exact, or so he said."

"I'll call him later."

Luther moved quickly through the second doorway, and then up the aisle to the big double oak doors and pushed his way outside.

Still, he was too late. Liza had disappeared, and he made a mental note to drop by the diner as soon as possible.

———

The day of Jack Anders' release from prison was at hand. He had one more day and night to endure, and then he would walk out into the sunshine of the free world, just as he had seen so many other men do during his two-year stint.

He had been assigned to the prison laundromat these two weeks, but on this morning, when he had left his cell and come down the metal stairs, a guard hailed him:

"You there, boy! Anders!" It was Markel, the man who had made a reputation for himself by mucking with some of the short-timers. Jack had feared such a summons, and now he considered walking on, pretending not to hear, but of course, that might only make matters worse. He turned, and Markel beckoned to him.

"Yes, Boss?"

"Fetch a pair of work gloves out of the shed yonder." The heavyset man's face was stern, emotionless, like marble pocked by harsh weather. "Then meet me out in the yard. Got some four-by-fours needs movin'."

"Yes, sir."

At least it wasn't hot out. His nose twitched at the pleasant dryness; the scent of wood smoke drifted to him from somewhere far over the land. "Follow me," Markel snapped. They walked in silence, with Markel several feet ahead of him, to the farthest corner of the prison fence and then turned to the right, away from the guard's tower, eventually making their way a hundred yards or so to a pleasant spot where the thick, dark limbs of a magnolia tree hung over the barbed wire above. There were tracks left by a tractor in the dry dirt all around, and about thirty feet away sat a stack of treated lumber.

"All right," Markel said. "This is where it is. I want you to pick up each one of them there posts and restack 'em right here by the fence."

Putting at bay the reasonable questions that occurred to him, Jack simply nodded his head and went to work. He strode over to the stack, picked up four of the eight-foot posts, carried them easily back, and dropped them in a great clatter by the chain-link wall.

"Easy with those," Markel said. "Two at a time is fine. We don't want no dents."

Back he went, taking a post in each hand, and then again, and again. He had moved about half of the pile when Markel, said, "Let's knock off for five." Jack was neither sweating nor winded, but he took off the gloves and rubbed the palms of his hands together. Markel was on one knee, resting a forearm against his thigh, the other hand placed lightly on the head of his stick (none of the guards inside the wire carried guns, of course). He removed his shiny, black sunglasses and pointed with them.

"Hey, boy," he said. "That a friend of yours over yonder?"

Jack looked up. Outside the fence about twenty feet, beyond the broad, black trunk of the magnolia, amidst its serpentine roots, was a negro woman – a girl, really, probably no more than fifteen or sixteen years old. But she had the full, plump body of a grown woman, with rich molasses-colored skin and dark eyes like chestnuts floating in milk. She wore a white cotton dress that rode up on her and showed her ample thighs, and a red bandana. Her hands were on her hips, and she stuck out her pink tongue at Jack and then sidled over daintily and disappeared behind the tree.

He blinked, uncertain of what he had just seen.

"She your cousin or somethin'?" Markel asked.

"I don't believe so," he said. "No kin of mine, sir."

"She acted like she might know you. Oh, well – best get back to work then, boy."

He turned and walked toward the stack of lumber, which had dwindled by half. He thought to himself: *So this is how he do it. Got to keep my mind on tomorrow.* But when he had lifted up the two posts and started back, she had reappeared, this time on the near side of the tree trunk. When he got close, he could see that the narrow straps of the dress were pulled down now and stretched tightly across her fleshy brown shoulders, so that the hem of the neckline draped precariously over her upward-peaking nipples, which were quite visible through the cloth.

As best as he could remember, she was the first female he had seen in two years, aside from the occasional secretary who might accompany a state inspector or other official visitor to the prison. Even his own mother, lacking a car, had not been able to come and see him, though she had written to him regularly.

"Would you look at that?" Markel said. "There she is again." He called out to her: "Come closer, girl, if you think you know this here boy."

Softly, she approached, stopping about ten feet from the fence. She smiled at him, her soft brown lips parting to show sharp, white teeth. Jack had been right – she was certainly no more than sixteen. Then, smiling all the while, her eyes locked on his, she lifted the front of her dress ever so slightly, reached a hand up inside of it, and from her panties, apparently, she produced a thin pint bottle filled with an amber liquid. She pulled out the cork and brought it to her lips slowly, carefully, still looking at him. Despite his best attempts otherwise, Jack could feel the steady rising down below, pushing hard against the stiff state-issue pants.

"You know, boy," Markel said, "I believe she is your cousin. Got to be. Now, I'll tell you, I don't never begrudge no man the right to meet with family. Lord knows it gets lonely enough inside this place. I'll tell you what.

You see that place in the fence right over yonder, by the metal post? It's buckled just a little bit right there. You see it, ol' Jack?"

He looked: there was a slight shadow where the links were indeed misshapen. "I done clipped out about a two-foot space right there," Markel said. "Done it myself in case if I ever get caught short when I'm on perimeter duty. Now, you look like you might just about fit through there. If you wanna slip on out there and visit with your cousin for a little while, I'd understand."

He gazed at her. She was plump, ripe as a berry, and she ran her long fingers down her supple throat, still saying nothing but telling him everything he feared to know with her eyes and her lips. He stammered: "Cap'n... Cap'n, now, you know I only got one more day to do. I'm s'pose to walk outa here tomorrow. If I go outside that fence, I gets more time."

Markel shook his head and looked sincere. "I'll never turn you in, Jack, I swear. I know how things run around here, and I'm tellin' you, you need to go out there and meet with your cousin. I know how it is for a man in this place."

Realizing that the protrusion from the crotch of his pants was now clearly visible, Jack turned his body sideways, but of course, this only made his arousal more obvious. In part, it was the excitement of naivety and curiosity, for he had never been with a woman – or a girl. He'd had lots of opportunities, but he was somewhat shy by nature, and his mother had counseled him against it: "Plenty a' these girls 'round here gonna lay a trap for you. But you cain't let 'em taint you. God don't like that." Nonetheless, he was a man now, and bound to make his own choices. In the moment, the risks didn't seem as great as he had expected. After all, it was only the three of them out here, and if Markel told on him, he could always deny everything. He could take her over behind that tree and just touch her, that was all, just touch her. Nothing more; and she could touch him, if she cared to. Even now, she was crooking her shapely brown finger at him. He could be out and then back inside the safety of the fence all within five minutes.

"I don't know, boss," he said, but Markel was no longer paying attention to him. He was looking past him, back toward the main complex, the cell blocks and administrative offices. Jack looked, too. There, with a plume of dust rising gently behind it, he could see the glinting hood of one of the prison trucks. As they watched, the hood grew larger, the plume taller.

"Aw, hell," Markel growled and spat on the ground.

"Who's that?" Jack asked.

"Perimeter guard. Comin' on shift early. Goddam ambitious rookie." Closer it drew, and now they could hear the low rattle of the engine. Markel looked straight at him, his face once again made of hard, expressionless slate. "Reckon your black ass got saved this time." Then, over his shoulder, he called loudly, "You best get on home right now, girl."

But when they both looked, she was already gone. They saw only the dark, sweetly arching, low-hung branches of the aged magnolia.

———

The moment MacDougal said it, Frank realized what was going to happen. He wasn't sure how it would all unfold, but he knew that it would; and he carried the knowing around with him all day, a sweet heavy burden, in the stockroom, on the floor, behind the register – it was with him, haunting him, taunting him like some ghost bound to take on warm flesh before darkness came on. He dreaded it, and yet he felt he could not contain his desire for it.

When he had come in that morning, stomping on the mat and then tossing his lunch on his desk, MacDougal had said, "Got to drive up to Raleigh today on business. Looking at some new goods. Have to stay the night."

"Yes, sir."

"I'll be leaving early afternoon. That means you'll be closing up. Opening up tomorrow, too."

"Yes, sir."

So, that afternoon, after MacDougal pronounced some final instructions and bid him a terse goodbye, he was not at all surprised when Mrs. MacDougal, wearing a yellow knee-length dress and a short pink sweater, opened the front door and came gliding toward him.

"Hi," he said.

"Hello, Frank. I thought I might give you a break and take you out for an ice cream. You look like you deserve it."

"I can't. It's only four."

"So?"

"We don't close till five."

Her laughter seemed to flutter around the corners of the shop like scraps of lace. "I don't think the boss would mind too much. I'm the real boss around here anyway, and I say you need an ice cream."

"Well..." He fumbled at the keys to the register. "Okay, then."

They got into her station wagon and turned right up Main Street, but then they went on past Stovall's Ice Cream Parlor and straight out of town.

"Got some homemade back at the house," she said. "Much better than any old store-bought stuff."

He nodded as if in humble and sincere agreement, but he was not comfortable. The more time that had passed since she had appeared at the foot of the guest-room bed, the more he had been able to convince himself that it had been a half-waking dream, that it had never happened. But now, as he studied her from the edge of his eye, he knew that it really had. Her dark hair was really right there at his shoulder, looping back over her right ear, and he saw again the real slope of her collarbones down into that mysterious shadow which was the very heart of his unknown yearning.

"My momma used to make homemade ice cream," he said. "We had a churn. That was in summer, though." She smiled, but he knew it had been the wrong thing to say – just plain stupid, in fact. Here you are, he thought, here you are riding in a car with a beautiful grown-up woman, and you say something like that. Gawd.

"Ever had shaved ice?" she asked.

"No'm."

"It's Italian, and it's delicious. Some people like it better than ice cream."

Now he remembered: she liked all things foreign, exotic, Mediterranean. And when he saw again the ornate wrought-iron gate at the end of the MacDougal driveway, it made sense. For a ridiculous moment, he imagined that they might have been somewhere in Europe, someplace he had once read about in a social studies book, instead of South Carolina, just outside of the town of Columbia. Up the long drive they went, a trajectory to his immediate destiny, arcing gradually up to the big house that – despite the passing fantasy of Italy – reminded him instantly of MacDougal with its massive, silent stone front. A sense of impending doom came upon him, but he fought the urge to tell her to turn the car around, to redeliver him to the store, to save him from this terrible mistake. He was merely a boy, after all.

Yet when she smiled at him again and then pushed open the front door so that he could walk through first, he felt a thrill skitter through him. And when they stood together by the broad granite counter after she had gotten the ice cream from the freezer and the two bowls from the cabinet, he realized that he was taller than she was by a good five inches: when had that happened? Her fingers brushed his as she handed him a spoon.

"It's good," he said, as he slid the first chilly, creamy bite across his tongue. "What did you put in this?"

"Some pralines. Oh, and some peaches, too."

When they had finished, he walked over to the sink and began to wash his bowl, but she said, "Just leave that. Come on out to the living room and sit on the couch."

"I should be getting back," he said. "I'm not sure if I turned off the lights in the store."

"You did. We did. Work day is over, Mr. Johnson. Like I said, I'm in charge now."

He sat awkwardly, stiffly, with his hands on his knees, and she sat very close to him. What was that smell she had on? In the car, he had breathed it in deeply, trying to decipher it. There was some vanilla in it, and something else just slightly spicy that almost made his nose itch.

"Actually, Mac doesn't talk much about the store. Almost everything I know about you, I learned at dinner that night. So, you like baseball?"

"Yeah." Baseball seemed like a long time ago, but what was it now? Only November.

"And Mac did tell me about your mother. She's ill?"

"She's not ill. She was. She died this past spring. I guess I lied to him about that."

She looked at him with the most sympathetic eyes he had ever seen. "Why?"

"I don't know. It's hard for me to say it. It's almost like it's... too embarrassing."

"I understand." She reached over and stroked his brow. Her hand was cool, and her eyes were deep and warm, somewhere between greenish brown and black. "It's very personal. I lost my mother, too, a couple of years ago.

You feel orphaned. You feel things that people can't understand unless they've been through the same thing."

He nodded.

"Frank. I think you should know that I didn't bring you over here just to feed you ice cream."

He felt his heart begin to pump rapidly, the blood thrusting into his temples. "You didn't?"

"Of course not. That would make you the child, and me the big bad woman, wouldn't it? The evil witch to your Hansel, I suppose. But I haven't just led you into a trap. I thought you needed to come here. You seem so...so all alone in the world."

"I like being alone," he said. "I used to hate it. I was so used to being around my folks, or around the team. Or everybody at church. There was always people around." He almost mentioned Liza, but held back.

"Well, I don't *mind* it," she said, "but I certainly don't like it either. I'm more of a people person. That's another reason why I wanted you to come over. I feel that you and I could be good friends."

"You do? But you're...so smart. Sophisticated." He was pleased to have come up with that word. "Me, I know exactly nothin'."

She giggled girlishly. "The truth is, you're closer to my age than Mac is. I think we *can* be friends."

"I guess we could."

She slid closer to him, her thigh alongside his. "Well, I know so," she insisted. "In fact, we could be very *good* friends."

And then, before he could turn his face or sidle away from her, before he could make any move at all, her face was drawing towards his, and then her lips, softer than anything he had ever felt, were touching his. He felt the tip of her tongue flick across his own. Her eyes were closed, but as she kissed him, she opened them again, and then he felt himself somehow pouring, sliding, swimming in those dark, warm pools.

————

Luther had been to the diner twice now to try and see Liza Applewhite. The first time, a Monday, was her day off, and the second time, yesterday, she had been so busy, balancing massive trays of heavy white plates and tall, sweating tumblers of iced tea, she had only had time to glance over and wave at him as he sat at the counter with his ham sandwich. Today, though, he made sure to come in around midmorning when she might be able to take a break.

She was. She clapped her palm on the bell in the server's window, called out something to the cook, and came over, pulling up a stool opposite him, across the gleaming blue counter. He had already finished his eggs and toast.

"Morning, Pastor Laite," she said.

"Miss Liza. How are you today?"

"Real fine." She smiled, but there were ash-colored circles under her eyes. "More coffee?"

"Why not?" She reached behind her for the silver pot, and as she did so, he noticed again that the sides of her carriage had more curve to them – she no longer possessed the tomboy's stringiness. He wasn't looking with any lurid interest: he felt a strong paternal urge toward this girl, just as he once had felt for Della Treadwell. He cared about what became of her.

"So," he said, "I'll get right to it. I saw you outside the church the other day. You looked worried, but by the time I got out there, you'd hightailed it. So tell me – how are you really?"

She leaned forward and put her elbows on the counter. "I guess nothing gets past you, does it, Pastor? The truth is, I did have a lot on my mind that day. But it's all gonna be all right. I've made a decision. A really big decision, and it involves you, too."

"Oh? And what might that be?"

"I'm getting married. We wanted to ask you if you'll perform the service."

He swallowed a hot gulp of the coffee and nearly sputtered. "Of course I will," he said. "but…who is *we*?"

"I guess you haven't met Carl yet, have you? He's a boy I met in here a couple of months ago."

Lord help us, he thought, but what came out was "Well, that's wonderful news, Liza. Congratulations. But I must admit, I am rather surprised. You're still fairly young."

"I'm nineteen. Tired of living with my mama, to tell you the truth. Time for me to get out on my own for a change. And Carl is so nice. He's – he's the right one for me, I'm sure of it."

So many times in these sorts of instances, Luther had held his tongue, as he would do again this time. You couldn't even explain to young folks when they were being foolish, when they were probably making big mistakes, when they were taking the wrong road. In most cases, you had to let them go on and do it. "I'd be happy to perform your marriage ceremony, but I typically do a brief counseling session beforehand. You know, just to discuss the seriousness of marriage, the sacrifices, the benefits, and the… the dangers involved. The kinds of problems most folks run into."

"Oh, I don't think we'll need that part. Carl and I, we're certain about this. We love each other very much. We know what we're doing. I plan to spend the rest of my life with Carl."

Is that so? he thought. The rest of your life? Well, your life can seem very short or very long, depending on how much misery you're willing to put up with. But instead he said, "But I have to do it, you see. The Methodist Church requires it." That wasn't entirely true, but it ought to have been, as he saw things. "In any case, we have some time to think about it, I assume. Have you set a date yet?"

"We were thinking about doing it on New Year's Day. Start out the year married. That'd be fun."

Hmm. Well, maybe. "All right, then. I'll tell you what, you give it a few days and then drop by the church office to start making some arrangements. We'll go from there."

She nodded, happy and satisfied, but when he was behind the wheel of the station wagon, a sudden thought struck him: her new shapeliness, her obvious distress out on the sidewalk that day… Could it be? He had seen it before, plenty of times. And if she were pregnant, he would, in fact, advise them to get married, so perhaps he should take a different approach to this matter, though he couldn't be very optimistic. Still, he thought, it doesn't do to jump to conclusions.

———

The day of Jack Anders' release from the South Carolina State Penitentiary came after all. Even as he passed through the gates, and then the door, hearing first the perfunctory farewell of the guard there and then the thunderous collision of iron tumblers, he did not feel a sense of jubilation, as he had expected. Instead, he noted calmly that he now knew a thing or two: he knew the long curve of time in prison, the trivialities of the days when one has no choice but to wait, but he also now knew, by the eventuality of this very day, that in truth, in the free world, every day could well be an escape of some sort from the mundane, a movement toward light. He vowed to try and remember that.

And striding intuitively toward the bulky white automobile he saw at the end of the walkway, wearing the same overalls and undershirt he had on when he had arrived here two years earlier, he knew another thing: he wanted to play ball again, for that was what he had missed most, besides his mother and her cooking. However, it was November, and he would have to wait till the spring... but he could do that.

To some degree, as he might have expected, his trust in men had been eroded, but sill he did not have the gnawing bitterness in him, like a stump that has been chewed up, that he had sensed in many other inmates. So, he would play ball again, he would do what was asked of him in order to do the things he wanted to do, and to see the places he wanted to see. That was how it worked.

The passenger-side door of the big white car opened, and this part was just as he had imagined, just as he had hoped. The woman who got out, in a blue-flowered dress, which he recognized instantly, was his mother. At the wheel, leaning over and smiling at him, was his Aunt Teeny. Wordlessly, as if one could actually step into the new world as if it were a robe someone could hold out to you, the man-child walked straight into the woman's arms, and he believed he heard the sound, like windblown branches on a roof, of two years' time sliding away into obsolescence.

Two

March through May, 1960

The old reliable pickup, which her mother's boyfriend had finally given her outright, bit heavily into the gravel as Liza turned down the lane that led to the house she shared with her young husband, Carl. She was Mrs. Carl Dixon now, according to the mail she got, but she supposed in some ways she would always think of herself as plain old Liza Applewhite. All she really knew was that she was happy. Their house was little more than a two-room shack with a stove and an attached bathroom; the iciness of late February made the nights and the mornings somewhat uncomfortable (the place was poorly insulated, but Carl was skilled in all manner of things and had promised to fix it), but there was nothing better in life than lying close to the man you loved under heavy quilts and with the curtains open, so that the sharp winter stars looked in on them, magnificent and affirming.

She was five months along with her baby, and she had made Carl leave the Christmas lights up because they reminded her that by *next* Christmas, they would have a child of their own, and their lives would be different ever afterward; the people they had been before would never be again, would be cast off like old skins or shells. She hardly ever thought of those dark days of her adolescence, and though she now realized that her association with the Treadwells, stained by misfortune though it was, had been a significant part of her own healing. No one had heard anything of Frankie since last August, and some, including Pastor Laite, said they feared for his safety; as for her, she was certain that he was all right, he was someplace, probably with that uncle, or else in some detention center somewhere. He was a boy, and she now could barely believe she had even imagined she might have had some sort of feelings for him once. He was not the man she had always needed, he was a boy who had cared only about a boy's things and who had run away, like a boy, when the reality of death had become more than he could handle.

Carl was nothing like that. He took care of things. He took care of her. He worked, he made money, and he could fix things. This very moment, she was smiling as she made her way toward the house, for she could see from the lamplight inside that he was home; she'd had to take an extra half-shift at the diner, but it felt so nice to find him waiting there for her, her man. Perhaps they would make love right away, as they often did in the evenings, worrying about supper later. He seemed not in the least put off by her ripe belly, but he was, of course, greatly interested in her ever-enlarging breasts. That was fine; in fact, it had never been so good. Despite her past, which had shamed her terribly, she had never really known much at all about men, about how good they could really be.

She had her house key, naturally, but she knocked because she wanted him to open the door for her. It swung inward, and there he was, shirtless despite the cold, smiling back at her. He was her man, by God, and she had given to him everything she had; shaking and frightened, although she had said nothing of its origin, she had given him her pain, and love had erased it.

————

Banks had made contact with nearly every man of authority and/or influence he knew, in South Carolina and beyond, but no one had ever heard of his nephew, Frank Treadwell. Of course, the Dillon County Sheriff's Office had published a missing-person report last summer, but nobody seemed particularly worried, aside from that preacher, who telephoned him once a week or so. Everybody else said the same thing: happens all the time, a kid turns fifteen, sixteen, something at home goes awry, and poof, he's gone. He'll probably turn up eventually.

Exasperated, Banks had been just about to give up on the whole idea when he suddenly remembered something Luther Laite had said in one of their first conversations after Bob's funeral: the kid was a hell of a ballplayer, an avowed phenomenon. If that was so, then he could not have achieved that sort of success without a special kind of obsession and a good deal of hard work, or so Banks believed, at least. Talent could only take you so far; Christ, everybody has talent of one sort or another. But how many people, even a kid, ever reach the point where others are willing to genuinely acknowledge someone else's success?

The point was that in about one month, in big and little towns far and wide, baseball was about to awaken again, to stretch, rouse itself, and begin its long season anew. Did it not make sense that a kid with that sort of obsession and skill would turn up on some green field someplace, in a youth league, maybe, or at the very least in the stands at a game somewhere? The trick would be to formulate a strategy, to figure out a way to sweep those places, as it were, in order to have a chance at finding him.

Karen came downstairs, sleepy and lovely in her sheer nightie, and she joined him at the marble breakfast counter. She crossed her long bare legs, the flesh of her thighs flexing and golden in the morning light that streamed in through the big bay window. "I love these winter mornings out here," she said. "Have you noticed how the water seems to be a deeper shade of blue lately?"

Banks nodded. "I'll start a fire for you," he said. As much as he had tried to grow bored with her, to find small things about her annoying, to discern reasons to move on to a new one, he had been unable to dismiss his growing attachment to this woman. She asked little of him, and she seemed unconcerned with pretense. The idea that he had money seemed to matter little to her; she enjoyed simple things – a hissing fire on a cold February morning, a warm quilt, and she performed the simplest tasks with a grace and naturalness he had not found in any other. Without makeup, this very moment, disheveled and still a little groggy, her hair unbrushed, she might have just emerged from the Forest of Arden.

"I'm fine," she said. "I'll probably go into town today, pick up some groceries. Are you going in to the office?"

"M-hm. You can give me a lift. Gotta make some phone calls."

"Have you heard anything yet?" She placed her bare feet on the rung of his barstool.

"Regarding?"

"Frank. Who else would I be referring to?"

"I guess I'm easy to read."

"Look," she said, running her cool fingers along his jaw line. "I'll say it again. I'm willing to help. Just give me a hint as to where to start."

He was about to say what he had already said a dozen times, that she needn't be bothered, that it wasn't her concern, but now it occurred to him that she really could be of some use in this matter. It required no additional commitment between them, and it was, after all, quite an undertaking for one person.

So it was that the look in her eyes passed from astonishment to avidness when he said, "All right, then, let's get started. You can help me begin compiling some information and some new lists of people to call."

"Great," she said, "I'll be ready in five minutes," and started to scurry up the carpeted steps, but then turned. "Oh, wait. Do you have a picture of the boy?"

Banks reached across the breakfast bar counter and picked up his wallet. He opened it and then produced two very small black and white photos.

"I clipped these out of his high-school yearbook." One was the standard headshot: Frankie gazed in near bewilderment at the camera, a half-smile just beginning to play at the corners of his mouth; he wore a checkered shirt with a collar; crew cut. The other was from the sports section: Frank in uniform, on one knee, one hand braced firmly upon the barrel of a bat, the handle of which ran along his upper arm.

"Handsome kid," she said. "He looks like you."

Banks made no reply, but slipped the pictures back into the wallet, and then in a single furious gesture, jammed the wallet into his back pocket.

————

For Frank, March, with its first suggestions of spring – small pockets of warmth such as a swimmer might experience when passing through drafts of sun-heated water in a dark river – brought an odd mix of feelings and impressions. Some were familiar to him, certainly, as they touched upon the membrane of his memory, his fast-twitch tendons and intuitive responses, all of which was the result of ten years of playing baseball, of aligning his body's rhythm with those of the weather and the grass and the dirt and the weight of a small, hard, horsehide-covered ball from spring until the autumn. But some of them were unfamiliar, for they were not of the child's world he had always known. For one, there was the strangeness of not being in school, of being far from the home he had known, of the great absence in his life which he could never quite grasp or even think upon deliberately: that of his mother.

And then there was Allison MacDougal. He could quite easily have recounted the events, the conversations, the small decisions that had led to their association, but he could scarcely imagine that he, Frankie, had actually been part of all that had transpired between them since November. Sometimes just thinking of her and of the things they had done and would do again thrilled him to his core, and other times it all made him unutterably sad, as if some great stone had been embedded in his chest and was wearing away at him from the inside out. In spite of the lustful flames that had burned in him as hotly as in any other male his age, he had always believed that coming to know a woman sexually would be part of his transcendence to manhood, that something inside him would be settled, that the trivialities and tortures of youth would begin to abate, but in fact this was not so. If anything, most often he felt more childlike, ruled by the absurdities that inflamed his brain and imprisoned his reason. Often he was angry with her for no reason at all, he would find suspicion in her smallest gestures and facial expressions, rail at her for what she was – a vivacious young woman who had married well but not for love, and who practiced abject and often tyrannical control over him with no fear of retribution and no remorse. He could not comprehend how she could be so elegant and yet so cruel at once.

At other times, the depth of his need for her startled him. Whenever they were together – and it happened each time MacDougal was out of town on business, and also when he was in town, in certain clandestine places (numerous times in Frank's small back room and even twice in the shop's stockroom), for him it was immersion in a kind of ecstasy unmatched in his experience, a new world of near madness with many doors to many unnamed pleasures, visceral tunnels that took him into places of such red and blinding passion that he thought he might simply mutate into some other form of life which would be something akin to an elongated, pulsing piece of flesh whose sole function would be to give and receive pleasure. And she had taught him everything – how to use his hands and fingers and mouth and that part of himself which she always referred to as "the object of her longing" all in order to satisfy her small body. Sometimes he believed they might actually devour one another, or that he might somehow fall into the seething pool that her body seemed to become, and lose all sense of himself.

Oh, sometimes they talked, lying there naked to one another in thought, word, and deed, with a half-consumed bottle of La Donna Rosa on the bedside table. At her place, they always used the downstairs guest room he had occupied on his very first night here, for he had at least resisted her attempts to take him up to the bed she shared with MacDougal (that would have been too much). At such times, the raw nerve of his pain would expose itself, and he had talked to her more than once of his mother, if only to recall aloud a few little things – the way she slept with her Bible on her chest, the way she hummed little tunes to herself – as if to scratch the bronze of the monument to her that he had built within himself. Once or twice he had been near tears, but then inevitably he would suddenly cast memory aside, turn to her, allow her to swallow him up again, retreat into her, hide in her, listen to her talk so sweetly about her own life: her father was Cuban and her mother was from Florida and her name had been Allison Lopez and she had been born and raised in Tampa and had once known how to speak Spanish but now couldn't remember much and she had met Mac quite by chance in the train station in Jacksonville and they had married after only a few weeks though her dream had been to travel the world and then her mother had fallen ill and died and they had bought this house and one thing had led to another and now she was stuck here and only saw her father once a year at Easter but all in all she was quite happy in any case and especially now that she had someone to talk to.

Then, when they would part, he would revel for a time in the scent she had left on his body, walking the streets of the town, breathing her in once again, feeling again the slow, rhythmic caress of her dark hair across his chest, the hot bands of her slender fingers on his shoulders and neck, the pressure of her mouth against his, and his only wish would be to return to her, be with her, without the worldly intrusion of time. That is, until he would at last go back to the store and see some object that reminded him of MacDougal – a fountain pen, a rumpled newspaper, a spare pair of boots, and then the horrible guilt would begin its slow, dreadful descent upon him. Why, oh, why had he allowed himself to get into such a situation, to be so ensnared, to so easily compromise every notion of decency he had ever been taught in his life? How could he so betray the man who had given him a job and a sense of order after his long, aimless journey, who had treated him like a son? To boot, he had betrayed the memory of his mother, and of the man his father had been in better times, and everything that Pastor Laite had stood for as well. He was only beginning to realize the meaning of all that he had heard in that church, in the Sunday School lessons, in the youth ministry campouts, and it was not just the sin of fornication; oh, no, it was far more than that: it was the sin of betrayal – betrayal of the living and the dead and of his own soul which had been untainted until only a few short months ago. Over and over, he determined that he would not go back to Allison.

It was in the clutches of such a cycle of desire and despair that he roamed out late one afternoon, after the two of them had met again in his little back-room hovel, far beyond the town limits to where the pastures had begun to show the first traces of green. He had forced himself to rise from between her supple legs there on the little cot, dressed himself, and stumbled out into the waning light. He had turned down a clay road, hardly knowing where he was, when he heard a familiar sound: it was the popping of baseballs in leather mitts. It was a small sound, even trivial, but for him there was great power in it. He rounded a short bend and there they were – a group of young men in gray sweats and caps, two lines facing one another, playing catch.

Instantly, a ball sailed over the split rail fence and directly for his head, and he reached up with his right hand and let it nestle silently into his palm. He shifted it to his throwing hand, looked down at the perfect red stitches, and then looked up to where the boy (or perhaps he was older) who had made the errant throw stood staring at him from roughly two hundred feet away. With no thought whatsoever in his head, Frank took a half-step and fired it back on a straight, sharp line, and the boy caught it at chest level. He realized that all of the players had stopped to watch him, but now they turned wordlessly and went back to their warm-up.

After a moment, a man in khaki pants and a short red jacket approached the fence, his hands in his pockets. He smiled, pleasant lines crinkling up around his lips and eyes. Good arm ya' got there," he said. "You a ballplayer?"

"Used to be," Frank said.

"Well, we're about to shag some fly balls. Why don't you stick around and take a few?"

"Ain't got a glove."

"I think I've got a couple extra in the equipment bag yonder. Then I'm gonna toss some batting practice to these fellas, too, if that sort of thing appeals to you. This here is the American Legion team, Post 3."

Weeks later, he would not be able to recall exactly what had transpired, and in truth, sometimes he would wonder whether it had even been real. He had simply poured his exasperation, his frustration, his joy, his emotional energy into two hours' worth of running, catching, throwing, and most redeemingly, in crushing those small, perfect white spheres with a wooden bat, farther and farther out into the most remote corners of the pasture and finally beyond the tall pines that had grown ever grayer in the lengthening afternoon.

At twilight, feeling greatly cleansed, washed, in fact, in the pure blood of his greatest love and the thing (as he saw now) that he was truly meant for, he returned to his little room. Allison was gone, but on his pillow was a little folded note. It read:

> *Mac is leaving tonight for Raleigh. I need the object of my longing. I long for it. I insist upon it. Bring it to me, please.*
>
> - *A*

He wadded it, turned, threw it into the metal waste basket. For the next half-hour, he lay on his cot, slowly smelling the sweat from his exertions at the pasture mixing with her scent, hoping to feel tired, wishing desperately for merciful sleep to come upon him. But sleep would not come.

He got up, went out to the shop's counter, put his hand on the telephone, waited. Then he picked up the receiver and dialed the MacDougals' number.

Her voice licked at his ear: "I'll pick you up in fifteen minutes."

"Fine," he heard himself say.

———

"Jackie! Supper!"

Having just turned back up the very last row of the bean field, he now paused at the husky sound of his mother's voice, looked up toward the house, and nodded. He removed the sling of the burlap bag from his shoulder and tossed it into the grass. It was still early spring, and the thin sheen of sweat across his shoulders cooled him as he trudged up the long furrow, and by the time he reached the porch, it had evaporated altogether.

It felt good to have been out in the field. He felt that since he had gotten home again, right on through Christmas, New Years, and then through the savagely cold days of February, he had done little except eat. He would sit down at the table, and before him would appear a plate of something – grits (sometimes with bacon), two peanut butter sandwiches, half a chicken, boiled okra with tomatoes and rice, a helping of beans with molasses and cornbread slowly soaking into it, and on exceptionally good days, pecan pie with ice cream or milk… Somehow, he never felt quite filled up; his stomach was like a hole that simply expanded with each mouthful, but oddly enough, with renewed physical activity, he didn't seem quite so hungry.

His mother turned from the big stove. "You going back out to the field before sundown?"

"No'm. Going to play ball tonight." He had waited to tell her, for he was uncertain what her response would be. He knew she still regarded baseball as a boy's game, even though she had never said as much, but he hoped she would understand that it was something he believed he had to do.

"What game you going to?"

"Just some a' them boys up from Taylorville. Making up a team."

She stared at him for a moment, her eyes narrow and black, and then she turned around. Silence seemed to fill the room like airy cotton.

"All right," he said. "I'll go back out to the bean field, then."

Now she set down the spoon and put her head down. "Son…" He looked at the angled set of her big shoulders as she leaned there, and he suddenly felt sorry for her.

"No, Mama. I feel like planting them beans."

"Son, it ain't that I don't want you to play ball. I want you to do what you like. It's just that I worry about you getting into trouble again."

"I don't intend to."

"You know as well as I do that it don't matter what you don't intend. It matters where you go and who else is coming."

"It's just a buncha them colored boys up to Taylorville. They want to make up a team, maybe get a few games. That's all."

She nodded, and then she made that small movement which is the iconic gesture of suffering mothers: she dabbed at the corner of her eye with the hem of her apron. "I know. I know. You'll be fine. Go ahead and go. Just be careful."

When he had found the worn, wrinkled glove below his bed and had left the house, passing beneath the thick, late-afternoon shade of the japonica tree and through the little wire gate, he kept thinking of her, how she had waited for him for so long, probably pined for him, all the while blaming herself for what had happened. He thought of the way she had forbidden specific people coming to the house since he'd been back, even Tol, who meant no real harm but who was likely to show up with a bottle. Even though he was eighteen, soon to be nineteen, he was her child, and he understood that, but she could not have understood what he felt as he turned up the road with his glove tucked under his arm, the jubilant wave of freedom that seemed to surge under him and lift him, the wonder that seemed to pour in at his eyes like streams of pure light, a bending road, an open sky, a line of evergreen tops rather than a turreted wall – those simple sorts of things the deprivation of which constitutes the true torment of the prisoner.

He began to trot, and soon, because it was that time of the day when the cool dryness of the air seemed to float through his body, so that there was no resistance, no separation between himself and the swatches of light and shadow all around him, he began to sprint. The cool air passed through him as through a humming engine, and before he realized it, he had traveled the two miles to the scraggly field where the boys, many of them in overalls, with no shirts or shoes, like himself, were milling about talking and laughing, some of them beginning to toss a ball around, one or two of them with bats, swinging away at invisible tailing fastballs.

A big-chested boy he had known for many years, Oscar, grinned and waved and came over to greet him.

"Heard you's back," he said.

"They wanted to keep me. Said they'd never seen nobody like me before. I woulda stayed, too, but Mama made me come home."

It was the old easy banter with someone he knew well, another thing he had missed without realizing it.

"When's the last time you hefted a bat?"

"Lemme think... 'Bout two and a half years, I reckon."

"Well, you back in it now. Let's throw some."

Thus his renewal had begun, and the ancient pattern of his folk continued to unfold: capture, oppression, and the worst sorts of degradation; endurance through patience, and finally, renewal and rejuvenation. On into the evening, even when they could no longer see the ball anymore except as a white, moth-like fluttering thing against the twilight (and yet still could catch it, fling it, strike it adroitly, as if it were bright daylight), they forgot for a little while whether they were grown men or small boys.

———————

For MacDougal, life was proceeding much more smoothly now that Frank had learned the store. The kid was smart, no question, and Mac had no qualms at all about taking the truck or the train up to Raleigh at least once a month on buying expeditions. He typically left on a Friday afternoon, so as to be gone only one day at a time, since a kid was still a kid after all; and after all, Allison could probably handle any truly important issues that came up.

How he had grown to love these trips, especially by train, despite the decrepitude of the north-running railway; he seemed to relax as soon as he put his hand on the polished wooden railing and hoisted himself on board. He hoped to bring his wife with him sometime soon. Still, it was satisfying to immerse himself in this man's world: the single car with the torn green-leather sofa and the aged, neatly attired colored porter bringing him his cigar and whiskey without him asking, and a newspaper. He had always loved trains, these hulking metal cars like sleek (if ailing) silver and red beasts, the smells of the oil and boiling coffee in the stations, and even though it was clear that the burgeoning interstate system would soon render the passenger rail obsolete, he clung to the experience not only because he had met his beloved in a train station but also because it reminded him of his father. When Mac was a child, his father had often taken him to Atlanta and Jacksonville on the train, and those journeys had filled him with wonder. He had a clear recollection of a slick-haired man who ran a snack stand at the Jacksonville station, who sold pineapple juice so sweet Mac's tongue still puckered whenever he thought of it, the rare, recollected sweetness of his childhood. He had even enjoyed the troop trains when he was in the army; there was nothing quite so nice as a pleasant card game by rail-car light, with a bunch of buddies around.

That – the army – was also where he had acquired his knowledge of goods. He had served as a supply sergeant at Fort Bragg during the war, never seeing overseas duty. The details of supplies had absorbed him entirely – handling them, recording them, and all the numerical accounting that went along with it. He suspected that such a life as he was still pursuing had damaged him socially; in essence, he sometimes felt that he did not know how to talk to people. That was one reason he liked Frank: the boy did not require much conversation, and often they would work through an entire day in the store with barely a word between them, either wrapped in a comfortable silence or with the radio going.

Allison was a different case, of course. He never intended being gruff with her, but he knew he often appeared to her in this way. It was not that he had no thought to offer; it was just that when he was around her, the words would not come, or else they got packed away deep down in his head somewhere. But he knew her, he knew that she tolerated his silences, and she cared for him and cooked and cleaned, and she went to church even on those Sundays when he had not yet returned from his buying trips, and the time went on. Sex between them (and for some reason, Wednesday night had become their "serata speciale," as she put it) was not exactly vigorous anymore, but it fell well within the range of "normal" marriages, he figured.

Petway opened the glass door, a half-tumbler full of amber whiskey in his hand. There was no club car on this train, but the thoughtful old fellow kept a bottle hidden someplace for his special customers. He flashed his toothy African smile and said, "Refreshment, sir?"

"Ah." He artfully slipped a dollar bill into the porter's palm as he took the glass. "You're a good man, Petway."

Petway removed his cap, thumbed the bill into the inside rim, and said, "Thank you for riding with us, sir."

His standard reply – "The riding is the easy part" – was the signal to himself: he was settled in, and he could now pull out the newspaper and stare at the photos, or simply look out the window and watch the fields and woods roll by. When he arrived in Raleigh, there would be a good steak dinner and a hotel bed with clean, cool sheets; in the morning there would be a factory tour, merchandise to scrutinize and handle, and then another good meal. And on Sunday, home and Allison.

"This ain't too bad," he said to himself, as he let the good, lively, friendly whiskey wash over his lips and gums like a warm balm.

———

The ritual of her two cigarettes with Robley, whenever they took their break in the lot behind the diner, remained Liza's only vice. It wasn't even the smoking so much as it was the conversation, for the comfortable and often comical banter between them had evolved into a genuine friendship, and here on the cracked and weed-fringed asphalt, amid random powders of broken glass and dirty puddles and seated upon two weathered old crates, they sometimes shared the intimate details of their lives.

Robley snapped shut his zip lighter with a metallic click. "Little Queen Bee really is a queen now," he said. "Carrying that little prince, ain't she?"

It was now late April, and she was well into the sixth month of her pregnancy. She patted her belly.

"Got a name for it yet?"

"We're just calling it 'It' right now. But if it comes out a boy, we'll probably call it after Carl."

"Nothing wrong with that. Daddy behaving hisself, too?"

"Carl can do no wrong. He gets his good nature from his mama, I think. That man works harder than just about anybody I ever met, up and gone with the sunrise and home late every night."

"Must be building a lotta roads 'round here these days." Robley swatted at the smoke that surrounded his smooth brown head.

"He's doing carpentry now, too. Traveling as far as Myrtle Beach and Hilton Head, some days. Says there's a lot of hotels and bars and the like going up there. And people putting houses on stilts."

"My, my," Robley said, rubbing his forehead. "What's next? Apartments on the moon?"

"I don't know, but I'm glad for it. We was gonna fix up that place we got now, but lately Carl's been talking about moving into town once the baby gets born. That way maybe my mama could help us sometimes."

"Mm-hmm. Nice to have family around, ain't it?"

"Funny how people start behaving so good when there's a baby coming. At first Mama and Roger was upset with me. Carl and I wasn't married then, you know. But now that everything is how it's supposed to be, she's been as sweet as pie."

"Having children can change you, that's sure." Robley stared at his shoes, suddenly lost in reflection. "I remember when my two boys was coming up. They was wild sometimes, all right, but I never could even raise my voice at 'em, let alone my hand. I was too soft. I left all that to their mother."

"Well, they turned out all right, didn't they?"

"Turned out right well. Both up in Raleigh now, you know. One drives a truck, and t'other paints houses."

"Good working men," Liza said.

"Got to. Can't depend on Mama and Daddy all they lives. Onliest thing is, it all went by so fast. I miss having 'em at home. Seem like the distance between hello and goodbye ain't no time at all. All's I can advise you, Queen Bee, is to try and enjoy 'em while they little."

"Oh, I will. And I'll tell you something else. How about I bring the baby up to your place in Moccasin Bluff sometime? Would your missus be willing to sit with it sometime if my mama ain't available? I'd pay her."

Robley grinned, removed the cigarette from his lips, dropped it, and crushed it under his boot's heel. "'Course she will, course she will. She'd love nothin' better."

"Wonderful." Liza patted her belly again and tucked in the front of her blouse. "Reckon we better get back to the salt mines."

Robley went back to his station at the big steel sinks, and she went back out front. In the deep yawn of the afternoon, the diner was deserted. Nevertheless, there was always plenty to do: refill salt and pepper shakers, replace ketchup, mustard, and mayo, bundle napkins and silverware, sweep and mop under the tables (especially where families with children had been sitting), and, if time allowed the luxury, count her tips for the morning. Usually the money was pretty good – her regular customers were reliable and appreciative; she was a good waitress, although – aside from Carl – she never allowed herself to become too friendly with any of them, the way some of the other girls did. Even when Luther Laite came in, generally at least once a week, she seldom stopped to chat, but he often brought paperwork in with him anyway and did a good deal of reading and writing over coffee and toast. It was reassuring to see him there, tall, dignified man in his light-blue seersucker suit (even in winter), high white collar, and graying hair.

Continuity – that was the word. She had only been in his church three times, that she could recall: on the occasion of the funerals of first Mrs. Treadwell and, shortly thereafter, Mr. Treadwell, and then for her own wedding. She would undoubtedly go there again when the time came to baptize her first child. And yet Pastor Laite seemed a significant par of her daily life in Dillon, as if he were as permanent as the oldest brick house in town, or the ancient, solid oak of which his own church's front door was made. Others might come and go, she thought, but Luther would always be here.

Frankie strayed into her thoughts, and some little spark deep within her scratched at the wall of memory, troubling her for a moment. All of that seemed long ago now, though it was only a year since it had all started. How quickly the wheel had turned, and how different her life was now.

And now suddenly, she realized that she truly wished to know that Frank was all right, that he was safe somewhere. Perhaps she would stop by the church office on her way home and see if there had been any word of him. Otherwise, she would have to wait until the pastor came in next for breakfast. It struck her that she had given him a photo of herself and a few 45 rpm records, but she had nothing of his, no shard or trace or trinket to show that he had even been a part of her life at all. Robley had said, "Seems like the distance between hello and goodbye ain't no time at all." Amen. There was truth in the man, certainly.

The little bell over the door rattled, and she turned her attention back to her work as the first customers for the lunch shift began to arrive.

———

Banks grabbed the jangling phone and stuck it to his ear. He had been gazing out the big jalousie window, tracing the steady progress of a sloop across the slate-blue bay, but as usual his mind had been very far away. He had deliberately moved his office out here, to this boathouse off a remote point, but now he found that work was the last thing he could focus on.

It was Karen's milky voice: "Hey, what are you doing?"

"Thinking."

"What are you thinking about?"

"You." That wasn't true, and she would know it, but he would have been hard-pressed to articulate the sort of strange thoughts that had been passing through his mind lately – of land, raw and untamed and wild with rivers and wild beasts, of great ships and their masters, of numbers running along an endless ticker tape, but most of all, of the nephew he had never met.

"I think I've got a lead for you," Karen said.

He stood up. "Say that again."

"I've got a lead for you."

He clutched at his collar and loosened it. "Come on, then, let's hear it."

"Give me a chance. What's your schedule tomorrow? We'll have to drive over to Columbia."

"We'll leave tonight. Now, let's hear it."

She paused in what he knew was an effort to calm him, but it only served to constrict his breathing even further. "There's a kid playing American Legion baseball in the Columbia area. They say he's head and shoulders above the rest of the league. A phenom. His name is Frank Johnson, and no one seems to know anything about him."

"How'd you hear about him?"

He heard the rustling of a newspaper. "I've been scanning the sports pages around the state," she said. "This is a headline from *The State*: 'A Man Among Men, Though Still Just a Boy.' It also says he's presently being scouted by the Cincinnati Reds, whose single-A affiliate plays in Columbia."

"Damn it," Banks said. "I've just suddenly come to the realization that I know squat about baseball. What the hell is 'single A'"?

"You've been working too much. You should take time out, enjoy yourself sometimes, go to a game. Single-A means they're pretty far down the ladder from the major leagues, but lots of players start there and work their way up. Triple-A is the highest level for minor leaguers. Somebody in the Reds organization must have heard about him, seen him play or something."

"Is there a picture?"

"No picture."

"Does it say how old he is?"

"Eighteen."

"Might not be him."

"Might not, but it might. Don't you think it's worth going over there?"

"Of course we're going over there. I'm just trying to be realistic."

They drove over that evening in the Plymouth and took a suite at the Sheraton Hotel, where they ordered room service (stuffed flounder, house salad, champagne) and made an early night of it. Still, Banks could not sleep. Various scenarios for tomorrow afternoon, when they would go to see Frank Johnson play baseball, kept playing through his mind. How would he approach the boy? Does one just walk up to him, he wondered, and say, "Hey there, son, I believe I might be your uncle." He entertained one plan whereby he might trick Frankie, if indeed he were the right Frankie, by simply calling out, "Treadwell!" And then, if it really did turn out to be him, what would his next course of action be? Should he inform the authorities? Persuade him to go home to Dillon? Wrestle him into the car and take him back to Hilton Head?

Such thoughts gnawed at his brain until he got up, walked over to the window, drew back the curtain, and stared down at the shadow-laden parking lot below. A few moments later, he heard Karen stirring. He had almost forgotten she was here; good girl that she was, she had known when to leave him be, and she had not even said anything when she had looked over his shoulder at the front desk, where he had signed them in as Mr. and Mrs. Banks Berenger. Now he heard the clink of the bottle, the glugging liquid, and then she approached him with two glasses of champagne.

"I know what's eating at you," she said.

"Do you?"

"Not enough champagne. And we didn't even toast."

"What is there to toast, exactly?"

She handed him the drink and then placed her soft cheek on his shoulder. "To family reunions," she said, touching the lip of her glass to his.

"Okay," he said, still gazing down to the gray and black murk below them, where no light seemed to reach. "Whatever you say."

————

"What do *I* think? You're asking *me*?"

Alison MacDougal stood with her hands on her bare hips, gazing at him where he lay on his back on the tall guest-room bed. As she extended her chin for emphasis, her plump breasts were jostled just slightly.

"Course I'm asking you," Frank said. "Why wouldn't I ask you? Who else would I? Who else even cares?"

"Mac cares." He was about to reply to this, but a subtle change in her facial set showed that she immediately understood the irony in her response. "Well, I know it seems crazy coming from me," she added, "but he really does."

"Maybe the two of you should just adopt me."

"Don't think it hasn't crossed my mind."

Unable to tell whether she was kidding, he sat up, pulled on his boxer shorts, and stood up. As was often the case after their liaisons, he had no impulse to touch her, even though she walked around the edge of the bed and stood very close to him, her face near his. "I have to go to the bathroom," he said.

"Anyway, aren't you too young to sign a professional contract?" she asked.

"Mickey Mantle was fifteen when he started playing semi-pro. Besides, they think I'm eighteen."

"No doubt you could pass for that. Nothin' little about you." She placed her hand on his chest and pushed him back onto the bed.

"Look," he said. "I can't stay. That fella from the Reds is going to be at the game again, and I want to be ready."

"Hmm." She looked him up and down wantonly. "How much did you say they're offering you?"

"They haven't offered me anything yet. But he mentioned five hundred just for signing. Two thousand for the rest of the season."

"Doesn't sound like much."

"It's damn good. Some of those guys will play for supper and a room."

"Then I suppose you really should do it. If they offer it, that is."

"Yep."

"I'll be there today. Look for me along the fence."

"Yep."

When he had gotten dressed and she had dropped him off at the store, and he had grabbed the little bag with the new glove she had bought for him, and then headed up to the field, he realized he had not really meant that business about wanting to be ready. Generally, he never even felt he needed to warm up. His arm always felt loose, his legs were always warm... It was as if his body was made for one thing, which was in actuality comprised of four things: running, throwing, catching, and hitting. And even though his days as a high-school player seemed long ago, he had at last seen with stunning clarity that it was all one, that these teams, their demands and degree of challenge, could come and go, and he would continue to perform, almost without thinking. He still believed it was hard, of course: it required concentrated effort, down to the finest detail, but he never worried anymore that he might not be as good as the other players. Truthfully, he knew that he was better than they were.

Yet, more than ever, he loved being part of a team again. He loved jogging with the team from fence to fence across the green meadow of the outfield, he loved sitting in the cool dugout and being part of the happy chatter, and he loved standing with the numbers one and two hitters (he batted in the three slot) in the on-deck area, bats across their shoulders, critiquing the opposing pitcher as he warmed up, kicking high. And when the conversation turned to women, even though he did not speak up about his experiences, a certain satisfaction glowed in him warmly, as he thought of the thorough and vigorous education Alison MacDougal had given him.

Whenever she attended a game alone, she stood by the fence, far down along the third base line so as not to attract too much attention to herself, where she would clap meekly and smile whenever Frank hit safely or made a play in the outfield. When Mac came with her, they sat together in the bleachers eating popcorn or hot dogs. He didn't mind: it reminded him of the old days, when his mother and father would both come to the games, and all was well. On those infrequent days when he made an error or struck out, then, as his parents had used to do, they would either say nothing at all or they would shout encouragement, and he would hear Mr. MacDougal's booming voice: "Shake it off, Frank. It's all right, son."

Of course, it didn't really matter whether they were there or not. He had gotten used to being alone, to doing everything alone. In the end, you were alone: you were alone when the ball was sent shatteringly high and deep into the sky over you, for only you could make the play, and you had to live with the consequences one way or the other. You were alone when you stepped into the batter's box and scratched out the ruts with your cleats, and you were alone when the pitcher looked down at you menacingly from the mound and then coiled into his windup. And then you were alone with the ball. Certainly there were those moments when you played for the team, when you would lay down a clean bunt to advance a runner to second or third, or make sure you got the ball in the air to the outfield to allow a teammate to tag up, but even then, there was no hiding. There was nothing in between utter success and abject failure, and there was no second chance at any play.

So it was that under the cold scrutiny of the scout from the Cincinnati Reds, he would feel no anxiety. He was excited, and he wanted to play well, but whatever must happen, it would happen to him alone and he would live with it. For now there was only the simple pleasure of trotting up the road leading out of town, arriving at the freshly mown, county-maintained field where the Post 3 team played their games in the bright sunshine, replying in kind to the happy greetings of his teammates, buttoning up and tucking in his uniform shirt, and taking his spot in the line for warm-up toss.

Banks and Karen attempted to appear inconspicuous as they gingerly ascended the faded green bleacher seats, feeling their way as if intoxicated, finally settling on the mostly vacant top row. Karen spread the red-checked towel on the seat in front of her and laid out the two sandwiches the hotel had made for them, along with two cans of soda, and then she glanced over at Banks and shrugged her shoulders as if to say, Well, at least we're here.

He smiled. "Kinda warm today."

"It's nice," she said.

A few parents sat here and there, the fathers reclining, elbows propped behind them, the mothers chatting with one another across their husbands' stomachs, rolling their eyes and laughing freely over stories of their errant sons' slovenliness and absurdities, then nodding approvingly at accounts of the same boys' good manners and honorable deeds. There were a few girls as well, all of them teenagers, as near as Banks could tell, in cutoff jeans and t-shirts, hair done up in sassy ponytails and French braids. A heavyset mother arrived, winded and apparently tardy for her duties, and opened the little portable concession stand behind the backstop; after a few moments, she swung the battered shutters outward and began rummaging in the steel cooler within.

Outside the chain-link fence on the third-base side were two more people: a thin man in a grey suit and yellow tie, with a small spiral notebook dangling from one hand, who was gazing out toward the tree line like a blind seer; a few feet farther down was an attractive woman in a simple white blouse and tailored skirt, who was too young to be a parent and yet too old to be a player's girlfriend. She was peering intently into the darkness of the third-base dugout, her lush, dark-brown hair spilling over her shoulder.

As for the players themselves, they all seemed to be between the ages of sixteen and twenty-one. It was easy to distinguish the younger from the older, for those boys who were still in high school were skinny and rangy, a bit less confident in their bearing, with blossoms of acne on their faces, while the older ones were beefier, with square shoulders and tough, protruding chins, some of them swathed by five o'clock shadow.

At a signal from one of the umpires (there were two of them, both in white short sleeves and dark pants, the one behind the plate holding his bulky chest protector and face mask along his side), the Post 3 team took the field, sprinting out to their positions.

"That's him," Karen said. "Number four. Plays center field."

Banks watched him run: there was an easy confidence in his gait, and he was one of the stronger-looking kids on the team. "I don't think that's him," Banks said. "He looks too old."

"Let's wait till we get a better look," Karen said.

Baseballs flew about during the final warm-up, as the outfielders made arcing tosses to one another and the first baseman launched skittering ground balls at his fellow infielders, amid spatterings of orange dust, as pleasant male chatter filled the air. And the pitcher, oblivious to all the activity around him, as if he were not even remotely involved in whatever was about to take place, gazed intently down into the catcher's mitt as though to read a tiny, inscribed message there. Then he took a step back, kicked his thick front leg up, slipped the ball from his glove, and fired it to home place. He then repeated this exact motion.

"Play ball!" the umpire brayed.

Suddenly, mysteriously, a curious tension filled the air. There was a buzzing chatter from both teams, jarring and nervous yet at the same time soothing, and there hung the sensation that something could happen, that indeed something inevitably *would* happen.

And yet nothing did. The first hitter struck out, the second walked, and the third hit into a routine double play, and Post 3 came in to bat. The aroma of broiling hot dogs had begun to float around them as the mother-in-charge at the concessionaire had apparently gotten things in order, and everyone present luxuriated in those few delicious minutes just before the catcher flung the ball down to second base and the leadoff hitter, his off-white uniform with blue letters suddenly blazing to life as he stepped into the bright sunshine, dug in at the plate. The Post 17 pitcher wound up, a short, nearly awkward motion, and threw a looping curve that seemed to buzz just under the hitter's chin. But it was a strike. The batter tugged at the shoulders of his uniform, nodded down at the first-base coach, and with new purpose in him, got set once again. This time the pitch came streaking over the outside corner, and the little leadoff man lashed at it, smashing it down the right-field line for a double. He pulled up, standing, at second and clapped for himself.

"There ya' go," Banks said.

The next hitter, a lanky high-school boy who appeared almost afraid, walked uncertainly to the plate. Frank Johnson, number four, came to the on-deck circle and began swinging two bats together, letting them flop first around his shoulders and around and down at an invisible ball between his knees.

"There he is," Karen said.

Banks looked at him intently, studying him. He was not particularly tall, but strangely, he seemed larger than he actually was. He was trim and muscular, with the hardness of a grown man about his neck and forearms. But it was the jaw-line, thin, taut, somewhat abbreviated, but with a twist to it that conveyed a certain brand of stubbornness, that made Banks lean forward. Recognition sparked in him, someplace deep down in a spot of memory he had long ago forsaken. And the forehead: it was short but intelligent, with a certain set to the eyebrows below it.

"It's him," he said.

Karen touched his arm and drew in her breath. "You're sure?"

"He's a lot bigger than Bob, but that's Bob's face, sure as shit."

A murmur ran through the sparse crowd when the number-two hitter backed out for a second time as the Post 17 pitcher hurled his big, slow curve at his chin. The third time, however, the curve did not break, and the hitter, in an unexpected show of fortitude, turned and took it full on the back of his left shoulder with a thud. Then he tossed his bat toward the dugout and trotted up to first base. Frank approached the plate with runners at first and second.

"All right," somebody said. "Show 'em what you got, Frank."

"Ducks on the pond, Frank."

"Whatta ya' say, four. Little base knock."

Intuitively, Banks glanced down to the fence that ran along the third-base side. The gray-suited man now rested his notepad in his palm, the pen poised an inch or two above it, as he looked at Frank as if he were someone he had known long ago and whose name he was trying to recall. Beyond him, the petite woman in the white blouse was watching the pitcher closely, biting her supple lower lip with finely-edged white teeth; a few seconds later, as the Post-17 pitcher gave an odd spring forward and delivered the ball, her scrutiny turned to the hitter, who waited patiently with the bat almost touching his shoulder, her eyes so bright and wild as to almost betray a kind of insanity.

Had he been called upon to do so, Banks could not have described what happened next, but here is what he believed he witnessed: it was the curve again, but breaking inward on Frank since he hit from the left-hand side of the plate, and this one had some bite on it as it wobbled out like a fan belt about to fly loose from its rotor, or perhaps like one half of a misshapen oval, and suddenly Banks understood that it was more than just a bending line – it was a deception of the highest order, an optical illusion that seemed to grow slower and then suddenly faster as it burrowed away at the air, an intelligent missile. And just as it was about to go slapping into its target – the big catcher's mitt that had not moved a millimeter – something else, something momentous and unstoppable occurred. The batter's back and shoulders twisted violently, like a tree racked by lightning, and although he did not see the bat meet the ball or even see it come around in its vicious slashing movement, he heard it: a single, sharp, rifle-like report like an echo off of a stone precipice. The ball left the park on a rising straight line, passing roughly ten feet over the left fielder's head and gaining another three feet of so before it began to die beyond the fence, skipped, and then bounded into the woods.

Frank had already rounded first base before anyone realized it was a home run. The woman at the fence was the first to understand, and she began to clap furiously, jumping up and down once or twice before she could restrain herself. The man with the notebook was scrawling away, not even looking up. Someone laughed out loud, someone else gave a low whistle, and then all applauded – a stately, almost reverential acknowledgement.

Karen's voice seemed to break the strange paralysis into which Banks himself had been cast: "Wow. That was a pretty good hit."

"Yeah. I'm going down to get a hot dog."

"But you just finished your sandwich."

"Still hungry."

He did not go to the concessions window but instead walked along the fence and sidled up to the man in the grey suit. They nodded at one another, and then passed a few moments of silence as they watched Frankie's Post 3 teammates spill out to home plate to greet him. The boys laughed, pushed one another, pounded on Frank's head, and then the umpire leaned over with his broom and cleaned off the plate for the next batter.

"So what did you think about that?" Banks asked.

The thin man turned, the knot of his yellow tie bobbing on his Adam's apple as he spoke. "Pardon? Oh, yes, that was a nice job hitting to the opposite field. You don't see that too much with these young fellas."

"You from the newspaper?" Banks asked.

"Oh, no. I'm a scout for the Cincinnati Reds organization. Just looking at a few players while I'm in town. We have an affiliate here in Columbia."

"Scout? So you do the hiring?"

"No, no. I just make observations and do the recommending, providing I see something I think the owners might like."

"All business, eh? I understand. My name is Banks Berenger, by the way." He extended his hand.

"Phil Seghi. You live here, do you, Mr. Berenger?"

"No, I...I'm just in town chasing down a few real estate tips, and I...I thought I'd take in a game. So what about this Johnson kid?"

"Good player. Good instincts. And good discipline. As I said, a lot of these young guys try to pull every pitch they see. You don't need a lot of power to do what he just did. Just a little bit of patience, generally speaking."

"But he is strong. At least he looks strong to me. If I may be so nosy, are you going to recommend Frank Johnson for the Reds?"

"Hard to say. It doesn't pay to make snap decisions. We'll see what else he can do. I will say, I saw another boy this week, colored boy that plays for the Taylorville team, who can do it all. Blazing speed, cannon for an arm, and he hits for power. Best I've seen so far this spring."

"Well," Banks said, mustering his best persuasive tone, "if he's better than this kid right here, he must be pretty damn special."

"He is, believe me. In any case, I'm told we can only afford one right now. If I had my say-so, I'd sign that black boy today. But management doesn't give me the say-so."

"Only afford one? How's that?"

"It's business, just as you said, Mr. Berenger. Budgetary constraints and whatnot. There's lots of talented players around, but only so much cash."

"I'd have figured pro ball to be a sure moneymaker."

"It's like anything else, I guess – a short trip from the bank to the breadline. Between you and me, there's rumors that the execs up in Cincy are putting the Columbia team up for sale." Seghi's flat Midwestern intonations were matter-of-fact, but this remark sparked on Banks' antennae.

"No kiddin'? Don't the Reds have money?"

"The minor league clubs are just affiliates. They're privately owned."

"I see. And what if nobody buys it?"

"We farm out the players with potential to other teams in the system. And the rest of them just go away."

"Hmm. Interesting. Well, in any event, Mr. Seghi, it's been nice chatting with you. Good luck with your scouting."

A nod, a handshake, and Banks was moving back up the walkway and then ascending the bleachers, his mind ablaze, so that he only vaguely heard Karen ask, "They out of frankfurters already?"

"Huh? Oh. Yeah, they are. Come on, sweetie, we need to get going."

"Go? Now? Don't you want to wait and talk to Frankie?"

"Oh, I'm planning to talk to him, all right. But right now we have to go. Got some calls to make."

"What's the matter?" Looking up at him, she shaded her brow against the brilliant early-spring sun.

"Gotta find out if we're solvent enough to buy a baseball team," he said.

Three

May/June, 1960

As far as he could recall, Luther had never before traveled out to Nettie Russell's place after dark. It made for a surreal drive, with the old wagon's headlamps catching on passing banks of fog and turning the spring's new insects into little flaming dive bombers as they moved deeper into the woods. Beside him in the passenger's seat, the Reverend James Jackson, monk-like and mute, stared into the thick black shadows as though pondering the essence of darkness on earth. The smoke of campfires drifted through the car's windows, mixing with that unmistakable, swampy smell of tannin.

The occasion for their journey was one which Luther had not approved in any official capacity, but it was one which – as he had at last realized – was critical. James's silence communicated to him that he, too, viewed it as a necessary unpleasantness; it was with near-disgust that he had carefully placed his 30.06 hunting rifle on the backseat in the place ordinarily taken up by the bags of groceries they delivered to the outlying poor families once a week. There it lay, cold, inert, its barrel protruding from a towel and showing dully in the dashboard's light, so that its presence there might almost account for the weight of silence that descended upon the space where easy conversation typically flowed without constraint. They were bound to a task that neither of them relished.

On their most recent trek to Nettie's clapboard shack, she had become increasingly distraught: the panther, she said, had come back; she could hear its long, gravelly call at night in the woods, very close by, and although she could see no traces, of course, because she was nearly blind, she swore that once the animal had even stolen onto her porch and looked in the window at her. She had made no mention of soliciting help from the mythical nephew.

"What do you think?" James had asked him on their way home the last time.

Luther had replied, "She could be going senile. She must be around eighty-five years old."

"Eighty-seven."

"Onset of senility is one possible explanation. Probably is some kind of critter out there. Panthers are still pretty rare, though, despite what occurred last August."

"Could be the same one. Tracking prey now that the weather's warming up."

"Yep," Luther reluctantly agreed. "I guess we shouldn't take any chances. She seems genuinely frightened. Thinks it's a demon or…or a spirit or something."

"I don't know about that. Sure enough gonna be hungry, though, after the winter we had."

"Well, what ought we to do, James?"

He could see that his friend had already thought about it. "You got a rifle?" Luther shook his head "I'll get out my old 30-nought," James said. "Ain't fired it in ten year, but it'll work. You busy on Saturday night?"

Luther had sighed and nearly said something about the odd and sundry demands of their vocation, but instead he had simply remarked, "Saturday it is."

Now they were here, the car's lights sweeping across the dirt patch and then falling upon the crooked old lady as she hobbled out onto the porch, the yellow light of a kerosene lantern glowing behind her. She peered in their direction, opened her mouth in a birdlike manner, and called, "Rekernized y'all's car engine. Ain't no mistakin' a preacher's engine."

"Evening, Nettie," James said, slamming his door. "We come to cure your panther problem."

"I know it. Didn't think you's comin' courtin'."

"No, that'll be next Saturday," Luther said, but Nettie did not smile back at him.

They sat in two of the cane-back chairs, as Nettie continued to stand there hunched, looking for them in the shadow of the overhang. James placed the rifle on his lap and unwrapped the towel.

"Whatchu got there?" she asked.

"Got my gun."

She shook her ancient head. "Can't shoot no devil."

"I'd say it's your best bet."

She stood there for a long while, and they were all silent under the spell of the cicadas and the misty spring night. Despite the dampness that coated his face in a thin sheen of water, Luther found himself dozing off as he leaned back against the wall. Finally, James spoke:

"Look here, Nettie. Why don't you go on inside. Go on to bed if you like. We'll let you know if that old panther shows up."

"I reckon I could get back to my sewin'. I cain't see them stitches, but I can feel 'em."

"All right, then. We've got the perimeter covered."

The two men continued to sit without talking to one another for some time, the night shadows seeming to close in on them ever so slightly. Luther thought that the tree trunks seemed to have gotten closer to them, and as though they were of a single mind, James whispered, "I think I figured it out, about the trees."

"Nettie's 'prayin' trees' you mean?"

"Yeah. This place hereabouts was once an old turpentine plantation, as I believe you know. There were numerous other houses – if you could call 'em that – like this one, where all the colored folks lived, most of 'em kin to one another. All gone, except for Nettie. I'm sure she somehow associates the past with these trees. They used to tap into 'em for the sap, but now, if you were to tap, what kinds of memories might come pouring out?"

"Old ones."

"No doubt. Ghosts, too, maybe. Spirits of the dead."

"I didn't take you for an occultist, James." Even as he uttered these words, Luther could not help recollecting that undeniable, startling sensation he had had that afternoon last summer when Liza Applewhite had come to his home, and he had felt in her physical presence, quite strongly, the spirit of the recently deceased Della Treadwell.

"Well, now, I know all about the Rapture and the Resurrection and all of that," James continued. I went to college, like you. Not the same college, by any stretch, but we studied the same books. But I'll be honest. I've seen some things in my life I couldn't explain. Heard a lot of stories from people I think are as clear-thinking as anybody I know."

"There's a lot we can't comprehend, I reckon."

"That's what you always say when we disagree, Pastor. Anyway, if there are such spirits about, we're doing a good job driving 'em away. What ghost wants to be sitting in one of these here trees when the bulldozer comes along, as it surely will? Gonna be solid concrete and asphalt one day soon, you mark my word."

In the momentary lull that followed, there came a sound, about fifty yards from where they sat and perhaps a dozen feet or so into the pines – just a slight shushing noise that could have been the wind in the leaves. All else was so still, it was impossible for Luther's ears not to have pricked up. Apparently, James had heard it, too, and now both men leaned forward and gazed toward the spot.

A gleaming yellow eye appeared, and then another, as some large animal moved among the trees. "By God..." Luther muttered.

James rasped over his shoulder: "Nettie! Turn down that damper. We got somethin' here."

Whatever it was, it was on the move, as the two small orbs flickered as the animal moved from left to right.

"Could be a raccoon," Luther whispered.

"Not movin' that fast. Too tall anyway."

In a column of black, the eyes paused, seeming to study them. And then from that column emanated a sound unlike any Luther had ever heard: it began as a low, guttural rumbling and then rose in both volume and pitch until it was like the hissing of a giant snake.

He could hear Nettie moaning inside the thin-walled house: "Oh, Jesus, help us..."

He glanced over at James, who had the rifle's butt tucked into his right armpit and the slender barrel raised. He was aiming carefully. When he looked back toward the woods, he was seized by terror at what he saw: the beast, entirely silent now, was coming towards them, gaining speed, covering the ground between themselves and it with incalculable swiftness. Incredibly, the eyes seemed to leap upward of their own accord, like two fireballs suspended across a taut trajectory, and in the millisecond or so that they hung in the air above their heads some twenty feet away, Luther thought he discerned the compact black shape into which they were burned, fully extended – he could distinctly see the hind legs.

The blast from James's rifle seemed to concuss within his skull, smashing at his brain, and a tongue of fire flicked from the barrel. Instantaneously, the glowing eyes vanished. A few moments later, when the great sound had ceased echoing off of the tree trunks that surrounded them, Luther noted that everything had fallen so still that even the cicadas had ceased their humming.

"I think I hit it," James said.

"I'll fetch my flashlight from the car," Luther said, and then when he stood up, he remembered the frightened old lady inside. He rapped at the door. "Nettie? You still in there?"

"Didn't go out for no walk, did I?"

"James says he thinks he got 'im. I'm going to get my flashlight and look around."

The flashlight's stream was feeble in the thick darkness, but they were able to trace the animal's spoor – heavy gouts of dark red, thickening blood – to the edge of the trees, and James said, "I for one ain't goin' in there tonight. Whatever there is to see, it'll wait till mornin'."

Given the cramped conditions in Nettie's home, and not wishing to invade the old lady's privacy, they slept under blankets in the back of Luther's station wagon, sealed against the night and the coming chill. Strange thoughts and visions floated through Luther's mind, and he lay awake for quite some time, as he listened to James's slow, deep breathing, a hammock of slumber in the midst of this wilderness. Black shapes, at once palpable and yet as vacuous as shadows, plummeted through his imagination, and fiery eyes danced like burning marbles. At last, with no idea of the time, he slipped into a fitful sleep.

A few hours later, with hot cups of coffee in their hands, courtesy of Nettie, and daybreak seeping through the pine trunks, they followed the spoor once again. It went for perhaps half a mile through brush and bramble, and their shoes became soaked with dew and their pants legs covered in sticky spurs; and near the trail's end, the new spring grass was flat where the beast, a very large panther (if indeed it was a panther – they had not actually seen it clearly), had lain and bled out. The blood, now black, had smeared the leaves and grass blades and seeped into the dark soil thereabouts.

For several minutes, Luther and James squatted there, their still-steaming cups poised level in their hands. They studied the grass, the ground, each of them wrapped in a kind of wonder, until at last, as if at a signal, they looked up at one another.

Clearly, this was the spot where the great panther had stopped to die. All that was missing was the carcass of the beast itself.

———

Frank sat in the waiting room of the Columbia Reds offices, which were built, beehive-style, right into the outer brick wall of the baseball stadium on Assembly Street, roughly a mile from MacDougal's store. The room itself was small but extraordinarily tidy, with neatly framed prints of former managers and teams, fresh dark-green paint, and a brilliant tile floor.

He looked up and smiled at the secretary, a fortyish woman with glasses and hair clamped down tightly by bobby pins. She smiled back and then rolled a sheet of onion-skin paper, along with the blue carbon, into her typewriter.

He was not nervous, although he knew that he ought to be. He had talked it over with himself (having said nothing to Allison, even though it was she who had relayed news of the phone call to the store and his summons) on the walk down, and he had decided that whatever they had called him in for, they had already made up their minds. Besides that, he believed that he was back in the old mindset, the one that made all of this seem spontaneous and therefore correct, as if he could never see what was *supposed* to be until it was actually happening. Playing baseball was like that: he knew that to most observers, the game seemed to be based on repetition, but in truth, every situation was a little different, even if it was only in the spinning of the ball, and therefore required a slightly altered reaction. Every situation required a suspension of the mind between thought and not-thought. He had no idea what the Reds would wish to say to him; his response would depend upon the spin.

Without warning, the door to the inner office opened and a man stepped out. He wore a navy blue suit and shoes as shiny as the tile floor beneath them. His face was tanned, his hair quite trim, and although he was rather small in stature, there was apparent physical strength in his bearing. Frank stood up and shook his hand.

"Hello, Frank. My name is Banks Berenger. Come in, won't you?"

He sat on the tweed sofa, and the man sat in the straight-backed chair next to it, rather than at his own expansive oak desk. As he poured them each a glass of water from a pitcher, Frank examined his face for a moment: there was something familiar in it, especially in the way the eyes would be downcast and thoughtful, but then suddenly they would fix on his own with a twinkle.

"So," he said, "what do you know about our organization here, Frank?"

He shrugged. "It's the pros, of course. Single A ball. Some good players have come through here. Frank Robinson…Ted Kluszewski."

"Indeed. Did you know that we're under new ownership?"

"No, sir."

"Well, we are. And consequently we're ready to shake things up a little."

"Yes, sir."

"And so…that means… Well, what does that mean to you, Frank?"

"I don't really know, sir."

The room fell awkwardly silent. The man tugged at his collar, though it was already unbuttoned at his throat; he took a swallow of water. "Look, I'll come to the point. I'm new at this. To be honest, I don't know diddley squat about sports. What I do is, I make money. Makes sense to me that the more this team wins, the more money I'll make, and I think you could help us win. Would you be interested in a contract with the Columbia Reds?"

He looked earnestly into Frank's eyes: there was something familiar in them, Frank thought. What had he said his name was? Banks Berenger – it didn't ring a bell. He glanced perfunctorily at the desk, but there were no photographs there, and the nameplate had been removed from its wooden holder. Otherwise it was a vast, honey-colored sheet of solid oak.

"I'd be very interested," Frank said.

A sense of relief seemed to pass over Banks' face, and then he was all business once again: "I can give you $500 for signing, and another three grand for the rest of the season. If it all works out, we'll find a spot for you with the Reds' winter-league team, get you ready for next year."

Frank sat in silence. He had been able to imagine this moment, even as recently as this afternoon, when Allison had told him he was to come down and meet with a Reds representative. Even during his walk to the stadium, he had envisioned a conversation similar to this one. For most of his life, in fact, he had been thinking of it, but the remoteness of it had kept him from dwelling upon it, so long as he still enjoyed playing. Certainly there had been the terrible finish to his final high-school season, but he had been able to put all of that away, in part, by resolving never to pitch again. He had come to believe that throwing at the Greenville High third baseman's head, hurting him, had been the only deliberately malicious act of his life, and he had regretted it. A baseball had been his weapon that day, but he figured that as a full-time outfielder, he would never again be tempted in such a way. And now, in the instant that he realized that he had at last achieved some unnamed, unknown thing, a thing kept secret even from himself, he felt a sudden longing to go home, to make things right there.

"I'll do it," he said. "But first I'd like to go home. Back to Dillon. Break the news to some folks there. See my daddy."

The executive's eyes grew wide and he swallowed a chunk of ice. "That I would not advise. I mean, we need you right away. This weekend, in fact."

"It's not that far by bus," Frank insisted. "I'll go home first. Then I'll play for the Reds."

"We can send you home in style, after the season."

"I'm sorry Mr. Berenger. It's the only thing I'm asking for. I need to see my father."

His brow thickly knitted, the executive stared down at his hands. Frank could see the pale shadows of old scars on them. "All right," Banks said. "All right. I understand. Just report for practice in ten days."

Just as Frank had stood up and was about to place his hand on the doorknob and go out, Banks asked, "So, what name, then?" He turned, confused.

"Name?"

"What name should we put on the contract? And on your new uniform? Johnson, or...something else?"

His heart thumped, but he recovered himself. "Oh. Yes, of course. It's Frank Johnson."

"I see. Fine. See you soon, Frank."

Outside, the streets of Columbia were alive with the business of the afternoon. A few men hustled about the town center, alligator-skin shoes scraping on the pavement. A colored woman in a blue headscarf came out of an apartment building and poured a pan of water into the gutter. Three elderly men reclined on benches in the freshly mown park, smoking cigars. Oddly, as he walked along, Frank felt both exhilarated and weary, like a man returning from a triumphant battle. He would not turn seventeen for three more months, and yet he had a contract with a single-A professional baseball club. Given what he had been through in the past year, it seemed nothing short of a miracle.

His mother might have said it really *was* a miracle. He wondered whether she would have let him sign. Probably not – she would say he ought to finish school instead.

Pastor Laite, now he might have agreed to the miracle interpretation, but he would have sided with her, of course. In any case, he would put the pastor on his list of folks to visit with back home.

The more he thought of it, the more people he began to remember. He would see them all.

Even Liza.

———

Luther felt all of the juices in his body sink and sway as he watched the young woman intently. His brain seemed to burn as she looked up at him from where she lay on her back, her slender, naked legs opened wide towards him, a small smear of sweat above her upper lip. She gave him a weak smile.

He had not wanted to penetrate as far as the delivery room, but when he had gotten word that Liza Applewhite had gone into labor some seven weeks early, he had come to the hospital right away. Then, having arrived, he was abruptly approached by a particularly strong-willed nurse who instantly hustled him into an anteroom where he clumsily donned a surgical mask and cap.

He had said, "I'm not supposed to be doing this."

"She asked for you," the nurse said. "She's a little bit scared. Dr. Tifton will have to perform a C-section. He says the baby is turned wrong."

"Where's the husband?"

"Still at work, she says. We sent for him, but he'd already left." Thus he was literally led by the hand into the echoing tile-covered delivery room, where he came to the rather strange realization that he had never seen a vagina up close. It startled him, and for an unsteady moment he sensed the sheer impossibility and miraculousness of all this. Could it really be that the perpetuation of a noble species came down to this? A woman lying on a her back in a sterile room, her reproductive canal raised and waiting to spout a sprawling, bawling thing earthward, and in so doing to add the burden of one more mouth, one more set of lungs, one more bundle of need to this mad, chaotic world? God help us.

The obstetrician turned from his tray of shiny instruments and gave him what may have been a grim smile from beneath his mask. Luther felt slightly dizzy.

"Are we almost ready, hon'?" the nurse asked.

"No, we ain't," Liza groaned, but the doctor stepped somberly into the space between Liza's legs, holding the scalpel out before him like a man about to cut a ribbon.

Instinctively, Luther moved around to the side of the table and took hold of Liza's right hand. When he glanced up, he saw a thin, bright stream of blood spattering up the doctor's forearm, and he quickly looked down again at Liza's face: her eyes were shut tightly, but otherwise it was calm, almost saint like. Luther held his breath, and the old words began to run through him, through the middle of his chest: *...hallowed be thy name... thy will be done, on earth, as it is in heaven...*

"It's all right, Pastor," said the nurse. "All she feels is a little pressure down there."

"Feels like something's died," Liza whispered.

But she was wrong, for beyond the upraised sheet, Luther saw the silent doctor lift a small, bloody thing and place it in a plastic bin on the table. It's thumb-length arms and legs paddled at the air, and then it set up a squalling far too loud for its tiny size.

"Gonna be fine. Fine boy."

"Can I see?" Liza asked. "Can I hold him?"

"Not yet," said the nurse. "It's important that we get him cleaned up first."

A half hour later, he sat in the waiting room, staring down at his shoes, elbows to knees. He had only been in the delivery room for a few minutes, but he was drained. It was his first time; the blood, the fluid, the blade, the smell – it had all been more brutal and expeditious than he had expected, and yet he had felt a Godliness in it. He hadn't realized it at the moment, but the Spirit had been in that room. The hands, hands working, grasping, joining with one another – it had been astonishing, really. And yet…yet it was the most common sort of experience, this way in which, more or less, all of us arrive here, naked and at the mercy of those who have come before us. He wished he could have been of more help.

On his way out to his car, he met Carl in the parking lot. He seemed hurried, out of breath. "Hey, Pastor. Sorry I'm late. Did I miss anything?"

"You missed everything."

"Dang it."

"At least you're here now. Better hurry on in."

He stood by the station wagon's door and looked up at the night sky. What was that constellation called, just above the tree line? He could not dredge it up from his memory.

He climbed in and put his hands on the old familiar wheel and headed for home.

———

MacDougal ran his hand along the two long, cool barrels of the shotgun that lay across his knees. He was seated in the rolling chair at his own desk in his own office downstairs in his own house, but oddly enough, he could not recognize any of the objects in the room. It was a sort of blindness he had never experienced, or like trying to identify things by reaching into a box.

He had been here for two hours now, he figured, while she slept upstairs. Strangely, he had not flown into a rage, had not even really felt surprise, when he had found the note she had left on the kitchen table. He had come in a day early, quietly, from a buying trip to Raleigh, and there it had been, on a single, yellow sheet of stationary in her fancy, curly handwriting:

> *One more night in heaven till he comes home. Can't wait to feel you in me and all around me once again. I long for the object of my longing.*
>
> *- Me*

It was the familiar, intimate language she had once used in her letters, long ago, to him, when they had first begun dating. Certainly he had never been fool enough, beforehand, to believe that he could be her first lover, and afterward, he had had the good sense not to ask her about her past. He had just counted himself fortunate to find so rare a dark-haired beauty willing to marry him, and then to stay married to him for getting on to eight years now. He had tried often to live up to it, but in the end, the simple truth was that he was a numbers man, a supply sergeant, a bean counter, bland, good with money – but he was not a poet. As soon as he had seen the note on the table, this old inadequacy, the weakness that he had covered up with gruffness and silence for so long, had come under a great, glaring spotlight, and he knew that a life without her, from this point onward, would be a condemnation.

And so it was, in this light (though the office was now swaddled in a near darkness), that he broke open the shotgun, exposing the chambers, and he shoved in the two shells. He shut it with a sharp, metallic click that seemed to echo throughout the house, but otherwise there was no sound. He rose silently, the gun's stock tucked under his arm, and he moved through the room and into the downstairs hallway in his stocking feet, the thick, expensive carpet absorbing any groaning that the floor below might have emitted, and by the nightlight tucked in by the kitchen, he placed one foot on the bottom stair leading to their bedroom. He looked up, but saw only a shroud of gray, and listening closely, he heard only her characteristic breathing, though he had no doubt that someone else was up there.

Another step, and he listened again: she rustled in the sheets, and her breathing turned into soft snoring. He smiled. It had never kept him awake, and in fact, there were times when it had even brought him peace to awaken in the middle of the night and hear her. She was a heavy sleeper, all right, but he never had been; half the time, he was a borderline insomniac, though he had never been terribly troubled by anything in particular; it was just in his makeup.

A third, and a fourth, and a pause, and then he quickly took the remaining steps and found himself poised on the landing, the shotgun now raised to his shoulder. The half-open door was before him, and he peered in, but could only make out the bulk of the bed and the twisted, bunched-up sheets.

Her breathing now was almost songlike, musical: he could hear in it her voice, her sweet laughter, those small, loving intonations which now would never be his again. He inched toward the doorway, reached out and into it with his left hand, and found the light switch.

In his slowed-down perception, it seemed a gaping eternity between the moment that he threw the switch and the irretrievable instant that the awful light flooded the bedroom.

When he had disembarked at the bus station, a block or so up from the old square he knew so well, Frankie headed even farther to the northeast, skirting the ragged edges of the town in order to avoid detection. He did not see his mission here as celebratory. For now he wanted only to see his father.

He had, for some days, been delaying, for after he had asserted himself, making clear his intentions to Mr. Berenger in the Columbia Reds front office, he had abruptly realized that there was no real need for him to go back after all; as far as he knew, no one there would welcome him; he wasn't altogether sure they would even *want* him, given all that had passed; and ultimately there was the possibility that no one there would remember him at all, for people's memories were short.

Except for that preacher, of course. He would remember everything.

Finally, though, it was Allison who had convinced him that it was time for him to make a return journey to Dillon. Only the previous evening, when he had rolled off of her, she – glistening with sweat and with that sleepy half-smile – had said: "I guess you saw my note on the kitchen table."

"Yep. Sorry I didn't give you a proper hello."

"Oh, you did, all right." She ran the back of her hand down the length of his bare torso. "So, what have you decided to do?"

"About?"

"You know what I mean. Don't pretend you don't. Are you goin' back to see your daddy or not?"

"I doubt it. He doesn't care about me."

She propped herself up on her elbow and flipped her dark hair over her smooth, tan shoulders. "Now, look, mister, you're going on seventeen now, I believe. And you're going to be a professional ballplayer, too. It's time for you to straighten up some."

"I am straightened up."

"Whether you like it or not, you're one of those people that's been called on to do something special, and that means you can't just act like a kid anymore. I mean, is a ballplayer a kid, or is he a man?"

Frank considered this. "Both."

"Well, be that as it may, you have to set an example. Let's say your daddy is still in bad shape, like you said. You can do him some good. Give him something, give him his pride. I know he'll be proud of you. He can't help it. It's in the nature of parents."

"How do you know? You've got no kids."

"Doesn't matter. I know what sort of mother I'd be if I had any. And anyway, I might still have some someday. I promise you your father will be happy to see you. Besides, you don't know – maybe he's changed."

"Doubtful."

"And besides that, maybe there's other folks there wants to see you. Old girlfriends, for instance."

"Never had none."

But of course, he had thought of Liza then, who had, in fact, been his friend, but not his girlfriend. He saw her as she had looked that day when they had walked down the road in the morning light, and he had thrown the rock and hit the mailbox in front of her old house: she had stood in the road, head tilted, just as Allison's was now, asking something of him, he felt, though he would never know what it was, exactly.

"I suppose maybe I should go," he said at last.

But was it for her? Or was it really to see his father after all? He wasn't sure, but in any case, he had hauled himself up from the bed and begun getting dressed. It was early, but he wanted to go back to his little room, get his stuff together, and get a good night's sleep.

"That's a good boy," she said, suddenly quite sleepy once again. "Just do me a favor and turn off the lights downstairs. Oh, and be sure to pick up that note off the kitchen table and throw it away someplace. We don't want to take any unnecessary chances."

"Okay."

Perhaps he would run by the station, he had thought, and if they were still open, he would go ahead and buy his ticket tonight. He'd catch the earliest bus he could get. Then he'd have the ride to think things over, to figure out what he would say when he saw his father.

Walking swiftly, he was halfway to town when he realized he had forgotten to pick up the note Allison had left for him. That was all right, though: he figured MacDougal would not be back until late afternoon tomorrow, and she would have plenty of time to put things back in order. She was always very careful about that. Somehow, he had reconciled himself to all of it, and now he found that he enjoyed her conversation as much as he did the other benefits; some of his best times over the past nine months or so had been simply lying next to her and listening to the words that rolled off of her tongue; sometimes they drank straight from the bottle of La Donna Rosa that perpetually sat on the bedside table. His regard for Mac had changed, too: he was gruff but kind in his avuncular way, and he could bear once again to look him in the eye; it was simply all a matter of compartmentalizing his life, at least in terms of those few people who occupied its sphere. When he was around him, he could play the loyal employee, but when he was with her, he was someone else – a demon lover, and an obedient companion; he found that these pseudo-personalities had emerged quite readily in him, practically of their own accord, but of course, he felt he was most in his own skin when he was on the ball field.

He would see how things went now with his father. Maybe it would mark a new beginning for them both. Then later might come a visit to the diner, too, for he was certain that he would find Liza there, just as always.

Walking swiftly now, with barely a trace of the boy he had been only a year ago evident in his stature and movements, he took the turn, the old dirt drive that led down to the river. His heart began to beat rapidly, and the profusion of sweat beneath his arms and on his back, having soaked into the new collared shirt he had bought, began to cool as the cool air from the river came up to meet him. The house came in sight, and there was the old pickup in the carport, along with another car, a Plymouth. He strode quickly to the door and placed his hand on the knob, but hesitated. It was funny – a door you had known for so long, had so many times thrown open in one easy motion, bounding in, happily exhausted, sweaty from practice, books and baseball gear tucked under each of his arms... both of them there, perennially, the mother in her apron and flowered cotton dress at the sink, the father seated at the table with his newspaper, and the smells of home emanating from the stove.

He removed his hand and knocked crisply on the door. Footsteps within, and then it swung inward. A tall man appeared there, and as if someone instantly dropped a gauze before his eyes, confusion filled him. He stepped back, nearly stumbled. The eyes were familiar. It was...yes, it was him – Luther Laite. He peered down at Frankie, nodded, and smiled.

"Pastor... what... are you?"

"Hello, Frankie," he said. "I'm so glad you're back. We've all missed you. Come in, will you?"

Part Three: The Divine Child

One

April, 1961

Frank Treadwell had at last become a great watcher of baseball. For him, playing the game had always been the preferable – and certainly easier – means of approaching its complexities, but as it is with all those to whom such endeavors come easily, a conscious awareness of the skill and craft of an art as difficult as baseball had been relatively slow in coming to him. Now as he stood at the twisted metal fence watching the tall, wide-shouldered colored boy swing the bat, he found that he perceived things he never had before.

For one thing, there was the explosive power that lay in the thick thigh and hamstring, held back and above the crouching right knee, so that one quick turn of the hips and the big shoulders, all driven by the buttocks, would turn the fat part of the bat into a great hammer falling upon the shell of the ball, thus turning hitter and bat into a kind of uncoiling cannon; except there was no recoil – only the follow-through, a perfect, tight arc that knifed efficiently through the air to complete the harmonious yet deadly forward advancement. That swing was the powerful force that could divert and even reverse the course of human events.

There was the first half of the swing, of course (although it wasn't half of anything, but rather the point at which two moving spheres might collide and the hitter's hands would begin to turn over), and this big black kid had the rare ability to adjust his stroke, to vary its angle mid-swing depending upon the location and shape of the pitch. He was patient with an outside fastball or a ball breaking away from him; he would bring the heel of the bat through first, essentially slapping the ball, changing its angle, letting its own momentum carry it out and down the right-field line. But when he got one near the middle of the plate, the slap became an eruption of muscle, wood, and leather, and the ball was sent scorching on a line just over the top of the batting-practice pitcher's protective screen, literally humming over second base, and striking the top of the fence in center field, causing the loose chain link to go shivering from one end to the other. "Damn," Frank muttered.

He knew that one did not have to be exceptionally strong to hit a baseball that hard, but if you had a good swing and a good eye (although the eyes were only a part of the instantaneous and intuitive vision required to pick up a small object flung towards you at ninety miles per hour), then being strong certainly helped.

"Nice job," he said. The colored boy had finished hitting and had come over to rest the bat along the fence and to have some water. He squinted up, the dust of the dry clay caked along his jaw-line.

"Thanks," he said. Then he grabbed his glove and trotted toward the outfield.

Frank had been about to ask the kid his name, but he knew it already, having asked one of the other players earlier. He was Jack. This was the all-colored team from Taylorville, and Frank had come upon their practice by accident as he was out for a training run. Now he leaned over, stretched out, and began the slow jog back to town.

Running for exercise was something he never would have thought about doing, but the Columbia Reds had an official trainer who made them do such things. They had a weight room, too, with lots of barbells, but Frank had not yet used them, for he was slightly concerned that adding muscle to his frame might slow him down; nonetheless, now that he had seen the beefy colored kid swatting those frozen ropes, he thought he would consider it.

At least he could count on Banks Berenger not to try and give him any advice, even though the team's owner had clearly taken a special interest in him. That would be hard to take, and besides, by his own admission, Banks knew almost nothing about baseball. It was hard to believe that all of that had happened less than one year ago: the previous summer, he had signed a professional baseball contract, played in his first few professional games (granted, he had played poorly, mostly riding the bench, but he had gone two for ten as a pinch hitter), and beyond all of that, like the scenes from some bizarre and rather grotesque film, the ponderous events of his own life had seemed to surround him, to orbit about him randomly, superficially, as if they belonged to some fictional character, and then to close in upon him.

In just two weeks' time he had been hired to play ball and had also been informed unceremoniously of his father's violent death. He wanted to feel something, to grieve over it, to curse the god who would indulge in such cosmic humor, but Frankie had neither laughed nor cried: it was as if deep down he had known all along that Bob Treadwell was gone, but the man who had died had little connection to the father who had driven him on those crisp early-spring mornings to his first practices, who had stood at the chain-link fence all those afternoons into the twilight, with pure pride in his kindly eyes. The love he had known, the unabashed and unconditional love, had been transformed by accelerated events to a distorted and strangely shaped memory. It was as if, during that long first year away from Dillon, he had changed too much to ever go back anyway. And he had realized that the life he had known there, his mother, his father, Liza (Pastor Laite was also the one who had told him, rather bluntly, that she had gotten married and had a child), his old school, his former teammates – all of that and all of them were now the odd events and shadowy figures of a life that was no longer his. Certainly he was saddened by all of it, but it was a sadness that seemed to reach him from a great distance, as if he were standing on a mountaintop looking down upon his own past.

The more immediate and distressing thing had been all the trouble with Allison. When he had returned to Columbia, where, at Banks Berenger's behest, he had agreed to take a small apartment owned by the Reds organization (cramped, but still a step up from his accustomed digs), he went to retrieve the few possessions he had left in the little washroom at the back of MacDougal's store. He had found it locked up tight, closed, with no lights on and no sign in the window. So, he had walked the two miles up to the couple's house, but had found it shut as tight as a stone as well, the lawn un-mown, red curtains drawn, and as he had stood knocking at the heavy oak door, a morbid sense had come over him. Later, it was only through bits and pieces of conversation, confirmed ultimately by a days-old newspaper clipping, that he finally understood what had happened: in some kind of despair and despondency, Mac had shot himself in front of his wife in their upstairs bedroom. The police were not aware of any motive, and apparently Mrs. MacDougal had been too traumatized to speak to them. She had gone into seclusion.

Frank had not realized then how shaken he was until he had sat down for a cup of coffee in a grimy little diner up the road from the stadium. *My God,* he had thought, *he must have come home not long after I left. What if he had found us in that bed downstairs?* He recalled MacDougal as a good soul, usually silent, often grumpy, but generous, and now he – Frank Treadwell, not Frank Johnson – was the source of the man's sad undoing. Once again he had been the errant son who, if he was able to act at all, acted wrongly. He yearned deeply to behave as he should, to pay some sort of price, and this was part of the reason, finally, that he had not rebuffed the Reds, had not told them to take their contract and stick it where the sun wouldn't shine. He saw clearly that he had a chance once again to fulfill the expectations of a father figure, to form a bond, to do something right for a change within his small sphere of personal relations. Besides, Banks had offered a compelling argument: he was ready to play at a higher level, and baseball would be not only his true life and career from now on, as he had always hoped; it would also be his final escape from whatever had troubled him in his own past. He really could be Frank Johnson now.

In mid-September, when it had become clear that his first attempt at professional baseball, such as it was, had been a failure, and he was prepared to quit, Berenger had said to him, "Look, it's going to be all right. You're by far the youngest player on the team. You can't expect to come in and light things up right away."

"I did terrible. I'm terrible."

"Look at what you've been through this past year. I'm amazed you can even get your shoes on in the morning. I may not know much yet about baseball, but I can look and see how hard it is. The whole damn game is about trying not to fail; hell, hit three times out of ten, and you're considered a good player. I never heard of such a thing in my life."

"I hit .600 in high school."

"That's because that was high school. This ain't. This is men who will choke you to death in your sleep in order to get your spot. Now, that's something I know something about, and let met tell you: the only thing is for you to take the same attitude, because the alternative is going back to sweeping floors and stocking shelves, or worse yet, going back to Dillon."

"I've got nothing in Dillon. I'll never go back there again."

"Then I suggest you start preparing for next season. Seems to me that's all you've really got."

It was hard to argue over. Aside from this forceful, clearly successful man, who sometimes seemed to treat him almost as a son, and on other occasions merely as a fascinating business proposition (though he did like the lady-friend – wasn't her name Karen?), he had no one and nothing left. He had scoured the countryside around Columbia, searching for Allison, but it was as though she had simply vanished from the earth, and he'd had no other connection to her besides Mac himself, who had blown his own brains all over their bedroom wall.

He had acquiesced, saying, "I reckon I could do some weight training now that it's the off-season."

Banks had grinned and said, "My boy, I have two words for you: Caracas, Venezuela."

So it was that he had taken a long bus ride down to Miami, and then for the first time in his short life, he had stepped on board a plane – a small, unsteady, cramped prop plane, to be sure, but nonetheless one that lifted him high above that white city and then over a glistening body of dark blue water, and set him down again in Caracas, where he would spend the fall and early winter months playing for the Caracas Lions of the Venezuela Professional Baseball League. Caracas – that was the sort of place in which he had never believed he would find himself, even in his wildest imaginings. How could he describe it, should someone (such as Allison) ask him about it: What was it like? It was like going to a different time, a different world, unrecorded in any book, that could only be captured by a painter, but he was not a painter, he was a baseball player. He would have to say it was all in shades of clay and white stones, with vivid green trees with glossy leaves growing plentifully along its waterways. It was full of the sounds of men shouting back and forth in its business districts and children in its pitted alleyways, and of small, boxy cars the very horns of which sounded like brassy women's voices. And the smells – there was always the smell of cooking food: roasting chicken or pork, peppery spices he had never experienced, and warm cakes. All of that was nestled at the foot of the green, misty mountains in whose lower folds, nearly toppling downward, were the straw and stick shanties of the poor, while higher up, the whitewashed villas looked commandingly out over the city.

In the three months or so that he spent with Los Leones de Caracas, he felt that he had played very well. He was relaxed, he saw the ball well at the plate and made solid contact, and he made several good plays in right field, after which echoing applause drifted out across the big, open stadium. There was typically jocularity in the clubhouse and in the dugout, and often the players of mythical stature who sometimes appeared at their games both in the stands or on the field – among them Cesar Tovar and Luis Aparicio – were pointed out to him by his teammates.

He had come back in January, picked up some part-time work bussing tables at the little diner where he had sat over his coffee six months earlier trying to make sense of the demolition site that was his life, and now that the season was almost here again, he felt rested and renewed. All that was pressing upon him now was his need to tell Banks Berenger about the colored boy he had seen twice now playing for the Taylorville team.

And his need to see Allison, of course. Every day, every place he went, every time he wandered out in the streets of Columbia, hers was the face he was searching for. He looked for her tossing, dark mane of hair at every bus stop, in every crowd, and when he was alone again, he would curse the day he had ever left their bed.

———————

Banks leaned away from the gleaming breakfast counter in the kitchen of his three-story, stilted home at Hilton Head, folded his hands across his paunch, and gazed at the lovely woman across from him. Karen was deeply absorbed in the sports section of the morning's newspaper. He had not yet discovered in himself any real interest in games, especially baseball, but she had become a fan; she read box scores with fluency, knew who the promising rookies would be around the league for the upcoming season, and understood the gravity and indisputable narrative conveyed by statistics.

When he was honest with himself, he was still undecided about her. She was by far the best and most beautiful woman in a long line of them, the most giving, and she asked little in return. He did not know why he had been unable, within himself, to commit to their relationship, but he suspected it was because all of his zeal still went into his business ventures, though there was less of that these days. Personal relationships, for him, had always been like dabbling, and he halfway understood that this was why he had ultimately turned his newfound connection to his nephew into an investment: it leant a certain gravity to it.

"What's on the slate for today?" Karen asked.

"What's today? Monday? Going up to Columbia to get some paperwork done. Purchase orders and what-not. Seems everybody wants my autograph."

"Let me know if you need somebody to do footwork. I've got nothing planned."

"Will do." That was another thing about her: she seemed to sense intuitively that his life was his work, that if she were to be part of it, she would be part of that as well. Perhaps it was a sort of cross that he must bear, but he knew now that it was the only way he could finesse things.

Although Frank's experiences had been different from his own, they had been just as rough. To have lost both his parents to such cruel deaths in relatively quick succession allowed for two consequences: juvenile delinquency, maybe mental illness, or early independence and manhood; fortunately, the latter condition had seemed to prevail. Still, he knew how hard that brief visit to Dillon must have been for him. As many times as he had practiced his speech ("I know this will come as a shock to you, but you and I are closer than you might think... Your dad was my brother..."), he had not yet mustered the resolve to deliver it. Luther had given him a full report by telephone of what had transpired at the little house on the Little PeeDee: he had gotten him inside, set him down, and for the better part of an hour, the boy had sat in silence as Luther said the things that needed saying, telling it all as directly and plainly as he knew how, all except for the chapters about the existence of an uncle and said uncle's real reasons for buying the Columbia Reds baseball team – for now he had left that alone, a curious riddle that a smart boy might very well solve for himself anyway. Luther described the way that Frank had sat there in silence, head bowed as the words seemed to rain down upon him, invisible barbs to make invisible wounds.

In the end, they had decided to put the house up for sale, and Frank had collected a few things – his old glove, some records and odds and ends, an old iron key from a kitchen drawer, a photo that was quickly slipped into his back pocket, and his mother's scuffed-up old Bible. Then he had accepted a ride back to the bus station. When the money from the sale of the house had come in, Luther had mailed it to Frank. Money wouldn't heal all the wounds, but it damn sure didn't hurt, Banks had thought.

Yet as he rolled it around in his head on the loping drive over to the Reds' offices, he could see that for him this had never really been about the money. It had been about the freedom to do as he wished, to build what he chose and never have a boss to ride him and watch over his every move. Buying nice things had not been an exercise in greed but rather a demonstration of his autonomy. He had always enjoyed crunching numbers and watching his projects grow, but now that he was settled in as owner of the Columbia Reds, he realized what a thankless task it really was: not only did he have to meet the budget ($5,000 to Spaulding, for instance, for new baseballs every season) and handle financial issues, he was also expected to be a frigging public relations man as well, and that meant drinks and dinners with people he didn't much care for, Chamber of Commerce functions, and so on. He had accomplished his objective of finding Frankie and straightening out his life for him, but it was all starting to wear thin. The boy had become a man, as far as he could see – perhaps it was time for him to move on.

When he arrived in Columbia around ten, there he was, waiting in the exterior office for him. In front of the secretary, they greeted one another in their ritualized manner:

"Mr. Berenger."

"Mr. Johnson."

Then, once inside the sanctum sanctorus, as Banks called it, he said, "Well, Frankie, what can I do for you today?"

"I'll come right to the point, sir. Does the team have any money left over?"

He set his briefcase down and turned to face him. "Well, I don't see as that's any of your concern."

"I beg to differ. Hersh Freeman says I'll be hitting in the two spot this season and…"

"I know that, too. I signed off on it."

"I found the player we need. Colored boy, plays for that traveling team from Taylorville."

Banks popped a peppermint into his mouth and gazed toward the window. "Taylorville, huh? Colored boy, you say?"

"Best natural swing I ever saw."

"Hm. We've never had any coloreds on the team since I've been here."

"I hate to be the one to break it to you, Mr. Berenger, but the Dodgers signed Jackie Robinson back in '47."

"I'm well aware of that. But the reality is that things haven't changed that much in some places. Around here, for example."

Frankie looked down at his shoes for a moment and shook his head. "You're right. But isn't the idea here to win some games?"

"You really think he's that good?"

"I saw Frank Robinson play in an exhibition game last fall. I'm not saying he's that caliber yet, but he could be."

Banks glanced ruefully at the accounting ledgers stacked sternly on the bookshelf. He sighed. "I maybe can find some money someplace. I'll come out and see him play later this week."

"I appreciate that, sir, but you've said you don't really know anything about baseball."

"That's true. But I damn sure know money when I see it."

When his nephew had gone, Banks stared at the door, where his spare sports coat was hung on the hook in a rumpled clot, and he mumbled to himself: "I wonder how much it costs to buy a golf course these days."

———

Luther Laite had never been big on grave-tidying, but he had taken this task upon himself because, foremost, there were no Treadwells left in Dillon. Nobody else was around to do it.

He tried to approach it as he approached his gardening, but that hadn't worked; no, though there was order here, the cemetery was not a domain of growth or spirituality for him. It was merely another place he had to go sometimes because it was part of his job.

He longed for the days when folks were buried in the churchyard, beside the building where they had been baptized and married and eulogized, but those times were gone. City health ordinances would not allow it. In secret, he wondered whether all bodies ought not to be cremated, or perhaps dumped into deep, muddy holes by the river, where the worms could go to work on them. After all, as the old song said, the body would become "just the house I once lived in, for my spirit by then will have fled." He had only ever doubted that once.

Often he had wondered what the sense of vacuity and desperation he had experienced at the passing of Della Treadwell had really been about. Was it the ache a lover feels when he loses his beloved? That absence which is the opposite of love? If so, then he was glad he had chosen a life of celibacy. One could never be subject to constant loneliness if he had not known constant companionship.

He did not view Christ as his companion. Such trivialization was not in his makeup. The Christ was in him and around him, and in the very molecules of the air. Certainly one can see Him in the face of an infant or of a sick woman, but that is only because all things are endowed and imbued and infused with Him, and without Him, they would not exist at all. Christ was here at the graveside, but He was also beside the cradle, and everywhere in between. Luther recognized that his view of God was highly metaphysical – a perspective he had learned from his father, he supposed, who had been essentially an ascetic masquerading as a preacher – but he had no one with whom he could share those thoughts except for James Jackson, with whom he visited only sporadically. He wished, in fact, that at times his church could be more of the "burning bush" variety, that there could be more joyful noise, more spontaneity, more clapping and shouting…but that simply was not his method of operation. His own faith was quite palpable, filled with strong imagery and impulses in his blood (how long had he struggled to overcome his innate anger, for instance), but what came out of his mouth whenever he was at the pulpit was restrained and filtered by the processes of his mind. To believe was logical, in the end; non-belief was nothing more than insanity. It made perfect sense that for the creatures who had been made to hold dominion on earth, those who possessed a conception of the future and who could learn from their past, for those who could wonder after the mysteries of the universe and actually recapitulate the act of Creation through art and literature, the body must be only a temporary vessel for something else that is eternal and Godlike.

In that case, then, why did he come here sometimes with a little broom and a trowel and tend these plots like somebody's little old grandmother? This was no more Della and Bob Treadwell's dwelling place than a shell was the true home of a peanut. We're made of dust, and there is a finite amount of dust upon the earth, and so why did he come here? Even as he stabbed away at the insidious weeds, he wondered. It is because we are bound here by the ties of the earth and the living, rooted, unable to take flight until we are pushed, he thought. We cling to the life we know, tooth and claw, and that means saying the words and praying the prayers and reading the books and writing the sermons, knowing all the while that it is insignificant, all of it, beside that meaning whose essence is hidden from us while we are here. And why is it hidden? That was easy: would you put a small child behind the wheel of a truck? Would you hand him a fortune and expect him to know how to spend it? Take that boy, Frankie: he still had quite a long road ahead of him, despite the strange brand of reserve he had shown at his parents' house that day last summer, and his seeming maturity, for Luther had seen plainly that he had not yet begun to deal with the magnitude of his losses. No, we only become fully human over a good many years, we must endure pain, we must get some miles on us, take a few bruises, break a bone now and again. Only then can we become ready for the next part of the journey.

The journey itself was of paramount importance, and so he had ceased wondering whether he had broken the law in not reporting Frank's whereabouts to the authorities, once he had found it out. Likely he had, but experience had taught that sometimes the law was inadequate to circumstance.

These past two years, in particular, had taught him a good deal. After the death of Della and the spiritual death that had ensued for him, and then the rebirth and renewal engendered by Bob's strange death, there had been growth. He had put away his anger and tamped down the vicious temper that had plagued him most of his life. He saw more clearly the way in which the cycles of this earth mimic what comes afterward, and now and again, in certain moments, a tremendous sense of peace would come over him, and he knew why "Peace be with you" had been such an important part of Christ's mantra, for strife is forced upon us every day. We must lay aside our anger. And our fear: this was why he had thought but little of the panther incident out at Nettie Russell's place. He was certain there was a logical reason the beast's tracks had disappeared – perhaps a sudden flash rain had worn them away, or perhaps a single, desperate, dying leap had carried it into the tall brush, but either way, he could not bring himself to believe in those sort of phenomena, for he put no stock in ghosts or evil spirits, though he did believe in the devil's presence in the world. Now, he thought no less of James Jackson because his friend had indulged himself in a bit of superstition (he had been quiet, somewhat harrowed, on the drive home the next day), and he truly felt it had nothing to do with race either (he knew white folks who were far more given to tall tales than James), but as for himself… his God was a God of the mind, not the imagination.

This was not to say by any means that he treated the New Testament stories as metaphor. In fact, he believed absolutely in the four Gospels' account of Christ's life. The miracles found therein were quite real, he knew. Just as with faith itself, it could not be that we are given some comprehension of miracles as suspensions of what we call nature's properties if such things had never occurred. And aside from the Virgin Birth and the Resurrection, they were just the sort of visceral displays a smiling god might use to reveal himself to men at that particular time in history: walking on water (Luther's personal favorite), turning water into wine, selective healings, raising a dead man from a crypt... Since he had been a boy, it seemed, he had encountered many more people who were predisposed to doubt such acts, who read those stories sardonically and mumbled over "scientific explanations." So be it, he thought; someday science will be the god of this misguided world.

He scooped earth and packed it in around the stems of the bluebells he had planted at the foots of the graves, and then he gathered his tools under his arm and headed for the parking lot. Liza had called the office and made an appointment to see him this afternoon, and he certainly did not want to miss her this time. Last time he had failed her, his absence had resulted in some great decisions on her part, and although he believed all had turned out well, he felt it likely that being present was the preferable option, in the Lord's eyes. We are creatures of free will, he thought. Let us exercise it.

———————

Liza shut her eyes and held the shower's nozzle above the back of her head, letting the warm water rush over her neck and bare shoulders and down the small of her back, hoping it would wash away all thought.

It was no use. "Damn it all," she muttered. "Damn them all."

Or maybe, she thought, I've just been standing here all this time, and I dreamed it all up somehow. One of those hallucinations, in which a split second seems an eternity. What seemed like yesterday morning was only a moment ago, and like a missing engine, time had clicked after a sudden hitching into its rightful gear. But this wasn't true, for as she had learned long ago, the truth had a cold and burning skin all around it, and that was all she could feel now.

She raised her face to take the water full upon it. "Satan," she murmured, "if you ever listen to prayers, too, if there are such things as prayers to you, then listen to this one. I want him dead. You evil angels down there and hereabouts, work your blackness upon him today and put him in the ground. And make it hurt, please."

But that was no good either – she didn't mean any of it in her heart. She felt mostly an odd bewilderment, like a person that has been shaken from a sound sleep, and even the awareness that she had been asleep had not yet dawned upon her. Carl had come home late last night, bathed, gotten into bed, and reached over to stroke her hair, and she had pretended to be asleep; this morning, he had gotten up before first light, brushed his teeth, and quietly left the house.

She had lain there a long time watching the first grey sliver of daylight lengthen at the edges of the blinds. How does this happen to me now? she asked of the dark walls. Why now? After everything I've been through just to get here? Sunday evening, between mouthfuls of macaroni, he had told her, "Big job comin' up this week. Probably miss supper." And just as he had said, he had come in late Monday night, too tired to talk, too tired even to go over to Little Carl's crib and touch his head, he said, as he nearly always did. Then yesterday, he had risen and left the house so silently she had not even been roused, and much as she had chastised herself for not making his breakfast for him, she immediately thought that she could make it up by preparing a nice lunch and carrying it down to him. It would only be a matter of stopping by the construction company's office and finding out where he had been assigned. So, around ten, she had powdered the baby, put on a pretty, summery dress, and cranked up the old pickup.

"Can you tell me what site Carl Dixon is working at today? I'm his wife."

The man behind the counter had looked up at her and blinked. His face was like an old paper sack. He swallowed once. "Sorry, ma'am. He don't work here no more."

She stood staring. The words made no sense. "Of course he does. Carl Dixon."

"Well. He quit last week. I'm sorry."

She felt Little Carl wriggling beneath her arm. "Did he say... Did he catch on with another outfit or something?"

The man shrugged his narrow shoulders. The air in the cramped room smelled of raw onions. "I can't say for sure. I don't know."

Now the heavy tock of the electric clock on the wall behind him came to her. "Okay, then," she said, and she left.

What had happened after that had been amongst the wildest, most diabolical of coincidences she had ever experienced. In her distraction, she had missed the turn back through Dillon, and ended up on a sloppy dirt road, the heavy truck wallowing out among scraggly pines interspersed with broken-down shacks and flimsy, leaning trailers. And suddenly she saw him, standing on a cinder block step in front of an eggshell-blue double-wide; she had known him immediately, even with his back to her, for he was bare-chested; those were without doubt his slim shoulders and sharp shoulder blades, and he stood in that 'Carl' posture, as if he were just about to suddenly walk away in any direction, like a distracted child. But he didn't walk away. As she drove past, the trailer door opened, and a redheaded woman appeared there and opened it just enough for him to slip through. Later, Liza had thought it odd that neither of them had looked over at her as she rambled by – cars must be fairly infrequent on this road. Perhaps they were simply too engaged in anticipation of whatever was about to happen inside.

She stepped out of the tub now and reached absentmindedly for her towel. She was a fool; it was her fault. She had been taken in once again, but in a much more deadly and undignified way than she ever had in high school. Anyone might understand how a young girl might be deceived, damaged, because she knows nothing of the world, but a grownup woman with a child? She would never get over this. She could never face her mother again.

On the other hand, she would have to go back to work at the diner now. There was no doubt about that, and she would have to ask for her mother's help with Little Carl. She looked over at her son, where he slept deeply and soundlessly in the crib Roger had built for him. She could not bring herself to think that he might one day grow up to be like all the other males she had known in her life, crude and lustful and ill-mannered, or if they had manners, they were the more deceitful for it. Yet she did not wish she had borne a daughter either, for a little girl might be doomed to some fate like her own, and she could not stand to think of that. There is no hope in the world, really, she thought, and the moment you put a little faith in somebody, something like this happens to you.

Then again, she could just leave. She had the truck, but little enough in the way of cash. It occurred to her that she could sell some of Carl's tools and get enough money together to maybe rent a motel room for a few days until she could find work somewhere. But she would still have the baby and nobody to look after him, and when she thought of the shitty little towns strung along the highways and the cheap diners and taverns (for waiting tables was the only kind of work she had done), it turned her stomach, and she saw herself as condemned to a life of enslavement, bacon grease, hairnets, scrounging pennies for rent, electricity, and water, never having anything left over, and worst of all, having to entrust her child to strangers. She felt she could not bear it. The first strains of desperation clawed at her.

There was one person she could at least confide in, though it was, once again, a man. Still, he was supposed to be a man of God – Pastor Laite – and he wasn't supposed to think like most men. He was supposed to be a... What was the word? A conductor? A conduit. A link. If there was some sort of meaning in all this, some sort of reason she had been made to suffer all over again, he ought to know of it. Her own mother had never been a churchgoer, but she had gotten some sense of how it worked through her association with the Treadwells: it wasn't meant to be just a get-together once a week to sing songs and pray and then feel better about things you had done the rest of the week, or a reason for old ladies to bake chickens and beans and yams and gossip through the long, sunny summer Sundays. She had witnessed the bravery with which Della had approached her end, and she reckoned that much of that strength had come to her from the church – if not exactly from the people there, if not from the folks they really were with all their faults, then from what they ought to have been, and she had lived her life up to now mostly thinking about what things and people (including herself) *ought* to be, *ought* to have been.

Anyway, there was no place else to go, nobody else to go to. She would make an appointment with Pastor Laite.

She went over to the crib and gently, merely by stroking her thumb across the small, soft crown of his head, she awakened her son.

———

Emerging from the dark days that had followed her husband's suicide, Allison MacDougal had suddenly found herself craving two things: her Catholic roots and the sea. The warm lure of each seemed to course through her, to appeal to her sanguine nature, and once she could concentrate again, they became her obsession. There was limited access to one – the Catholic Church – in Columbia, and none at all, of course, to the other. She would have to leave this place.

She barely knew where she had been anyway since that night she had awakened to see Mac at the foot of their bed with the shotgun pressed under his chin, the lower part of the barrel held in his extended palms, with his thumb on the trigger. He had looked at her with great sadness in his eyes – the only time she had ever seen such an expression on his face – but said nothing in those moments before the deafening explosion. She could not rid her mind of the sound that followed a millisecond afterward: that of the back of his head hitting the wall behind him.

There had followed only a blur: a fumbling telephone call, several hours at the police station, and then several nights in a dull-green hotel room where she neither slept nor woke but lay in a state of suspended animation, all of it tumbling over and over in her mind. Finally she had gotten up, gone to the house for some more clothes, and then left, driving away from the life she had known for eight years. The house? Leave it to the banks and the lawyers, she thought, for she no longer cared.

She'd headed straight for Tampa and the sunny streets of Ybor City, where she had grown up in what now seemed another lifetime, where her father had an apartment. He was an amiable, animated, dark-haired fellow of sixty-three, and he had welcomed her with a great flourish of sympathy and with dinners at a little café at the corner of the block. With its flower boxes and fruit trees and the old smell of tobacco from the cigar factories and the workers everywhere and their vigorous conversations in a language she had forgotten, the neighborhood was the closest she had ever been to the Mediterranean, where her heart truly belonged.

Her father had insisted that she take over his bedroom. He would sleep on the couch for the duration of her stay, and she would have her snug privacy and her own shower and a little balcony where she could be alone and gather her thoughts.

It was here, in a little rectangle of sunlight with her coffee, that she sat for the first time in weeks and allowed herself to think about Frank – not about what had happened or about the fateful note she had found in Mac's office and tucked into her pocket before the investigators came, or any of the remorse that clung to her, but just about him. He was a good boy, but a boy all the same, when all she had ever desired was a man, and a man meant someone who could give to her his strength and his quietude and allow her to dwell at the core of his being. In the end, she felt pity for Mac, because she was goods on a shelf to him, and when he had at last seen the superficiality of it all, he had destroyed himself. Oh, she was to blame, no mistaking, if only because she had allowed herself to live that life. When she thought how it had taken a boy to clarify things, a boy with his boyish obsessions and excitations and his pouting and chest-thumping, she felt foolish. Nonetheless, it had been an extremely valuable lesson, for she saw, too, that the man she needed, the man who could satisfy her body, mind, and soul, had likely never walked the earth. He was a thing of her imagination, and she would be alone for the rest of her days.

Resolved and reconciled to this, she went inside to the kitchen, rinsed out her cup, and then descended the twisting iron stairway to emerge into the bustling street. The sun poured down between the cafes and warehouses, pasting the wild shadows of iron posts and lamps here and there upon the stones, and everywhere were the faces and voices of the Hispanic workers, the Central American and South American immigrants. Several times a pair of dark male eyes would catch her own, inviting, seducing, telling her in an instantaneous flash of light that her reawakening womanly needs could be satisfied right now, here, up a quick flight of iron stairs or in a narrow alleyway, tucked in behind a green, flowering shrub.

Yet she walked on, with only a slight smile to acknowledge that she knew what was behind those eyes. She was a woman alone with her burden of pain and remorse.

She did not realize how far she had walked until she heard the sound of her own steps clearly against the fading roar of Ybor City. She was at the edge of the district and ready to turn back when something caught her eye – a sturdy-looking brick structure with a tall iron gate before it, and bronze lettering in an arc atop the gate:

OUR LADY OF PERPETUAL HELP

A church. Was it her church? She thought, Well, if ever a person needed help, it's me. Is this where I am supposed to go now? If the woman she had been six months ago could have observed her now, she might look down on such a pathetic soul and admonish her: you've done this to yourself; now straighten up and take responsibility for it. But she was no longer that woman, for care and loss had worn away her sharp edges. Perhaps if she could just speak briefly with a priest - not to tell him everything necessarily but just to be in the presence of someone who might offer her a little hope...or even if she could light a votive candle or kneel at the altar... She approached the iron gate, and placing her had on it, found that it had been warmed by sunlight. It moved inward an inch or two, as it was not latched. Beyond, the clay-colored church itself rose upward into the heights of the fugacious morning.

She looked up and down the street, as if someone she knew might be watching her, but oddly, there was utter quiet now.

Two

An ashen twilight had fallen over Columbia, and the street lamps and headlights and the orange glow from the windows of shabby apartment buildings now threw a dull reflection over the town, but Jack Anders was barely conscious of the passage of time. He had stood looking at himself in the mirror at Frankie's apartment for at least half an hour, turning this way and that, pulling the new, stiff hat down over his eyes, first glaring out ferociously from under the bill, then smiling broadly. He couldn't get over the rich crimson of the shirt with its raised, stitched white lettering on the front. He turned his shoulder again to glimpse his name on the back: ANDERS.

That was when Frank came back in suddenly with a sack of groceries, startling him so that he was frozen in his pose, staring stupidly at himself. Frank only smiled.

"Don't worry about it," he said. "I did the exact same thing. Hey, I got us some oranges."

From behind his back, he tossed a piece of fruit at Jack as he crossed towards the tiny kitchen. He held it under his nose, sniffed its sunny freshness, and caressed its dimpled surface with his thumb. "Thank you," he said.

He did not yet know what to make of this white boy. His only experiences with whites (crackers, his cousin Tol called them) had been less than reassuring: there had been only the deceitful boy selling bags of peanuts at the game on that fateful day nearly three years ago, and then there were the guards at the prison, but that had been all. His mother had worked in white people's houses off and on for as long as he could recall, riding the bus to and from town, but she never said anything at all about that. Only once, when she had come home tired and sore and grumbling, he had asked her, "What's wrong, Mama? Don't they treat you good?"

She had looked at him over her glasses and said, "They good. They good as gold," and then she placed her hand on his close-shaven head.

Naturally, when Frank had approached him after practice that day and told him that the Reds were interested in him, he had been skeptical, even suspicious. I don't know how it usually happens, he had thought, but I bet it don't happen like this. Still, it was true after all; a man in a dress suit had picked him up in a big car and had taken him down to the stadium, and he had signed his name to a contract that very afternoon. Two thousand dollars was more money than his mother could make in two years time, but when he got home that night, he had it in his pocket – cash money, two thick rolls of fifties. Oh, she had been a bit upset, of course, when he told her that they wanted him to move into town, but somehow she could not manage to keep from smiling at him.

He had not told her, however, that he would be sharing Frank's apartment; that would have elicited a good deal of fretting and then a heavy dose of advice, and he thought that he could do without that for now. Within himself, he concluded, he would put aside what he knew of the shiftlessness and trickery of white folks. He glanced over at Frank, who had cut a whole in the top of his orange and was sitting on the couch, sucking out the juice. He supposed he would give the boy a chance.

––––––––

Banks had believed that it was an untenable plan, but now he knew better. Unequivocally, in fact, it had been a stroke of genius. The big office in Cincinnati liked it, for it helped fill the colored bleachers at both home and away games, and it made Columbia look "progressive" at a time when all the national news would paint South Carolinians as querulous racists and South Carolina itself as a bastion of the Klan. To Banks, and indeed to most of the people that he knew, black and white, the troubles and sit-ins in Greensboro and even in Rock Hill somehow seemed far-away, like somebody else's fight, but a miasmic fog seemed to hang over them nonetheless. But a colored player and a white player not only getting along well in the locker room and in the dugout, but sharing an apartment, too... Who'd have thought of it?

He knew very well that Jackie Robinson and Branch Rickey had crashed through the race barrier back in '47, but in the southern minor leagues, especially the smaller towns, it was another matter; the barrier remained in place. Banks had grown up in a time when segregation – separate and unequal – was the state of things between the races, and such was still the case: separate water fountains and bathrooms in the Winn-Dixies and Piggly Wigglys, "whites-only" lunch counters. Real old-timers sometimes talked about the days when whites and Negroes lived in close proximity to one another, in the country, performing the same farm work, sweating into the same dirt, sharing the same food – hominy, beans, the foods of poor people. But industrialization and new economic competition had separated people, isolated people from one another. He never met any blacks, sellers or buyers, in his real estate ventures, though he had hired plenty of poor men, white and colored, as construction laborers, and they were pretty much the same; they arrived, they worked hard, but the shared humor was gone. And then they simply moved on.

Of course, he thought, there were those who would chide and even abuse Frank for his friendship with Anders (though Frank himself had remarked, "Friends? Hell, we ain't friends. We're ballplayers."), but he knew as well that there were those who would aggrandize him, and that might be a worse consequence. As for himself, he had two ideas about it: either the boy was acting out of raw naivety to social restrictions, or given what had happened to him these past two years, he just didn't give a shit what people thought.

He was inclined to believe the latter.

As if she could read his mind, Karen, who had come downstairs and sat across the breakfast counter from him, said, "He knows more than you think he does."

"Who?"

"Frank. He's not the doe-eyed kid you see him as."

"I see him as a company employee."

"Sure you do, Uncle Banks. Someday you'll have to acknowledge that not all your relationships are business arrangements. And you'll have to tell him who you really are, because you care about him. He's your brother's kid."

He looked down into the dark depths of his coffee mug. "I can't argue with you," he said. "It's my curse...my cross, I guess. To be honest, I never knew how to do anything other than make money. I saw my mother – mine and Bob's mother – struggle all of her life. She made two unhappy decisions, and I looked at that, the cheap flea-bag trailers, the barrooms, and always at the mercy of some landlord or boss, and you never get a break. I swore that would never be me. Consequently, I learned to see the whole world in terms of dollars. I look at something or someone, and a dollar amount pops up. I can't help it."

"That is a burden," she said. "Wonder what my number was the first time you saw me."

"Wish't I had a joke to answer that with, but I don't. I could have gone back to Dillon. I knew where my brother was. But it rang up a zero whenever I thought about it. Do you think a man can unlearn that? Is it too late for me?"

She looked at him steadily; it was that look, bright, blue-eyed, with genuine interest and curiosity, and softness. Was that what love looked like? "No," she said. "It's not too late. You're getting there."

"I hope so."

"What's on the schedule for today?"

"'I've got to ride out and look at a property on the point. After that, I'm going to head over to Columbia, try and catch a ballgame. You're welcome to come along with me if you want to."

"I'd like that."

The April sun had burnt away the sea mists that hung over the coastline, a vast pinkish stretch of sand turning to brown, as the two of them rolled along the King's Highway out toward the Grand Strand. It was still mostly empty, with a few strips of garishly painted motels and lonely gas stations, and here and there along the shore a few scattered tents, probably belonging to northern college kids who hadn't made it as far as Fort Lauderdale (or who hadn't signed up for JFK's Peace Corps, Banks thought wryly) – thrown down between the spindle-legged commercial piers that were like gigantic insects making their way into the water. The water as yet had no color; it was a great moving web made of reflective fibers, and once the air had cleared, only the occasional silvery tanker in the far distance disturbed the flat line where ocean met sky.

———

Luther sat on his back porch and held his glass of tea to the sunlight that poured over the edges of the old weathered fence and across the upturned dahlias and lilies in the flowerbed. If he looked closely at it, he could see the fissures in the ice cubes, the small crystals and cut surfaces against the golden-brown hue. "That's it," he told himself. "Relax. Breathe."

More and more, he found that he marked changes in his own life and outlook according to Della Treadwell's death; it was a gash on his personal timeline, and he would think, "Well, that's the first time that's happened since she's been gone," or, as in this case, "It never would have happened that way when she was alive." Today, he was proud of himself, for he was certain that he had rid himself for good of the old sin, the old Demon Wrath. How could it be otherwise? He had just this moment realized that his first and strongest impulse after his conversation yesterday with Liza had been to wrack his brain for means to assist her, to address the problem at hand, to get her and her child through the next few weeks. The old Luther…well, that old sinner would have been gripped by uncontrollable rage, possessed by it completely; he would have gone out immediately in the station wagon to prowl the streets around Dillon and then lain in wait for the bastard to show his face, and then he would have yanked his bones right out of his skin. But the reformed Luther, what did he do? Why, he sat on the porch peacefully drinking iced tea and looking at his flowers, and thinking of ways he could help. Maybe that was where the whole idea of sainthood had derived: someone shows you through her own grace the proper way to love, and then once she's dead, you spend the rest or your own time trying to do the same. Saint Della.

In any event, he had come up with a plan. He could not have her come and stay with him (though he certainly would have done so, had he not known that certain members of his own congregation would say vile things, and then he would be in no position to assist anyone), but he could offer to help with Carl Junior. The church ran a nursery part-time and it would not be difficult to make room for him, and then in the afternoons, when necessary, he could redeliver the boy to his mother's hands. Liza herself would be moving back in with her mother temporarily, and going back to work at the diner, but she would land on her feet. She would be all right.

But what a time she'd had, poor girl. What was she now, twenty? Nineteen? As a lifelong bachelor, Luther believed he had a certain objectivity on these matters, and he had perceived again and again the pitfalls that awaited young women who gave themselves away to the sorts of young men that were once called "bounders." Now she was strapped with a baby and no money, and a grim future before her. On the other hand, having never known physical intimacy with a woman himself, he did not know the catches in the heart, those raw and tender places that made such choices and such mistakes possible. Only Christ had known them and understood them without having experienced them, and he had forgiven them through the power of love. What else could have taken Mary Magdalene out of the prostitutes' doorways and brought her ultimately to the foot of the cross?

As far as the men in these parts, it was the same old struggle: either they could not grow up at all and languished in their depravities, as if existence itself were a great joke, or else they became hardened and unable to show compassion. In the worst cases, a whiskey-fueled anger drove them to physical abuse, and the infliction of pain upon others became their only real pleasure. He had once done some prison ministry, but he had learned that that kind of meanness was nearly impossible to rehabilitate; rare was the man who, having seemingly handed his life over to Christ while in a cell, could sustain such a commitment once plunged back in society. Once he had counseled a man on Death Row, sat with him in that cold, confined space through the dark hours, listened to his tear-laden pleas and prayers, but when the guards came for him, he saw the old resentment and smugness in his eyes; he loathed their authority and would have slit their throats given half the chance. But then the grimmest and heaviest authority of all, of the sort wielded by King Herod, fell upon him, and as they led him down that shadowy hallway, his body had sagged and he had fouled his own pants, and all who were there to witness it had seen the awful power of death to annihilate hope, to expose us as the weak and cowardly creatures we are. As Hamlet remarked, this fell sergeant is strict in his arrest. He had seen it close-up himself, and once it had almost laid low the faith that his father had rooted in him as a child.

Now he knew how hard it was, coming back from that. The odds are against us, he thought. It is one thing to talk a good, straight line, but another to come to terms with one's mortality, let alone learn not to fear the greatest of unknowns. We live in an age, he believed, when God is less inclined to speak to us openly, though he had felt His presence quite clearly in certain moments, many times; but the burden is upon us, mostly, to look for Him, and once we have opened our sleep-thickened eyes, we will see ample and compelling evidence that He is among us.

He might have meant the near-decimation and renewal of his own faith, or the finding of a lost boy, or his need to reach out to a brokenhearted girl wandering in the tunnel of her suffering… Then again, maybe it was simply the glow of the sun in a glass of iced tea.

———

Frank could smell the field before he saw it, the organic taste in his nostrils of the grass, the freshly raked soil of the infield, and the first hints of roasting wieners floating thinly on the air above them. He had known all of it for so long, and now it was not much different, really – just a little bigger, a little grander, a little more expensive. Then, emerging from the dimly lit corridor into that wide expanse, his heart leapt in the old way, and as always the old secret – that he was meant to do this and would always do this – was whispered to him.

There was nothing quite so fine as jogging out onto a baseball field with your teammates before a game, playing some catch, taking infield and outfield, some batting practice, as the crowd gathered, and then watching the other team do the same. The umpires would come out in their blue clothes, and they would meet with the managers at home plate, and soon it would be time to start the game. He liked these guys, all of them, even the opposing players, even the somewhat ineffective Hersh Freeman, even the managers and coaches of the other teams, even the umpires, for goodness sake. There were assholes among them, no doubt, but meeting an asshole at the ballpark was still better than meeting one on the street. Although many of the players were men several years older than himself, it was still the best kind of fellowship he knew, and there was always laughing and joking and horseplay right up until the pitcher would wind up for the first time, at which point suddenly everything was condensed, all minds focused, and then came the pitch, the first swing, the first catch and throw, each one the smallest bit different from every pitch, swing, catch, and throw that had come before. And yet they were very much the same. He felt he would never get tired of this.

Jack Anders was fitting in well – as best he could, anyway. The Reds had since signed one other colored player, Haywood Peterson, who was a cheap, capable utility infielder, but who would probably sit the bench for much of the season and often was not included on the roster for road games. Of course, the white players kept to their own small cliques, groups of three and four who roomed together, ate together, frequented the beer joints around town together, while in contrast, he and Jack lived a relatively sedate life in their little place on East Broadway. At home, often there were long periods of silence between them when they read magazines or watched the small black and white television that Banks Treadwell had bought for them, and sometimes Frank glanced at the 45rpm records that had belonged to Liza and thought about buying a record player. But in the dugout and on the field, their fondness for one another was much more in evidence; this was where their connection became kinetic, their teamwork and communication in the outfield – Frank in center and Jack in left – for those who watched carefully, was an exercise in grace, humility, and strength. A ball that was hit into the gap that would ordinarily fall in for an extra-base hit would now be succinctly snuffed in the pocket of one of their outstretched gloves, as Frank would yield right-of-way to his teammate's superior short-burst speed, while Jack would back away from a long fly ball if there were runners on base waiting to tag up, realizing that Frank's stronger and more accurate arm could turn a runner's certain advancement into a deadly risk. Their strategy on sinking liners in shallow left-center was simple: Jack would mount a full-sprint attempt at making the catch, as he often did, while Frank circled behind him in the event that the ball should get through. In this manner, they held even the fastest and best hitters in the South Atlantic League to a single at best.

True, they were only ten games into the season now, and fast approaching the month of May, but such had been their feats thus far in the broad green meadows where Fate had given them the chance to roam. In the stricter confines of the batter's box, each practiced his subtle art in the comparative loneliness peculiar to the odd endeavor of hitting a baseball, although Frank, who was now batting second in the lineup, found many ways to use the fearsomeness of Anders, who hit third, sometimes exhibiting the sort of easy power that those who had seen Mantle and Mays in earlier times must have shaken their heads over, for it was one thing to possess muscular arms and shoulders, but it was altogether another to make one's hips open up and bring one's whole being to bear upon a ball that seemed to dive away from him in desperation and to launch it into the upper limits. In general, the physical motion itself did not differ greatly from that of other hitters, but the results were of another, more mysterious category. The additional and perhaps more important meaning of Jack's power was simply that Frank must always find a way to get on base. He learned to engage the pitcher's psyche, to cunningly steal an inch or two here and there, create the illusion of space on either side of the plate, to foul off pitch after pitch when he was uncertain of their location, to be ahead in the count at all times, and to bunt for a base hit. Therefore, a double off of Anders' bat ensured a run, and a dinger, of course, meant two.

For most of the other Reds players, as typically happens in such cases, their energy and enthusiasm were infectious. As a single-A minor league team, the organization saw two breeds of player: those who believed themselves fit for the majors and were on their way up and in, and those older men who had been reassigned, relegated, and who were headed down and out. Even Kleghorn, who at thirty-five had spent four years with Detroit in the American League and another five with Cincinnati (never hitting higher than .230), showed hustle, fiercely running out the routine grounders that clunked weakly off of his bat. The younger players, most of them raw country boys culled from the southern woods, found themselves in a salubrious competition with one another, the sort of concentrated and pure effort, judged solely on its own merit, that can make sport worth watching even to the most ignorant or jaded observer.

Only one of them had seemed to suggest any resentment at all toward the early success of Jack Anders and Frank Johnson, and even that had not been overt: twenty-one year-old Talmadge Biggs, who played third base and owned an arm like a whip, would sometimes steal a glance at the two of them from beneath the bill of his cap, a certain slant to his head, his lips moving in a way that made Frank wonder what he was muttering under his breath. Only once had Biggs actually made a remark out loud, and even that was merely a joke, the sort of thing that men say to each other under these circumstances, a little dig that meant nothing at all probably, a dirty little comment that ought to have been tossed into the bin of stupid words quickly forgotten, but for some reason he had not forgotten it. He had arrived at practice a few minutes late on Monday, uncharacteristically enough, having had the trainer tape a slightly swollen ankle as a precautionary measure. Jack was dealing with some sort of equipment problem and had not yet shown up either. Frank had stepped down into the dugout, put his glove on, pounding its palm, and then he had gazed up toward the empty outfield.

Biggs, who was standing a few feet away, said, "If you're looking for your boyfriend, he ain't here yet. I'm having him sweep up in front of my locker."

Two other players sitting on the bench guffawed. Frank smacked his fist into the glove again, cleared his throat, and looked contemplatively across to the bleachers behind first base. "Funny, Biggs," he said. "Very funny."

Then he had jogged out to center field to shag some fly balls.

———

Liza just happened to see Sunday's newspaper because she had picked up her first shift at Trudy's Diner since before Carl Junior had been born and a customer had left it on the counter. She had tucked it away, and when she was finally able to sit down for a few minutes around two that afternoon, she opened it up.

It had been a rough morning. She had dropped off the baby with Pastor Laite at the church office, and had come rushing in just in time to take a table of six. It had been nonstop after that, a steady stream of pre-church early risers, during-church infidels, and post-church gluttons, and she was already so tired, so worn down by heavy trays, streaked with bacon grease and peach jelly, she could hardly read the newsprint before her eyes. But on the front of the sports page, a picture caught her eye. It was under a headline that read COLUMBIA A-LEAGUERS OFF TO A FAST START. That was a benign enough statement, but the photo showed a young man in a baseball uniform shaking hands with a colored man who was stepping on home plate. His face was turned slightly downward and in shadow, and he was smiling, but she recognized him immediately. He had grown – he was taller and slenderer through the hips, and his chest and shoulders had filled out considerably, but there was no doubt in her mind that it was Frankie Treadwell. She read the caption: *Reds center fielder Frank Johnson congratulates Jack Anders on another round tripper.* Johnson my foot, she whispered. That's a Treadwell if there ever was one.

The article, which somehow managed to be even duller than the headline, contained further misinformation. It said that Frankie was nineteen and "haled from" Horry County. Either this was some of the shoddiest reporting ever to see print, or somebody was telling deliberate lies. She looked around for someone to share this travesty with, but she found she did not really know any of the other girls on shift. She got up and walked back past the kitchen to the big steel sinks, where she found Robley hosing off the last couple of plates from brunch. He smiled up at her.

"Well, if it ain't the Queen Bee, in all her glory," he said. "I heard you was coming back. How you doing, Miss?"

"I'm fine. How bad did you miss me?"

"Every day, every day."

"Want to take a break for a ciggie?"

"Sure. Give me five minutes."

As she waited in the grimy back lot for him, she opened the sports page again. Could it have been a look-alike after all? All boys that age – athletic types anyway – look somewhat similar, especially in uniform. No, no: it was him, no question, now that she was able to hold the page in the bright sunlight. She had that odd feeling she got whenever she was suddenly jerked back to some point in her past, as if she had been living in some kind of dream or a made-up story, or as if time had somehow been warped and the arcs of two lines that had separated were once again about to converge.

Robley came out, smiling broadly. "So how is the young prince?"

"The baby's fine. I'm not so good. Carl and I split up."

His brow plunged. "Mmm. Sorry to hear about it. Mighty tough on you, I guess."

"Probably a case of good riddance. How's your wife and kids?"

"Everybody's fine, far as I know. Saw the boys at Easter time." He tapped his pack of Camels on his brown forearm and held it out to her.

"Thanks. Hey, Robley, let me get your opinion on something." She leaned over as he held a match up for her, then opened up the sports page with a dramatic rattling of paper. "Who does this look like to you?"

He studied it. "I'm afraid I don't recognize him. Is he supposed to be somebody famous?"

"Doesn't it look like Frank Treadwell to you?"

"Who?"

"You know. Frankie. Played ball for the high school."

"Oh, all right. The one that was sweet on you. Came by here to see you a couple times after his mama died."

"That's the one."

"Hmm. I'm not rightly sure. I only saw him for a minute or two, but I guess it could be."

"It definitely is him."

"Well, that's something, ain't it? From little ol' Dillon and got his picture in the paper already."

"This says he's doing really well playing for a professional team over in Columbia."

"How about that? Well, you never do know, do you?"

Robley clearly was not impressed, but then he must have read the dismay in her face, for he said, "Professionals, huh? I bet he *will* get to be famous. You know, if I didn't know better, I'd say you're the one kinda sweet on him now."

"No. I just haven't seem him in a long time."

"You should go up there and watch a game. Say hello."

"Who's got time for that? I've got the baby, and work now... In fact, you're going to be seeing a lot of me around here again, Robley."

"Suits me just fine." He dropped the remaining butt and ground it into the asphalt. "You always was the only one would talk to me anyhow."

"Long as you don't mind hearing me bitch about Carl."

"Don't you worry," he said. "We'll get it figured out."

Max Bass knew things about people. He knew secrets, and because he had kept a few himself, he could see the secrets of others as plainly as if he were looking at an x-ray plate: he could see straight into the insides of people. One or two shots of gin on the train or the bus to clear his head, and he almost always made the right choices concerning the players he was scouting, and by God, it had nothing to do with the old "Good-hit, no-field" formula.

In his two seasons with the Senators organization, he had referred twenty-three players, and twelve of them were now in the major leagues – a damn good record for any scout. He had been all over the country, in every little Podunk town from Smoke Hole to La Jolla, looking at players of every size, shape, and color, and he had learned one thing for certain: what he saw on the outside was nowhere near as important as what he saw on the inside. Every place he went there were good players, and lots of guys could hit and run and throw, but very few had the mental toughness or the cut-throat instincts it took to climb over the competition, or the willingness to gain an edge by whatever means necessary. Playing American Legion ball or high school or even single-A was one thing, but the grind and stress of a major-league season was another experience altogether. That took solid steel balls.

He had recognized Frank Treadwell the instant he saw him. He'd been passing through Columbia and had gone to a Reds game on a whim, expecting only to buy a 7-Up, load it up using the flask in his back pocket, take in a few innings, and then prowl the local taverns in search of a girl; such was his existence. His eye fell upon the young man trotting out to center field; the back of his shirt read JOHNSON, but it was Treadwell. He'd realized only sometime later that he ought to have been more surprised, but he had also known all along that the kid possessed the tools – maybe he had the toughness now as well. Some real-life experience, at any age, could make a lot of difference. But when the game was over, he had seen three players – Treadwell, that colored boy Anders, and Talmadge Biggs – that he thought the Senators might be interested in. Frank had looked damn good, going two for four at the plate and gunning a runner out at second base, but Jack Anders had impressive size and strength. As for Biggs, he was just plain nasty, stealing second with his cleats aimed at the infielder's knees, and when he was holding a runner close at third base, taking pains to step on the tender tops of his feet. If he'd had to pick one of them that same day, he'd have taken Biggs.

Of course, if he allowed himself to stew over it, there had been an old wound inflicted in his dealings with Treadwell. His career as a coach (such as it was) had been pre-empted by the kid's antics, and Max still believed he had been the one to turn him in over that business with the girl. Nonetheless, it had all worked out; hell, maybe he should thank him, for his reputation as a scout continued to grow.

He had phoned the Senators' office immediately afterward to tell them what he'd seen. "Stick around for one more look," Neidermeyer had said. "We'll talk about it when you get back. If we can free up some money by June, we'll send you back down there to make an offer." No qualms; sure enough, money talked, and the Senators would not hesitate to buy out a young player's contract with another team. Max knew that the time was coming when professional athletes would be making staggering amounts of money. The market potential was already in place, and it would simply take some bright lawyers to figure out a way. Shit, Willie Mays was being paid $80,000 this very season by the Giants.

So it was that he found himself two nights later in this drafty, echoing stadium, leaning on the railing along the left-field line (from here he could observe the mechanics of the left-handed hitters, and then in the fourth he could shift over to the other side to see the righties). He had been hung over all day, nursing his swollen head and aching bowels, downing handfuls of aspirin and drinking water, until finally he had been able to drag himself to the park just in time for warm-ups. He had bought a hotdog and then promptly puked it up into the toilet, but a cold beer had at last settled his stomach somewhat, and now he stood at the corroded rail and watched the wrappers and bags and other trash swirl across the infield, where they were lifted by invisible funnels of air and hefted into the seats. With only a little to-do, the game began, evening fell, and the lights blazed up against the glimmery-gray sky; the air was dead still tonight, and it was one of those evenings when he could clearly hear the umpire's calls, the undertones of half-chatter from the dugouts, and even the whirring of the ball as the pitcher flung it up to the plate, where it was abruptly met by a leathery thud or a piercing crack of wood. The first two innings were scoreless and nearly hitless, save for a skittering ground ball from Talmadge Biggs that found its way between the second and third basemen. It was shaping up to be a pitcher's night, and Max strongly considered strolling down to the corner bar where he had spent most of the previous afternoon and evening, but he decided to stick it out a little longer.

It was one of the great strokes in his life that he did so, for the events of the third and fourth were unlike anything he'd witnessed before in baseball.

First, the floodgates opened for the Reds, as the Knoxville Smokies' pitcher suddenly fell to pieces, walking the first two batters and then giving up a home run to the leadoff man, at which point he was mercifully pulled. The reliever, however, a pot-gutted right-hander of about thirty-five, had clearly seen better days as well. Treadwell came to the plate next, and Max already knew what was about to happen. Sure enough, after whipping two fastballs way off the plate and stubbornly shaking off the catcher's desperate signs, Chubs came inside with the change-up; it was almost as if he had deliberately worked on this particular pitch for this particular situation, as if he had asked himself beforehand: "Now, if I do face this ambitious youngster tonight, how can I best serve him? What might be the most lame-assed piece of crap I could throw him in order to make him look like the next Mickey Mantle and make my own team look like a bunch of assholes? I know – when I have him ahead in the count, right where I want him, I'll give him the change-up. He'll simply crush it." And so he did, though the ball did not leave the park. It traveled almost on a straight line to the deepest wedge of right field, just inside the foul pole, ricocheted off the top of the concrete wall, and pin-balled around in the corner where the breathless right fielder finally corralled it as Treadwell was rounding second base. The relay throw had little chance of getting him, but Frank dove headfirst anyway into third base, just for the fun of it, it seemed.

Jack Anders was still laughing as he stepped into the batter's box, tapped the head of his bat on his shoes, and then settled into his relaxed stance. Later, Max thought that perhaps it was this, the laughter, that led to the ugliness which ensued, though he could not be sure, since Anders hit from the right, and he couldn't fully see his face. He did see, however, the change in the reliever's demeanor: he seemed to summon the strength of his youth, to breathe life, as it were, into the passionate fires that once sustained his dreams; he sucked in his gut, glared at the batter, allowed the tension to rise taut in the air between the mound and the plate, and then, completely ignoring Frank's extravagant walking lead at third, he curled into his windup. A sharp fastball, maybe around eighty or eighty-five miles per hour, rose in like a flare, and Anders had just enough time to turn his head and duck a couple of inches, so that the ball caromed with a nauseating thunk off of his left shoulder instead of his skull and then rolled halfway up the screen behind him. A deeper hush fell over the sparse crowd as Anders growled in pain and then turned and flung the bat toward the Reds dugout, though he did not touch his shoulder. He turned his body fully to face Chubs, his broad chest heaving with anger, his feet planted.

The pitcher raised his middle finger at him, and in a voice loud enough for everyone in the stadium to hear him, he said, "Come get some, nigger!"

No one saw Treadwell striding toward the mound from third base except for the Reds' third-base coach, who first put his hands to his head in a kind of theatrical panic and then dashed out, throwing his arms around Frank's legs and pulling him to the turf. A melee ensued as both teams' benches cleared, outfielders and bullpen pitchers sprinted in to the infield grass, and coaches and managers on both sides rushed out yelling at the tops of their lungs. Frank and the third-base coach rolled over in an awkward way, as if they were on a hillside rather than a level expanse of ground, and players began pulling each others' shirts, separating one man from another, pushing, shouting, and the umpires pointed vigorously this way and that in an effort to send individuals back to their proper places. The crowd took notice, cheered, booed, and when order had been restored, turned back to their hotdogs and beers. Max laughed. "Good stuff," he muttered.

Because no one had quite understood what had happened, no one was ejected, and so the bloodletting by the Reds' hitters continued. At last, as the sky turned the color of a nasty bruise, the Smokies' catcher leaned over into the stands seemingly out of sheer embarrassment to make an unlikely catch on a pop foul, and the side was retired at last, though not before the Reds had scored five more times. With the score 8-0, Max closed up his notebook and was making his way toward the stairs when he looked up to see the same hapless, beleaguered pitcher walking slowly to the mound, his bulging stomach swinging in front of him like a sack of oats. Cruel joke, he thought, sending the poor son of a bitch back out there again. Or perhaps he was no more appreciated in his own dugout than he was by the opposition, but in any case, he had the reluctant bearing of a man approaching a chopping block, and so Max took the seat nearest the exit. There was no way he was going to miss this.

This time, Treadwell was first up in the inning. He seemed quite relaxed, as if the earlier incident had played out in some other life, some other game that had happened long ago, as he took a few easy practice swings, stepped to the plate, and dug in without even looking up. But as Max knew, ballplayers do not easily forget such things, and Treadwell, with all his weight on his back leg, patiently watched the first two pitches sail high, arms and back swinging loosely out over the plate between pitches – one, two, three strokes. And then came Chubs's final error, the one which would make him the stuff of lore, mentioned in the same breath with other famous victims of freak, career-ending incidents, such as Roger Goff, who permanently damaged the tendons in his ring finger while trying to remove his wedding band just before a salacious rendezvous in a hotel room after a road game, and Clarence Blethen, the 1920s pitcher who slid into second base and skewered himself on his own false teeth, which he always kept in his back pocket during games. It was a good pitch, actually, a sinister fastball that came whistling into the lowest part of the strike zone, and Frank went down to get it, smacking it with the meat of his bat so that the ball rocketed out at an incomprehensible velocity, an intelligent bullet that honed in on the reliever where he stood, spread-eagle after the effort of his delivery, burrowing in fatefully toward his exposed crotch.

There was a sound like a raw chicken being flung against a wall, and then the audible drawing in of breath by those two thousand or so witnesses who suddenly realized what had happened; this was then followed by several seconds of silence as time stood still, and then the heavy body fell sideways, toppling like a man cut in half by shrapnel. Treadwell took a leisurely trot down to first base and stopped there, turning, his foot on the bag, his hat's bill pulled low over his eyes, his broad grin brightly visible below it.

"No cup," Max muttered.

That night, the next day, and for several days after, the story would travel quickly around the league – indeed, around the ranks of professional baseball – of the vicious feat of retaliatory hitting by the single-A outfielder in the South Atlantic League. As for the pitcher, they said, he would require two surgeries to repair tears in both testicles, and ultimately one of them would have to be removed.

However, Max Bass, who was there, would always say that it was merely a strange coincidence, if not a case of utterly blind justice, for as good as any hitter might be, it is virtually impossible to hit a live baseball with that sort of pinpoint accuracy. "Anyway," he would say, "you should always drop your hands on a low fastball and try to drive it right back up the middle. It was just damn good hitting."

———

The hurly burly of the diner was at full throttle, resounding with the rattling of coffee cups and the constant hiss of the griddle. Liza picked up the sports section of the Saturday newspaper and tucked it under the counter until she could take her break. There was a stack of them there now, as she deliberately kept them as a kind of diary of Frankie's exploits; she had remembered that she had saved the clippings from his high school days, too –

they were probably at the bottom of a cardboard box someplace, but she was quite sure she had them. Why? It seemed to her that someone ought to do it, and Frank himself would never have thought of it.

Besides, it helped to break the monotony of the day. She couldn't recall when or why she had learned to read a box score (perhaps it had been from Frankie's father), but she knew enough that she could piece together the story of any particular game and determine how well he had played. Overall, she ascertained that he was doing very well, playing in every game and batting .373 so far for the season. Once in a while, his picture would be in the sports section with some banal cutline:

Center fielder Frank Johnson goes back to the wall to make a catch against the Jacksonville Jets on Thursday.

or…

The Reds rallied to beat the Hornets 8-7 last night as Frank Johnson went 3 for 4 at the plate..

She had carried the burden of her secret for three weeks now (except for having blurted it out to Robley on that very first day). In essence, there was no reason to share it with anybody, since his parents were both in the ground, and given the sudden surging of his career, he would probably never come back to live in Dillon again. She supposed that the sheriff still had a missing-person report out on him, but what if they found him? What could they do with him? Bring him here and put him back in school? It was nonsense to think he could return to Dillon High School and fit in, and it would be laughable to think of him playing ball there. At least they had gotten shut of that bastard of a coach,

Bass, and Liza still felt some satisfaction to know that she had perhaps played a part in that, having reported him for unseemly relations with at least one female student. And obviously, if Frank couldn't play ball, the he couldn't begin to function. There would be no point.

Deep down, she did have a desire to see him once more, though she had no inkling what he might be like now; he could well be an arrogant fool, as he had certainly shown potential for that in the past, and she needed no more of such men. She had considered an act that others might have judged unwise: she could, in fact, drive up to Columbia, provided the old truck she had gotten from Roger would make it that far... But what about Carl Junior? She couldn't very well take him with her; Frankie wasn't exactly ready for that, and she couldn't even think of calling upon the pastor to baby-sit without feeling spasms of guilt. Sometimes she imagined a life which just might have some degree of normalcy, wherein she and Carl would reach some sort of reconciliation and arrive at a settlement (though she hadn't yet found the time or the heart to look into divorce proceedings – they were still married, even though she had not seen him since the afternoon that redheaded woman had opened her trailer's door for him) and Carl Junior might grow up knowing his father, and she might even some day go on a date again, for she was still quite young. In the meantime, an afternoon drive to Columbia was but a fantasy.

She did know of one other person in town who retained an interest in Frank Treadwell, and that was Luther Laite, of course. She had been trying to think of a way to broach the subject with him, as he sometimes brought Carl Junior into the diner for a late breakfast when she was working (in fact, she expected him anytime now), but she couldn't figure out a way. For all she knew, as a pastor, he would go strictly by the book and call the authorities on him, and that would ruin everything. At last she had hit upon a plan, and when Luther did enter the diner with the now-toddling Carl Junior in tow, she took a deep breath, smiled at them, walked over to their table, and kissed her son on his round cheek.

"Morning," she said, and she placed a cup of coffee and today's sports section in front of the pastor. There was Frank Johnson again, this time sliding into third base. This she had never done, and as far as she knew, Luther had no interest in sports.

"Thanks," he said. Carl Junior cooed and reached toward her hairnet, and she pecked at him again before bustling off to tend to her other customers. When the crowd had thinned somewhat and she went back to check on them, Luther pointed at the paper and said,

"Hey, I just noticed something."

"Oh?"

"Yes. It's baseball season. I hear they're playing some good ball up there in Columbia. We should ride up there sometime and catch a game. You always liked baseball, didn't you?"

"Sure I do. But what about Carl Junior?"

"Why, we'd take him with us, of course. It's baseball, for goodness sake."

"I don't think I can."

"Well, when's your next day off?"

"Not till next month."

"Perfect. Find out the exact day and we'll plan on it."

As he looked back down, she thought she detected a slight smile, but he was a hard man to read sometimes. He had to have recognized the boy in the picture, if he had even glanced at it, but she couldn't be absolutely certain. She plucked the pen from her hair and pulled her notepad from her front pocket. "Over easy?"

"You know it," Luther said. "Scrambled for my friend here."

As she turned away, the words to herself were on the tip of her tongue: what had just happened? But she suddenly saw something that froze her mid-stride. There was a form on the other side of the big front window, and a pair eyes close to the glass. It was Carl, his long, tan hands cupped around his face; he was wearing his trademark sleeveless white undershirt. He was not smiling but wearing an expression that, she suspected, was intended to appear pathetic, sorrowful. They stared at one another for several seconds, as anxiety gripped her stomach.

"Something wrong?" asked Luther, behind her.

"No." She jammed the notebook back in her apron pocket, averted her eyes, and hurried off to collect dirty plates from the idle tables.

———

"Okay. What's wrong?"

Ordinarily, the silence in the little apartment, broken only by the soft pulsing of the television or their monosyllabic communications regarding dinner, was a comfortable one, but ever since the chaotic events that had taken place in the game against Knoxville, the tone of it had changed, as if something in the air surrounding them had gone afoul. Even when Frank asked, "Spaghetti okay?" Jack had merely shrugged his shoulders and said,

"Fine."

So, when he had put the steaming bowls on the coffee table and found *The Andy Griffith Show* on the little black-and-white, he asked again, as casually and un-provocatively as he could – what was wrong?

"Ain't," Jack said. He poked a forkful of noodles into his mouth and chewed.

"Have you heard from your mama this week?"

Jack nodded but said nothing.

Frank set down his toast, looked up at him, and swallowed. "Come on now, roomie. It's obvious there's something eating at you. Anything I said?"

The thick silence hung there for a couple of minutes as they stared at the screen, watching Barney Fife roll his eyes as he led Otis, Mayberry's town drunk, to a jail cell. At last Jack blurted, "I don't need you fighting no fights for me. If it needs fighting, I'll do it."

"Oh, so that's what this is about," Frank replied. "I suppose I know how you feel, but I'd have done the same for any teammate."

"You know how I feel? *You* know how *I* feel?"

"Sure."

"Boy, you got no idea. Trying to help me deal with that kind of trash ain't going to get us nowhere."

"Why not? That's what we do. You'd do the same for me, wouldn't you?"

"But it ain't the same. I ain't crying or complaining that I was born colored, but I got things to do. Got some things to show some people, and if I can't do it myself, ain't nobody going to respect me for it."

"Everybody needs some help once in a while."

"You don't understand. You won't ever understand. Don't you read the news? Those negroes in Greensboro that sat down at that lunch counter didn't get no help. If a colored man wants something in this world, his best chance is to just take it and don't say nothing. Just take it and don't apologize and don't need no help."

"That's a pretty sad way to go around."

"Well, that's how it is."

There was much more that Frank wanted to say: he wanted to explain that perhaps he was the exception, but he had seldom ever even thought about a person's skin color (and especially not in baseball), and that although he had heard and read about the trials and troubles of Jackie Robinson and Frank Robinson and Larry Doby and Roy Campanella and others, he'd always believed it should be easy to see who had been right and who had been wrong in those instances, for every man had a right to play baseball if he chose to; he wanted to say that in the modest house where he had grown up, there had been virtually no talk of race at all – that his mother had merely taught him not to appoint himself judge of anyone else, that all are worthy in God's eyes; he wanted to note that even though he had not grown up around blacks, those that he had come in contact with had been decent folks; he wanted to argue that it wasn't his fault they had put the negro school way out in Marion and that he had hardly ever found reason to set his foot in those communities, unless it had been to play a baseball game. Nevertheless, given the stony expression on Jack's face, he perceived that anything he might say now would simply fall awkwardly and heavily upon the taut silence that had overtaken the room.

So, the two of them stared at the television and ate the now-cold spaghetti, as the laugh track spilled out of the little box numbingly, a garbled soundtrack for the inane actions of the caricatures on the screen before them.

———

Banks lay sleeplessly on the bamboo chaise lounge beside the swimming pool, his whiskey sour balanced on his bare chest. For a while he would look out to the stars above the bay, and then he would contemplate the woman's face in the soft light. How lovely it was, how smooth and sweet and untroubled in her sleep, like that of an ancient statue in some remote jungle. He wished that he had a better way with words – he might write a poem for her and leave it on the breakfast counter for her to discover in the morning. No matter what he wrote, she would appreciate it, but he could not stand to do a thing badly.

Yet it was for those same reasons that he had determined he must break off their relationship. He felt befuddled over his own condition, and the idea that he might care for her genuinely, unconditionally, frightened him. That was deep water, and he needed numbers, exact depths, foreknowledge of costs and expenditures; he had always made his way and his wealth through deliberation, analysis, and plan of attack, but in her there was only this great warm depth and he had decided he could not subsist in it, for he knew that he could drown. He would have to end it.

The other great change at hand for him was his plan to sell the Columbia Reds. He hadn't told anyone of this, but he knew the time had come. In a way, it was quite similar to his dilemma over Karen: he could have continued as owner of the team had he been able to view it as trafficking in human flesh and blood, just as he might have dealt in livestock, but he had found that he could not. He saw them as young men, even boys, but not as commodities, and it wasn't just because he had bought the team in order to hire his nephew to play for it. It was quite clear that Frank had the ability to succeed in baseball on his own merit and talent, and all that Banks had done was to provide his first real opportunity, and he had done it in part (as he saw now) to try and make up for those years he had neglected his own brother. Well, that was done, a debt had been paid, and he would sell the team with a clear conscience, but only after he explained to the boy how things had really happened. Frank was bright, but in his youthful naivety, he had not yet seemed to ascertain that Banks's interest in him exceeded the parameters of the owner/player connection; at least, if he suspected the true circumstances, he never said as much. Banks expected that it might not make a pretty scene to tell him, for he knew Frank well enough now to see that he was fiercely competitive and would not abide any suggestion of an unfair advantage. Still, it had to be done if he were to tie everything up neatly.

Likewise, he would break things off with Karen and have no remorse, for he could never again quantify their connection – it had become too complex. This was what love felt like, he supposed, and he disliked it. He needed the orderliness of accounts, acreage, square feet, and dollar amounts. As he examined her lovely face, he wished that he could feel sad. He did not believe he had ever felt sorry before, for himself or anyone else. Life in his mother and stepfather's house had not been so bad; he had never been whipped, that he could recall, but it had not exactly been easy, either. He had always had to work. Sometimes he wondered what Bob's upbringing had been like, back there in Dillon on the Little PeeDee River. River rats, some folks called them. This place, this grand house on stilts that he had built for himself, with its sweeping view of the saltwater and the golden grandeur of the sun over open blue vistas, or as now, with the great velvet dome above with the new summer stars sprayed across it, and this beautiful half-naked woman sleeping within reach on a hammock – it was a million miles from the place of his birth. He was glad about that. Bittersweet: that was the word for it.

Perhaps the best thing about her had been that she had seemed to care sincerely for Frank as well. There had been nothing in it for her, but she had been of great help to him in finding the boy. At first, when he had purchased the team and subsequently arranged a contract for his nephew (albeit one he had been bound to get anyway), she had been the one quietly encouraging him to forge a relationship with him beyond the ballpark, suggesting from time to time that Banks invite Frankie to join them for dinner someplace in town or even bring him out to the house some weekend, if there were no games scheduled. But bless her, she hadn't pushed too hard, for she saw that it was not in his nature to get too close to the boy.

He would try to make it quick, get it over with in the next few days, though it would not be simple. It never was. She had never presumed to spend his money, as she came from money and seemed to have plenty of her own, and she had never interfered with the things he wanted to do. But change is the water in which we go, he thought; sea change, river change, any sort of change. If we don't change, we drown.

He was quite surprised to see the first paintings of the dawn seeping beyond the long, dark horizon. He had lain here for hours, thinking, drifting in and out of sleep. Fine. He had never needed much, and he hated sleeping, in general. It was a curse to a man who always had things to do.

Jack Anders knew that everything he had tried to say back at the apartment had come out wrong, but as soon as he had emerged from the tunnel for practice the next morning, the long green outfield and the sun seemed to scour it all from his brain. At least he had tried, he had spoken up, but in the end, none of it seemed to matter much beside the glory of the day, and Frank was his lively old self. And whatever had happened, whatever awkwardness had been between them, it was gone.

He knew he had sounded as if he despised white people, but this was not true. Despite what had happened to him, despite his undeserved term at the penitentiary, there was no lasting bitterness in his heart, no bur, though it was true that as yet he had seen no evidence that he ought to trust any of these people unequivocally. His idea had been to keep quiet as much as possible and to stay out of sight whenever he was away from the ballpark, but of course, the better the team did, and the better he played, the more difficult this became. Even on the long bus rides, even when he sat by himself on the very back row, after a while Frank would get up and come back and sit with him; that was fine, because generally they didn't talk anyway, and in the middle of the night, in the dark and lonely little towns, it was nice just to have the company. When they stayed at a motel, he would wait outside while Hersh Freeman, the manager, herded the other players in to sign their names and get their room assignments, and then Frank would come out and wordlessly hand him a key, and they would take their bags in. That was how it was done. It was well-known that the Negro American League was no more, and that was a good thing, he thought: fewer blacks would get to play, but those who did would earn more; he still marveled at the rather incredible idea that he received a healthy weekly paycheck just for playing ball, and his mother, in turn, marveled when he turned most of it over to her. On the other hand, it had made pro baseball a rather solitary experience for players such as Jack.

Nevertheless, as he tugged his cap down tight and jogged out for warm-ups, he would not let any of that bother him. Here he had no color: he was just a man standing on a grassy field, throwing, catching, throwing, catching, and everybody around him doing the same. He loved the feeling, the looseness in his arm, the sweat beginning to break across his shoulders, the sun on his face. The ball hitting his glove, pop!, and then out again, in his hand like a small, smooth rock, suddenly to be whipped so quickly and precisely that his partner (usually Frank) had only to hold his glove still in front of his chest, and the ball would snap into it as if tied to an elastic string, and before it could begin to nuzzle and nest there, out it came again, and then the whole cycle of movement was repeated. After that, infielders and outfielders would split up, and the pitchers and catchers would amble out to the bullpen to work. A good outfielder always reminded him of a hunting dog, the way he could go bolting out across an open field in the pursuit of a falling object, and that was all for the joy of it, but then the dog would turn back into a man when it came time to make the throw – hop, hop, opposable thumb and palm and then the flapping sound of your shirt sleeve on the flesh of your arm, the shoulder rotating better, more powerfully and artfully, than a piston engine, and away the ball went, getting smaller and smaller until it disappeared into the shortstop's glove. When the time came for them to hit, there prevailed an odd mix of happiness and intensity; no doubt, it was fun to hit a baseball, to crush it, hear that distinctive sound of wood on horsehide, to watch it go speeding out into the air, a super-endowed but short-lived bird, the temporal victory of human willpower over the force of gravity. However, it was difficult, and the mechanics of it (much of which was not natural) took effort and patience to master, so that what now looked quite easy and intuitive for a good hitter had most often been achieved through painstaking repetition and refinement. And even then, even after the hitter had paid dearly with his own sweat, failure was always imminent. Certainly it built confidence to take batting practice, to swat the practice balls that came ballooning up to the plate, but that confidence was fragile. In a game the balloons turned into guided missiles, zipping into what seemed a grossly enlarged strike zone, so that it sometimes seemed impossible to get the meat of the bat anywhere close to the pitch. And if the pitcher had his stuff working, it was as if horsehide and bat had become repellent magnets; the man towering over you on the mound would gaze down on you, a god of terror, cruelty, and remorselessness, who cared not for your physical and mental well-being. To swing mightily and hear only the whistling of the air, to twist in the humiliation of the empty follow-through, to walk away alone in failure and frustration, the victim of that superior intellect sixty feet away…there was no greater suffering for any man on earth.

Yet miraculously, each time, in a game, the fragile belief was restored, and the hitter would return to stand in among that collection of imaginary rectangles, squares, and polygons and renew the psychological combat. And the instant would arrive, every third time or so for a good hitter, when the hours of labor in the cage and in BP were redeemed once again, and ash-wood would strike stretched horsehide and the ball would soar out and land where no fielder could catch it, and now the batter would be the usurper, the terrible assailant, the man dashing viciously down the base paths. In contrast, while in batting practice there was no momentous victory, by any means, it was a chance to work on details, to be freed from the tyranny of the pitch count, to study motion and physics, and to do it all under the auspices of good-natured camaraderie and with the compulsion to laugh at one's own mistakes.

And when it was over, he had the feeling of satisfaction that comes with mental and physical effort and the smell of one's own sweat, that happy tiredness, then the shower, then dressing in the new denim and cotton clothes that he had bought for himself, the new leather two-tone shoes. And in a few minutes, he was out on the street again, happy and tired. Granted, in this part of town, his face was one of the few brown ones among the hundreds all around him, but still he could almost feel sorry for the poor souls who had spent the workday in grim offices and gaudy shops and against whom the odds were great that they should ever earn their livings playing baseball.

Luther knew that at some point we are all tested. Sometimes it was God who, for His own reasons, tests our faith now and again; very likely, such temptations were intended to illustrate either our strength or weakness in a given moment. Job remained the best example of such testing, and appropriately, Job himself does not know why he is made to suffer. Worse, though, were temptations by the devil, and Luther believed in them wholeheartedly. Without question, he valued the intellect and saw Christianity as a rational belief system, but he could never align himself with the symbolists, who perceive only metaphors in the story. Nor did he associate himself with the mystics. True, he could not bring himself to believe that the sighting and physical evidence of a predatory animal such as a black panther, in a place where panthers had dwelt for thousands of years, amounted to a demonic manifestation, but he believed it was quite dangerous to say that the person of Satan is merely a representative figure; in fact, he would have said, that is exactly what the devil would want us to believe. To dismiss demonic possessions, for example, as this or that brand of psychosis, gives the demons the covertness they desire. Such possessions were real – Luther had seen them.

As a boy, he had watched his own father put his hands on a member of his congregation, a young woman whose body had been wracked for days, pretzel-like, with all of her muscles tensed in tight bunches, who spoke to him and cursed him in a strange voice that was not her own. Not knowing what to do for her, her family had brought her to their house and placed her tormented body on the dining room table, and his father had prayed over her, had read aloud over her, and at last placed his hands on her head and commanded the spirit to leave her. He recalled it vividly: he had watched the man's hands turn blood red and swell up, and even from several feet away, he had thought he could smell something beginning to burn. And then, just when Luther believed those hands would burst or suddenly be engulfed by flame, the woman's body eased, slumped before their eyes, and she had taken a deep breath and then looked around at all of them.

"Am I at home?" she had asked.

Aside from the fact that he had witnessed this, he found it quite reasonable now to believe that the devil is active among us, but we will seldom, if ever, know when he is present. He is a brilliant opportunist. Look with what conniving he appears to Christ in the Gospel of Matthew: when Jesus has not eaten for forty days, and when He is alone in the wilderness with no one to help Him or provide moral support, Satan offers:

"If you are the Son of God, tell these stones to become bread." The vulnerability, the appeal of it... And later, when he has conveyed Christ to the highest point of the temple, he says,

"If you are the Son of God, throw yourself down. For it is written: 'He will command his angels concerning you, and they will lift you up in their hands...'" Again, to do as his tempter suggests, even in such a dangerous spot, would be to misuse God's authority. Finally:

"Again, the devil took him to a very high mountain and showed him all the kingdoms of the world and their splendor. 'All this I will give you,' he said, 'if you will bow down and worship me.'"

Each time, Jesus does not waver, but look at the genius in Satan's attempts. He appeals to our most fundamental physical and emotional weaknesses: he offers to ease His hunger under extreme duress; then he introduces our primal fear of falling, that sensation that has caused each one of us to awaken with a racing heart from a sound sleep; and at last he appeals to the human need for more comfort, more wealth, more food, further quenching of our sensory desires, for our greatest fear may be that this world is all we shall ever have. Indeed, Luther thought, all accounts of temptation in the gospels share a common theme – they involve the prideful challenging of God's authority and the ego's demands to be fed.

The demon that preyed upon him now was a familiar one. His old anger had been rekindled by Liza's errant husband, Carl Dixon, who, predictably, had reappeared and was trying to "get back together with her," as she said. Luther's dilemma was clear but irresolvable, in his view, for he believed deeply in marriage (especially those officiated by himself), thought that couples ought to stay together in all circumstances, and viewed legal divorce as a stain upon society; in essence he believed in the sacrament. However, he could not support a reunion in this case. Some actions deserve punishment, and in this case, at the very least, the act of adultery compounded by the subsequent abandonment of a child should be taken seriously. If the boy were sincere, then perhaps his contrition would merit consideration, but as Liza had told it in the church office the other day when she had come to drop Carl Junior off, his demeanor had been less than solicitous.

She had spoken quietly as the toddler sat nearby on the rug, playing with a toy truck: "He won't let me be. He comes by my mama's apartment every afternoon, right after he gets off work. I won't let him in, but he stands there in the doorway, practically begging me."

"He probably hates going home to an empty place."

"Well, he ain't lonely for very long. I've had three people tell me they've seen him up at Silky's Tavern several times, with several different girls."

"I thought you told me Carl doesn't drink."

"He doesn't drink very much. But he does like to go out carousing, apparently."

"You've done the right thing, not letting him in."

"He does look right pitiful, though."

Pastor Laite leaned forward at his desk. "Listen, Liza. I've seen his type before. He'll try and play on your sympathies until you change your mind. You can't let him manipulate you."

"He says he's changed. Says he's been thinking everything through."

"Doesn't sound like it to me. Not much time for thinking when you're out at the bar with different women all the time."

The distress welled up in her eyes. "I should have known better, with Carl. He's sweet and handsome – I shouldn't be surprised that the girls are attracted to him. Maybe I was smothering him too much or something."

Luther thought carefully before he spoke next. He couldn't say what he really had in mind, so he told her, "I've performed lots of wedding. I've seen lots of men get married, some of the worst specimens you've ever seen. Some of them mean as snakes. And I've seen women, too, some no better than prostitutes. Drunkards. Remarkably, many of them really do change, they become model husbands, wives, mothers, and fathers because they come to realize that this is the way we are meant to do. To put away the old vices and habits and understand what's important in this short time we have here on earth. Others never do. He's given the best life anyone could ask for, a home, love, but something in him causes him to throw it all away. Give him a second chance, and the whole thing happens all over again. Bad for all concerned. Best thing is to let him go."

She nodded and daubed at her eyes with her sleeve. "I know. You're right. It's just...I get lonely sometimes, too."

"Loneliness is one of the worst things we experience, but we come through it. Heck, then you get to be my age, call it by some fancy name like 'contemplative solitude,' and suddenly people admire you for it. Let's change the subject for the moment. I hope you haven't forgotten about our plans to take Carl Junior up to Columbia to see a ballgame, have you?"

"It's been so busy at the diner. I haven't even thought to ask for | time off."

"Well, I checked the team's schedule. Why don't you ask for next Friday? We can leave around three. The game's at six."

She took a breath and looked over at the child, who had been watching her closely; he was sensitive to his mother's smallest movements, and his small brow was knitted in passing concern. "Okay," she said. "I'll see if they'll let me."

That had been Sunday afternoon, and today was Tuesday. For much of that time, especially away from the tasks that presented themselves at the office, Luther had made the mistake of allowing himself to stew over Liza's remarks, and now he found himself engaged internally in the old struggle, the great conflict in his heart. He knew what he wanted to do, all right: he wanted to drive over to the apartment Liza shared with her mother, park around on the side of the building, and wait for that little bastard to show up and start in on her; but he would never get to the door this time. Luther would approach him, take him around to the alley – drag him if necessary – and explain his options to him. If he wouldn't accept his options, a knee in the gut was always a persuasive tool. Demon Wrath licked hotly at the back of his neck, made his knuckles itch.

He closed his eyes. "Help me, Father," he muttered. "Help me not to yank this boy's testicles out through his throat." But he again saw only his own father's hands as they were seared against that young woman's scalp, growing redder and more swollen by the second.

––––––––

Frank bounded down the steps of the apartment building and onto the sidewalk. There was purpose in his step: he had been asked to come in and see the team owner, and had been given an appointment time. He felt certain it concerned recent news swirling about his relationship with Jack Anders; the papers had gotten wind of the incident a few weeks ago in the game against Knoxville, and the *State* had run a story – "Standing Tall for a Teammate" – with a photo of him and Jack next to one another in the dugout. Frank had refused to give an interview about it, of course, but that had not stopped the reporter from asserting that "Johnson has stood up for integration... How refreshing to have a voice in minor-league baseball carrying on the struggle

fourteen years after Jackie Robinson broke the color barrier in the Majors."
Worst of all for him had been facing Jack afterward, but the young outfielder
had been understanding this time.

"Don't sweat it," he'd said. "You don't control what they write."

He was not sure what the organization might have to say about it, but
he had some words to say himself – an earful, in fact, and they concerned
Talmadge Biggs, whose resentment of Anders had only festered. He routinely
cut into the water-cooler line in front of Jack during practice, and during games
he muttered ugly remarks whenever Jack failed to reach base (which was rarely)
or when he couldn't get to a sinking liner (even more rarely). The last straw
for Frank had come on a road trip to Charlotte the previous week. As Frank
had come out of the motel's office and handed Jack his key, Biggs had said
quite loudly, "Why can't that nigger just sleep on the bus? Management'll shit
if they find out we're hiding a darkie in one of the rooms." Several other players
laughed out loud at this, but Frank's first impulse had been to put his fist in
Biggs' fat face, but then he remembered the terse conversation in the apartment.
As for Jack, his face might have been made of chiseled granite.

There was no reason, however, that Banks shouldn't be made aware
of tensions in his own team's ranks.

So, when he sat before Banks, with the office door shut and the little
window fan blowing warm, thick air around the room, he fully expected to see
the newspaper clipping on the big desk. He did not. Instead, Banks said nothing
for a few minutes, making notes in a little pad, and when he raised his head, his
eyes looked very tired.

"Morning, Frank. This won't take long," he said, and Frank realized
that the weary owner had apparently forgotten that it had been Frank, and not
himself, who had asked for the meeting. "I've been trying to think of a way to

put this," Banks continued, "but I guess the best way is to just come out with it."

"Yessir?"

"I'm putting the Reds up for sale. I've thought about it quite a bit, and it's time for me to move along." He sat back and put his hands behind his head; despite the sweep of the fan, there were dark circles of sweat under his arms.

"Yessir."

"I expect to get some offers right away, given the attendance we've had. It'll probably all be said and done by July."

"What does that mean for the players?"

"Oh, I don't know. Probably not much. There's really nothing that needs fixing. I will tell you that a couple of other franchises have shown an interest in trading for you. They seem to think you might be ready for the big leagues in another year or two. A fella from the Senators phoned the other day and said they're trying to decide who they want between you and Anders. One of you will get an offer to move immediately to their triple-A affiliate in Syracuse. "

"Me or Anders."

"That's right. Proverbial golden ticket. Next step after that is the Majors. But then I don't have to tell you that."

His walk back was a slow and thoughtful one. This was the life he had chosen, after all, and every ballplayer was, in essence, a kind of journeyman. To pack one's bag and board a train for a big-league town or even a triple-A club would be...like putting out to sea in a small but sturdy vessel, maybe, or maybe like those strange dreams one has wherein one's body becomes so light the forces of nature are suspended and one gains the power of flight. But he had made a home in Columbia, and although moving, for him, would be merely a matter of packing his duffel bag, he enjoyed the routine of walking to the same ballpark, dressing out in the same locker room, the rituals of game day, and even the wearying bus rides that made coming back to the little apartment that much sweeter. He had not known such a stable existence since he'd been a child, back before his mother had gotten sick. If only he could see her again, and Dad, too; wouldn't they be so proud of their boy?

Of course, as Banks had said, the Senators were looking at Anders, too. If they took him, Frank would be left behind, at least for this season. He himself was awed, sometimes, by Jack's grace and power; as a pure athlete, he was clearly better. He was older, too, and Frank had come to regard him at times as a mentor. It took character to absorb the kind of treatment he took when...

Abruptly, with a flush of shame, he realized that in his selfish worries he had forgotten to present his case concerning Talmadge Biggs' offensive behavior. But it was too late now – he was supposed to be at practice in twenty minutes.

———

It was a small but happy band, the three pilgrims who rode in Luther's station wagon to Columbia that bright Saturday morning in June. To anyone who saw them pass by, they seemed to be a family – although he was one of those well-seasoned men who never quite look as old as they really are, Luther might be taken for the father of Liza and grandfather of Carl Junior. Liza was in pleasant spirits, a doting mother to her chubby boy, and easily taken for a devoted daughter as well. She had packed a lunch of chicken salad sandwiches from the diner, and she passed one to Luther, smiling; she was now absolutely certain that her real motive in this journey was the same as his, though it remained unaddressed.

She would remember the car ride about as well as any of the other events, momentous as they were, that would occur that day, for the rattling old station wagon, though not completely comfortable, possessed character, and it suited Luther. And Carl Junior did very well on his first trip out of town, crying only once for some unknown reason, but alternately sleeping and smiling thereafter. Mostly, however, it put her in mind of those old days when she would ride to Frankie's games with Mr. and Mrs. Treadwell, back when she was only a girl. That was when summers had been golden, she thought, and everything was a game whose outcome had mattered little – back when there were no Greenville boys and no Carl Senior and no death or thoughts of death.

"So he stopped coming around," she said.

"What?" Luther glanced over at her.

"Carl. He stopped coming over and trying to talk to me."

"Well, that's good, isn't it?"

"I guess so. He filed for a divorce. Probably shacked up with some woman."

"Hmm." Luther veered out into the passing lane and pulled around a big logging truck.

"Pretty weird," she said, "the way he just all of a sudden stopped coming around."

"I reckon so."

She had never been to Columbia before, but it was not much different from other towns she had been in: first there were the trailers and shacks, the shabby industrial parks, and then the woods disappeared and the traffic thickened, and the odors that came through the car's vents grew mustier, sweatier, laced with the diesel of busses, and then, like that, they were in the midst of the city.

They found the ballpark with no difficulty (Luther had phoned for directions before they left), and she awakened Carl Junior, put the extra sandwiches in her purse, and then turned to find Luther gazing at her thoughtfully.

"You ready?" he asked. She nodded.

Here was another new experience, for she had never been to a professional sporting event. It was only the minor leagues, but she felt the excitement immediately – it seemed to sing in the air above them as they walked toward the stadium among a crowd of fans, and as they drew near, the dull trundling of the turnstiles and the cries of the vendors and the smell of popcorn and roasting hot dogs touched some nerve in her; the openness of it all invited some strange sort of glory, and she wondered whether Luther and Carl Junior felt it, too.

They made their way to their seats in the left field bleachers, and as soon as she sat down and the field came into focus, she spotted Frank, and a little mixed current of joy and angst ran through her. The Reds players were warming up in their crimson t-shirts without names on the backs, but she didn't need to see "JOHNSON" in order to pick him out. Frank Treadwell was unmistakable in the way he threw, caught, and ran about in the same sort of happy dance he had done as a boy. He was bigger, of course, broader in the shoulders and thicker through his chest, but she would know him anywhere.

Finally she heard Luther's voice. He had apparently been saying something to her, but she only heard the question that came at the end of it: "Do you see him?"

"Yes," she said, staring down into that green bowl. "I see him."

————

Luther could think of no better place to be on an unseasonably cool Saturday in June than in a baseball stadium. He wondered why he had not made the trip sooner, for this was a pleasant place, and it was far from the daily trials of his duties as pastor of the United Methodist Church of Dillon. He felt quite free here, with the breeze on his face and the cheerful sounds of people gathering as though for a Sunday picnic, except that in this case the spiritual thirst that drew them was for baseball.

It was all meaningless, he knew that. Nothing at all depended upon a game played by overgrown boys, but that was precisely what one needed sometimes – to sit in the middle of a small sea of baseball fans, conscious of the privilege placed at their feet for such a pittance. It was not so much a spectacle as it was performance art, one that directly involved everyone in attendance in various mystical ways. It occurred to him briefly that America would indeed win what Bernard Baruch, a South Carolinian, had called the Cold War, if for no other reason than Americans would never tolerate the lack of baseball.

Of much greater immediacy to him, however, tedious though they were, were the problems he had left behind in Dillon, and not the least of those had been the one Liza had brought up during the drive this morning: that lout of a husband of hers. Yet somehow, it seemed, it had abruptly been resolved – and Luther had had nothing to do with it.

Oh, he had struggled mightily with his temper, but he had kept the Demon Wrath at bay. With an odd sense of achievement, he had ticked off the things he had not done: he had not driven over to Liza's abode and lain in wait for him; he had not pulled the boy into the alley and pummeled him; he had not damaged anyone's personal property; he had not even threatened anyone.

And yet the problem had solved itself. He had let her alone, and providing the boy did not have some sinister motive, Luther could only account for these circumstances in one way: it was the answer to his prayers. In fact, the answer had been twofold, for God had helped him to put down his anger, and He had also protected Liza in her vulnerability. Even though Luther believed in the power of prayer unequivocally, it always amazed him on those rare occasions when one of his own was answered directly.

Besides, this God knew something about anger. Luther saw no discrepancy at all in the differing depictions of God in the Old and New Testaments and His transition from a wrathful God to a loving one over the course of the story, for God's story is also our story. Do we ourselves not have to learn to love over and over again, to realize the power in forgiveness, and to set aside that which twists from within? Luther could only think of fathers he had known, ill-tempered men who had been changed immeasurably by the birth of their children; the flame of love is lit, and the old ways are left behind. Should not our perception of God's dynamic nature also reflect this kind of change?

But let all of that go for now, he thought. Here you are in a baseball park with a vivacious young woman who is yet full of life, with many years before her, and who even at this moment has the blessed chance to learn from her mistakes and straighten herself out. And there is her child, who as yet knows nothing of wickedness but who will be mostly shaped from this time on by those who come into his life, either by fate, chance, or choice.

And there was the reason for their presence here, to meet again the man-child, once lost and still unaware that he had been found, jogging in his bright red t-shirt among the other red t-shirts back to the dugout and then through the passageway to the clubhouse. Now all that remained for all of them was to wait for the game to begin.

―――――

As Banks Berenger sat alone in his private box (the only private box in the Reds' stadium, it was little more than an over-sized storeroom with a picture window and room for a small bar), he felt none of those things he believed he should have. He had never felt them. He felt no sense of munificence or even control, as he gazed out over the green grass and the brown dirt below and watched men work and people of all shapes gather in the seats to view a spectacle he had never really understood. Was it because he had never grasped the "team concept"? As far as he could see, success in this arena depended greatly on the talents of the individual; the so-called sacrifice, for example, was really nothing of the kind – it was an individual player executing a skill that increased his own value to the team. Any batter, and especially a pitcher, was isolated; he performed at great risk to his own financial standing, and though he might hear all sorts of encouragement from teammates and coaches, ultimately he was on his own, a man at the edge of a cliff. Given all of that, Banks ought to have been able to generate greater enthusiasm for his position here, but a kind of apathy or anemia always gripped him whenever he came to the ballpark.

He was essentially a loner. He had procured the wealth long ago that would have enabled him to join any leisure club, any business organization, or to have traveled to any exotic locale in the world, to have hobnobbed with the "haves" at glossy bars around the globe, but those things had never interested him. Hell, he only owned one suit and a few ties, when he could have gone to the fanciest haberdasheries in London and Italy and had the finest clothing sewn for him by the finest tailors in the world. And women? In his limited circles, mostly at private dinners hosted by real estate clients and rotary club members and chamber-of-commerce bigwigs, the most beautiful among them had practically flung themselves at him.

He had suffered greatly over his decision to break off his relationship with Karen. He knew very well that he would never find a better woman, more giving and tolerant and less interested in shopping and cars and the other things to which women of her rank were typically drawn. Perhaps it was he who was not good enough for her, and he was only hastening the inevitable, but in any case, he knew that he did not have the sensitivity or the patience or the will to sustain such a connection. Evidently, his brother Bob, despite his weaknesses, had done a much better job at sticking to a good woman.

He and Karen had played out the sad drama on the veranda of his house at Hilton Head, out on the pool deck. He needed some time to himself, he had told her, and as he said it, he was filled with self-hatred. She had kept her small apartment in Charleston but had resisted when he had offered to pay her rent for her; he had felt some sense of waste in that, but now he felt relieved that she had maintained her own place. She was silent for a time, sitting there beneath the big potted palm tree, and then she'd said, "I'll have to collect my things."

"I'll put them in a box and send them over."

Another long, slow silence fell between them like the shadow of a passing cloud, and then she said, "Okay, then," and stood up, looking about distractedly for her keys, which were in her hand. She had only a single truly bad moment, when she was at the door and she turned back toward him, eyes brimming; she was about to speak, and he held his breath, but then she suddenly opened the door and went out.

That is how it is with people, he thought, scrutinizing the odd rituals occurring below him on the field. A series of awkward farewells. It is always best not to start such things, because they inevitably end in this manner, or worse. The same would soon be true with Frank, too, but it was time for both of them to move on. He had done his duty by his nephew, having yanked him out of a future that might have consisted of mediocre American Legion teams and store clerking, at best, and he had set him down upon a path where glory awaited, if only he would seize it. And it was not merely the glory of personal triumph; it was the best sort of success one could have in American life, in which the triumph you enjoyed was within your own body, raw skill, and in which even your name had monetary worth. Banks had worked very hard for his own kind of success, and although he knew little about baseball, he knew that everything Frankie did in that meadow down there was driven only by pure animal love.

He saw now that both teams had gone to their respective dugouts and the managers and umpires were meeting at home plate. He had been informed by telephone that the Senators would have a representative on hand today who would offer him a deal to obtain the rights to Frank Johnson's talents. That would be cause for celebration for all concerned, but strangely, as he looked out broadly over the park where the seats were now nearly full, he felt only a vast and seemingly ancient sadness sinking slowly into his breast.

———

Max Bass had turned up a day early in Columbia, for a fellow scout had told him about a decent whorehouse just west of town. It had turned out to be so, and he had spent the night with a girl who went by Tammy Lin, who said she was eighteen but then again might have been thirty. He had awakened with a pounding hangover and had gone to a diner and sat staring dumbly into a cup of coffee until he was able to check into his hotel at noon. Then he had slept it all off and risen again at six, not entirely clearheaded but ready to go to work.

It was the familiar cycle of sinfulness followed by suffering and then rationalization. He was okay – no one had forced anyone to do anything, all had been done by consent, and no one had been harmed. He would put on his checked sport coat and his tie and go down to the place where all could be forgiven and where redemption hung ripe in the blue sky as though the place were a cathedral, or a place of towering air, where perpetual human longing could be occasionally fulfilled.

Today he felt particularly good about his mission, for he carried someone's destiny in his breast pocket – a contract offer of twenty-five grand, the sum the Senators had decreed could be offered to Frank Johnson. Max, of course, knew that Frank Johnson was in actuality Frankie Treadwell, but on an intuitive level, though he did not know the specifics, he understood why the boy had been compelled to abandon his old identity. What he had witnessed in May had shown him plainly enough that now the thing that had been missing before – the toughness, the savvy necessary to succeed at the professional level – had indeed emerged. Clearly the boy had taken that most treacherous inward journey and come through it as a man.

In turn, Max thought, here was his own chance at absolution. Whatever wrongs he had done to Frankie Treadwell could be made up to Frank Johnson. He would be the messenger angel, a herald with a man's future in his pocket and the will to make it happen. He saw that he had missed his chance before to nurture real talent, even to become a father figure to a malleable lad, because of his own selfish indulgences; yet now, he could still correct it all, still be of great use in this unfolding story. He would not drink tonight, and he would not go out into the humid night to lie between some strange woman's legs. He would perform his job, and once again Max Bass would be respected, even revered. He couldn't wait to see the expression on Frank's face when his old coach came striding into the locker room.

He climbed the steps and found his seat behind the third-base line. Ten thousand restless conversations swirled about his ears, punctuated by the sudden random explosion of an inflated popcorn bag, while down below all of those eternal and universal sounds – the happy chatter of the home team's infielders as they gathered in the skittering ground balls thrown by the first baseman, and the popping of the catcher's mitt as the pitcher wound up – rose like an orchestra tuning up in a great theater and disappeared into the early-evening sky above. It brought back to him the vestiges of his own youth, little threads of memory of himself as a player, hungry, angry, ready to murder, to take a chunk out of somebody, with arms like thick cords of steel and legs like springs. You never know what you have inside you until you look up to see a ninety-mile-per-hour fastball screaming towards your head.

The Reds' pitcher certainly had his stuff tonight, striking out the side in the first inning with consecutive nasty sliders; still, he thought, the opposing hitters would adjust and catch up to him by the fourth, no doubt. The first batter for Columbia grounded out, but due up next were the three that he had scouted back in May: Talmadge Biggs, Frank, and Jack Anders. Biggs showed the patience of a much older man, taking a pitch low and outside on a 3-2 count and being rewarded with an easy trot down to first base. Max watched carefully as Frank Johnson strode up to the plate, waved the bat's barrel through the strike zone and then got set. There was no tension in his stance at all, just an easy grace, as an excellent swimmer treads water effortlessly and never tires. Nonetheless, clouds of doubt passed through Max's mind as Frank stared confusedly at a change-up right down the middle and then swung awkwardly, corkscrew-like, when the pitcher came back hard on the inside. Had Max made the right decision? Would the Senators think him a fool? Perhaps the eye for talent on which he had prided himself was beginning to fail after all.

Then, just as abruptly, all was well again. Ahead 0-2 in the count, the pitcher knew his craft, firing a low, sinking fastball just off the outside edge of the plate; it was the perfect pitch, virtually unhittable, and yet somehow, either through desperation, courage, or sheer terror at failure, Frank thrust the bat out into the vacuum that deadened all in proximity to it, that life-devouring cylinder that was the path of the pitch, and with a sharp crack he poked the ball into shallow right field for a single. Most observers would have remarked that he had "gone with the pitch," but Max knew it had been more than that: it had been an insane action driven by mortal fear. Max breathed, greatly relieved, and then he felt even better when Anders came up and struck a loping grounder to the shortstop; it was an easy double play, but he was quite pleased to see the vicious way in which Frank went hard at the second baseman, who leapt high to avoid the glinting spikes aimed at his knees, pirouetted in midair, and made a nice throw to first to end the inning.

The time for acting – the controlled violence necessary to the act of hitting – had passed, and now the stage was set for that period of reacting – the quick reflexiveness essential to defense, which the home team called the bottom half of the inning. Max had been a center fielder himself and knew the athletic demands and the truth about the highly-strung nature of the man who played this position, for he must be like a patient sprinter whose starting gun is the sound of the bat but to whom the distance of the race was unknown until all was set in motion. He had always believed that any ball hit into the outfield could be run down if only the player had enough desire and will; he believed that Frank had the desire, if not the speed, but the truth was he had not really seen enough of his fielding at this level to say whether he was much good; the Senators wanted hitters, and that's what he had found for them. He saw now in Frank's easy jogging, hopping about, and teasing with Anders between innings the same sort of playful demeanor he had shown in high school, that easy confidence, but that would mean little without the tools to go along with it. This time around, however, he did not have to wait long for simple answers. For the very first out, Frank came charging in on a weak pop behind second base, covering at least forty yards at a dead sprint, called off the shortstop and made what would have been a difficult catch for most players look routine. The crowd did not react, for they did not see that an instantaneous reaction and extraordinary agility had made it possible. Max saw.

It was what happened in the top of the fourth inning, however, that all of those in attendance that day at the Columbia Reds stadium would remember for the rest of their years on earth. The opposition had runners at first and second with two outs, and the number-eight batter for the Knights, their Spaniel-like second baseman, came friskily to home plate. He had looked bad in striking out earlier, and his face bore a look of mixed dread and sinister intent. He fell behind in the count by two strikes, those same mean sliders their hitters had seen all evening thus far. Then, even as Max looked on intently, something in the manner and psyche of the Reds hurler shifted subtly, and he missed badly to the outside; then, unintentionally, he came way inside, just below the Spaniel's chin, and a murmur went through the crowd. When it happened again, even harder this time and headed for the man's ear, there was a collective sucking in of breath and then scattered applause among the more sadistic fans. The hitter, angry and frightened now, threw down his bat and glared at his adversary, who shrugged his shoulders as if to say, "Sorry, I have no idea what's happening here." The umpire mulled the situation for a few moments, and decided not to intervene. The Spaniel dug back in and waited.

The big pitcher, greatly alarmed, went to a slow windup now instead of the stretch, and both runners instantly took off. He moved far too carefully, too predictably, and lobbed up a balloon toward the fat middle of the strike zone. It would not even have made for a crisp batting practice offering, and the Spaniel's eyes grew wide, for he had likely not seen such succulent meat since his own high school days, and he shifted his weight back and waited for it. Accordingly, the blast that came from the batter's box was probably unlike anything that he had ever achieved before.

The ball was clearly bound for the first row of the bleachers in dead-away center. Max watched it and laughed. Never a dull moment, he thought. But then, another sort of drama began to take place. Frank Johnson, who had been playing somewhat shallow, did not seem surprised by such a towering drive off the bat of such a diminutive man, and was at top speed within three seconds. It was strange, Max thought, the way in which his muscles, legs and arms, seemed to fold into themselves and become almost wheel-like, a white and red blur. He could only think of some kind of predatory animal seeking a dying bird as the ball began to plummet towards the wall. The wind had held it slightly, though it still had enough distance to carry it out of the park, and Frank timed his leap perfectly. He sprang off of his right leg and extended his entire body and right arm so that he was no longer a wheel but a flying spear, and he went up, up, carried by his own momentum, his glove raised like a flag until half of him was above the wooden fence, and to the stunned amazement of all, even Max, who had seen everything, the ball disappeared into the pocket of his glove, a white spark suddenly and completely snuffed. The ferocity of Frank's leap, however, carried him even higher, beyond that point at which the laws of gravity ought to have prevailed.

With his superior vision, Max could clearly see the expression on Frank's face. He was serene. The ball was safe, at least, and he finally turned his head to consider, with grim amusement at first and then a boyish grin, whatever lay below him.

From the perspective of the man in the field, time during a baseball game passes in any number of odd ways. Hardly anything is measured in minutes or hours, but rather by the distinctive pace of a pitcher's windup, for instance, or the obsessive and repetitive movements of a hitter settling himself in the batter's box. Time stretches, lays itself out in the mid-day sun like picnickers in a Renoir picture, but the player must not be fooled, for at any moment the picture can explode into action which will then be measured in the strictness of terms which do not even include seconds or milliseconds; they are more like the sudden appearance of atoms in quantum physics. The ball that was in the pitcher's hand suddenly appears in the first baseman's glove. The base runner who was idly watching with his hands on his hips abruptly becomes the irresistible moving body in an imminent collision with the shortstop.

Distances and angles, however, must obey every law of nature no matter how cruel. Sixty feet. Ninety feet. Ninety degrees. There can be no variation, no interpretation. A man who cannot run very fast must face the humiliating likelihood of being thrown out upon attempting to score from second on a base hit, for although it is one and hundred and eighty feet, we must add another fifteen feet or so to account for the turn at third, and for a slow runner this means death. The fleet outfielder launches his spear, and the wooly mammoth goes down, and like twisted Neanderthals, the hunters gather around and laugh over their stricken prey. Then there are those distances that vary from park to park but are no less strict in their arrest: distances to the outfield fences, the height of those fences, the proximity of the lower deck seating to the foul lines, and so on. Some parks are friendly to hitters, others to pitchers. An outfielder operates mostly by intuition, a sixth sense that tells him where he is, even at a dead sprint as he chases a fly ball, in proximity to the fence. Most pro stadiums utilize the so-called "warning track," a broad dirt path running the length of the fences to let the hurrying player know he is approaching the impassable boundary between the field of play and the world "out there," but a true outfielder does not need it. He knows where the fence is.

The outfield fences at the Columbia Reds' ballpark were indeed just that – fences, constructed of plywood, painted dark green but with a bright yellow strip at their very tops to facilitate an umpire's ruling on such matters as fan interference. Because they were wooden, they were somewhat more forgiving than the cement or brick walls found in some parks, or worse yet, chain link, in which an outfielder's cleat or hand might get caught up, resulting in an ugly injury. The fences at the Columbia park were eight feet high, give or take an inch here and there depending on the forces of weather.

The observer might reasonably ask, "Does the player in the field think about any of this when he is standing out there alone?" The answer, of course, is that he does not. Yet he knows it, just as a pilot knows about the air and land and water, though he is focused chiefly on the task of flying. There is indeed much to think about – wind direction and speed, a batter's tendency to either pull the ball or hit to the opposite field, whether to throw to the base behind a lumbering base runner, to name only a few – but by and large playing the outfield is about reacting to stimuli. The difficulty is that although those stimuli often seem redundant, in truth each one is slightly different from all the rest; hence, it is mysterious.

No outfielder with the same experience and skills understood these things better than Frank. Because of his peripatetic approach and his freewheeling style of play, the small-town reporters like to say that he "roamed" the outfield, but truly no movement was wasted, and every journey had an objective. He had made many excellent plays at his position and a few that could rightly be called spectacular, but it should have been so, for his physical gifts were exceptional and he had never learned to fear the fence because he had the intuition, and he knew all of this about himself. He expected to make those plays, and in fact, he believed in his heart that there was no ball hit in the air toward center field that he could not reach, as long as he always did what he was capable of. Only fate could control the final outcome after that.

In the top half of the fourth inning of the game against Shreveport, he thought of the usual things – the breeze, the hitters' habits as he had read them, the nature of the Reds' own pitcher to throw inside or out in certain situations – but his belief about himself dwelt in his bloodstream and his breathing. With two outs, he carefully scrutinized the man coming to the plate; it was the Shreveport second baseman, whom he knew to be a tenacious and consistent hitter, though his demeanor gave him the appearance of emotional instability. Frank moved in to play him shallow in the hopes of catching a sinking line drive or at least preventing the runner on second from scoring in the event of a ground ball up the middle. He did this with some reservation, recognizing that the small batter, though no slugger, possessed some power, born of will, and was just as likely to smack it over his head, thus clearing the bases. Frank looked to the dugout for instructions, but Hersh Freeman seemed distracted by something on his scorecard. Forbes, the Columbia pitcher, worked ahead in the count quickly with the slider that had been working for him all evening, but after the second strike, Frank saw that something was now different. Perhaps it was in the lethargic way Forbes received the return throw from the catcher, but by whatever subtle shift had occurred, Frank saw that fatigue had suddenly come pressing down on the big man; it happens this way with some pitchers – exhaustion strikes like a boulder rolling downhill, and the worst was when the hurler himself did not even realize what was happening to him. Such was the case with Forbes.

The next three pitches, all balls veering weakly off the plate (the third one nearly plunking the batter), affirmed Frank's suspicions. He did not feel at all good about any of this. When, as though in slow motion, Forbes went to his windup on his sixth pitch, Frank believed he understood the rationale: get the out, focus on the batter; he's the guy that can hurt us.

And hurt them he did. With the count at 3-2 and two away, the runners on first and second took off at a gallop. The problem was that Forbes' delivery was slow, and in this case it was even slower given his exhaustion, and as he unfolded himself in a long, lazy fashion, Frank saw clearly what was about to happen, for he saw the compact batter's eyes bear down on the floating white sphere. He turned and began to sprint even as he heard the sound of the bat, and that extra step, he believed, would allow him to get to the ball. In addition, the wind was favorable, blowing in, and as Frank gathered speed, he felt quite confident that he would make the catch.

As always when he was in such pursuit, his brain emptied of everything save the throbbing urge to impose himself upon what must have seemed inevitable to everyone else. That is the way with those who believe: it is logical, for instance, based upon what we know of this world, that we are creatures bound to destroy ourselves. We ought to have done so long ago, based upon the evidence. Yet a handful of the believers keep going, and so we remain. In any case, Frank Treadwell, the happy, eager boy, and Frank Johnson, the man of great will and determination, melded into one being once again, and a mighty ball of speed went streaking towards dead-away center field, the deepest part of the park. He knew exactly where the fence was, and timing his leap, he extended himself, catapult-like, his body traveling not in an arc but rather in a precise, rising angle. The ball settled in his glove as if drawn by a magnet.

In this unexplored space, his first feeling was one of exhilarating freedom. Childhood dreams of flying fluttered again somewhere in his mind, petals moved by a breeze. Then, with a strong sense of the comedy in which he was the protagonist, he realized that he had not – had never, in fact – anticipated the other side of the fence. He looked downward, and the dream gave way to a morbid dread of the mundane, the gray asphalt, blowing trash, beer slop, peanut shells, all of which seemed a thousand miles from the emerald green environs he had just left. He felt his kneecaps hit the bright yellow two-by-four on top of the fence, and then his body tipped wildly, his spine striking something hard, unforgiving – the bleacher railing, as it turned out. Now he was headed straight down, another five feet or so, the top of his skull striking the pavement first and the remainder of his flailing body's weight crashing behind it in the manner of a pile driver.

He did hear, for just an instant, the sound of the crowd (Were they screaming? Cheering?) and then, like a river bound for other shores, it ran away in a great current, leaving at first a sad trickle, and then, finally, a vast, dry silence.

Three

Those first few minutes in the emergency room were quite vague in her recollection. She remembered the sickly pale pink paint on the walls, those peculiar medicinal smells, and the way Carl Junior had looked so frightened at first; yet after only a few minutes, her son suddenly seemed quite grown-up as he sat there with his little legs up on the plastic chair and a pensive expression upon his face. The well-groomed man from Bob Treadwell's funeral was present, too. She tried to remember: was he Bob's brother? Frankie's uncle, then? She had forgotten about him altogether, but here he was now, to her amazement, with his collar askew, and looking clearly quite distressed.

Liza was very glad, in the end, that Luther had brought them. At the ballpark, in those few surreal minutes after Frankie had disappeared without a trace beyond the outfield fence, they had risen, cheering, but in another moment had become numb and unspeaking; many others in attendance at the game had also been stunned into a disbelieving silence, but then the moaning of the ambulance siren had brought them all back to the moment, and Liza had realized that her hands were shaking and her face had drained of blood, and it was Luther who had touched her shoulder and said, "We'll find out where the hospital is. You ready?" He was her rock through those first few deadly minutes and then hours, although the tall man said little during the tedious time that ensued; his mere presence gave her a sense of comfort she had not experienced before. Several times he had taken her hands and they had closed their eyes, but they offered only silent prayers; no words were needed, for their purpose was clear.

Other than that, all she could really recall was the neurosurgeon coming out to the waiting room to speak to them. Some of it was doctor talk – "contusions, concussion, lacerations, subdural hematoma..." – but most of it was quite straightforward. Frank had hit his head, his brain had swollen up, and they would have to operate to relieve the pressure; he had also fractured his backbone on the railing, but there was reasonable certainty that there had been no permanent nerve damage. Finally, he had also cracked both of his knees on the top of the fence, tearing the big muscle behind the left one, and that would have to be sewn up as well. In all, provided the swelling in his brain went down, he would be all right, though most certainly he would not be playing baseball anymore. At least not for a very long time.

"After the surgery, we'll likely keep him sedated for a couple of days," the doctor had said. "He'll be in traction with that spinal injury, and that's not going to be very comfortable."

They stayed overnight, the three of them, and in the early morning, with the sun seeping in through the waiting room blinds, the same doctor, now looking haggard and pale, had come out and given them a brief report: the procedure had gone well. Now it would be a matter of waiting to see how much of it had worked.

In the swirl of these happenings, she had been sure of only one thing: I must wait, she thought, I must be here when he awakens, whether it turns out to be two days or two months. Perhaps it harkened back to those days when they were little, when he was five and she was seven, and she had gone with his family to picnic at Lake Norton, and she had felt a strong protective urge, a great need to keep him away from the fire, and also from the unknown darkness beyond the trees as he laughed and ran about, to guide him away from danger. He had gotten away from her somehow, he had wandered off into the night, but she would wait for him. So much had happened to them both since she had rejected his adolescent fumblings and he had left in bitterness over that and over his father's decline, and most of all, because of his mother's death, but each of them had changed. With a kind of desperation she had never felt, she wanted to talk with him, to tell him everything.

The problem, of course, was that she had Carl Junior to think of; she would have to lay aside her own desires and take him home. Yet Luther seemed to read her every thought these days. Some time after the surgeon had left and they had settled as best they could back into the uncomfortable plastic chairs, he had looked over at her thoughtfully. "I have a proposal for you," he said. "This is just an idea, mind you. I figure there's nothing more that I can do here right now. Suppose I go on back to Dillon, tend to things there, and take the little fella with me? He knows me well enough, I think, and he'd be better off back home than in this place. I can keep him with me during the days, and then drop him off in the evenings at your mama's place, once she gets off of work. That way you can stay here as long as you need to."

"You'd do that for me, Luther?"

"He's an easy kid to be around. He's good company, in fact. You should stay here till there's some more news."

She had not known what to say, but she had promised herself that she would repay him someday, somehow. In the meantime, once the two of them had left, she had gone down to the gift shop, bought herself a toothbrush, and then with some cajoling and a bit of pleading, she had convinced the head nurse on his floor to let her build herself a little nest in the soft armchair in his room.

Now as she sat there, she remembered she hadn't seen his face up close in nearly two years. He had filled out; it was the squarish face of a young man, deeply tanned, with the shadow of a beard and the beginnings of creases around the eyes – all that squinting out there in the sun, she assumed. But the boy was in there still, in the untroubled visage and the strong, even breathing. His body, too, was broader, more solid, his forearms thick, his fingers long and powerful; it was obvious to her now that he had been made for the sport of baseball, but the specialist had said he would probably never be able to play again. That would be a terrible adjustment for him, he would fight, and then he would grieve, but at least she would be there with him. They had their whole lives ahead of them – if he would still have her.

She had not paused to consider that he might not care for her anymore, and then what a fool she would seem. After all, he had been a high-school boy when she last knew him, and if there was one thing she knew about, it was the lustful and capricious nature of high-school boys. But they had always had far more than that, hadn't they? They had a history, they had been children together, they had grown up together, down there on the Little Pee Dee River, and they had come through some things, together and apart. Once in a great while, the old guilt hovered over her with dark wings, but she had learned to turn away from it, to remember that her only real fault had been her naivety, her stupidity. There was always another side to things – despite the idiocy and brokenness of her marriage to Carl, for instance, she had been given a wonderful son. For the first time in months, she felt certain that everything would turn out okay. Such thoughts, as well as the hospital cafeteria's food and the candy bars and coffee from the nurses' station, sustained her through the hours as she waited.

On the afternoon of the third day, just as the doctors had said he would, he opened his eyes. Immediately he looked at her directly, clearly, and he did not seem at all confused.

"Can you play that one song again?" he said. "I like that one."

"What song?"

"The one about the dream. You know the one."

"Of course," she said. "I remember now, Frankie."

She began to hum it softly.

———

Although it was made in brilliant sunlight along a shimmering two-lane highway, for Banks the drive home on the morning after Frank's fall was one that was undertaken in the most desolate spiritual darkness he had ever encountered. His first reaction, when it had happened, had been an overwhelming sense of responsibility. From his box behind home plate, what he had seen had been almost unbelievable: his nephew made an astounding effort, leaping far higher than he would have believed any athlete capable of, as if his legs were made of more than simple human flesh, and then he had disappeared; the way his body had soared high above the fence and then careened over its top edge, he must have plummeted sharply, right onto the top of his head. Banks had never witnessed such physical fearlessness before.

"It is my fault," he kept whispering to himself, as he watched most of the other players and many of the fans gathering about the spot where Frank must have landed. He saw that Frank was unconscious when the stretcher came, his arms flopping over the sides until they strapped him in, and then as he had driven behind the ambulance to the hospital, he had thought again, "My fault. I should never have told him about the damn contract. That kid always overdoes everything anyhow." Now, on the drive eastward, Banks was uncertain why he had done any of it. Why had had bought that damn team? What good had it really done anybody? Why hadn't he done as any normal human being might have done, and once he had learned of his nephew's whereabouts, turned the matter over to the authorities? No, not him, not Banks. He had always had to let money rule over all; he was compelled to try and buy or sell the odds in any set of circumstances that presented itself, and this was the inevitable outcome of such a fraudulent approach to life.

He despised himself. He saw with sickening clarity what he had always suspected: he was a shallow man who had forgotten everything he had ever known except for the ability to accrue more money, a knack he knew others envied in him but which he now recognized as the curse it had become. Where love for family should have been, where his need for redemption for the abandonment of his own brother, there had been only a yawning hole that he had filled with monetary gain, which was no real sort of gain at all in the end. Even now, ostensibly, he was returning to Hilton Head to meet appointments with potential property buyers, real estate clients, whom he loathed almost more than he loathed himself, but in truth something sick inside of him had made him leave the injured boy's bedside.

It must have been the self-hatred. Or fear. He was terrified of the moment when Frank should regain consciousness and he would have to say something. And then again there was always the chance that he might not wake up at all. The surgeon had said that it was almost certain he would ultimately recover, but you never really knew about these things, did you? There were lots of cases like this in which things had gone badly, and you were talking here about a young person's brain, a free-floating organ, for God's sake, sloshing around in there inside a cracked skull. Or the back injury – suppose Frank should never be able to walk again let alone chase after a silly ball? No, the body is fragile and unpredictable and we cannot count on its survival. Granted, he had left instructions with the girl and with Luther Laite to phone him immediately should any complications arise, but he had a morbid feeling that something would indeed go awry, that there would be complications, and that his real suffering, his penance was only just beginning. All because he, Banks, had used money in place of love in order to see that he got the things he wanted. Soon, he began to wish that he had never gone back to Dillon for Bob's funeral, that he had never met that preacher, never even known of the existence of a nephew, and certainly that he had never taken any interest at all in buying a baseball team. He hated baseball, for God's sake. Most boring damn thing in the world.

If only Karen could be there when he got home, but he had destroyed all of that as well. He had sent her away. He wanted desperately to find her sitting at the breakfast counter with her coffee when he arrived, but he had tossed her back into the maw of the shallow, rootless world of country clubs and dull dinners, that deadening, colorless landscape in which he had found her to be the only living spirit and the only jewel. He had thrown away the pearl. She would not be there, nor would she be able to tell him to do the things he already knew he ought to do, and so he would not do them. He was not stupid; he knew that it was quite likely she had already found someone else, someone better, someone more grateful, more giving. Someone else would already be enjoying her extraordinary beauty and her generosity, while he, not stupid by any means but certainly a fool, could only return to a dark and lonely house.

When he arrived, he pulled sadly into the garage and then mounted the steps robotically. He fumbled for his keys, barely aware of his own hands, numb to all, emotionally emptied. The place was dim, a perennial twilight in comparison to the brilliant light and the green waves beyond the picture window, a sight that moved him not at all. And there was the telephone, mocking him with its deadly black silence from the kitchen counter.

He walked over and put his hand on the receiver. Then he removed his hand, walked over to the bar, and poured himself a scotch. To call her now would be to admit his weakness to himself. And how could he do that, even if it were true, when he was the one to whom the wisest of investors entrusted their vast wealth? He was to meet this very morning with a man who intended to hand over a great sum of money so that Banks could subcontract the building of a luxury hotel on the island, the sort of hotel most people could only dream of staying in, let alone constructing from the ground up – Italian marble,

Honduran mahogany, all the very best of materials. And to think he had started out twenty-five years ago with no capital and some scrap lumber and only his own hands and head to work for him. There would be other women, just as there always had been; they would come to him as certainly as the mail would bring the architect's drawings and the cost estimates and then the checks with his name on them.

He stared at the phone again, rolling the crisp scotch over his tongue. What did he have left to lose, after all? He had an empire at his feet, laborers at his beckoning, men who wanted to give him great amounts of money to raise their garish buildings, and yet he stood here a broken man. He was in the midst of selling a baseball team, for Christ's sake, at a substantial profit, and yet to her he was a cad, no doubt. If she answered at all, what might he say that could possibly hold any meaning for her now? He had opened the door and swept her out like so much dust. But he could not help himself, for a desperate man, when he is on his way down, will grasp at any handhold.

He downed the remaining scotch, and with a last, deep intake of his breath, he raised the receiver and dialed her number.

———————

Six months later to the day, Luther Laite bought himself a Christmas present at the Dillon Hardware Store. Although Howard entertained him with a couple of benign jokes and the familiar, friendly banter, on this particular day the absence of Bob Treadwell, his former employee, hung heavily in the air between them. Then, when Luther stepped back out into the bright afternoon light, he thought about how only a couple of years earlier, it would not have been unusual to have met Frankie on the sidewalk, or perhaps just around the corner, leaning there on his bike as he waited for his father to finish up at work.

Bob would have hoisted the bike into the bed of the pickup and then taken them home, where Della would have had supper waiting.

The present Luther bought for himself was a new set of gardening tools, as he had already vowed to himself that this spring he would finally get everything in order, keep things weeded and watered, and nurture greater patience in himself. He had fallen into the bad habit lately of expecting everything to happen too quickly, from Frankie's physical healing to the restoration of the emotional connection between the young man and Liza. It would all happen, if it had to be so, but it would take time, and he would have to know when to butt out. That is one more mark of the real Christian, he thought: knowing when to act upon circumstances and when to allow God's will to unfold itself and simply to accept it. Banks Berenger, for example, was a good man, but he had not yet fully realized that he was just a poor maker and not THE Maker; he still believed that he could move the earth, if necessary, or wreck it, if he saw fit, and he had been damned lucky that woman of his had been willing to have him back again at all, much less marry him. It had only been last August that Luther had officiated at their wedding, but it had been a summer to remember. When Frank had at last been allowed to leave the hospital, they had taken him to the house at Hilton Head to care for him, where, as Luther understood things, he lived rather like a young prince.

Luther would always reckon that it had been Frank's spectacular accident that had compelled his Uncle Banks to marry. Perhaps he had finally felt the hard truth that when things start to go sailing out of control, so to speak, one must have somebody or something to hold onto. Of course, Banks had also at last revealed to Frank the real nature of their relationship, and by Liza's account, they were both handling it well, though they didn't seem to like it much.

Luther's thoughts turned to her now, as he lined the shiny new tools up on his back porch: the spade, the trowel, the hoe, and the rake; though there were traces of the season's first couple of frosts on the ground, he could envision a potting shed, just there by the steps. Liza's strength had been the most surprising thing of all, for she had scrimped and worked and sacrificed, and now she was part owner of Cindy's Diner, and she had just put a down payment on her mother's old house on the Old River Road – not bad for age twenty-one. Heck, not bad for forty-one. Somehow she had also found time to write to Frank nearly every day and to go up and see him for a few hours every Sunday. They had taken to calling Carl Junior "CJ," maybe to help her dispel past regrets, or maybe to make things a bit easier on Frank, at such time as he should move back to Dillon. There would be lots of things to think about there, however, for although he had matured considerably, he certainly was not ready for step-parenting, chubby and cheerful and well-adapted as the child seemed to be.

Ah, Luther thought, this would be the time they would remember most fondly. He had never experienced it himself, but he had seen it many times: because they were mostly still apart, but also now knew that they loved one another and always had, they were filled with constant longing and wonder and anticipation, and when the moment should finally arrive when they could really be together, the sweetness would be almost unbearable for them. He hoped another wedding might soon be in the offing.

Yet with all of that, marriages and children and such, life on this earth had shown its other face again as well. Nettie Russell had died. He and James Jenkins had gone out to her shack on the old turpentine plantation to deliver her groceries and found her seated on the porch, her eyes (which had been nearly sightless for many years) fixed upon her "prayin' trees." It reminded him of the posture of Bob Treadwell's corpse when he had been found down in the scrub oak grove by the Little Pee Dee River, except that in her case there had been no panther attack. She had gone peacefully.

He found that the panther had never left his imagination, however, and after the county coroner had come out and fetched the small, dried-out shell that remained of Nettie, it was James who had spoken of it first, on the ride back. "I got this all figured out," he said. "I know what it meant now. I know why that big cat used to come around here."

"Oh?" Luther heard the skepticism in his own voice.

"He wanted to show us he was for real, that he really had been the one killed your friend – Bob. But it wasn't an act of evil. It was a favor."

"Mm-hm. Go on."

"Well, more than a favor, then. It was God's way." James looked out at the tree trunks sliding past them, as though seeking for his words there. "He was a good spirit, don't you see? That boy's life could not have been shaped in any other way. He might have ended up drinking like his daddy, or worse yet, having to take care of him like some old nurse. No, it was a good thing that ol' panther did, and he came here to let us know about it."

"But you plugged him," Luther said. "I saw the blood spoor."

"We never did find him after, though, did we?"

"My friend, I reckon there are some things you and I will just never see eye to eye on."

James grinned, his broad, dark-brown cheeks forming two shiny orbs. "You are a smart man, Luther, but there's plenty you've yet to learn."

"An educated fool, eh?

"You said it. Not me."

There was no doubt about the veracity of that remark, he thought, admiring the neatly arranged tools. He said to himself, I do have a lot to learn. I have to learn when to do and when not to do. Here is to do, for instance: I will invite James Jenkins to come and deliver a sermon at the United Methodist Church, along with any of his church's members who would care to come along. We will have some colored folks in our pews, because I have seen the ugliness that grows out of isolation from one another. And if he invites me again to his church, I shall go. We believers must stick together and talk about our common belief and not about our trivial differences. It will not be a popular act with all parties concerned, but I will do it anyway.

Especially difficult was the not-do. He would try not to do too much arranging between Liza and Frank, though he had a strong streak of old-lady matchmaking in him. He would stand back, but as he thought it over, he began to see two distinct scenarios: In one of them, things did not go very well, and he sought not to dwell upon that vision, but briefly he imagined Frank Treadwell despondent and depressed, bitterly resentful over the turn his life had taken, lonely, his face a tablet with suffering written upon it; and there was Liza, too, growing older in the bleak old house down by the dark river, haunted by the ghosts of those who had abused her throughout her youth and then again in her womanhood. And the unhappy, recalcitrant son was nowhere to be seen, having abandoned this place of misery years earlier.

He preferred the other picture, for in this one he saw a table set upon the grass beside a well-kept, snug little home with a flowerbed that he himself had helped to plant. And around that table were gathered friends and relations, children who had not yet been born, a loving uncle and aunt, now a grand-uncle and grand-aunt. And there was Liza herself, smiling and chatting as she served up something from a great dish of food. It was a communion in the truest sense. And over there at the edge of the yard was Frank, tossing a baseball with CJ, now a strong high-school kid, and there was little trace of the old wounds to Frank's body as he moved, except for a slight hitch in his stride whenever he planted his left foot and threw. Luther himself was not in either of the scenes that he imagined, which he thought a little odd, considering how much he had become involved with all of them. Still, he knew that he would be an important part of it all if he could just sort out the doing from the not-doing.

And that, of course, would be the object of some of his most earnest prayers.

The sun fell quickly, even precipitously, behind Frank as he sat on the pool deck at his uncle's house and looked out toward the Atlantic Ocean. He had a blanket over him, although he was not cold, and a book on the little table beside him, although he had not read a single page and did not even know its title, having plucked it at random off of the shelf inside. He still found it somewhat difficult to concentrate on anything specifically set in front of him, and within the house, though it was quite roomy, the turmoil of Christmas with its stacks of boxes and the tree with limbs loaded with lights and baubles all made him a bit uneasy. Out here, however, the crisp air helped him to keep his head clear, and those grey, cleaving waves and that chalky sky fascinated him endlessly.

He could feel himself getting stronger almost by the hour. He was walking quite steadily now, if a bit crookedly, and tests at the clinic in Charleston had shown significant improvement in his motor skills and his memory. He could remember some of what had happened now, even up to the instant when he had sprinted after that fly ball (he had been pleased to learn the umpire had ruled that his catch had been good for an out). After that, though, there were long blurry stretches over the days and weeks when he had been hospitalized, and afterward, too – for instance, he could not recall arriving at the home of his Uncle Banks. He recollected well the feel of the strange, taut traction cables and the relentless pain in his back and his knee, and he knew that Liza had been there quite a lot, but he remembered little of what they had said to each other in the first couple of weeks after he had regained consciousness.

Sometimes, in that hospital bed, he had awakened from the heavy sleep induced by pain medication, and he had not even known his own name; at such moments, he was an utter stranger to himself and to the world, separated from his identity, and it terrified him. At other times, particularly when he would first awaken, he could not understand why his mother and father were not in the room with him. Where were they? He realized that something had happened and that he was in a hospital room; the bed was familiar, but he had it confused with the bed they had set up for his mother in the den at home. At other times, he would see Liza, all grown up, and it would come back to him with devastating clarity that his parents were both dead and that he had been out on his own for a long time now and that he had been hurt in some sort of freak accident on a baseball field. It was a little like being strapped to a great roulette wheel, and sometimes his number would land on some odd moment in the past – a birthday party, or the Fourth of July, or a certain little-league game, and at other times, he would catch a glimpse of smiling young men in crisp uniforms – there was one with the name Johnson stitched on the back, an older version of himself, and that would fill him with confusion. Once in a while, the wheel would land him smack in the present moment, and there was Liza again and the spare hospital room, and that was where he wanted desperately to remain because he knew intuitively that it was real, but he never could. The wheel would spin once more, and he would slide away with it, at the mercy of the whims of his subconscious. Many times, he found himself in the little outboard they'd had a dozen or so years ago, sitting beside his father, drifting ever so quietly and softly over the darkness of the Little Pee Dee River, its water so black and reflective it was like flowing enamel paint, and then an unspeakable serenity would come upon him. Yet all would soon turn to confusion again, and worst of all were those half-dreams in which he would find himself once again seated in the armchair in his mother's old sick room, in the house by the river, when she lay in the tall hospital bed they had brought home for her: he would see her again, withered and pale and dried-looking, the dark veins in her arms exposed, and then suddenly she would be gone and he would see himself in that same bed, unable to move, with some great but invisible weight pressing down upon his chest, and he would awaken with a start to find that he truly was in such a bed after all, and unable to move.

Finally, though, his head had begun to clear. He was startled to recollect that he really had been a professional baseball player – that this had not been someone else's life after all. The Reds' owner, Banks Berenger, had begun coming to visit him with some regularity as well, and more recent events had come back to him at last, his teammates (many of whom, he was told, had also come by when he was still in the haze created by the anesthesia and then the pain medication) along with Hersh Freeman and all the rest. Jack Anders had come, too, Banks said, but Frank had been really out of it then, ranging far and wide in the landscape of his dreams, and Anders had had to leave for Washington the next day. Haltingly, Banks had broken it to him that the major-league contract intended for Frank had been offered to him instead. At first Frank was unmoved by this news – he truly did not seem to care. Over the course of the next few days, however, he had wondered whether he ought to feel jealous; finally, when he was reconciled to having very little reaction one way or the other, he was able to feel glad for Jack. He deserved his shot as much as anyone ever had. He still felt that way, sitting here right now, wrapped in a blanket on the pool deck. Perhaps Anders had finished the season well with the Washington Senators, but Frank did not know: he had not turned on a television or even taken much interest in the game since his injuries. And the

Christmas card, when it had arrived, made no references to baseball or batting averages or contracts or any of that kind of thing. It simply read, "Hope you're doing better. Happy Christmas. Jack Anders."

By contrast, the toughest thing for him to swallow had been Banks's bombshell. Nevertheless, since the past had gotten all muddled up with the present, Frank had begun to believe that he did indeed remember his father mentioning a brother once or twice, but he could not recall the specifics. Maybe they had assumed he was dead or else in some place so far away he might as well have been dead.

"As you can see, I'm more or less alive," Banks said. "We weren't full brothers, though. Nobody in Dillon knew it, but Bob and I had different fathers. Mine was a man named Berenger, who came from Charleston. People called him Hatchet. Sordid tale, won't trouble you with the ugly details."

"So you're telling me that you and I are blood relations?"

"Correct. I'm your uncle."

"And then – now let me get this straight – then you bought a whole baseball team just because you found out I played ball?"

"Seemed like a good idea at the time."

Frank knew that his reaction to this news ought to have been indignation, but when he had thought it over, he found once again that he didn't care that much. It was amazing how much indifference could be induced by a significant head injury and a broken back, especially in matters that were not within his control. He had proven his ability beyond any shadow of doubt, to himself and everyone else who had cared or mattered, and besides that, anything he had ever done on a baseball field had been solely out of his own heart's true desire; in a way, all of it had been the lucky answer to a boy's wish.

Recognizing that he still had family, though, when he had been certain that all traces of Treadwells and their kin had been erased except for himself, was a different matter. There must have been some queer design in all this that he couldn't yet begin to fathom, and the more he thought about it, the more he saw that wherever he had gone, whatever had happened to him, various sorts of family had seen fit to come to him, to help him in some way: there had been the truckers and the drifters, those first few months out on the road, and then Allison and Mac had been there for him, too, and then the Reds (particularly Jack), and now it was his true uncle and aunt. You couldn't begin to get around the idea of family even if you wanted to.

As if on cue, Karen opened the sliding glass door and smiled at him. "Need anything?" she asked.

"No, thanks. I'm just fine. Great, in fact."

And, of course, Liza had come to him. For a while he had believed that she, too, was merely an image of the past, tucked away in the ragged mental scrapbook of the old life in Dillon. Sometimes she seemed to have perished along with his mother and father and all the rest of them, and – as he now saw that it usually goes in this life – he had ended up only with little bits of her, a few objects, some 45-rpm records and a wallet-sized high-school portrait, just as the others had merely become names written in an old bible and an iron key. But it wasn't so this time: she had reappeared in the flesh, a beautiful, brown-eyed reincarnation of herself, lively, still young, someone he had never deserved to have in his life and still didn't, but here she was. As his mind had continued to sharpen itself, he had often thought of Allison McDougal with nostalgia and with gratitude and with crushing guilt; he would always care for her, though he was quite certain he would never see her again. Liza was different, for she had known him when he was small, and he knew that she had never been very far away from him and never would be somehow.

Of course, the previous summer, when he had gone home to see his father, when he had first signed with the Reds, he had heard from Luther all about her marriage and her baby. But now the marriage had broken apart. She was firmly in his life again, though Frank had no idea where or how things would go; he only knew that he could not now imagine how he could get along without her from here on out. It was almost as if he had reawakened to his real existence, his true identity, and the past could now be connected to the present moment. But how would they proceed? Slowly, that was for sure. For instance, he had a good deal of trouble envisioning himself as a stepfather at this point in his life, and he had said as much to his Uncle Banks a couple of nights ago, out here on the chilly pool deck.

"Don't think of it that way, then," Banks had said. "Can you think of yourself as a friend? Can you be any sort of a help? Can you add something good to that kid's life?"

"I really don't know."

"This might sound a bit odd coming from me, but I'm just now figuring a few things out myself. You can't ever get shut of the people who are truly meant to be in your life, no matter how hard you try. Sometimes you just have to stand back and let love do the work."

"That's all easy for you to say," Frank said. "You're rich."

"No argument there. Much to the embarrassment of us all, I am rich, though I should add that none of my money was free. Believe me, a rich man has most of the same troubles as a poor one, only they're more expensive."

In any case, Frank had thought, there will be time. He knew that Liza would indeed be a great part of whatever came next for him, but he had also made a mental checklist of some other things he needed to do, too: he must go back to the old church and sit down and talk with Pastor Laite about many things; get reconciled to a few things he had done and had not done; visit a few old teammates maybe; and he wanted to finish his schooling, too – they had night classes for people like himself.

The doctors had told him he couldn't play ball anymore, but he wasn't sure he believed it. Besides, he thought, there is always somebody around making a living at telling other people what they can and cannot do, but you can't put too much stock in them. His body had begun to feel quite strong; oh, he had a good deal of stiffness in his leg and his neck every morning, of course, but if he could get out and run a little bit, throw a ball, swing a bat... that might help hasten his recovery. He could see it: whatever he'd lost in the way of speed in the field, he could make up for with positioning and smarts, or maybe he could learn to play first base, where there wasn't as much range needed. And hitting was all in the mind; there had never been a time when he had not believed that he could hit, and that had not changed. What he needed was to get a bat in his hands and find somebody willing to throw him some pitches. It came back to him in a rush, the feel of the smooth handle, the stepping in towards the ball, the rotation of the hips and shoulders, the soul-redeeming impact as wood meets horsehide, all done without thinking but with a consciousness beyond thought, the way a kid does when it's simply part of his nature. The need became too great, and as a thirsty man tries to put the idea of water away from himself, he reached for the book on the little table, opened it on his lap, and stared at the words.

Learning to wait was a good thing, and he'd had some practice at it. At last he had seen that the true beauty of baseball lies in the careful balance between the patience and quietude of a monk and the instinct to act appropriately in a unique dimension in which the smallest calculations matter. If you could live your life that way, it would be the best kind of life. In a strange way, this same sort of patience, the feeling of it, seemed to him inherent in other things, too – in the lovely green spaces and in the river and in the people and places that he loved. Dillon itself seemed to wait for him, patiently, as only your own hometown can wait. Go on out and see some of the world, your town says, but I will be here waiting for you when you get tired of all that and you decide to come back to me. Change comes, but my streets are much the same, my shops and my old brick buildings, my churches, my people, and their stories, by and large. And the river, too – that would be the same.

As he watched the churning ocean, his vision drew him farther down the coastline, traveling like a disembodied eye past Edisto Island and all the way to Winyah Bay, there turning back to the northwest, riding like a hawk upon the slight wind that flowed above the Little Pee Dee. Below, the river was patient and yet moving, waiting for him, and now the hawk hurtled downward and its eye became a boy's eye, just peeking out over the edge of a small boat's bow above the slow, dark water, just slow enough that in its dark surface he could see his own reflected face, a boy's face, as the voices of his mother and father, warmed by the timbre of love, seemed both to caution him and encourage him at once. Still, like one in a familiar dream, he did not need to look up at them, or to the wide bend that lay glistening just ahead where the light broke through the treetops, to know that they were nearly home.